TAKEN

MARY ANNE MUSHATT

Quills & Quartos
PUBLISHING

Edited by Ellen Pickels and Kristi Rawley

Cover Design by Cloudcat Designs
On the cover *Pani Barbier-Walbonne*, 1796, François Gérard
On the back cover *Gretchen's Favorite*, Johann Georg Meyer von Bremen

ISBN 978-1-951033-41-5 (ebook) and 978-1-951033-42-2 (paperback)

TABLE OF CONTENTS

prologue

March 1807
Matlock Manor, Derbyshire

THE HOUSE WAS STILL, ITS OCCUPANTS ASLEEP SAVE PRESCOTT Fitzwilliam, Lord Matlock, who sat in his overstuffed leather armchair, pondering what the morrow would bring. His booted feet, propped against the grate of the fire, toyed with a half-burned log fallen from its perch. Although dying, the flames were the only light or warmth in the chilly room. As he sipped his brandy, his mind revisited the previous week's events. George Darcy was dead, and Matlock's mind whirled with possibilities. *I must get young Darcy out from under the thumb of that woman.* He rose, unsteady from the time of night and the half-bottle of brandy he had consumed. "Sticking her nose in where it did not—*does* not—belong."

He stumbled to the sidebar for another drink. "And then there is my *sister. I* could have moulded George if not for Catherine's obstinate demand that the boy marry her 'little Annie.' She mucked it all to Hades! When my Anne died, George was ripe for the pickings, save for that Darcy woman. How dare *Alexandra* prance about like a queen, barring me and mine from Pemberley!"

The man rubbed the greying stubble on his chin as a twinge of culpability infected his mind. *That nasty business. I had forgotten about that…nasty business. Shocked even me.*

As if shaking off a bad dream, he returned to the safety of his chair, kicking the grate as he settled in to enjoy his brandy. *That was when I could have taken George and his money. But no, that sister of his kept him locked up with her and the duke.* He threw the dregs of his glass on the flames, enjoying the fire's flare. "That"—he wagged his finger at the glowing logs—"that was my mistake. Totally miscalculated tactically. Should have played on his sympathy *and* kept Catherine away from young Darcy."

His hand pushed his silvering locks from his eyes. "That was another mistake I can no longer afford. But now, what could be more natural than my comforting the dear boy, offering the wisdom of my experience?"

He looked into the fire, greed filling his heart. "It is but a matter of time before *I* control Pemberley, steering young Darcy into one or two schemes in which I happen to have an interest!" With a predatory gleam in his eye, he threw another log on the fire. *For now*—he rubbed his hands together—*the boy is mine!*

The sliding of a wooden panel interrupted his reverie, and an involuntary grimace edged across his face as a woman, also in her fifties, appeared in the room that even his wife dared not enter. Reed thin and wrapped in total black, she bore on her face the marks of cruelty.

"Prescott, what are you going on about? I could hear you halfway down the corridor!" Lady Catherine de Bourgh demanded, coming into the flickering glow of the fire. Seating herself in the adjacent chair, she continued. "I wish to speak to you, Brother."

"What is on your mind, Catty?" Placing one hand on each arm of the chair, he looked at her as a cat cornering a mouse. "I shall listen… for the time being."

"I should hope you will. I want your word that you will do all you can to move forward the alliance between—"

"Leave it!"

She slammed her fist on the chair arm. "I shall not leave it! This cause is one to which I have given great effort—too much to abandon it now. I have *sacrificed*, and I shall *not* have you push it aside for your convoluted dreams of stealing young Darcy's fortune."

"Oh, and your aims are so altruistic, are they?" She faltered, and he leaned in with malice. "No, I thought not. You want your share of the bounty as much as I." He looked away before returning quickly to face her. "But I tell you: this moment is precisely the wrong time to force that particular issue. That woman will be lying in wait, expecting us to make such a move. No, it is better to wait, bide our time, and build young Darcy's confidence in us. Lure him back into the family web as it were, *then* make our move."

"I disagree."

He waved his hand in dismissal. "That is what we shall do, sister. I am head of this family, and my word is final." A threatening note coloured his voice. "Now, leave me. We have a long day tomorrow. I expect you to suitably grieve over the loss of our dearly departed George."

Lady Catherine stared at her brother, her eyes narrowing with disdain. Without another word, she rose, swishing her gown before retreating through the secret door. As the panel slid back, he filled, then drained, his glass. "Patience, sister dear. You have earned this, and if you wait but a few years, perhaps less, Pemberley will be thine."

Behind the nearly closed door across the room, a woman softly gasped and staggered back to her chamber. As soon as she was able, Isabelle Fitzwilliam entered her room, closed the door, and firmly turned the key in the lock.

One

January 1812
Longbourn, Hertfordshire

*E*LIZABETH SHIVERED FROM THE COLD. A*ND THE WET.* R*IVULETS OF RAIN*
ran down her arm as she ran as fast as her young legs could manage.
Even though the cloud-ridden night gave no vantage, she continually
looked behind her. Fighting the need to cry, she ran faster and tumbled
over a large log. She swore, the cackling laugh of her tormentor
ringing in her ears as she hit the ground. Her head struck a large rock,
and she lost consciousness of where and who she was.

Elizabeth's eyes flew open as she furiously scanned her environs.
Still caught in the frightening dream, she stared straight ahead till the
familiar furnishings of her bedchamber at Longbourn reassured her she
was safe. Pulling her knees to her chest, she inhaled, holding her breath
to the count of three before exhaling and closing her eyes. Still feeling
the damp cold of her phantom forest, she repeated the words of her
rescuer. *It was a dream, only a dream!* she repeated, working hard to
anchor herself in the present and rocking in a vain attempt to soothe the
panic overwhelming her again. "They are getting worse. I could handle

my dreams when they revived my years with Papa and Mama Bennet, and I still felt safe…and loved. *Those* dreams I welcomed.

"But the horsemen have returned, and the cat has re-emerged from the dark. And soon, Jane will no longer come to wake me when the dreams become too much. Mr Bingley has claimed her heart, and I shall be left alone to face my demons. Now more than ever they tug at the veil to what I was before…before coming to Longbourn." She shook her head, crying into her knees.

"Lizzy!" Jane Bennet rushed through the door and embraced the young woman who had been her sister for over a decade. Stroking Elizabeth's dark curls with one hand, she wrapped her other arm around her sister's shoulder. "It is your dreams again, is it not?"

Elizabeth nodded, her head now cradled in Jane's embrace.

"They are getting worse, are they not?"

Again, Elizabeth nodded.

"Oh, Lizzy." Jane crushed her to her heart. "I shall ask Charles to take you with me. Surely, he will agree. Many brides take their favourite sister with them when they marry. And Charles is so wonderful. You will see—it will be just like before…when Mama and Papa were still with us. Only better."

"Oh, Jane, I could not." Elizabeth looked up through teary eyes. "You and Charles deserve time alone."

Jane only smiled, pushing an errant, tear-soaked curl from Elizabeth's face. "No matter. Dearest, of what did you dream? Perhaps it would help for you to unburden yourself."

Elizabeth nodded. "It was night…*that* night. I felt everything I felt then—the rain pelting my arms and my cheeks, each breath burning my lungs."

Her hand clasped her night-rail to her chest. "I felt fire in my legs from running for so long. I ran and ran till I could not hear them anymore—ran as fast and as quietly as I could. Jane, I felt the despair of not knowing where to go—not knowing where I would be safe. It was because I kept looking back, expecting one of those men, or worse, her—"

"Her? The cat?"

"Yes. Catty-cat." She looked at Jane. "That is what we called her."

"You knew her?"

"I must have."

"And then?"

"And then I fell and knew no more."

"Till Papa found you."

"Yes." Elizabeth finally smiled. "Until he did."

THE NEXT MORNING, Elizabeth took her drawing supplies and walked out, her dreams from the night before infiltrating her waking consciousness. Rambling beyond the family's estate, she was inexplicably drawn to the place Edwin Bennet had found her nearly sixteen years before. The log was still there, decayed yet surrounded by a stand of young, hardy trees.

Her mind turned back to that terrifying time. "Thank the good Lord that Papa Edwin and Mama Gloria found me." She chuckled. "My second 'birth' he called it."

"The day we found you is the day we shall celebrate, Lizzy. It is the day you were given to us." She smiled until darker visions faded into the hooves of a magnificent sorrel horse flying over the fallen tree and the handsome rider with kind eyes turning in surprise to see a frightened, unexpected child, crouching to make herself as small as she could beside the ancient log.

Not wanting to be drawn back any further, Elizabeth shook herself, forcing herself to concentrate on the charcoal sketch of Noah's Puddle that she was determined to complete before returning to Longbourn. It was no use; with only two days until Jane's wedding, her mind refused to be diverted away from the small, frightened child she had once been.

Putting her sketchbook back on the ground, she picked up a stone. She looked at the lines of embedded quartz then threw it into the pond as far as she could. *How shall I endure Longbourn without Jane?*

Gathering her supplies, she walked along the clearing, recalling their first meeting with Charles Bingley. It was there that she and Jane encountered the new owner of Netherfield. It was there that Jane and their kind, cheerful neighbour began to fall in love.

Elizabeth wrapped her arms about her as a feeling of emptiness enveloped her. *Now it feels unlike a friendly place. Its magic is gone.* A sudden rush of startled birds surprised Elizabeth, and she called out,

"Jane!" With a sense of growing unease, she hastened back to Longbourn.

On the Netherfield side of the pond, a man stepped from the foliage, advancing as she turned and retreated. The tall figure placed a booted foot upon a large rock, staring after her. *I wonder what other sights this little hamlet of a village might offer. If she is any indication, I can see why Bingley was so eager to stay.*

Netherfield was ablaze in candled glory as the Bingley family held the last fete before the following day's nuptials. Friends from town were standing about drinking, dancing, and gossiping. The best man strode along the periphery of the crowd, nodding to acquaintances and trying to avoid his hostess. *At least after tonight, Bingley will have another to fill that role.*

Standing a head taller than most of the crowd, Fitzwilliam Darcy kept his gaze averted as one and all tried to claim his attention. Looking about, he saw Bingley with his bride-to-be. *She is tolerable, I suppose, but not cultivated enough to tempt me.* He let his eyes wander about the room, judging all beneath his notice. He avoided the local gentry as if they had a pestilence, and not being in a humour to converse, he delayed furthering an acquaintance with any of Bingley's friends, men still tainted with trade who had made the jaunt from town.

On his second ramble around the great room, he heard someone laugh: pure, joyful, and unrestrained yet not overdone. He turned and moved unhurriedly in that direction to give the laughter time to spoil into something brittle, something to ensnare or belittle. But it never came. Rather, he found it repeated for another measure before schooling itself, first into a youthful giggle, then into a melodic voice. Positioning himself nearby, but not close enough to excite attention, he stood and gazed about the room to locate the source of his beguilement. There she stood—*the lady of the lake. I should have guessed she would have such a pure, joyous laugh.* He stepped closer.

"Lizzy, how can you say that?" asked a girl who would be rather fair looking if not standing next to one of the most bewitching women Darcy had ever had the pleasure of observing.

Lizzy, he thought, taking a quick glance to see how the name suited her. To avert any suspicion, he turned his head yet remained attuned to every word.

"But it is true, Charlotte. You know how the Bingley brats went on about *their* Mr Darcy, but good lord, I do not believe the man has spoken one word…to anyone! How impolite."

"Well, he is very rich, Lizzy," Charlotte replied.

Darcy's spine straightened, but he felt a stirring of hope that he might hear something—anything but the accustomed fawning that usually accompanied his status.

"Ah yes, and the rich may be offensive at any time, but for it to be here, on Jane's night? Insupportable."

"And what would you do about it?" Charlotte asked.

She looked at her friend, apparently trying to stifle the laughter bubbling forth. "I shall waltz right up to him and say, 'dear Mr Darcy,'" she began in perfect imitation of Miss Bingley's efforts earlier that evening. "'How wonderful of you to attend this ordinary little affair. But pray, your valet seems to have neglected to include an essential in your impeccable attire.'"

Charlotte laughed, and Darcy felt his own lips twist when the girl fluttered her eyelashes.

"'And what could that be?'" asked Charlotte in a false baritone.

"'Why, your *manners*, dear man…'"

The girls burst into laughter, and Darcy felt a cascade of delight wash over him.

After an angry matron tut-tutted them, the young women attempted to compose themselves, and deciding to add fuel to the fire, Darcy straightened his waistcoat, took a deep breath, and walked by the duo. Passing this 'Lizzy,' he murmured so only she could hear, "Excuse me, but I must find my valet."

He felt a satisfaction, the likes of which he hadn't felt in years as, after a moment of what he assumed was shock, the fascinating Miss Lizzy let out another peal of perfect laughter.

"M<small>R</small> D<small>ARCY</small>," Miss Bingley's voice came from behind him. "Pray, do share your mind on the society into which my brother has most regrettably immersed himself."

Bowing, Darcy observed both Miss Bingley and her sister, Mrs Louisa Hurst. "It seems a bit rough, but it *is* the country, madam."

"How I do wish you had come earlier. Perhaps you would have been able to assist us in dissuading Charles from offering for..." Miss Bingley allowed her eyes to drift to her brother who was dancing with his intended. "To think—no fortune, no connexions, and the family she does have..."

"I shared a rather enlightened discussion with Mr Bennet—" Darcy began.

"But that is not her father," Louisa added.

"No?" Darcy asked, surprised. *Perhaps there is something to what they say about Charles's choice. Not that there is anything to be done about it at this late date.*

"Mr Bennet is her uncle," Miss Bingley interjected. "Miss Bennet's parents passed on a number of years ago, and she and Miss Elizabeth remain at Longbourn only by the grace of Mr and Mrs Bennet. Do say we may count on you to persuade Charles to distance himself from that family. I mean they are not her true family after all—and really, can you see any of them visiting us in Mayfair?"

Again, Miss Bingley shuddered. "Especially Miss Elizabeth."

"*I* hear she will be cast out of Longbourn as soon as Jane weds," Mrs Hurst added. "She is to be farmed out to an aunt, and the only Bennet relations I know of in town are tradesmen living in Cheapside."

"If you will excuse me, ladies, I believe I shall go and speak with your brother." Darcy bowed, then before leaving, he turned to address them. "But be assured, you may count on me to convince your brother to dissuade his new wife from her family, for his sake as well as hers."

The sisters curtseyed, their smiles filled with calculation and malice. Though he could not see them, Darcy shuddered as he found his friend, who was speaking with his bride-to-be and a dark-haired woman.

"Bingley," Darcy called out when he was but a step away.

"Darcy! How grand to see you here on this night of nights for me." Bingley's joy was infectious, reflected in his lady's eyes and that of her companion. "You remember Miss Bennet, but I do not believe you have met my soon-to-be sister, Miss Elizabeth. Miss Elizabeth Bennet, Mr Fitzwilliam Darcy."

"I am pleased to make your acquaintance. I know Mr Bingley and his sisters have lamented your absence."

"Yes, I have heard." He smiled.

"You will be standing up with Miss Elizabeth, Darcy. It is good that you at least have the chance to meet before tomorrow."

"Indeed." He again smiled and was disconcerted when her eyes refused to quit his features. She shook herself, and her discomfiture was so adorable that, despite the uproar he would cause, he pressed on. "Would you, if you are not previously engaged, dance the next with me?"

Surprise spread over her fair cheeks, widening her sparkling eyes, and Darcy drank her in. Her soft, "I thank you, yes," was music to his ears. His hands twitched with the anticipation of leading her to the dance, and a tickling irritation grew against the tiresome conversation of last-minute wedding details, but he revelled in his ability to remain close to her.

"Oh, Jane, how Sir William Lucas will lament the loss of the 'jewel of the county.'" Elizabeth's hand swept her forehead. She turned to Bingley. "I do not think he will forgive you, Mr Bingley. But I shall, for you have made my sister incandescently happy."

Darcy was struck by the brilliancy of her joy as she took her sister's hands in her own. It was an intensely private moment, and Darcy was surprised that he felt no impropriety in the display. *The emotion brightens her eyes.*

The music changed. "Miss Elizabeth, I believe this is our set?"

Nodding, she took his offered hand, and he led her away. Darcy breathed in her scent. *Delectable—the tang of citrus like the blush of spring. Magnificent.* Both their steps had a natural ease, and Darcy felt himself well matched for a change. *She is grace personified. Feeling the music, she lets it move her.* His eyes focused on her rhythmic motion and the swell of her breast as she skipped back to her place after dancing a tantalising circle around him. He struggled against turning to keep her in his sight. *Get a hold of yourself. You are no mooncalf. You are Fitzwilliam Darcy. Think, man. This is the one who will be cast out to live in Cheapside!* He straightened his shoulders to rein in the tumult of her nearness. *But surely, one dance will do no harm—especially one so far from the glare of London.* And with that, he scoffed at any thought of damage to his reputation, forgetting that one doyenne of society had him firmly in her sights. And the rare smile that graced his handsome face was not pleasing to Miss Bingley—not at all.

After leaving Elizabeth at the side of her uncle, Darcy was again struck by Mrs Hurst's warning regarding Elizabeth's future. *So, the beauty goes to London, eh?* He found a glass of punch. Turning, he saw her dancing with one of Bingley's friends from town, and his eyes darkened. *That is Rathborn, I believe. But he cannot afford her*, he thought as he took a sip, wishing for a wee drop of brandy. *'Tis a sad fate for these gently bred girls of great beauty and few potential suitors.* He allowed his thoughts to dwell on the gallants to whom this particular gently bred girl might consent.

THE WEDDING of Miss Jane Bennet of Longbourn to Mr Charles Bingley of Netherfield was a brilliant success, held on a brisk winter's day with clear blue skies full of crisp sunlight bringing everything into sharp relief. Felicitations had arrived from throughout the kingdom as both Mr Bingley and the Bennet household maintained a lively correspondence with family and friends in all quarters of the realm. Elizabeth and her cousins Mary, Kitty, and Lydia looked even more beautiful than usual next to the pinched and supercilious looks of the groom's sisters. Jane tried to make peace between the factions of her family, old and new, but Elizabeth would have none of it. Her quick mind saw through the veiled insults and the oppressive air of superiority that the 'Bingley brats' exuded.

Standing in the reception line, Elizabeth chuckled at the continual nonsense spouted by the 'brats.' Elizabeth looked at her younger relations. *They are not always…silly.* She smiled. *Especially when one engages their more devious talents in a noble cause.* Looking up, she found Mary's eye upon her, and she blushed. Turning her head, she found Franny Bennet, current mistress of Longbourn, starring at her and obviously misconstruing her response as something more teasing with the wealthy and accessible gentlemen in the room. She rushed towards Elizabeth.

"You listen to me, Miss Lizzy," she hissed behind clenched teeth and a forced smile. "One word, one blunder, and you will be out of Longbourn. Forever!"

"Then it is a good thing Elizabeth will be leaving with me." Both Frances Bennet and Elizabeth turned as Mrs Raleigh approached.

"Aunt." Elizabeth curtseyed, her cheeks red with mortification.

"Elizabeth," said the woman reassuringly. "Mrs Bennet, I believe Admiral Raleigh has arranged everything for Elizabeth's removal to town? I was assured before my husband departed for Ireland that all was in order." Mrs Raleigh secretly delighted in Frances's discomposure. "If you were not informed, I suggest you take that up with *your* husband. I have long wished for Elizabeth's company, but I would not consider taking her away from Jane. Now that Jane is happily settled, I shall take my sister Gloria's child—"

Frances Bennet huffed. "Her stray."

Mrs Raleigh stepped closer till her face was mere inches from that of Mrs Bennet. "Madam, it is fortunate that we are in company, for if not, I would strike you and strike you hard. Such incivility borders on the cruel and is not to be borne," she hissed before turning to Elizabeth. "Come, my dear," and with that, she led Elizabeth away to speak with Mrs Bennet's more pleasant relatives, the Gardiners.

two

March 1812
London

MISS ELOISE HAVERSHAM HAD MARRIED CAPTAIN STEPHEN RALEIGH
soon after Elizabeth arrived at Longbourn some fifteen years earlier.
Due to her love of adventure, Mrs Raleigh had accompanied her
husband until hostilities had forced her off the high seas, and she had
spent many months at the home of her sister, Mrs Gloria Haversham
Bennet. During their time together, she had doted on her nieces. While
she loved the maternal leanings of little Jane, it was the bright and
witty Elizabeth to whom she drew closest. When Gloria died while not
wholly bringing life to her son, Mrs Raleigh had kept Elizabeth with
her as much as possible, but her marriage to an untamed war hero
played havoc with her domestic life. Rising quickly through the ranks,
the now-Admiral Raleigh enjoyed taking his wife to distant lands and
experiencing life in new and exciting cultures. She maintained a close
correspondence with Elizabeth, learning by proxy of the increasingly
difficult nature of the girl's relationship with Longbourn's current
mistress, Mrs Thomas Bennet.

While the announcement of Elizabeth's coming to live at Raleigh House was spontaneous, the decision had most decidedly been well thought out. Admiral Raleigh was of a similar bent as his wife as he, too, had been charmed by the vivacious child who had grown into a remarkable young woman. He was more than happy to have custodial care of their niece.

During the first three weeks at Raleigh House, the women divided their time between shopping and exploring the booksellers they both enjoyed. When the girls were younger, the Raleighs would bring Elizabeth and Jane to town whenever feasible, and the girls would spend hours among the stacks of dusty tomes, each seeking a hidden treasure on the booksellers' shelves. Elizabeth was hoping to indulge this passion again and, after promising to behave, had convinced her aunt to allow half an hour of unescorted time at Battswell's, a bookstore she and Jane had visited regularly. She had become rather a favourite of the proprietor who had marvelled at her range of interest and her knowledge of up-and-coming writers. It was his habit to follow her tastes when ordering new authors' works. Many of their patrons enjoyed her selections, and Battswell's had thrived by being on the cusp of the new and interesting. Consequently, they indulged any special order Elizabeth requested.

"ELIZABETH," Darcy whispered, looking out at the street from the shelves of Battswell's. There she was, the woman haunting his dreams, no more than five feet away with the sun glinting off her curls. His connoisseur's eye trailed to the ringlets about her neck—that, he noted with satisfaction, was long and graceful—and he found himself wishing to drag his lips along its length. From there, he drank in her shoulders and her frame, inch by inch, appreciating the bounty of her bosom, her slim waist, and her hips. He eyed her with an unabated hunger. *A man could get lost in those hips.*

As his body responded, he exhaled in relief when she moved away. *Yes—go, Miss Bennet,* he thought. *Go find yourself some ribbon or lace to adorn that magnificent body. It is not fair to tempt a man so,* he silently chided as he tugged his waistcoat and returned his attention to the book he was holding. The bell atop the door jingled, indicating a new customer, and Darcy stiffened. *No, no it cannot be! What would such a woman be doing in a bookstore?*

Unconsciously, he slipped to the back of the shop as she wandered through the stacks. Struggling to focus on the book in his hand, his eyes returned to follow her as she traced the spines of various books catching her interest. She smiled at a title, and as her slender fingers tugged it off the shelf, he thought his breath would never return. *Those eyes! They sparkle and dance!* Aware of the impropriety of watching her, he could not command his eyes to abandon their quest, and they returned again and again to this goddess as she breathed deeply, savouring the smells of paper, ink, and leather.

Passing by a bookshelf, Elizabeth slowed her pace, allowing her eyes to read each and every title. She found a large book on the reign of Queen Elizabeth and, leaning against one of the shelves, pressed the book close to her chest. Chewing on her lower lip, she opened the tome and began reading, completely unaware of the gentleman watching every move.

When she headed back towards the counter, he followed until they were each at the end of their aisle. But while she moved forward, he hung back. *I cannot—shall not—make a complete fool of myself over her.* Taking a random book from the nearest shelf, he feigned interest in order to eavesdrop on whatever conversation she might have with the proprietor.

"Ah, Miss Elizabeth!" Mr Battswell said, coming from behind the counter to take her hand and bow. "It has been too long."

"Well, I shall be a more frequent visitor to your emporium, Mr Battswell, as I have recently moved to London. But I forget myself. How are you, sir?"

"Well, very well indeed. Please, wait here. One of the books you ordered has come in."

"Wonderful. Thank you," she called out as he went behind the curtain at the back of the shop. In a minute, Battswell returned with a leather volume in his hands.

"It took a while to find a copy, but as you see, I was successful."

The bookseller's satisfied smile widened when Elizabeth took the book and, cracking it open, gasped at the illustrations. "This is the exact book I was looking for. It is a present for my sister, Jane. She is recently married."

"Well, please give her my best wishes for her health and happiness."

"I shall, and indeed, I thank you on her behalf."

"And who is the fortunate gentleman, if I may ask?"

"Of course you may, sir. A Mr Bingley."

Darcy's head jerked up hearing of his best friend. *Bingley!* He smiled. *It would be impolite of me not to ask whether she has any word of her sister and my friend. He is the perfect entrée. Now I know what other people feel when using a connexion to further an aim of their own.* And with that, he stepped forward, interrupting the ongoing conversation.

"Pardon me for interrupting, Miss Bennet." He nonchalantly approached the counter. It took a moment for Elizabeth to place him. Surprised that she did not immediately recall their former meeting, he added, "Fitzwilliam Darcy, miss. We met at the wedding of your sister"—he enjoyed the blush spreading across her lovely cheek, especially as it flushed lower to the enticing edge of her dress—"to my friend, Bingley." He smiled broadly, knowing its effect on women. Yet she maintained her distance. He stepped closer.

"Ah, Mr Darcy!" Battswell said, "I was unaware you were still here." Darcy sent an irritated glance to the bookseller till his eyes returned to Elizabeth.

"Tell me, how long is your stay in London?"

"My stay is indefinite," she replied.

Noticing her rising discomfort, he backed away. "I wish to introduce my sister, Georgiana, to Mrs Bingley and hope to include you in that invitation." She smiled at the mention of both her sister and his, and Darcy felt something in his chest spring open, a sensation he could not recall before. Their conversation shifted to the books Elizabeth had ordered, and making sure to include Mr Battswell, Darcy discerned that her tastes and custom influenced the variety of authors offered by the store.

After another twenty minutes of the most stimulating conversation Darcy could recall having with a young woman, a startled Elizabeth exclaimed, "The time! I am late. What will the admiral say? Will you have these sent 'round, Mr Battswell?" She headed towards the door.

Darcy called to her, "It was a pleasure, Miss Bennet." She only nodded before hurrying out the door. Keeping his eyes trained on her, he asked Battswell, "Admiral? Which admiral would that be, Battswell?"

"I believe that would be Raleigh, sir."

Darcy stored the information while placing his selection on the counter. "I believe I shall take this, and perhaps the latest volume by the *lady* recommended so enthusiastically by Miss Bennet."

"Very good, sir."

Darcy left Battswell's Booksellers to enjoy the afternoon fencing match arranged with his cousin Richard.

Longbourn, Hertfordshire

Dearest Lizzy,

Longbourn suffers greatly from the cruel abandonment of its 'greatest jewels,' as Sir William continues to say. You and Jane are sorely missed, and life here is not the same, as you can well imagine. Mama continues to crow over Jane's good fortune until even Kitty and Lydia tire of her constant braggadocio. And yet, I see in her eyes the fear that we have lived with for so long. 'Three daughters to marry!' is her constant refrain. And our most recent visitor only made matters worse, at least for a time.

As you are well aware, Longbourn is entailed away from the female line, and the next to inherit is Mr William Collins who wrote Papa, offering an olive branch. Believe me, if Mr Collins is what our good Lord intended as the bearer of that first olive branch, I fear the story of Noah and the flood would have ended rather differently indeed. He is nothing like Rev. Colter, self-possessed and compassionate. No, our Mr Collins reminds one of the bellows Hill uses to stoke the fire, yet he is twice as useless. I do not mean to be cruel, truly, for Mr Collins has done my family and me a great service.

Remember, he came to Longbourn, olive branch in hand, and as the eldest, it was my duty to accept said offering. But I could not, and despite Mama's lamentations, Papa stood by me, and we, or rather I, have been saved from that particular hardship. Mama had spread the word about the village that Mr Collins would join himself to our family in general, and me in particular, in such a way as to ignite the fire of Mr Waverly's ardour, and the morning of Mr Collin's disastrous proposal, my dearest Michael, as I may now call him, came and defended his right to love me. For love me he does, and after an altercation with Mr Collins where Mr Waverly punched Mr Collins in the cheek, my brave and besotted Michael went down on his knee to me and proposed marriage! Marriage, Lizzy! I, Mary Bennet, am to be married and to the man I love! Come this July 27, I shall be Miss Bennet no longer but Mrs Michael Waverly.

Please say that you will join us on this happiest of days, dear cousin. Please? I miss you more than I can say and hope that you and the admiral and Mrs Raleigh are in fine health. In the coming months, I shall travel to London to begin the fittings for my wedding clothes. I shall try and convince Papa to accompany me, as Mama will have many details to arrange here at home. We shall stay with the Gardiners, and I hope we shall have ample opportunity to visit.

I miss you, Lizzy, and remain,
Your faithful cousin,
Mary Bennet

MR BENNET's letter to Elizabeth offered a wry assessment of the absurd nature of the Reverend Collins and the ease with which he had transferred his attention in the span of two days from Mary to Miss Charlotte Lucas. His letter also included a bit of local gossip regarding the Netherfield ladies, who had tarried in Hertfordshire longer than expected. Sitting in her room at the Raleighs' spacious home, Elizabeth read of John Lucas's tales of the unexpected advances of Mrs Hurst. Staring out the window, she pondered the nature of the family Jane had joined and thought, not for the first time, that no one could really know everything about another, and that was especially true about the house of Bingley.

DUE TO THE admiral's reputation for nautical victories, his family's connexions, as well as his wife's social grace and wit, the Raleighs moved in the first circles of London society. Once it was known that they had returned from Cumberwait, their estate in Northamptonshire, invitations to social events flowed in. The Montridge ball was a highlight of the season, and Mrs Raleigh insisted they all attend.

"Dearest, you know I have little patience for the pettiness of the dance hall," her sailor lamented.

"The Montridge ballroom is hardly a dance hall, and you will put on your best evening coat and dance the night away! Think of Elizabeth stuck here night after night with us old folks. She is young and must have her share of amusement."

"If you insist," the old seaman grumbled with a twinkle in his eye.

Mrs Raleigh turned to her niece. "Now then, Elizabeth, we must see about a gown." Heading to the door, Elizabeth in tow, Mrs Raleigh turned to salute her husband. "Until this evening, my love." And with that she swept out of the room.

Their efforts at Madame LeSage's atelier was well worth the hours spent pouring over design books and decoding the patterns into a look that would show Elizabeth's figure and perfect skin to their best advantage. Their creation showcased Elizabeth's assets yet was comfortable and easy to wear. The fabric was a rich, ruby-red satin that nearly glowed in the candlelight. Mrs Raleigh decided there and then to lend Elizabeth a set of ruby jewellery her husband had designed for her while serving in India.

Unfortunately, the day before the ball while walking on a newly washed marble floor, Mrs Raleigh slipped and fell, twisting her ankle. When the housekeeper, Mrs Ketchum, called the footmen to assist her, Mrs Raleigh could not stand on her own.

"Oh, Aunt, are you in great pain?" Elizabeth ran in from the music room. "Shall I send for Dr Clements? The admiral?"

"No no, dear. It is but a sprain, 'tis all. Do not fret so, Elizabeth." Mrs Raleigh hobbled, leaning heavily on her footman. "Come, help me up the stairs. I shall retire to my chamber. Mrs Ketchum has already called for the physician. There is nothing more to be done."

It took much convincing on Mrs Raleigh's part to convince her husband and niece to attend the Montridge ball without her. "Elizabeth, it would be a shame for you to miss this opportunity. You were so patient with Madame LeSage, after all, and must reap some reward for all those hours being pricked by her pins."

Elizabeth saw the gleam in her aunt's eye. "The dress can wait, Aunt."

"Elizabeth, did not your aunt tell you of the rule?" Admiral Raleigh asked.

"The rule, Uncle?" Elizabeth asked, assured that a story was commencing.

"When we were in India, we made the acquaintance of a Mrs Smith-Hyde—or was it Hyde-Smith? In any case, she informed your aunt that a gown has one good evening to it, and that evening can never be replaced. Of course, I believe her interest in the dressmaker's salon your aunt frequented influenced her beliefs. I swear your aunt obtained more gowns during that tour than in the three years hence."

Laughing, Mrs Raleigh chided, "I did no such thing."

THE MONTRIDGES HAD OUTDONE THEMSELVES, decorating the sumptuous ballroom with hothouse flowers and candles glimmering in crystal chandeliers. The guest list matched the décor as the first circles of London society cavorted and cajoled with each other amidst the excess. Yet, despite the abundance of fabric and sparkle of jewels, when Admiral Raleigh crossed the threshold with his niece on his arm, a pervasive hush fell over the great hall. Elizabeth was partly correct in her assessment that the pause in conversation was due to the return of the distinguished Admiral Stephen Raleigh. Before leaving for India, the Raleighs had been the delight of the *ton*.

Absorbed in her thoughts, Elizabeth missed the collective gasp at her entrance as the attending males perked up and the women scrutinised her natural elegance, contrasted to their primped and acquired finery. Her eyes—deep, dark, and luminescent—drank in the splendour and shone with intelligence. Her satin gown draped her figure in a most alluring manner, and more than one gentleman's resolve succumbed to the bounce of chocolate ringlets when she turned to speak with her uncle. The curve of her neck drew the masculine eye to the swell of her breast. Murmurs regarding her identity rippled through the crowd, and more than one man schemed to obtain an introduction.

Elizabeth was in high demand, her name bandied about, and depending upon the gender of the speaker, the conversation either praised her or ripped her apart. Watching nearby, Miss Bingley gasped when Elizabeth Bennet took to the floor with none other than Viscount Ravensbrook. So great was her stupor, she failed to notice Darcy, who approached her from behind to fulfil his obligation to Bingley to "keep an eye on Caroline and mitigate any trouble she may provoke."

Just before he reached Miss Bingley, his cousin Viscount Braddleton approached him. "I knew I would find you among us this evening," Braddleton spoke though his eyes never left Elizabeth. "It seems there is fresh blood in the market."

"I thought you were otherwise engaged." Following Braddleton's gaze, Darcy was stunned to find Miss Elizabeth Bennet, ravishing in her satin gown and partnering Ravensbrook. *What is she doing here?* He struggled for composure. *How magnificent she truly is!*

Braddleton tore his eyes away from Elizabeth momentarily. "The tables can wait, while some things should not be missed, no?"

"I happen to know for a fact that Miss Bennet—"

"Bennet? Excellent work, Darcy. For once, you are one step ahead of me."

"Miss Bennet is a gentleman's daughter. Her sister—"

"All very interesting, I am sure—perhaps another time? Happy hunting, Darcy." The viscount waved his hand in dismissal, adjusted his cravat, and headed to the opposite end of the hall where Ravensbrook was escorting the belle of the ball. Darcy turned his attention back to Miss Bingley.

Miss Bingley hissed to her sister, "I cannot believe *she* is here. And she was dancing with the son of an earl! How did Elizabeth Bennet obtain an invitation to an evening such as this?"

"I do not know. But fear not: once word circulates of her *obscurity*, I am sure it will be the *last* event she attends." Mrs Hurst quirked her eyebrow, giving her sister a knowing look.

Indulging in another glance at Elizabeth, Darcy's heart beat faster. Miss Bingley cackled, causing the hair on the back of his neck to rise, and he forced his attention back to their diatribe.

"I shall see to *that* myself. Passing herself off as a woman of society indeed. Who does she think she is?"

Deciding he needed more information, Darcy interrupted the sisters. "Miss Bingley, Mrs Hurst." He bowed his polite greeting.

"Mr Darcy, it is good to see you. We have not seen you since our brother's wedding."

"Yes, to the delightful Miss Bennet, now Mrs Bingley," he said while his eyes took in the enticing Bennet whose hand now lay in his cousin's as he accompanied her across the floor. A fire flared in his body as a rush of adrenalin compelled him to supplant his fortunate rival.

Miss Bingley continued her invective. "You have noticed your cousin's *unfortunate* choice of a dancing partner…"

"And Lord Ravensbrook's," Mrs Hurst added.

"Unfortunate?" Darcy asked, his mind envisioning a change of partner for the lovely 'unfortunate.'

"She is Miss Benn— I mean Mrs Bing—" Miss Bingley could not help the shudder that ran up her spine. "She is my new *sister's* sister… of sorts. She is not related, really, not truly so."

"No?" This piqued Darcy's curiosity. "How so?"

Miss Bingley leaned in to whisper in his ear though she intended her voice to carry. "She is a foundling! They say she was discovered on the side of the road!"

Darcy was so stunned, he spoke before thinking. "But how could a babe—"

Mrs Hurst regained her tongue. "She was four years old—"

Dormant images crawled from the dark recesses of Darcy's mind, held at bay by years of denial. Caroline drew him from any sort of self-reflection. "She was nearly five. Even then she must have been tiresome."

"Tiresome?" Darcy asked, looking at the engaging smile and enchanting eyes that sparkled as the viscount led her off the floor. Darcy was surprised when his cousin left Miss Bennet in the company of a much older man. "The admiral," he whispered.

"She has an impertinence that is ill placed in one such as she." Miss Bingley left off when she, too, saw Elizabeth's companion. "Well, that explains the gown *and* the jewels..." She left her thought unspoken, watching Darcy digest the implication.

"Indeed. Well, if you will excuse me, ladies, I must go and speak with my cousin." He bowed to the sisters of his friend, who curtseyed. As he took his leave, they smiled in mutual smug satisfaction.

Competing streams of information merged and battled through the great hall regarding the unknown Elizabeth Bennet. Trying to quell the unsavoury murmurs reaching his friends and allies, the admiral let it be known that Elizabeth was under his protection, unaware that his words might be misconstrued. Those of his immediate circle understood the family connexion, and although they were not silent, their voices were less voluble than the envious and covetous tongues inclined to heed rumours spread by the likes of Miss Bingley. Elizabeth's obscure origins and the unspecified connexion to her distinguished escort fed the desires of those willing to tear her down as well as those hoping to gain her favours for themselves. Those old enough to remember recalled a woman of similar features and great beauty from generations past and remained on the sidelines, sipping their punch and recollecting previous balls when they themselves were young.

Therefore, it was of great interest when Elizabeth was again brought to the dance floor by the most eligible of London's bachelors, Mr Fitzwilliam Darcy. Miss Bingley fumed as the handsome couple moved flawlessly through the steps. Mr Darcy's gaze was hard to decipher, and so intent and focused was he on the sparkling eyes before him that Caroline could not determine whether he approved of the upstart or not. This was a new aspect of the personality she had studied for the last five years, and it puzzled her. Even more disconcerting to her, as the couple ventured from the floor, was the rarest of sounds rumbling through the hall: Mr Darcy laughed.

LATER IN HIS PERSONAL CHAMBERS, Darcy reviewed the evening over a glass of brandy. Although accustomed to it, he was appalled by the bitterness of Miss Bingley's attacks on her new sister. His thoughts moved from the Bingleys to the alluring and enigmatic Miss Elizabeth Bennet. He had surprised himself in asking her for a set. *I do not, as a rule, dance in public with one of such dubious connexions. And there is the question of her birth.*

He took another sip of the smooth liquor. "And yet there *is* something about her…"

Stumbling to his nightstand, his thoughts lurched. *Elizabeth,* his mind cooed, her voice reiterating their earlier conversation. *She impresses more and more…* He splashed water on his heated skin. *Now that is an understatement.* He smiled. "Indeed!" *I cannot fathom why she chose this Raleigh. Perhaps she likes her freedom, and his being at sea…I wonder…perhaps she would consider a change of arrangements? The house on Townsend Street would do nicely. A good neighbourhood but not close to Uncle's latest folly.*

His internal ramblings were interrupted by echoes of his parents' pleas to honour the Darcy name. "I shall not think of them—not now."

He punched his pillow before placing it behind his head. *Much better to think of her. How she glowed when speaking of her sister's happiness. A pure joy to witness. Her eyes sparkle so.* He sat up, suddenly. *I have seen that sparkle before!* Again, memory tried to solidify a connexion as recollections intruded of women he knew who possessed such vivacity. Without warning, his mind shut that mental door, enticing him to a more carnal path involving himself and Elizabeth. Visions of visiting together the isolated bookshelves of Battswell's and Darcy House, and as his eyes closed in peaceful sleep, he saw her pressed against the bookshelves in the fashionable home he planned to establish once she was under him and his *protection.*

April 1812
Darcy House, London

DARCY LOOKED OUT THE WINDOW, AT WAR WITH HIMSELF. THE MAN beholden to his father's principles struggled against five years of Fitzwilliam tutelage, the prize being the intoxicating Elizabeth Bennet. *How can it be that…that a country girl has taken hold of my soul in one conversation and what—two dances?*

He paced the floor. "I am a Fitzwilliam *and* a Darcy"—he gesticulated wildly—"destined to marry the daughter of a peer!" The bluster went out of him as his mind recalled the shrill voice of his aunt, and he added, "Or Anne." He paced again, hands behind his back. "Elizabeth is *perhaps* a gentleman's daughter." He took a step. "Yet she already may be cognisant of her options." He took another step. "And she *has* left her family in Cheapside for the protection of this Raleigh." He sighed. "I heard more than one of my friends bemoan the fact that the admiral was there first."

He rubbed his chin. "But it is odd that he would bring his…." He could not finish the thought. "She is a jewel though." The memory of her eyes, her laugh, and the way her body swayed in the dance filled his mind.

"I am a Darcy, and Darcys do not... We are above *that* sort of arrangement." He turned sharply towards the sidebar, refilling his glass. "What is this hold she has on me? Why can I not rid her from my mind?" As if returning from a stupor, he stared at the bottle and glass in his hands, looking at them strangely. Setting them down as if they were poison, he shook his head. His fist landed on the table. "How can a country miss do this to me? Who is she? Who are her people? That is a question not even the clever Miss Bennet can answer," he snorted. Smug in his mental sparing with her image, he caught sight of the miniature portraits sitting on his desk.

The eyes of his departed father looked out at him: calm, settled, eyes that knew right from wrong and lived in that certainty. The eyes of his mother, Lady Anne, were kinder, more compassionate: eyes that still lived in his sister, Georgiana. His mother's familiar refrain echoed in his heart: *"Who are you to judge the misfortune of another? Their incentive is always a mystery. Always."* It was a theme taken up by his father's sister, Alexandra, before...before his father died when the two of them had tried to counter the imperious pride of his Matlock relations and diminish their influence. Alexandra Darcy Elliston, Duchess of Northampton, had married into the nobility, commanding society and legions of dependents, yet it was *she*, especially in the year after his father's death, who called on him to remember his humanity. It seemed her mission was to ensure that both Darcy and her son, his cousin Julian, retained their compassion, mercy, and sense of humour.

"After Father's death, the duchess would not come to Pemberley— too many memories." He sighed. "She could afford to remain at bay. *I* was the one forced to remain, living with the enormity of my loss, my days filled only with fading recollections of Mother and Father." An unsettled memory surged beneath his exalted self-control, shifting in his brain. Darcy shuddered, recalling the sensations of overwhelming loss and suspicion. "That time nearly ripped my family apart." Darcy returned to his desk. "Nothing was the same after... Time has healed much and yet...once Father was gone, Georgiana would visit Green Haven to see the duchess. But me? I was trapped, stuck with the responsibility that is Pemberley. And with Lord Northampton in service to the crown, my cousin Julian was abroad, too, as his attaché.

"My life was empty, and my Matlock relations were only too happy to fill the void." To his surprise, Darcy felt hot tears on his cheeks, thinking of the mercenary principles they encouraged him to embrace. Bitterly, he muttered, "A Matlock looks out only for his own and never backs down."

Unwilling to dwell on the disparity between his ideals and the reality of his life, Darcy's mind returned to happier days when the duchess's laughter had filled the halls of Darcy House—memories of her wit and adventurous spirit, entertaining through lazy summer after-noons and dark winter nights when she would thrill them with her best stories. When she married the Duke of Northampton, she made him a better man, peeling away the stoic nobleman to reveal a man unafraid to allow his heart to lead him. Sighing, Darcy remembered Pember Lake shimmering in the August sun as they sailed with the Northamp-tons. He saw himself as a young boy swinging on trees and racing Julian to the highest limb. The boys frequently visited each other at either Pemberley or Green Haven, the Elliston estate in Northampton-shire. They would fish, fence, and make elaborate forts both outside and within the ancient walls, using whatever cushion or chair was at hand, to the chagrin of both mothers and housekeepers. Julian was like a brother to Darcy, and even now—although increasingly less frequent —whenever Julian was in England, they would still meet and break bread.

Yet, when I needed him most, he was gone. Darcy sighed, wondering how such wonderful people had slipped away from him. He had left again, that time for Vienna, "and could not be *bothered* to help me with Wickham!" he spat.

"So sorry, old chap," Darcy intoned in a singsong manner. *"I shall inform my mater and pater, but duty calls."*

"Duty!" Darcy said, derision heavy in his voice. "His duty was here with me. *I* am his family. That"—he pointed out the window—"is when I learned who my true family was." He bounced his hand against the glass. "Of all the people in the world, I am beholden to the Matlocks. And *that* is not something they will ever let me forget."

The house of Matlock was notorious amongst the *ton* for the care they took in promoting their place in society. They encouraged Darcy to cleave to their values, trusting in his position to secure his happiness. Under their tutelage, Darcy discovered he liked the deference of others, which befitted his role as master of Pemberley and grandson of an earl. He liked the impenetrability he found in feeling superior. He was proud of his heritage, of all he had accomplished and possessed. And he longed to possess more, much more.

As dawn broke, Darcy's weakening will remained caught between the principles his parents had instilled, the demands of his heart and body, and the demands of the Matlocks—increasing demands to abandon all hopes of a warm and loving home and marry his cousin Anne de Bourgh. "And yet what choice do I have? I owe my uncle everything! If not for him, Georgiana's shame would be broadcast about the *ton* and all chance of her happiness forsaken."

Again, Elizabeth's image danced across his mind, and he chased it. *If I offer for Elizabeth,* he thought, *my aunt and uncle's demands become less unctuous. I shall have Elizabeth with me...forever. For, once she accepts me, nothing and no one will force her from my side. Lady Catherine may lay claim to Pemberley, but I shall have Elizabeth.*

Pleased with his decision, Darcy headed to his chambers for a bath. Disrobing, he took in his reflection in a mirror. Looking himself in the eye, he saw his mother, releasing waves of doubt throughout his body. *How can I?* he asked himself, shamed by the arrogance shaping his features. "And yet, how can I not?" he asked the man in the mirror. "No decent man will offer for her. Her liaison with the admiral is common knowledge. Miss Bingley is sure to broadcast *that* about town. And once Braddleton discovers it, I am sure he will make her an offer."

He wiped his face again. "I shall be doing her a favour! I shall be good to her, true to her. I shall not leave her." He pushed himself away from the washstand he gripped for support. "And if Anne becomes my wife, then I *deserve* the solace of such a remarkable woman. Someone shall have her; why should it not be me?"

WHEN MRS RALEIGH had accustomed herself to using a cane, the Raleighs arranged to take Elizabeth to a performance of *The Marriage of Figaro,* as Mozart was one of her favourite composers. Elizabeth was stunning, her lustrous curls elegantly arranged atop her head, her cheeks rosy, skin creamy, and her eyes gleaming like diamonds with depth and the ability to communicate on many levels. She wore a silk gown the colour of burnished peaches, and she radiated a grace and elegance beyond the normal range of beauty.

"My dear, you are magnificent," Admiral Raleigh said, offering her his arm. Blushing, she looked at her aunt for confirmation.

"Oh, Elizabeth, truly you are stunning—perhaps even more so than at the Montridge ball." Blushing even more, Elizabeth smiled, nodding her head to acknowledge the compliment.

Covent Garden was a whirl of activity as the *ton* and their following meandered about, gossiping over the exalted personages in attendance. Tongues wagged as the Darcy carriage pulled up. Although initially disappointed when Colonel Richard Fitzwilliam emerged, the tittering tongues of the *ton* redoubled when he handed out his young cousin Miss Georgiana Darcy.

Nearly ten minutes later, a hush overcame the crowd as the Raleighs emerged from their own conveyance. The admiral turned to hand out his companion, and a collective gasp unnerved Elizabeth as she left the carriage. Sensing her unease, Raleigh squeezed her hand before turning to hand out his wife. If any of their party noted the appalled expressions as they made their way to their box, they were too genteel to comment.

As the various aristocrats settled in, more than one pair of eyes locked onto the triad seated in the Raleigh box. Many were relieved when the orchestra diverted their aroused curiosity regarding the temptress who seemed more enticing than any opera. It had been said that she was Raleigh's mistress, but Mrs Raleigh's presence at the theatre appeared to contradict that line of reasoning. Colonel Fitzwilliam, along with most men approaching their thirties, was more attuned to and interested in the machinations of the *ton* than those on stage, and he followed many of his fellow bon vivants with his opera glasses.

"I say, she is delectable."

"Who is?" Georgiana asked as she took in the diverse audience.

Years of being in the company of her brother and cousin made Georgiana immune to their coarser inclinations.

"That woman!" He nodded in the direction of the Raleigh box. "Beautiful women come and go, but she is a rare breed—utterly irresistible."

"Regretting your alleged courtship of Lady Mariah?" Georgiana asked in a mix of sweetness and pungent disapproval.

The colonel looked at her sharply. "What do you know of Lady Mariah?"

"Enough," she said, raising the opera glasses to her eyes. *Enough to know you care about her about as much as I care about the velvet covering this banister.* Georgiana swept her eyes across the rows of seats till she found the Raleigh box. She, too, gasped before composing herself. "For once, I must agree. She is everything a beautiful woman should be."

"Do you know with whom she sits?"

Georgiana looked at the older couple engaged in what appeared to be a delightful conversation with the unknown beauty. "She looks familiar."

"You know her?" Richard leaned forward in his seat.

"Not *her*, the woman she is with. That is Mrs Raleigh!"

"Mrs Raleigh," he repeated, trying to assess where that name fell in the social register.

"A sometime neighbour to my aunt Northampton."

"I see." He leaned back yet kept their box in his line of sight. "Pray, why is Mrs Raleigh but a *sometime* neighbour."

"Her husband is an admiral and is often at sea," Georgiana offered, unaware of her cousin's lingering interest. "Mrs Raleigh travels with him."

The colonel folded his arms across his chest, thinking, *At least he is of rank. But what of her?* "And she is their daughter?"

"No, that cannot be. My aunt has often commiserated with her on their lack of children."

"Your aunt has a very healthy son, Georgiana, as you are both aware."

"I know. It is just that…" Georgiana lowered her head. "It is just that the duchess still grieves."

"I swear I shall never understand women," he snorted. "The girl was taken more than a decade ago. You would think they could let it rest."

"Lady Elizabeth was their *daughter*! She was taken from them at Pemberley—my *home*!" The disdain in her cousin's expression stunned her. "Surely, she may be allowed to grieve as long as necessary."

The colonel relaxed his protective posture. Although never truly believing the rumours, his pride recoiled at the innuendo and ostracism he and his family endured because the duke's family believed his eldest aunt, Lady Catherine de Bourgh, had a hand in the kidnapping of young Lady Elizabeth Elliston. Though a hardened combatant, he could not reconcile that someone of his blood could orchestrate the presumed killing of a four-year-old child. In the field of battle, he drew on this instinct to persevere and win, regardless of the cost, yet in moments such as these, he questioned the kind of man he had become.

DURING INTERMISSION, Georgiana and the colonel made their way to the Raleigh box to pay their respects and attempt an introduction to their mysterious guest. However, the line of swags and tittering women was too thick, and they were forced to retreat as the second act began.

"I say, Richard, do not be so dour. There is always the second intermission," Georgiana said with a giggle and a sly smile. Noting her cousin's interest, she continued. "You are familiar enough with the score. When we are five minutes out, we shall leave and forestall the competition, arriving at the Raleighs' door before any others!"

Smiling at her plan, Richard gave Georgiana a brilliant smile. "Brava, Georgiana. Brava."

AT THE END of the second act, Admiral Raleigh rose to order champagne. Opening the door, he nearly threw Colonel Fitzwilliam off balance. Although of different military units, the colonel had enough respect for rank to click his heels and salute the superior officer.

"Admiral Raleigh," he began.

The older man took a hard look at the officer standing before him. "Colonel Fitzwilliam, am I correct?"

An engaging smile lit the colonel's face. "Yes, sir." He let his eyes wander past the shoulder of the older man. As he did, Raleigh peered over *his* shoulder at Georgiana Darcy, who remained to the side.

"Can it be? Miss Darcy, how good to see you!" Raleigh stretched his hand to the young woman as he spoke to his wife. "Dearest, come see who the cavalry brought us. It is the duchess's young niece!"

"Admiral, it is a pleasure." Georgiana beamed at his warm welcome. "Will you do me the honour of introducing your guest?"

"Lizzy, my dear, come and meet the niece of one of our dearest neighbours at Cumberwait."

"It seems we have a surfeit of nieces this evening, Uncle," Elizabeth said as she approached along with her aunt.

"Georgiana!" Mrs Raleigh exclaimed, hugging Georgiana. "Oh, my dear, how you have grown. You and Lizzy are terribly unkind to grown up so fast. It makes one feel positively ancient."

"Elizabeth, may I introduce you to Miss Georgiana Darcy, niece of my dear friend the Duchess of Northampton."

Elizabeth's head swam with echoes of her past ringing in her ears. *"Not even Northampton will stop me now!"* The room swirled, and she reached for the back of a nearby chair. Though her aunt was busy with the introduction, her response was lost on neither military man. Raleigh steadied her at the elbow as Mrs Raleigh continued. "Miss Darcy, this is my niece, Miss Elizabeth Bennet. She is staying with us, and I hope you will come and visit while we are in London."

"How long do you intend to stay in town, madam?" the colonel asked Mrs Raleigh.

"Our stay depends upon the admiral's responsibilities, but we hope to remain throughout the Season."

"Excellent." Colonel Fitzwilliam smiled. "Miss Bennet, from where do you come?"

"Hertfordshire, sir. My family..." Elizabeth stumbled over her words, and Mrs Raleigh quietly took her hand. Elizabeth gave her a diminished smile. "My family's estate is near a lovely little town in Hertfordshire: Longbourn, near Meryton."

"But that is where my brother's friend Mr Bingley resides!" Georgiana added.

Elizabeth looked at the young lady, making the connexion to her dancing partner. Blushing, she recalled the feel of her hand in his—*the way he looked into my eyes. So fascinating...* Sensing that a response was required, she continued. "Indeed, Mr Bingley has the delightful fortune to have recently married my sister."

"You must send them my best wishes for their happiness when next you see them," Georgiana added.

The colonel spoke next to his young cousin. "Well, we must return to our seats, poppet." He turned to the admiral. "It was a pleasure, sir."

The older man bowed his head, watching as the couple turned to leave.

"You must come to see us, Georgiana, and we shall have a long visit," Mrs Raleigh offered. Georgiana nodded her head and smiled as she took her cousin's arm to leave.

four

AFTER A TRIO OF SLEEPLESS NIGHTS, FITZWILLIAM DARCY LABOURED at his desk over the profitability of a proposed investment, his mind besieged by a proposition of another kind. His thoughts clung to Elizabeth Bennet though they had only shared one engagement since her arrival in town. He also saw her during intermissions of *Othello*—in the company of her Cheapside relations, the Gardiners—and he was enchanted by her observations and novel interpretations of the play. It moved her though she never indulged in a vulgar display of sentiment. She teased and cajoled a curmudgeonly lord into a new perspective, and her gown was a sight to cherish. Not even her being in company with those *Gardiners* dampened his pride at the bevy of men appraising her charms.

Being in her presence fuelled his imagination to increasingly fascinating scenes he ached to enact. His favourite occurred in his house on Townsend Street, part of his mother's dowry. It was in a fashionable part of town, and he would be unashamed to be seen leaving it if he could ever tear himself away from her. He pictured her hosting succulent dinners for him alone. Another favourite fantasy involved Elizabeth the morning after a night of passion, allowing him to dissuade her from dressing; frequently, Elizabeth was continuously in his bed...

Darcy was startled from his daydream as the Earl of Matlock and his sister, Lady Catherine de Bourgh, burst into his study. Grateful that he was sitting at his desk, he only raised an eyebrow.

"Nephew!" the lady demanded. "It is customary to rise when your superiors enter a room."

"Yes, and it is the custom for that to occur right after my man finishes announcing their presence in my house."

"Darcy," the earl bellowed. "Your manners!"

"I believe we have had this conversation before, Uncle. Let us get to it. Tell me to what I owe this...singular event of *both* my esteemed Fitzwilliam elders' presence in my home?"

Lady Catherine sat regally in the chair, facing her nephew. "I demand to know what you are about with your atrocious behaviour. Honestly! Dancing with that...that *woman* the other night at the Montridge ball! And then engaging her attentions last evening at the theatre."

"I beg your pardon?" Darcy blinked at the rapidity of gossip spreading throughout the *ton*.

"You know full well that you are pledged to Anne. You are making such a...spectacle...with that unknown...nobody. It is not to be borne."

"Aunt, I am not engaged—to your daughter or any other lady. And until that day, *you* will remain silent on the matter of whom I partner with."

"I will not!"

"Catherine, Darcy is a man of the world, and he is entitled to a few *last* liaisons before he settles down to honour his *family* obligations." Lord Matlock glared at the younger man.

Although Darcy's thoughts ran in a similar vein, he rankled under his uncle's attempted dominance. While Darcy could only picture *Elizabeth* as his lover, he knew his uncle kept a string of mistresses whose leave-takings were becoming increasingly brutal.

"Be that as it may," she continued, "there is a time and a place for such things, and an event of the magnitude of the Montridge ball is most definitely *not* the place to parade one's paramour. It insults my daughter, and I shall not stand for it. Do you hear me?" The older woman stood, fury in her eyes, spittle gathering in the corners of her mouth. "No one humiliates Lady Catherine de Bourgh!"

"Miss Bennet is *nothing* to me, Aunt." *Yet.* "And it behoves you to remember this. There are laws of slander in this country."

"Do not be a fool, Fitzwilliam. She is no one, not even a Bennet!" Lady Catherine raged. "Oh yes, I know of her *dubious* lineage, and I repeat—this will not stand."

With each word, she pointed a bony finger at his chest. "You were formed for Anne, not some charlatan who parades her assets for the pleasure of every rake in town."

"Enough, Catherine. You have said your piece. Now go and find Georgiana," the earl ordered. Glaring at both her brother and nephew, Lady Catherine reluctantly left them. Taking the seat she vacated, the earl tented his fingers. "Darcy, I undoubtedly understand the *need* to supplement the affection of the marital bed. If this Miss Bennet takes your fancy, then offer for her. You have the house on Townsend Street. Give it to her. Give her a carriage—two even—with a generous allowance. With little inconvenience, you shall have it all. A man in your position is entitled to his pleasure, and if you follow my advice, you can fulfil your obligation to your family *and* have the heat of your desire."

Darcy snorted. Catching his response, the earl snapped. "It is your *duty* to marry, and you *will* marry Anne."

"I had thought the choice was mine."

The two glared at each other. "You are a Fitzwilliam, and as the head of this family, it is *my* will that you and Anne marry."

"You overstep yourself, Uncle." Darcy stood firm.

The older man sought signs of weakness, a vantage from which to launch the next prong of his attack. "You know you would be forbidden to introduce Georgiana to this country whelp. If you insist on keeping Miss Bennet's company, I might question your competency if you keep her here with you."

Darcy straightened, his glare hardening.

"Georgiana is at a delicate age, Darcy. One false step in your standing and her future could falter"—he leaned closer—"especially after your nearly tragic oversight last summer at Ramsgate. One transgression might be overlooked—but two?"

"You would not dare!" Darcy barked. Though he maintained an icy stare, he inwardly shook. *I had not thought that even Matlock would stoop so low! No one threatens my sister. No one.*

"Have you *ever* known me to make an idle threat, Darcy? Lady Catherine presses for this daily. Marry your damned cousin, and be done with it."

"I do not love her!" Even to his own ears, the argument sounded weak.

"Love? Do not be a fool. Take Anne as your wife, and make this Bennet chit your mistress. It is what men of our station do—and have done for generations. There is no shame in it."

Darcy hung his head, shards of indignity piercing his consciousness. Hearing his own plans on his uncle's tongue made his skin crawl. Flashes of his parents and the Northamptons plagued him. *How could they feed me to the jackals?* he thought, looking at the corpulent man glaring at him like a wolf. *That we should think alike at all is hard to bear.* Darcy turned to the window, catching his reflection in its mirrored surface; instead, he saw Elizabeth's sparkling eyes and flashing smile. "I need time."

"A month—not a moment more. You need to marry soon if she is to give you an heir and live long enough to raise the child as he ought to be raised."

"'Ought to be raised'?" Darcy was incredulous.

"As a Fitzwilliam."

"The child would be a Darcy."

"You are one of *us*, nephew, and your child will be the same. *Never* forget that," he blustered, advancing on him. "Your Darcy relations have done you no good—none whatsoever—for all their connexions, their fortune!"

The earl softened his rage with false warmth. "*Your* wealth and *my* power will make us unbeatable." Enthusiasm grew as he spoke of the future. "We shall petition for a title, and you will join the House of Lords. Together, we shall rule this land…"

With an iron fist, Darcy thought.

"…and return England to her glory."

"Enough, Uncle." Darcy sighed as the burden of his future closed around him. He looked at his uncle, knowing the difficulty of maintaining a longstanding opposition. He had tried, but Georgiana's near elopement had undermined his confidence. *Matlock is right. Another blunder and Georgiana would be ruined.*

Elizabeth flashed through his mind, and his eyes darted towards the man who watched him as a hunter would his prey. *If I could have her, this might not be so intolerable.* Glancing at the window, he saw the reflection of the miniature portraits of his parents and sighed. *But what would you think of me?*

"I shall give you my answer in a month."

"A month, Darcy—no longer."

AT DARCY'S FRONT DOOR, Lord Matlock and Lady Catherine separated, and she descended to her carriage. Lord Matlock watched not only his sister's departure but also the traffic on the street, taking pleasure in the fashionable young women parading in the park across the street. Eventually, he nodded, and the coachman opened his carriage door. Descending the stairs with more gusto than usual, he stumbled, using his cane to stabilise his sizeable frame. With the aid of his coachman, he drew himself into the carriage and was off.

Twenty feet away, another carriage followed the earl, maintaining a constant distance till the earl's conveyance turned into Townsend Street.

RIDING through Hyde Park early next morning, Darcy saw the enticing figure of Miss Elizabeth Bennet as she walked with a young woman he assumed to be her maid. The weight of his despair was lightened as he glimpsed the skin between the rim of her bonnet and the collar of her coat, and he noted a flush on her cheeks from the exercise. He licked his lips as he noticed the delightful smile animating hers. *It is like a dance. She is so graceful simply walking.* Hearing her melodic laughter, he urged his horse Attila closer.

"Miss Bennet?" He triumphed at her surprise as her beautiful lips parted, forming a perfect circle that he imagined putting to good use. *Whoa, boy. Do not get ahead of yourself.*

"Mr Darcy?"

Bringing his horse around, he dismounted, noting that she backed away when his horse shied towards her. Her voice shook, eyes locked on the beast. "What brings you out so early this morning?"

"I often ride at this hour. It allows Attila his head to recall what being a horse is about."

She turned away. "Well, I thank you for stopping, but I would not wish to interrupt your ride." Then Elizabeth stopped, looking around the nearly deserted park. She tentatively took his offered arm, and they strolled along the secluded path.

Once they had completed nearly a quarter of the length, Darcy spoke. "Miss Bennet, if I may be so bold as to ask, are you happy?"

"Happy, sir?"

"Yes. Happy."

"I am afraid I do not take your meaning, sir."

"Certainly, you cannot be content with the admiral…giving your affection to a man of his advanced age? Is this all you believe the world has to offer?"

"Age? Offer? Mr Darcy I must ask you to speak plainly as I do not take your meaning."

"I…you must forgive me, madam. I am unversed in these matters."

"What matters do you mean?"

"In arranging…"

"Arranging…what?" Elizabeth stopped, placing her hands on her hips. "I ask again, Mr Darcy, please speak your mind and let us be done with this."

Biting his bottom lip, he tore his eyes away from her delightful anger. "What I propose, perhaps a bit prematurely, but I find myself pressed for time…"

Seeing she was about to interrupt, he continued, holding out his arm for her. "My family…um, the Earl of Matlock and Lady Catherine de Bourgh are not persons to be denied, Miss Bennet."

Presuming her silence to be recognition of her proper place, he continued. "They have imposed a time frame upon some rather personal decisions regarding marriage to my cousin Miss de Bourgh, but before I forge ahead with my engagement, with the…my plans to wed my cousin and join our two estates, I wish to secure my happiness…with you."

"Lady Cat..." Elizabeth whispered, seeming lost in thought.

"Yes, Lady Catherine de Bourgh," he repeated, irked that she was not attending. "Do you know her?"

"Miss Bennet?" Elizabeth's young maid stepped forward, casting a scornful glance at the tall, brooding gentleman.

"Yes, Markum, what is it?"

"You asked to be apprised when it was coming on seven o'clock. You know how your *uncle*, Admiral Raleigh, dislikes any delay in the morning meal."

"Your *uncle?*" Darcy sputtered, confusion evident in his eyes. "The admiral? He is your...your uncle? I thought..."

He stepped forward, but Elizabeth stepped back.

"Miss Bingley made no mention of an admiral."

"Neither I, nor Jane for that matter, are in the habit of parading *our* relations about as mere stepping stones to increase our social standing." She paused, understanding growing on her countenance, coupled with rage. "Just *what* was the relationship your twisted mind had conjured between the admiral and me?"

He felt himself blush, and the fire in her eyes flared.

"You...you thought that he and I...were...?" She turned from him. "Oh, you *are* insufferable."

"What other conclusion could I draw, seeing such a beautiful woman on the arm of a much older—"

"He is married to my aunt!" She turned to gather herself. "I had thought better of you, sir. But you are just like so many other wealthy, young men it seems: thoughtless and careless with your assumptions."

"I had my reasons." He sounded petulant even to his own ears. "I... must marry...my cousin Miss Anne de Bourgh. I felt with you...with me...I could..."

"Could *what?*"

"Have..." He could not say it aloud.

"How dare you!" she hissed.

Her eyes glared, drawing him like a magnet. Before he knew what he was about, he kissed her, so quickly that she had no time to move before his lips claimed hers. In a flash, she withdrew, slapping him hard.

Darcy was at the extreme ragged edge of his vaulted self-possession. "That hurt!"

"It was meant to." She stepped back. "Aargh! I knew by the way Miss Bingley spoke that you must share her disdain for the feelings of others, but I had *hoped* your friendship with her brother, now *my* brother, would acquit you of such malice."

She stabbed her finger into his stunned chest. Even the heaving of her agitated breast could not dissuade him from the fire in her eyes. "I see, however, that my *first* impression of you was correct. You, sir, are *no* gentleman, and you are the last man from whom I would ever accept a proposal—*of any kind*!"

Her anger dissipating for the moment, Elizabeth stepped back. "Good day." She turned, joining her maid as they left the park.

Darcy could only stand there, mouth agape. *I have never!* He twisted about to see who, if anyone, witnessed his humiliation. Gathering Attila's reins, he cast a mournful look at her retreating form as he mounted. Before giving his horse a kick in the sides, he said, "I shall not see her again."

As she walked from the park, Elizabeth had to focus on placing one foot in front of the other. Furious with Mr Darcy, she knew to contain herself until reaching the sanctum of her chambers. Yet, with each step, she felt compelled to scream. They picked up their pace, and Markum escorted her charge upstairs to the lady's apartment.

Throwing herself onto her bed, she broke into uncontrollable sobs. *How could he? How could he ask me to consider such a thing? That is not my destiny. Never! I would rather starve than…than sell myself to some man just to take the chill out of someone's arranged marriage!* The unceasing taunt of Frances Bennet came unbidden: *"No decent man will ever offer for you, Miss Lizzy."* She feared her step-aunt might be right, and her tears increased, quelling the unspoken hope that a man such as Mr Darcy would ever offer an *honourable* proposal to her. Rocking her body, she sobbed into an exhausted sleep that gave her no peace…

Elizabeth was walking down a beautiful path, shaded by

*ancient trees, happy and assured of being loved. She was at
peace, a state of being she had not felt since Edwin Bennet's
death five years earlier. As she explored the oddly familiar
pathway, hooves galloping towards her at breakneck speed
intruded on her idyll. Before she could move to safety, an arm
reached down and scooped her up mid-stride. The horse
continued at break-neck speed as she dangled, suspended in the
air. She screamed, crying out for release, but the unseen
abductor only slammed her in front of his saddle. Pulling free
from his grasp, she drew a breath before hurling herself from
the horse, only to be roughly caught by the man's companion
and pushed into a waiting carriage.*

Fearing her mistress's growing distress, Markum sent for Mrs
Raleigh. By the time she arrived, Elizabeth's dream had unveiled the
face of the one in the carriage. After years of endless night terrors,
Elizabeth came face to face with the person holding the riding crop that
had inflicted searing pain on Elizabeth's four-year-old back.

Rushing to her side, Mrs Raleigh caught Elizabeth up in her arms,
the admiral looking on helplessly while Elizabeth screamed. "No, no!
Please! I will be good! I will!" Stephen Raleigh hurried from Elizabeth's door, calling for the physician while Mrs Raleigh rocked Elizabeth in her arms. Markum wiped Elizabeth's fevered brow with a cool
cloth.

"Lizzy, child, please...I beg you...calm down." Holding Elizabeth
to her breast, Mrs Raleigh frantically scanned her memory for a way to
comfort her niece. She tried recalling her sister's letters for any
mention of techniques Gloria and Edwin had used to calm Elizabeth
years ago. When the little girl first came to Longbourn, she had been
tormented by dreams so terrible that it took hours for her sobs to cease.
More often than not, it had been Jane's gentle ministrations that calmed
the frightened child. Mrs Raleigh thought of all Elizabeth had endured
since Edwin had found her. Gloria Bennet's death had necessitated a
move with Thomas Bennet to Longbourn when Elizabeth was nine, as
Edwin felt he needed Thomas and his wife, Franny, to help raise *his*
girls. But letters from Edwin and Jane—and even oblique references
from Elizabeth herself—informed Mrs Raleigh that, rather than a

mother's love, Frances Bennet tormented Elizabeth as an unrelated foundling.

Edwin's death five years ago had removed the last barrier to Franny's wrath. And now, Jane's marriage had broken her only link to those happier days. Realising the depth of Elizabeth's sorrow, Mrs Raleigh's heart ached anew for the waif she had instantly claimed. From their first meeting, something about Elizabeth had captivated her. She was never sure whether it was the little girl's spunk that took such strong hold of her heart, or whether it was the unaffected beauty of her unending curls and intelligent eyes that spoke so eloquently and decisively. But her own marriage, and subsequent travel to the Far East with Stephen, had given them little time to build the bonds that could fully protect or comfort Elizabeth.

Such were her thoughts as Dr Clements entered and, to Mrs Raleigh's great relief, found nothing physically wrong with her niece. "Thank you, I shall see to it personally that my niece abides by your recommendations."

Chuckling, Dr Clements finished putting away his instruments. "Of that, Mrs Raleigh, I have no doubt. Anyone who can keep Admiral Raleigh in line with a doctor's orders is a force to be reckoned with."

A knowing smile crossed the good doctor's face; he nodded and, taking up his bag, he made for the door. "Good day, and please do not hesitate to call should your niece's condition worsen."

"Thank you, Dr Clements. You are most kind."

"Not at all." And with that, Mrs Raleigh returned to rocking her niece in her sleep.

ELIZABETH'S BAD DREAMS CONTINUED, AND MRS RALEIGH SCOURED her attics for her sister's letters, now yellowed by time, seeking clues to relieve Elizabeth's tumult. She read first to herself and then to Stephen of the night terrors, of Elizabeth's excessive fear of horses, of the bruises and open wounds criss-crossing her back, and of a fever that rendered her unconscious for days when first found. She read in excruciating detail of the beautiful dress Elizabeth wore, though it was soiled with wear and the blood of numerous beatings. Of the finest silk, it was trimmed with roses embroidered along the hem, collar, and sleeves. Gloria and Hill laundered it until only the faintest of stains remained on the back, and they fussed over its preservation in her hope chest.

"Her chest—Elizabeth's hope chest!" Mrs Raleigh jumped from her chair. "I must write to Thomas and see whether they still have it. Perhaps it will aid Elizabeth to have a small piece of her life with Gloria and Edwin." She wrote an express letter to Longbourn, requesting Elizabeth's chest be sent to Raleigh House and giving a brief description of Lizzy's tumultuous state. Then she carried the bundle of letters to confer with her husband on the latest idea perco-lating in her head.

Later that afternoon, both Admiral and Mrs Raleigh took tea with their niece. For only the third time since the incident, she was well enough to sit in the parlour. In addition to the refreshments, Elizabeth found a bundle of letters Gloria Bennet had written to Mrs Raleigh, recording details obscured by the passage of time and the love of her adopted family. "When you are ready, dear"—Mrs Raleigh patted the neatly tied bundle—"we"—and she looked at her husband who nodded —"feel it may do you some good to read how loved you were at Long-bourn—the joy you were to both Gloria and Edwin and their contin-uing love for you, Elizabeth."

Tears crested along Elizabeth's cheeks, but they were not the hysterical tears of days before. Elizabeth nodded and tentatively took hold of the packet. Reverently placing it on her lap, her fingers explored the folded parchment. "I may keep these?"

"Yes, of course, dear."

A grateful whisper was all she could summon. "Thank you…"

Pemberley, Derbyshire

ALTHOUGH NOT YET NOON, Darcy refilled his third glass of fine French brandy—one of the spoils of war accumulated by his cousin Colonel Fitzwilliam. Emptying it in one gulp, he stumbled to his desk where he buried his head in his hands, subsumed by the weight of the last year. *First Georgiana, and now I fall upon my own sword.* He looked up through bleary eyes. *I am no better than that animal Wickham, dishon-ouring a woman!*

Lifting his glass, he addressed the empty room. "What he tried with Georgiana, *I* did to Elizabeth. Only *he* had more finesse!" He finished the glass and looked around the room. A deep shudder of revulsion crept up his spine, and he returned to the sideboard, empty-handed. Steadying himself, he grabbed the crystal decanter, making his way to the safety of his desk. His heart grew heavier, and he fought against the tears trickling down his cheek. His head ached from the spent emotion, and he banged his fists against the desk. "I was more concerned with propriety than protecting Georgiana! How was she to know Wickham hid such evil behind that simpering flattery, wooing women without raising one iota of suspicion. *I made you his perfect victim, sister.*" His gaze landed on the portraits hanging in his study. "I failed you too— Mother, Father—in so many ways."

He felt their accusations from the grave. "What was I to do? I had an estate to run, and…Northampton was consumed with grief. The duchess was so focused on his recovery when he fell." He replaced his father's portrait on the credenza behind his desk. "That left Matlock. Thank heavens *he* had time for us. His sense of honour—of *family*— rallied him, and he came to our rescue. But at such a cost, Mama"—he looked at his mother's image—"at such a cost."

Darcy's voice fell away. "And now? Now I have lost the only woman I believe I could ever love. She is a country girl—no more than a gentleman's daughter. Yet she is everything enchanting. So light and pleasing, her mind is quick, and when she is happy, she is astounding. I believe I…I feel…I love her."

Darcy choked back another rush of tears. "And she is lost to me." He put the portrait down absentmindedly, and making his way to the window, he looked across the vast expanse of land that had been his family's heritage for centuries. Yet he saw nothing more than Elizabeth's eyes as they had flashed and sparkled throughout the brief span of their acquaintance. "And that is all I shall ever have of her."

Closing his eyes, he felt crushing defeat, his mind tormenting him with her voice, her smile, and always, *those eyes!* "Will this never end?" He banged his hand against the window frame. When he opened his eyes, he could see the dust rising behind a substantial carriage barrelling down the long tree-lined drive. It cleared the trees, and he groaned when he recognised the crest on the polished door. "What on earth does she want with me now?"

ELIZABETH SETTLED into the bay window of her room overlooking the little park affronting Raleigh House. There was a lovely stand of trees whose branches were plainly visible between the newly sprouting leaves. Hoping to focus the turbulence of her mind on the interplay of line and light, she brought her stylus to the parchment, drawing long, slashing lines across its surface, creating branches intersecting one atop another. Elizabeth's mind spun, unravelling the curtain protecting her from that awful night she was taken from her family. As if a cloud moved past her eyes, she saw the carriage with her younger self crouched in one corner, legs tucked beneath her to avoid touching any of the frightening adults surrounding her. The racing wheels of the great coach hit a bump, sending the large man next to her crashing into her small frame. The man with the big moustache exclaimed as she screamed, her body slamming against the carriage wall. Pushing her small body upright, Elizabeth looked up as the Cat pulled at the man's riding crop and struck her. Elizabeth turned her back to them to protect herself.

She saw it play out before her as she sat, her stylus striking out against the paper now strewn with lash-like lines. All the emotion suppressed from years of survival burst forth on the page as Elizabeth drew what her heart felt. Her mind had no connexion with the design; all she knew was that she finally was purging that pain from her body. "Please, God, let it end! Please!" she cried, over and over until, finally exhausted—the stylus dulled beyond use—Elizabeth could draw no more. Her mind was a blank. Without looking at the parchment, she replaced it in her portfolio and dragged herself to bed, succumbing to vital rest. To her surprise and supreme delight, she slept a deep, dreamless sleep.

THE DUCHESS OF NORTHAMPTON walked with single-minded determination up Pemberley's stairs. Without preamble, the door opened, and the footman bowed. She continued until approached by the housekeeper, Mrs Reynolds.

"Your Grace?"

"I must speak with my nephew. He is at home?"

"Yes, madam, but he is—"

The duchess quirked her brow, eyes glinting with determination. "Not accepting callers? Good—see that we are not disturbed." Continuing on, she steeled herself to her purpose and shut out the memories. Throwing open the door, she entered, shutting it with such force that the sound reverberated down the marble hallway.

"Duchess?" Fitzwilliam Darcy rose from his armchair.

"Yes, Darcy, it is I." She approached but halted when an offensive odour assaulted her. "Good lord, when did you last bathe?"

Darcy looked down, appearing chagrined. "I am pleased to welcome you back to your ancestral home. It has been an age, has it not?"

"What are you about?" The duchess stepped closer till her nose verified her suspicions. "I truly must recommend that you attend to your…personal habits."

She sat, and Darcy did as well. "I have received a report of an alarming nature and have not come to hear it denied, for I trust my source. I have come to find out what you and that blasted *family* are about."

"Forgive me, Duchess," he said with an unmistakable disdain. "But I do not like your tone or your insinuations against my *family!"*

"Darcy!" the duchess replied, shocked.

He held up his hand. "I think it highly disingenuous of you to come here and insult the people who came to my res—who have supported me in the past."

The duchess paused, and he recalled another brow that challenged him in the same manner. He stared at her much longer than appropriate. She took his measure with a quick glance at the nearly empty decanter on his desk. "Pray tell, just how did the Matlocks *support* you, nephew."

"You mean apart from all the years after my father's death? Take, for example, in just this last *year* while you tarried at Green Haven, my uncle Matlock was busy, working assiduously to…to quell the rumours." Darcy flushed angrily. "*He* arranged to have Wickham silenced, requiring more modest sums than I could have arranged. Of course, I would have killed him…"

"You pay him? Still?" the duchess asked sharply.

Darcy looked offended and sheepish simultaneously. "Yes…but as I said, only in small amounts."

"Darcy!" The duchess rose, hesitating to reach out to her now-agitated nephew. Instead, she sat on the arm of a nearby chair, her face a mixture of anger and sadness. "The duke and I bought Wickham's debts to ensure his silence. It was the *duke* who threatened that he would see Wickham *hang* if he heard of any rumour regarding Georgiana! And now? Now you say that your uncle—"

The duchess went to Darcy's desk, pouring the remains of the bottle into his discarded glass and emptying it in one gulp as Darcy looked on.

"What on earth are you talking about?"

"Sit," she commanded, and like the young boy he once was, he did. "Julian spoke to us before he left the country, and of course we responded—not with words but with action." She came and sat across from him. "The duke was still convalescing, so Julian and I launched an investigation of our own—"

"But Julian left the country!"

The duchess looked at Darcy with such sympathy that he had to turn away. "*Before* leaving, which he delayed until the investigation was complete." She watched Darcy take in this information before continuing. "We had Wickham tracked. Rothem, our steward's brother, unearthed the swath of debts and other damages that man unleashed across the kingdom." She sighed and, coming to his side, took his hands. "We methodically bought up his debts and, when we found him hiding at a hideous boarding house in St. Giles, presented our ultimatum. He could be silent and never get in touch with you or Georgiana, yet remain free, or he could work off his debts in prison, or be deported."

She smiled at Darcy's shocked expression. "Julian says the coup de grace was when he informed Wickham of the duke's threat and that if he ever heard any word of Georgiana's near elopement bantered about the *ton*, he would see to it *personally* that Wickham was hanged in the public square in Lambton."

She rubbed her brow trying to remove the tension gathering there. "I cannot understand your ignorance of this. The duke wrote you—"

"He did not!"

"I do not lie." Her challenge cut through the haze of misconception.

"But how…is this possible? Matlock said—"

The duchess snorted again. "*Matlock* is a deceiver of the first order. It was his loose tongue that started the last round of rumours."

"What? What rumours?" Darcy's agitation soared.

She took his hand to lower his distress to a reasonable level. "Please. It has been taken care of."

"How? When?" he demanded. "I had not heard of any rumours about Georgiana..."

"That is because I—well, Julian really—took care of them."

"But when?"

"Before he left the country this last time. It seems that he and Matlock share a penchant for a particular courtesan. Julian swears it is because she was a spy in the French court and has many useful associates on the continent. I say rubbish to that. She is a beautiful woman who knows how to please a man.

"Matlock was mouthing off to a Miss Natalia with whom he had a recent liaison. Julian was in the next room—exchanging state secrets, no doubt—and heard your uncle commenting that his niece had narrowly escaped a similar fate to the one that led Mademoiselle Natalia to her current predicament."

The duchess smiled ruefully. "Julian said Miss Natalia was none too happy about *that* remark, but later he was able to persuade her to forget she had ever heard the name 'Darcy.'"

"He mentioned Georgiana by name?" Darcy looked horrified.

Seeing his distress, the duchess only nodded. "Will you not ask me why we acted the way we did?"

It took a moment for Darcy to rally, but he whispered, "Why?"

"Why did your uncle deceive you? That answer you must ask of him." She took hold of his hand and squeezed, waiting until he was able to look her in the eye. "As to why *we* acted in your behalf? Because we love you, and we *are* your family. And we have learned that there is nothing so wondrous as family or more worth protecting than those one holds dear." She smiled at him. "You are part of us, and perhaps we should have written more often and come to you, but you know how difficult it is for me to come here."

For the first time since crossing the threshold of her childhood home, the duchess's eyes wandered around the room that was once her father's study and then belonged to her brother. "Now this is yours. And I am proud of all I have seen and heard of life here. But..."

Silenced, they searched for a way through the moment.

The duchess spoke, her voice unsteady. "There is no excuse for ignoring you and Georgiana. There could never be one. I tried—truly, I tried to return. But I—I could not. After your father died, I could not… so I sent for Georgiana to come to Green Haven. And she did until… first there was the duke's diplomatic travels, then for so long we were unsure whether he would live, and afterwards, whether he would walk again.

"By the time we were able to be of use to you, it seemed that the Matlocks had taken hold, and all we could do was watch from the sidelines."

Bitterness filled her, but she rallied and spoke with humility. "I am sorry to have forsaken you when you needed us most. Julian tried to warn us of your need…of the extent the Matlocks…"

The duchess fell silent for a moment. "But to make such an improper suggestion to a gentleman's daughter! Even for a Matlock, that is low."

Darcy collapsed into his chair, looking defeated. "How did you—?"

"I refer to your cousin Viscount Braddleton. He danced with Elizabeth, the niece of Admiral and Mrs Raleigh, our dear friends in Northampton. Braddleton danced with her at the Worthington ball and soon after made her an unseemly offer—in a *public* park for God's sake! Has he no shame? Elizabeth said not a word. She has been… unwell ever since."

The duchess wrung her hands. "And the admiral…well, he did not become the commanding person he is by sitting idly by. He interrogated Markum, and *she* described the miscreant perfectly: tall, dark hair, curls, a deep voice, impeccably dressed."

"The lady is unwell?" Darcy's voice was pained.

"She has not been the same since that day."

Darcy hung his head. "Braddleton has always been a careless rake but—"

"Careless?" the duchess exclaimed. "Do you mean to say that *you* would have offered your *protection* without the sanctity of marriage, regardless of her respectability if she was not connected to Raleigh?"

She rose. "And if she had refused as she did? If she were alone in the world, would you have left it at that? Accepted her choice? Or would you have forced her hand? Demanded she give herself over to you? Would you have taken what she would not willingly give?"

"I...no! I am not such a depraved being."

"No?" the duchess demanded. "Mrs Raleigh was distressed enough to write, to risk our friendship over a lack of depravity in one who is perilously close to you."

"I am here, am I not?"

"What does being at Pemberley have to do with anything?"

"I was in a situation once," he hedged. "Reminiscent of that one"—his arm made an arc about him—"and I removed myself from London...to..."

The duchess took in her nephew's distress. *So like his father.* "To remove yourself from her?"

"I...held ambitions for her..." He was unwilling to clarify the situation to his aunt.

The duchess thought this through and softened her voice, looking at Darcy and seeing her nephew suffered sorrow more than shame. *The rest must wait for another day, but I promise you, Fitzwilliam Darcy, that I shall get to the bottom of this.* After what felt like eternity, she retook her seat. "I have also heard among my friends that pressure is being exerted on you to marry your cousin Anne."

Sighing, Darcy slumped in his chair then leaned forward to rest his elbows on his desk, his hands clasped before him. "Yes."

"I see."

"Do you?" Anger coloured his voice.

"Yes, I do. I know first-hand of the Matlocks' determination in achieving their goals." She looked him directly in the eye. "They stop at nothing—"

"Yet you left Georgiana and me to their wiles!" His tone was heavy and laden with the absolute despair of having been abandoned.

"Yes, I did," she replied unflinchingly. "I did, and for that I *am* sorry. I could do no more than have her at Green Haven. When George died, you were tied to Pemberley."

Darcy looked up to see his indomitable aunt tremble, her lower lip between her teeth. When she was able to speak, she whispered, looking into his eyes for absolution. "I could not."

Darcy went to his knees before her, taking her hands gently in his. "It is in the past."

"But you suffered for my weakness. Please, I beg you, forgive me." Their eyes locked, and there was peace between them. When his beautiful aunt gave him a weak smile, the tension of the last year lightened just enough for hope to creep in. Her tears were a surprise to him, as were her hands on his cheek and the kiss to his brow. "My darling boy. What a sorry lot we are, are we not?

"Now, tell me why the Matlocks feel obligated to force your hand, my dearest nephew."

"Your *only* nephew," came the well-worn refrain.

"Yes, my *only* nephew." She chuckled. "Come, tell your auntie what it is that troubles you."

Darcy took the chair adjacent to hers. "Since last year's disaster, Lady Catherine has been nearly continuous in her demand that I marry Anne. While Lord Matlock promises to protect our name from ruin, Lady Catherine threatens the opposite—to expose us should I not agree to her demands."

"No!" she gasped. "Why did no one—? Belay that...I did not deserve your confidences then. But now I *will* have my share in the conversation."

Smiling, he nodded. "It has been a difficult position to maintain when one's family—"

"—forces you to choose between saving Georgiana and saving Anne."

"Saving *Anne*? I hardly see it that way." Darcy rubbed his temple.

"I cannot believe that even Lady Catherine would be so cold or calculating as to wish her daughter to marry any man who would have her."

Darcy's apparent confusion amused her. "Think, nephew, other than bullying *you* into her bridal chamber, what kind of man would willingly unite with the house of de Bourgh? At least with you, she is assured of kindness towards that poor creature."

Darcy nodded, amazed.

"Still, to force the two of you into a loveless union—at least, I assume it is...or rather would be...loveless?"

"I feel pity for Anne but nothing more. And although Matlock spoke of an heir, I do not believe she would survive childbirth."

The duchess quirked her head. "That would tangle things, would it not? To wish to marry her to you, knowing that doing so endangers her life…well, more than most. Although Lady Catherine—the entire Matlock clan, really—seems to possess remarkable powers to see and believe only that which suits their aims."

"At least she has let go of that absurd idea that Mother wished a union between Anne and me."

"Yes"—she gave him a rueful reply—"I believe Philip and George set that lie to rest." She looked towards the window, lost in a distant memory until Darcy took her hand. Returning to the present, the duchess assumed a smile and patted his hand. "The question remains— what are *you* going to do now?"

She could see that he was lost for answers. "Please know that Philip and I shall do whatever we can, whatever is necessary, to help you if you wish to avoid this marriage."

"I wonder whether it is what I deserve."

The duchess held his hand tightly. "No one deserves to live without love. Your father *and* mother would wish nothing less for you than to live with one who loves you—not the name, the estate, or the fortune, but you. Remember that—it is God's truth. But you must be strong and fight for love when it comes."

He looked ashamed. "It was not"—he swallowed—"Braddleton."

"I see."

"I—"

She held up her hand. Taking one breath and then another, the duchess looked at her nephew's sunken cheeks and the circles under his sad eyes. *And his neglect of his hygiene!* She sighed. *Just like George, punishing himself so much more than another ever could.*

Recalling what helped her older brother, she spoke. "I am willing to *overlook* this transgression as it is obvious that you punish yourself mightily for it. *And* because I understand from Mrs Raleigh that Miss Bennet retaliated by slapping you."

He nodded.

At his honest dismay, her heart softened for the motherless boy before her. "Again, I ask—what do you plan to do about it?"

"What can I do? She is lost to me. I cannot imagine she would accept any offer…any word from me…not now." The sadness returned to his eyes.

She watched him closely. "What would you ask of her now?"

Darcy looked up, and her heart cried for the child he had been, the boy who still looked so lost. "For her hand, Aunt." He took a deep breath to steady his shaking hand. "Just knowing I have harmed her cuts deeply. I was mad and cruel and selfish, and I know I have relinquished all hope of righting things between us."

He ran his hand through his unwashed hair. The duchess took in his distraught appearance and wondered what this woman could be to her nephew. "Since that day in the park, I have come to realise a great many things about myself, none of them pleasing—except that I recognise how extraordinary Elizabeth Bennet is. In the brief moments I have been favoured with her presence, I have felt alive, truly alive. And I enjoy the feeling."

The duchess noted the animation returning to her nephew and sent a silent prayer that somehow this would resolve itself in his favour.

"Without her, without the hope of her, nothing seems to matter. My heart tells me that somehow I must convince her to accept me—my hand—that my happiness depends on having her with me always."

He looked sheepishly at his aunt. "I know it may sound foolish, but that is how I feel."

"Good," she said.

"But what of Georgiana? They threaten to take her from me if I—"

"Let the duke and me worry about this. Surely, we can come to some arrangement. After all, what use is all our money and connexions if not to help our nearest and dearest. And you *are*—you and Georgiana." She patted his hand. "And grovelling is never pleasant. But as the duke rightly knows, in love, there is no shame."

Six

May 1812

Lieutenant George Wickham looked up from his assigned paperwork. As one of the few educated officers, he was tasked with contracting provisions for his militia unit. When his mate Denny led in the unshaven but well-dressed horseman, he was surprised. The man was tall and gruff, and when he shot Denny a blistering look, Wickham dismissed his friend. "Thank you, Denny."

Looking askance at the curt dismissal by a man who owed him nearly fifty pounds, Denny huffed but left them alone. The stranger took a seat, leaning heavily on the rough wooden table the lieutenant used as a desk. Wickham took the measure of the man, unnerved at the unrelenting glare in his eyes. He coughed to clear his throat. "What may I do for you, my good man?"

Glancing around the empty room, the man answered in a hushed tone, "My mistress requests your presence, Mr Wickham."

Smiling, he wondered which of his paramours requested his services. "And who would your mistress be?"

"Lady Catherine de Bourgh, sir. And as you know, she is *not* a lady to be gainsaid."

Wickham attempted to mask his discomposure. "No, no she is not." He looked into the man's face and found no malice or threat. "What —?" He cleared his throat and began again. "What business would your mistress have with me?"

"Her ladyship does not share her thoughts with the likes of me."

Wickham nodded. "When?"

"As soon as may be. You know Rosings does not like to be kept waiting."

"I have Sunday free."

"Sunday it is." The man rose to leave, but before opening the door, he addressed Wickham one final time. "Be assured, Mr Wickham, that should you not keep the appointment, I am advised to come and get you." The man's grin sent Wickham's heart racing, and the hair on the back of his neck stood on end.

The man tipped his head, replaced his hat, and left the room. Wickham tried to focus on the report he was writing—knowing that he needed to cover *misdirected* funds—but he found it increasingly difficult to do so. Unable to discern her purpose in asking for him—of all people—he recalled her obsession with uniting Pemberley and Rosings. Later, undressing for bed, he spat. *Why should Darcy get it all? True, Anne de Bourgh is no beauty, but she is rich.*

He laughed outright at the thought of actually doing his nemesis a favour. When his head hit the pillow after assiduously working through his plan, he fell asleep with one word on his lips: "Rosings."

GEORGIANA ENTERED the breakfast room at Ridgedale, the town home of the Matlock family. Although never close to her Matlock relations, Georgiana found herself more frequently in their company since her uncle Northampton's accident nearly three years ago.

"Aunt…" she began a week into her visit.

"Yes, dear?" Lady Matlock continued to peruse a review of a recent exhibit of Turner's paintings.

"Did my brother seem…out of sorts to you?"

It was not so much *what* she said but *how* that caught the countess's attention. Placing the paper down, the elegant woman cocked her head to the right. "I...did not notice anything particular."

Smoothing the paper along the polished table, she refocused on the article. "Georgiana, I believe we shall have an outing of sorts. Lady Bambridge speaks very highly of this Mr Turner and his work. I wish to see it, and you shall accompany me."

"WILL YOU NOT TELL ME, ELIZABETH?" Mrs Raleigh asked amongst the sea of pillows on the young woman's bed. Smoothing the wayward curls from her niece's brow, Mrs Raleigh reviewed the names of men Elizabeth had danced with at the Montridge ball. *I have asked directly whether it was Braddleton, but she says nothing.* Mrs Raleigh reviewed the other possibilities as she stroked Elizabeth's hand. *There was the duchess's nephew, Mr Darcy, but she assured me it could not be him. Then there is Lord Ravensbrook, but I am certain he knows our connexion to Lizzy. That leaves Braddleton! It must be him. He is notorious for his lascivious and reckless behaviour. Oh, my poor Lizzy!*

Elizabeth shook her head. "It signifies not. I shall never see him again." When she pulled back, Mrs Raleigh was horrified to see despair in Elizabeth's expressive eyes.

"Dearest, please." Mrs Raleigh clasped the girl to her. "Tell me what pains you so."

"Mrs Bennet always said that no decent man would ever offer for me." Elizabeth looked searchingly into Mrs Raleigh's eyes. "She said I would be alone, that I was destined for such a fate."

Mrs Raleigh had to strain to hear the last. "Nonsense! I defy you to find two farthings worth of sense in anything that woman has *ever* said!"

Mrs Raleigh took Elizabeth's hand and looked her directly in the eyes. "This is most definitely not the time to remember anything *she* chattered about. First of all, you are *not* alone, and second, not only do you have your intelligence, wit, beauty, *and* connexions, but you also have a substantial dowry so that you *are* mistress of your future, unlike *her* unfortunate daughters. You and Jane have always been cared for. My sister and her husband could do no less than ensure you were protected, always."

"It is not only that." Elizabeth bit on her lower lip. "Miss Bingley has said something similar to me."

Mrs Raleigh gasped in horror. "I did not know she could be so brazen."

"The woman holds no love for me and is an unrepentant gossip. I fear she spreads the lie about the *ton* that Uncle and I are—"

"I shall have her hide hanging on the wall!" Mrs Raleigh muttered under her breath. Mastering her fury, she saw the humour in Elizabeth's eyes. "What do you find so amusing?"

"I was picturing Miss Bingley in your sitting room, her brightly coloured gown a magnificent accent to the indigo of the walls."

Catching the tease, Mrs Raleigh relaxed and patted Elizabeth's hand. "You leave Miss Bingley to me. Stephen and I are known well enough to society that no one of importance will believe her. And they know that you are our niece as I have regaled them with tales of your escapades for years. Now, come, let us dress and face the day. I believe you will enjoy the exhibit at the Gallery. I know I have been all anticipation myself."

Leaning against the headboard, Mrs Raleigh looked at her niece, relieved that a modicum of strength was returning. "Elizabeth, I cannot say I agree with keeping this *man's* identity secret."

"It matters not, Aunt. I shall not see him again."

GEORGIANA AND LADY MATLOCK walked the exhibit rooms of Mr Angerstein's gallery. Marvelling at the paintings of J. M. W. Turner, they strolled until the strident tones of Caroline Bingley, accompanied by her sister and brother-in-law, were heard. Attempting to stifle an involuntary groan, Georgiana was nearly undone by her aunt's half-hearted effort to do the same.

"Miss Darcy," Miss Bingley called from across the chamber.

Rolling her eyes, Georgiana turned to greet her. "Miss Bingley, Mrs Hurst, Mr Hurst. How…pleasant to see you."

"I must say I am overcome by the loss of your company since my brother made his…unfortunate marriage." Miss Bingley turned on Georgiana's relation and almost purred, forcing an introduction to the lady. "Lady Matlock, it is an honour of the highest degree."

The older woman barely acknowledged the upstart. "I have heard of your brother for years through my nephew Darcy, of course. It is a pleasure to meet you at last." Her words dripped with insincerity.

Miss Bingley let her eyes roam the gallery, preening to all witnessing her triumph. As she surveyed a distant archway, she caught sight of Elizabeth and an unknown woman. In a loud aside to her sister, Miss Bingley continued. "Speaking of 'unfortunate,' there is Miss Bennet now. Who is she with, Louisa?"

Momentarily forgetting her company, Miss Bingley craned her neck to see the fashionable woman accompanying Miss Bennet. Georgiana took a surreptitious glance around the room, startled to see the niece and wife of Admiral Raleigh engaged in a lively discussion before one of Turner's larger paintings. So engrossed was she in the party across the gallery that Georgiana failed to notice the countess's response.

Lady Matlock was paralysed, staring at the women directly across the cavernous room. Slowly, she walked towards them. Georgiana was surprised as her aunt's gown brushed against her.

Trying to re-direct Miss Bingley's attention from the countess's unusual behaviour, Georgiana bravely took the arms of Miss Bingley and her sister, leading them towards another painting. She then disengaged, saying, "Pray, forgive me. My aunt tends to become absorbed in art. I shall be but a moment." She hurried to collect her wayward relation.

As she reached her aunt, Georgiana was surprised to find that she was only steps away from Miss Bennet and Mrs Raleigh. Steeling herself to be bold, she called out, "Miss Bennet, Mrs Raleigh, how lovely to see you both again! If I had known your interest in art, I would have invited you to join us."

Lady Matlock was brought out of her stupor by her niece's speech. "You know this woman?"

Georgiana nodded. "Mrs Raleigh is a friend of the duchess."

"Northampton?" the countess asked.

Are all of Londoners a bit daft? Elizabeth pondered before turning to the fretful girl. "Miss Darcy, it is good to see you."

"Yes, Miss Darcy, how lovely." Mrs Raleigh's eyes darted back to the countess, whom she believed to be the stepmother of the man who had accosted her niece.

"May I introduce you both to my own aunt? This is Isabelle Fitzwilliam, Countess of Matlock."

Miss Bingley's strident approach circumvented further discussion. "Miss Darcy, I thought we had lost you," Caroline called from halfway across the chamber, her sister Louisa Hurst huffing after her. Arriving next to Georgiana, she said, "I am sure your aunt has better things to do than be introduced to Miss Bennet."

Turning upon the interloper, the countess spoke in an agitated and condescending tone. "And why would that be, Miss Bribble?"

Caroline sputtered, but quickly sizing up her intent, Elizabeth replied, a sparkle of mischief returning to her eyes. "I believe, your ladyship, that Miss *Bingley* wishes to convey that a peer would not wish an acquaintance with a foundling such as myself."

Lady Matlock's voice trembled. "You are an orphan?"

"I was taken from my family when I was not yet five."

"Aunt!" Georgiana cried as Lady Matlock collapsed to the floor.

PANDEMONIUM ENSUED as carriages and a physician were summoned and the distraught countess was transported home. Elizabeth and Mrs Raleigh made to follow Georgiana, but they were blocked by Miss Bingley, her eyes filled with hate. "I believe *you* have done enough, Miss Bennet." She leaned in, whispering menacingly. "Why do you not crawl back under the *log* where you were found. Truly, it would be best for all." Miss Bingley spun on her heels to follow Georgiana and Lady Matlock.

Stunned, Elizabeth began shaking until Mrs Raleigh's arms embraced her. Even with soothing words of comfort whispered in her ear, she could not focus or move. *For a moment, everything was…clear before it was swallowed up in darkness. Again.* Realising that Elizabeth was deeply moved by the meeting, Mrs Raleigh spared but a moment to send a withering glance at the retreating harridan before returning Elizabeth home.

WICKHAM KNOCKED AS he had been instructed: three raps, a pause, and then a fourth. He heard someone slowly approach the door and then the sound of a lock turning before the heavy wooden slab opened. As his eyes adjusted to the dim light of the fire and single candelabra, he heard the strident but tired voice of Lady Catherine de Bourgh.

"Come, Wickham, and be quick."

"A pleasure to see you, Lady Catherine, as always."

She pointed to the prepared seat. "I wish to conduct this matter and be done with it."

Wickham raised his brow. "No offer of hospitality, your ladyship?"

"Do not reach above your station, boy."

"Indeed, it is late, and—"

"There is a reason it is late. Do not trifle with me," she spat. "I know you. Step out of line with me, and I shall *know* how to act."

Wickham felt an involuntary chill trickle down his spine, and covering his response, he sat, taking in the ornate room. *Even in a simple side parlour, she gilds the lily.*

Lady Catherine began. "I want you to reach out to my nephew Darcy."

"Why would I do that?"

"Because you have letters from my simpering niece that you will threaten to publish unless he meets your demands."

Wickham leaned back, watching the woman holding him in a hard gaze. *What is she about?* The steel in her eyes gave him pause, but his greed overcame his trepidation, and he entered the game. "That is a costly proposition, my lady."

"I expect no less from the likes of you."

"Especially as I have no such letters."

"Make them up, man. I had thought you more resourceful."

He coughed then pressed his luck. "At present, I have no female companion trustworthy enough to aid me in this. And my hand *is* that of a man."

"Anne will assist you."

He nodded with a quick smile then crossed his arms. "My fee is three thousand pounds—in advance."

"Half now—half when the results are in."

"And just what 'results' are expected?" he asked, knowing the answer full well.

"Darcy's agreement to marry Anne."

Ordering his thoughts, Wickham hesitated. *Darcy is not that much a fool.* He stroked his chin. *Although he would do anything to protect Georgiana...*"Lady Catherine, while casting no aspersions upon your daughter, Mr Darcy has never expressed a desire—"

"Silence! They are formed for each other, and I shall not endure your idle conjecture."

Wickham held up his hands in supplication. "I shall do as you ask, but I must insist—three thousand now."

The older woman sat back, eyes afire with malice. "*Two* thousand now—not a farthing more—and an additional thousand when it is done."

"I believe we have come to terms."

"Come back tomorrow, and you will have your money."

"Excellent." He stood. "Until tomorrow?"

Nodding, Lady Catherine rose and pulled the bell cord. "Harvis will open the door. Give him five minutes then leave."

Wickham bowed and headed towards the door.

TWO DAYS LATER, a large carriage with the Northampton crest rolled up to the Raleigh town house. While neighbours in the country, the Northampton and Raleigh families were seldom concurrently in town, so the visit was rare indeed. Admiral and Mrs Raleigh watched from their door as the duke emerged and handed out his wife.

"Your Grace," Mrs Raleigh offered, happy to see her friend. "Your Grace." She bowed to Philip Elliston, fifth Duke of Northampton.

"Mrs Raleigh, Admiral," the duke said solemnly, taking in the worn appearance of the couple, friends for over a decade.

Nodding, the admiral held out his hand. "Your Grace, it is good of you to come." They entered the richly appointed town house and then a warm, inviting parlour.

Once tea was delivered, the duchess began. "How is your niece, Mrs Raleigh?"

The duke and duchess exchanged worried glances as a deep sorrow overcame their friend. Mrs Raleigh looked up, unshed tears in her eyes. "I am afraid this incident has evoked painful memories for her. This seems to have triggered memories of the events that brought her to Longbourn."

"How did she come to Longbourn?" the duke asked as his hand sought his wife's.

Raleigh responded. "She was found by my brother-in-law, Edwin Bennet, nearly fifteen years ago." His brow cocked on hearing the gasps of his visitors. "Are you well, sir?"

Elizabeth, pale and drawn, had entered the room. "Pray forgive me, Aunt. I was unaware you had guests."

"No, no, my dear. Please come in." The admiral was still studying the Northamptons' responses. "Your Grace?" Rather than a response, the couple simply gaped, open-mouthed.

Mrs Raleigh attempted to defuse the strange atmosphere in her parlour. "Lizzy, come, let me introduce you to Their Graces, the Duke and Duchess of Northampton."

Curtseying, Elizabeth looked at the woman who remained standing, eyes open in wonder. *Those eyes,* she thought as a flood of buried images burst free in her mind. As she collapsed, a single whisper escaped her lips. "Mama..."

Seven

M RS R ALEIGH RUSHED TO E LIZABETH AS SHE FELL TO THE FLOOR while the admiral called for assistance. The duchess backed away as if seeing a ghost. *No, no, it cannot be!* She felt trapped between doubt and hope. Looking at her husband, she found the same confusion and fear in his eyes. They gazed at the prostrate young woman, her head cradled in Mrs Raleigh's lap, and the duchess moved forward slightly, daring to take a closer look.

Disbelieving the dark curls cascading across Mrs Raleigh's lap, the duchess felt the world sway and time shift. "Elizabeth," she called, as her mind returned to a long-abandoned memory. In those earlier years, her young daughter, Elizabeth, would escape the nursery to climb into her bed. With her beloved girl lying across her chest, the duchess would run her fingers up and down the child's arm. As her luscious chocolate curls unfolded across the duchess's night gown, they would chat, Elizabeth questioning her mother on whatever came into her head until a maternal touch relaxed her enough to drift into sleep. The duchess gave into the temptation and looked at the young woman, and even though every rational thought screamed: *No, it cannot be! Not after all this time!* her heart pulled her forward. As if of one mind, she and the duke stepped forward.

Feeling all the pain of long years, despairing of their daughter's return through the endless false promises ending in futility, the duchess drew closer to the still-unconscious young woman. Reaching the cushions of the sofa, she dropped to her knees and trailed her fingers up and down her covered arm as she had done with her own child years before.

Tugged by a hidden memory, Elizabeth woke, lifting her eyes with a smile. When the duchess saw her unfeigned peace, she clasped her daughter's hands to her lips and cried in a soft wail, her heart rejoicing that her child had finally come home.

Surprised by this uncharacteristic display, the admiral stepped back as Mrs Ketchum and two footmen entered to lift Elizabeth from his wife's embrace. Both he and Mrs Raleigh saw the tortured expression on the duchess's noble face as Elizabeth was carried up the stairs to her bedchamber. The duke helped his wife to her feet and took her in his arms.

"It is she, Philip. Elizabeth!" The duchess sobbed into her husband's chest.

He said nothing but held her tight. Trusting an explanation would follow, Raleigh left the room to see about the physician.

When they were alone, the duke spoke, his voice shattered. "Alexandra, please, let us not get our hopes up too soon."

"Did you not see her? It was as if my mother lives and breathes!"

"I know, I know. I simply...to come so close...I do not know whether I could bear it again."

Realising that he needed her strength, she crushed him to her and held him there as he shook. His loss was as great as hers was, and his feelings were as bereft and strong as those assaulting her. She pulled back, looking him in the eyes. "It is she, my love. I know it. Those eyes—did you see them when she woke? It was like when she was young and would escape the nursery to come into our bedchamber. I would help her into our bed and run my fingers along her arms until her questions ceased and sleep took her."

The duke chuckled, no doubt recalling many mornings that he woke to find Elizabeth sprawled across her mother's body. He stroked his wife's hair. "Promise me that you will let us discover the facts before surrendering your heart to her."

The duchess looked up. Sensing both compassion and fragility in her husband's eyes, she recalled the false claims made by impostors during those first horrible years, and the duchess did something she rarely did. She capitulated.

ANNE DE BOURGH placed the pen back on her desk, trying to avoid the splotches of the last four letters. Despite the desire to aid her mother in securing her cousin Darcy, she felt Wickham's distraction acutely. *His eyes,* she sighed, working the crimp from her right hand. *They are so blue…I could look into those eyes for the rest of my life.*

Anne had never fancied herself an attractive woman, but she had no need for female attributes. Her mother had seen to her *arts* being more substantial and less susceptible to the ravages of time. Her allure to the male of the species was purely financial. And for Anne, that was enough. She sat back in her chair, allowing her eyes to drift from the handsome face of her companion to his impressive physique. Adjusting her gown to relieve this sudden burst of heat, she dropped her wrap.

"Madam." He retrieved the shawl from the floor.

"Thank you, Lieutenant Wickham." She gasped as his hand swept her spindly curls from her neck, caressing her shoulders as he smoothed the cashmere along the top edge of the gown hanging loosely about her frame.

"It is my delight to be of service…to you," he whispered in her ear. "Dearest Anne."

She looked at him with wonder at such bold words addressed to her. *Such a gentleman, so handsome and friendly.* Anne sighed into his sky-blue eyes.

"Who knew, when your mother asked that we work together, that it would be such bliss?" He drew his lips closer to her ear.

She looked at him with doe-eyed awe. "Truly?"

"Oh yes, dear Anne." Wickham took her hand, stroking his deft fingers along her thin wrist. Without warning, he brought her hand to his open lips, dragging them across the responsive skin. His eyes held hers, now half closed with desire.

Anne shivered. "George," she whispered as in a dream.

He drew her to his chest, hands flying over her gown, pressing her into his embrace. Physical evidence of his desire rose between them, and feeling it, Anne's eyelids flew open.

Taking advantage of her surprise, Wickham thrust his tongue into her mouth. Instead of a maiden's response, Anne surprised Wickham by taking his measure in a most intimate and arousing manner. Pulling back to see her response, he smiled in reply to the wicked gleam in her eyes.

"Extensive reading opens one's mind to all sorts of possibilities," she purred into his ear. Wickham grunted as Anne ran her fingers along his length, unfastening the buttons of his fall. Feeling his ardour rise, he got straight to the point of his seduction, and there on the desk of her private study, Anne de Bourgh became a maiden no more.

WITH ELIZABETH safely asleep in her chambers, Mrs Raleigh returned to the parlour, anticipating a singular conversation. The admiral waited for her outside the door, surprising his wife. She raised an eyebrow at him, and he replied, "It looked like they needed a moment alone."

"I can only imagine." Mrs Raleigh entered his open arms, and they clung to each other. "Do you think it possible?" she whispered.

"Anything is possible, dearest." He gave her a quick squeeze. "But we shall substantiate this claim thoroughly before relinquishing Elizabeth to anyone."

"Thank you, Stephen, thank you." Mrs Raleigh swept away an errant tear.

They entered the room where the Northamptons sat on the couch, obviously in as much need of reassurance as themselves.

The duke spoke first. "How is she, Mrs Raleigh?"

"She rests. Fortunately, some of Dr Clements's tonic remains, and she will sleep uninterrupted."

"Tonic? Is she ill?" The duchess looked up, great concern in her eyes and voice.

"No, it is…since the…encounter with the viscount, she…" Mrs Raleigh clasped her hands together, missing the look of disgust spreading across the duke's face while the duchess seemed to be lost in thought. "Her dreams have returned two-fold."

"Bad dreams?" The duchess grasped her husband's hand. They exchanged glances—hers of compassion, his with a burning anger.

"Yes. They have not plagued her for many years, but she admits that, ever since Jane married and left Longbourn, they have returned."

The duke interrupted, unable to contain himself any longer. "Raleigh, Mrs Raleigh, I must ask you, is there any chance that your niece is...could she possibly be..." He looked away for a moment before plunging ahead. "You said she was found...?"

"Yes, yes she was," Mrs Raleigh replied.

The duke squeezed his wife's hand. "When was she...? You mentioned nearly fifteen years ago. When precisely did she join your family...the year?"

"Two years before I completed my time at Miss Edrington's. September 1794—no, later in the fall I believe."

The duchess unconsciously rose from her seat. "I must go to her."

Mrs Raleigh placed her hand on the grand lady's sleeve. "Madam, what is this about?"

"I—" She looked at her friends as if emerging from a trance. "She...she is my daughter."

"But how can that be?" Admiral Raleigh weighed in.

The duke spoke. "Our daughter, Lady Elizabeth Aubrey Rose Elliston was taken from us in November of 1794 by, we believe—"

"—Lady Catherine de Bourgh," the duchess spat.

"Catty..." Mrs Raleigh whispered.

"Catty?" the duke asked. "What do you know of her?"

"That is the name Elizabeth rails against in her dreams."

"It is the name Elizabeth called my brother's sister-in-law."

Raleigh crossed to the sideboard and poured a round for all. When each had another fair sip, the admiral spoke. "It is a miracle."

"True enough," the duke responded. "True enough."

"When may we see her?" the duchess asked, looking at her husband. "How do we tell her we are her parents?"

"I suppose there is no way like a direct assault," the admiral offered.

"But, Stephen, she is so fragile..." Mrs Raleigh argued.

"Fragile?" the duke asked.

"Yes." Mrs Raleigh turned compassionate eyes to the duke. "You know of her...encounter with Braddleton?" The duke nodded. "Elizabeth was well loved by my sister, her husband, and their daughter, Jane. Jane and Lizzy, Lizzy and Jane—they were inseparable.

"When Gloria died, Edwin—my brother-in-law, Edwin Bennet of Longbourn—it was he who found Elizabeth. She was...well..."

"Perhaps that is a tale left for another time, my dear," Raleigh interjected.

"Yes, of course," Mrs Raleigh agreed. "Those first years were blissful for the Bennets. I met Elizabeth half a year after she came. Oh, she was lovely—still is, of course—but such a beautiful child. Such curls and smiles—and her mind!—quick and sharp and kind.

"But after Gloria died, Edwin wrote his brother, Thomas, to bring his family to live at Longbourn. Thomas was a barrister in town, and he and his wife, Frances, came to Longbourn. Edwin felt his girls needed a woman's *gentle* hand," she scoffed. "As if that would ever happen."

"Mrs Raleigh," the admiral warned.

"Frances Bennet did not take kindly to Elizabeth. She accepted Jane since Jane is beautiful and sweet as the day is long, and she was Edwin's flesh and blood. But Lizzy? Lizzy was too smart for Frances and did not make much of an effort to hide what she thought of 'Aunt Bennet.' All was well, relatively well, until Edwin died nearly five years ago."

The duke collected his emotion at hearing his daughter's life told by others. "The bad dreams?"

"I believe they began September last?" Raleigh looked to his wife for confirmation. "When Mr Bingley came to Netherfield."

"It was when Jane was being courted that Elizabeth noticed the nature of her dreams had changed," Mrs Raleigh added. "She started remembering more. At first, her dreams were of her time with Edwin and Gloria. But when Jane became engaged, the dreams changed. They turned to the way she first came to Longbourn, revealing more and more details from an earlier time—being found in the woods, coming to Longbourn, waking from the fever."

The duke's throat was suddenly dry. "How was she found?"

The admiral explained. "Bennet said she was huddled alongside a fallen log. He had been inspecting the fields at the adjacent estate, Netherfield, for a friend. He was riding home, and he thought he heard a child crying. His horse jumped, and he saw movement. It was Lizzy, and he brought her home."

"Was she…harmed?" The duke's hands clenched into fists.

The admiral waited till the duke could look him straight in the eye. "She was beaten, sir, badly so. Edwin told me that for a time they feared for her life. If he had not come by that morning, well…"

The truth of Elizabeth's averted fate hung between them.

The duchess sobbed, and it took her husband a full five minutes to control the unadulterated rage tearing through him. Raleigh turned away, offering them a moment of privacy. Mrs Raleigh came and placed her arm around the duchess, who sobbed into her shoulder. When she was able, she looked up, her cheeks wet but her eyes clear.

"Thank you. Thank you both," she whispered.

Uncomfortable with the emotion, Raleigh nodded and returned to his chair. "I must ask, what makes you think Elizabeth is she?"

"It is more than a mere thought. I *know* that young woman is my child," the duchess said defiantly.

The admiral continued with an acknowledging nod. "But how? I do not mean to be uncaring, but Elizabeth is my primary concern here." He was prepared for the straightening spines of those sitting across from him. "Please, I am not denying the possibility. I only wish to understand. How can you be so sure?"

"When I first saw her, it was as if I was standing before my mother, Aubrey Rose Darcy," she began.

The duke looked at their staring faces. "It is as if…as if Mother Darcy lived and breathed before me. Her hair, her colouring, her eyes. I just know. Your niece is my daughter." He looked dazed. "My flesh and blood—after all these years, alive!"

As a man accustomed to interrogation, the admiral could handle nuance. As commander of a warship, he had learned to read the fervent emotions of men—knew when to push and when to retreat. Sensing that the shock of Elizabeth's identity was ebbing, he redirected the conversation to the topic of security. "Sir, you did not seem surprised that Elizabeth—forgive me, Lady Elizabeth—remembered a woman named *Catty.*"

The duke sighed, wiping a tear from his eye. "Each year in the fall, before Elizabeth's disappearance, we…all of us…would visit Pemberley, the duchess's ancestral home in Derbyshire. She and her brother, George, were always close, very close. And while Lady Anne Darcy was offensive at first, she seemed to soften once removed from the influence of her family. When Elizabeth was born, however, Anne's sister, Lady Catherine de Bourgh, began visiting Pemberley at the same time as ourselves, invited or not." He sighed. "She changed, became more abrupt, volatile. Her daughter, Anne, was nearly three then, a peckish child, irritable and sullen."

The duchess took up the tale. "Lady Catherine would taunt Elizabeth, urging her to be more like Anne, not to play in the mud, not to trail after our son Julian and Fitzwilliam, my brother's son."

"Ah." Raleigh crossed his arms.

"She would lecture me on the proper sphere my daughter should aim for, and that *woman* believed my daughter…" The duchess took a deep breath to quell the emotion surging through her blood. "…that *my* child was less worthy than that sickly creature she kept at Rosings."

The duchess's ire flushed her cheeks. "She would go on about Pemberley and Rosings being destined to unite and the desirable outcome *that* would be."

"Lady Catherine sounds awful," Mrs Raleigh said, taking the measure of this unseen threat to Elizabeth.

"That is not the half of it," the duchess snorted.

The duke rose and paced about the room. "Lady Catherine can hold a grudge longer than anyone I have ever known, and she has always held one against me, I fear…"

Both Raleighs turned to look at the duke.

"She felt I should have offered for Lady Anne or even herself. We had words in a park one afternoon. She was furious when I did not accept an invitation to tea. Even then, she was rather…unstable."

The duke paused to take up his glass for another sip, gathering his courage to face the eyes that were trained upon him. "She was incensed that I sought out Alexandra before she was officially out. Not only that, but Lady Anne, her own sister, refused to go along with her schemes to entrap me as she only had eyes for George Darcy. Lady Catherine knew how close Alexandra and George had always been. Even before Elizabeth was born, George and I…we would talk nonsense about our children marrying. Little did Catherine know—or at least that is what we thought."

He walked to the window. Taking a deep breath, he turned, standing with the glass at his back. "George Darcy and I spoke of a wedding contract during that visit. We were not in earnest of course. How could we be? We were merely discussing our children's happiness, but who could have known—" Emotion choked his throat.

"You could not have known…" The duchess spoke for his ears only.

"Known what?" Mrs Raleigh asked.

"That *Lady* Catherine de Bourgh is inhuman!" the duchess spat. "Not only did she eavesdrop on a private conversation, but she left that afternoon—stormed up and down Pemberley, calling for her carriage and disrupting our plans for the day. She returned late that evening—no word, no explanation—barely in time to dine."

The duchess stood still, eyes lost in the past, and spoke in a hollow voice. "Not five days later, the children were spending the morning near Pember Lake. It was a favourite spot for the Darcys at that time of year, so near the orchards when the harvest is in progress. They were having a row. Young Darcy and Elizabeth were always sparring over something. We, Lady Anne and I, were asked to rein them in."

"I gather she was a spitfire even then," the admiral added.

"We called them to the house, and Elizabeth was so involved in the tiff with her cousin that she left her doll, Maisey. It was her favourite—my mother had made it by hand—and she dropped it in the meadow by the lake. She was very upset about it during dinner." The duchess wrung her hands. "She wanted to retrieve it, but I insisted she wait until after her nap." She sobbed, and the duke embraced her.

"We thought she was upstairs in the nursery, but she left the protection of her nurse and family to find Maisey. There was no other reason for her to leave the house."

The duchess stopped, recalling a long-ago moment. "Tucking her in for her nap, I kissed her, and that was the last time I saw my daughter until this morning."

Mrs Raleigh held out her hand, and the duchess took it.

"You say this Lady Catherine kidnapped Elizabeth, believing she would prevent a marriage that was at least—what?—over a decade in the future?" Raleigh asked. "What will be her response to Elizabeth's reappearance?"

"Do not fear, Admiral. We shall not fail her again. No harm will come to Elizabeth," the duke affirmed.

"But what of this Lady Catherine?" Mrs Raleigh turned to the duke. "I mean, if she did that when they were both so young, what might she do now when they are of age?"

"I do not know. But again, I pledge to you both, we shall not fail."

"But how?" Raleigh was persistent.

"Fear not, Raleigh. The Matlocks have made mistakes through the years—and enemies. They are weakened. Their influence wanes." The duke resumed his seat. "We—George, Alexandra, and I—always suspected Lady Catherine's involvement. We had no proof, so we could not proceed further. However, I have kept the house of Matlock in my sights and have learned enough to keep Elizabeth safe. Should they make a move, I shall know how to act. They shall not harm my family again."

Looking at the duke, Raleigh spoke up. "Perhaps I shall request some of the cadets to watch her goings-on about town."

"Raleigh, I believe that is my responsibility."

"You would take her…from us…so soon?" Mrs Raleigh asked.

"Mrs Raleigh, please understand. She is my daughter." The duke's voice was irrefutable.

"But she…" Mrs Raleigh struggled for words.

The duke spoke more softly. "We know Elizabeth has grown up with you as her relations. We shall do nothing to keep her from you or you from her. But you must understand—she is our child, our blood. And, forgive me, my friend, but you must realise that, although we do not make a fuss, we are distantly connected to the royal family. Elizabeth, even in a small way, is—"

"—of the blood royal!" Mrs Raleigh looked at her husband, who was as surprised as she was.

"Of course," the admiral said as he took his wife's hand.

"I cannot promise that criminal action will not be taken against the house of de Bourgh. However, I believe Bedlam is where she belongs, and I shall do my best to ensure that she is mandated to the care of their *able* physicians. But I pledge on my honour, Lady Catherine *shall* be brought to justice."

Taking a moment, Mrs Raleigh tried to lighten the conversation. "Imagine, our little Lizzy of royal blood! Wait until Frances Bennet hears this! I wish to be there when she learns that the girl she snubbed every chance she could has royal blood in her veins. I confess to more than a bit of satisfaction in that."

"You said Elizabeth looks like your mother, madam?" the admiral asked.

"She is the exact replica of my mother." The duchess smiled.

"She is truly a beautiful woman," Raleigh continued. "Just the other night—when was it?—we both remarked as she came down the stairs, dressed for the Montridge ball, and we knew. Our feelings were confirmed that Elizabeth's family must be exceptional."

The Northamptons beamed. Mrs Raleigh looked towards the stairs. *But the poor child has endured so much since then.* "Your Graces, you must understand…there has been so much tumult in her life these past months."

Mrs Ketchum came through the door, dropping a quick curtsey. "Ma'am, Miss Bennet is awake and asked for tea to be sent to her chamber."

"Please prepare the tonic Dr Clements advised, but do not administer it yet. I would like to speak with her before she takes another dose."

"Yes, ma'am." With that, the housekeeper left the gathering, and all eyes focused on Mrs Raleigh.

"Duchess, I understand your wish to see Elizabeth as soon as may be. But I would like to speak with her first." Mrs Raleigh's heart tore as the duchess's face fell. "I simply wish to prepare her and assess whether or not she is strong enough."

"Strong enough? I am her mother, not one who comes to do her harm!" The duchess's disappointment turned to anger. "How dare you keep me from her!"

"Alexandra, please!" The duke tried to console her. "Mrs Raleigh only wishes what is best for Elizabeth. Think what all of this means for *her*. We have each other and know more of her story while she has lived with a mystery that is unravelling at what must be a frightening pace."

"I only wish to make this easiest for her." Mrs Raleigh patted the distraught woman's hand. "I beg of you...patience."

The duchess nodded, attempting a smile, and Mrs Raleigh rose, heading towards the door. Before leaving, she turned. "Perhaps you would come and wait in Elizabeth's sitting room?" The hopeful smile blossoming on the duchess's face was a joy to see, and she leapt to her feet. The two women linked arms as they went upstairs.

ASCENDING TO THE SECOND FLOOR OF RALEIGH HOUSE, THE MEN WERE adrift in their emotions. The admiral, commander of men in battle, and the duke, master of great estates and diplomatic missions for the crown, were unsure how to proceed. Shaking off their stupor, they entered the admiral's study. Raleigh walked to the sideboard, offering a snifter of contraband French brandy to his guest.

"Spoils of war," he said, holding up the rare vintage. Raleigh poured two full snifters, but neither man drank after the first sip.

"Do you have a bit of parchment, Raleigh? I need to send an express or two." The duke rose from his seat.

"On the desk, port side," the admiral said, indicating the portfolio on his precisely laid out desk. "There. Quills and ink—starboard."

"Indeed," the duke said under his breath, then aloud, "I say, you can take the man away from the sea but not the sea from the man."

"No indeed. Orderliness, besides being next to godliness, is essential when your living space is a hammock in a room five by five feet square."

"Come now, Raleigh, it has been many years since you suffered such constraints."

"Aye, but they formed my habits."

"Truth in that." The duke gathered his supplies and began his task. Aligning the second sheet of parchment, he paused, twirling the tip of the quill against his chin before filling the page. When finished with his fourth letter, he hunted for sealing wax. Then, removing his signet ring, he affixed the Northampton seal. "Would you arrange delivery?"

"Of course." Raleigh rang for his butler then returned to his seat. "May I be so bold as to ask the nature of your missives?"

"Not at all." Returning to the armchair nearest the admiral, the duke took up his brandy. "Magnificent, Raleigh, truly a treasure."

"Thank you."

"The first letter was to my nephew, Fitzwilliam Darcy." Noting the quirked brow of his host, he continued. "I have only seen it once or twice, but I know there is a portrait of Alexandra's mother hanging in Pemberley's dower house."

"In the dower house?"

Northampton nodded. "Aubrey Rose Darcy passed on shortly after Elizabeth's disappearance. The image was too painful for Alexandra, and her brother, George, had it moved. I have asked that young Darcy bring the portrait here to town."

"But why?"

"What my wife said is true. Elizabeth looks like my wife's mother. The portrait was done for her presentation. They could be identical twins—separated by a generation, of course. We thought it might help convince Elizabeth…"

"…and us?"

The duke nodded. "Despite Alexandra's outburst, we realise we are all working for the same purpose—to make this as easy for Elizabeth as possible. And we understand how profoundly difficult this is for *everyone* concerned."

Rousing himself from the memories overwhelming his composure, he coughed. "There is one other matter." The duke shifted in his chair. "My daughter has a birthmark it seems that all Darcy women carry."

The admiral blushed. "Is it on her…" He patted his backside.

The duke chuckled.

"Jane used to tease Elizabeth about it, and not being privy to the secrets of your wife and her family, I did not know…"

"Of course."

"And the other three?" Raleigh nodded to the letters on the adjoining side table.

"One to Julian who is in Brussels on some business for Liverpool." He picked out one of the sealed letters. "This is to my grandmother."

He nodded at Raleigh's surprise. "Yes, she still lives and will inform the proper royal ministry that my child lives."

Raleigh's voice choked with emotion. "And the third?"

"My solicitor."

"Ah." Raleigh nodded. A sense of loss overcame the admiral, and he covered his eyes with his hand.

Seeing the dejection on his friend's face, Northampton leaned towards him. "Raleigh, Elizabeth considers you and Mrs Raleigh family, more so than either Alexandra or me, most likely for some time to come. We must all work together to create a balance between us for Elizabeth. We do not intend to simply take our daughter and abscond with her to Green Haven. She needs you, and truth be told, I believe that Alexandra and I—and even Julian—will need your guidance on how to acclimate Elizabeth back into our family."

The admiral gave him a sad smile. Running his hand around the back of his neck. "What say you to a game of chess until we are summoned?"

"Capital idea, man. Capital."

UPSTAIRS, Mrs Raleigh settled the duchess in a chair by the fire before disappearing through the connecting door of Elizabeth's chamber. Sighing at her distraught niece, she hurried to her side.

"Lizzy." Mrs Raleigh engulfed Elizabeth in her embrace. "Oh, my dearest, dear girl."

Mrs Raleigh thought of how her sister, Gloria, had wished Elizabeth would reunite with her true parents. Now, as Gloria's fondest wish was coming true, Mrs Raleigh felt strangely betrayed. *Oh, I shall miss you, Lizzy.* Closing her eyes, she pulled Elizabeth closer, feeling her sister's dear heart encouraging her to let go.

"She *is* my mother, is she not?" Elizabeth whispered with a mix of trepidation, excitement, and hope.

Mrs Raleigh nodded. "Yes, I believe she is."

Elizabeth glanced towards the door.

"She waits in your sitting room. Would you...are you ready to meet her again?"

"Yes, oh yes, Aunt..." Elizabeth grabbed Mrs Raleigh's hand, and an unspoken emotion crossed between them. Mrs Raleigh caressed Elizabeth's cheek.

"While external appearances will change, you are and will always be one of us." She wiped a tear from her own cheek. "There will always be a place for you with us. You are part of us. I love you as I would my own child."

Smiling, Elizabeth nodded, and they embraced.

"Thank you, Aunt Raleigh. I love you too."

They tightened their embrace before separating. Mrs Raleigh went to the door, opening it and calling for her friend to join them. "Elizabeth, it is time to meet your mother. She is anxious to speak with you, as is your father."

"My father," Elizabeth said with reverence.

"Yes, Elizabeth," came a voice from the door. Elizabeth looked at the hesitant duchess and held out her hand. The duchess hurried to the bedside. The grand lady dropped to her knees to take her daughter's hand. Instead, Elizabeth wrapped her arms around her mother, who rapturously held her.

"Elizabeth, my darling girl." She hugged her to her breast as tears streamed down their cheeks. "How I have prayed for this day."

"Mama," Elizabeth sobbed.

DARCY STOOD BY THE WINDOW, re-reading the express delivered that morning. *What is Northampton about?* he thought for the hundredth time. *Three years without direct contact from him, and his first missive is to request—nay, order!—me to locate Grandmother Darcy's portrait.*

His long fingers drummed against the window sill. *And bring it to London? Since when have I been an errand boy? I am not ready to return to town.*

He pushed away, staring into the empty room. "I cannot face her.

Not now. Not yet. I shall send the portrait and perhaps stop in to see what all the fuss is about."

He paced the room, hands clasped behind his back. *But Northampton is not one for bluster and false summonses as are some of my other relations.*

He took another turn, unsettled in the unfamiliar sensation of indecision. "What if something has happened to Julian? He has been on the continent, and God knows what kind of trouble… I shall go to London and be of service to my family."

With a relieved look of certitude, Darcy summoned Mrs Reynolds. "I am required in London. I shall accompany Grandmother Darcy's portrait."

"I shall have it brought over from the dower house. Jameson will pack it in a crate, so it will be ready by tomorrow morning. I shall have Westervelt prepare your bags, sir. Is there anything else, Mr Darcy?"

"No, thank you, Reynolds."

The housekeeper turned to leave.

"Do you recall why Grandmother Darcy's portrait was removed from the main gallery and sent to the dower house?"

Sadness filled her eyes. "It upset the duchess too much, sir. She could not bear the reminder. With her loss"—Mrs Reynolds dropped her voice—"and then Lady Anne's death, your father removed the painting. It was a time your father feared greatly for his sister."

Darcy nodded. "Thank you, Reynolds." *I completely empathise with how you must have felt, Duchess.*

Alone with his thoughts, Darcy paced more, his impending journey weighing on him. *I shall not call upon Bingley and risk that particular reminder. Damn, I may never be able to see Bingley again! What in God's name possessed me to blurt out such a thing! In Hyde Park of all places. What she must think of me.*

Darcy clutched his chest, feeling as if his heart was breaking. *I shall not see her again. All that is left to me is ashes. I have no right to believe…to hope that Elizabeth…could ever…would ever…forgive me. I may as well finish it.*

He went to his desk and sat down. Opening the desk drawer, he withdrew a large, flat box containing duelling pistols and a small, velvet-covered jewel box. Placing them on the desk, he ran his hands over their differing surfaces. He opened the larger box, retrieving one of the finely balanced firearms. "Northampton gave these to me for my fifteenth birthday. Then after we all made a fuss, both he and Father took Julian and me aside and forbade us to ever use them on another human." Darcy chuckled. *We both thought it ludicrous to have such fine pistols and foreswear using them.*

Memories of his Northampton relations renewed his spirit, recalling his last conversation with his aunt. Sitting perfectly still, his mind raced with conflicting images. *Fight for love—eh, Duchess? Is there a chance of forgiveness?*

The sensation of his aunt's embrace, the tendrils of her love, a love he thought once lost, wrapped around him, easing the grasp of his fear. Feeling the pure joy of this love, Darcy's spirit woke. He chuckled. "I *will* ask the duke for lessons in grovelling." A rare smile spread across his face as images of his esteemed uncle on his knees before his aunt played through his mind. Closing the lid, he returned the pistols but kept the ring box on his desk. Taking a quill and parchment, he wrote.

Lady Catherine,
Due to family obligations, I shall be unable to make my annual visit. Should things resolve themselves to our satisfaction, I may be able to attend you and your daughter later in the spring, or perhaps by mid-summer.

I remain your nephew,
Fitzwilliam Darcy

That should hold her. "Who knows, perhaps after speaking with the duchess, I may yet find another way…perhaps…"

He reached for the portrait miniatures that travelled with him from London. "What would you say, Father? Would you accept a foundling for a daughter? Would you consider her a disgrace even though she is intelligent, witty, kind, beautiful, and she…" He sighed, recalling their dance and conversations and the fire in her eyes. "When I am with her, I feel alive! As if all things are possible."

He paused. "With love, all things *are* possible."

He looked at his mother's portrait. *When you accepted Father's*

proposal, your family was in an uproar. You were destined for a duke.
Darcy's mind dropped another piece into the puzzle. "Northampton, if
I recollect. Instead, it was my Darcy aunt who joined the highest
ranking peerage! No wonder the Matlocks hate us so."

As another bit of family history slipped into place, Darcy marvelled
that he had missed the cause of the Matlock ire. "My aunt thwarted
their plans to lift themselves in society when she fell in love with the
fifth Duke of Northampton. And no one holds a grudge like the
Matlocks.

"Now I understand my father's warning against trusting them. No
longer is it inconceivable that they had a hand in Northampton's
misfortune. With Elizabeth's abduction, life changed at Pemberley.
Grandmother Darcy's portrait was the least of what we lost. Mother
withdrew into a shell—from shame, no doubt."

Darcy fell into his chair, holding both portraits of his parents.
"Should I win her heart, I believe your sister will stand by me, Father,
even if yours will not, Mama. But the thought of living without Elizabeth is too painful to bear. Even if I must humble the Matlock pride
and throw myself at her feet, I shall beg for another chance."

Taking both miniatures and the ancient velvet box, he headed
upstairs to pack them in his trunks.

OVER TEA, Elizabeth agreed with both mother and aunt that a shopping
expedition was in order. The trio set off as early as possible for the
stylist who was on the cusp of fashion and whose discretion was unas-
sailable. It had been decided that, until word had been received from
the royal ministry, they would make no official announcement.

The drive to Bond Street was full of cheerful chattering as mother
and child learned about each other. Mrs Raleigh's presence as a neutral
party filled the gaps and patched over any misunderstandings. She
monitored Elizabeth's adjustment to becoming Lady Elizabeth Elliston.

Arriving at the epicentre of London's fashion world, the trio of
beautiful women caused a stir among the men trolling the streets and
the women hoping to be seen. According to plan, they entered the
dressmaker's shop without encountering anyone of their acquaintance.

Together with Madam LeSage, they expanded Elizabeth's

wardrobe. Only the finest silk, velvet, linen, and muslin would suit, and Elizabeth felt her head might simply burst with the variety and volume of choices. Protesting the extravagance, she bobbed a curtsey to her mother. "Ma...madam"—she turned and gave another to Mrs Raleigh—"Aunt. I believe there is a bit of lace on one of the shelves that we simply have not yet seen."

"But, Mademoiselle, I shall..." Madam LeSage began.

"No, please. I need a breath of fresh air from all this...business." She glanced over the stacks of fashion plates and fabric draped about the furniture and the three matrons.

"Do not stray far, Elizabeth," Mrs Raleigh pleaded.

"Yes, we shall be done here very soon, Eliz..."—the duchess quickly corrected herself—"Miss Bennet, and we shall return to Northampton Place for supper."

Eyes twinkling in no small delight that her mother understood her, she again curtseyed to them all and left their private room to peruse the stacks of fabric, gaining a modicum of space and time to adjust to the demands of being Lady Elizabeth Elliston. Wandering about the ribbons, she took in the luxurious fabrics. Beginning when she was a child, she would let her mind drift when thoughts threatened to over-whelm her. She would leave the confines of the house and go off in the woods to calm her mind—caressing the trees, the tall grasses, the wood of the fences and stiles or inhaling the clean, fresh scent of the woods after a rain. Focusing on touching each tree trunk, listening to the wind with her eyes closed, or feeling the rays of sun on her cheeks and uncovered hair lulled her into dropping any disturbing thought. *And with Franny Bennet around, there were many.*

She smiled, thinking of the changes in her life. Instead of wild meadows and forests, she had the exotic delights of Madam LeSage to lighten her heart. *And Mama!* Elizabeth revelled in the warmth spreading through her heart. *I cannot explain nor understand how or why I feel so much...love when I am with them. But I do. And that is enough. It is more than I have ever had, even with Jane. I feel...I feel... with them, I feel I am home. And nothing...not a single soul can take that away. Ever again.*

IF CAROLINE BINGLEY was caught unawares at seeing Elizabeth Bennet in Madame LeSage's shop, she did her best to conceal it. Instead, she proclaimed in a loud voice. "I was unaware that women of your calibre were allowed, *Miss* Bennet." She sauntered over, close enough to whisper in Elizabeth's ear.

"I do hope you will consider changing your name, Eliza. It would be a *shame* to tie the houses of Bingley and Bennet to the disgrace of *your* fate. It is not unheard of for a woman in your position—no?"

Instead of the shame Caroline half expected to overtake the upstart, she was surprised when Elizabeth laughed uncontrollably. Nervously looking at the fashionable women who watched them with avid curiosity, Caroline turned on her heel to leave the store after firing a parting shot. "I find my desire for a new gown overpowered by my need for a breath of fresh air."

THE DUKE OF NORTHAMPTON sat in the nursery, rocking in the chair that had soothed both his children. Not even the maids were stirring. *From the first time I saw her—those big, brown, Darcy eyes—I was a lost man. And her giggle. She must have been nine or ten months old when she began. And she laughed all the time. Such a happy child. Stubborn too. She would walk as did her brother...attempt most everything he did.* Memories flooded his consciousness. "Elizabeth and Julian—nothing could come between them. Except Fitzwilliam."

That boy was always trying to get her attention, and she just wanted Julian. That was what... The duke's visage darkened recalling the row that ripped his family apart. *All those years lost—wasted while she lived not thirty miles away!* He slapped his thigh. *All the tears, the years waiting...wondering. Where was she? Was she alive? Safe?* Sadness overwhelmed him, and he wept.

WICKHAM LEFT the well-appointed bedchamber with a satisfied smirk. Any servants that may have seen him enter were sleeping off the doctored wine Anne had provided. Straightening his jacket, he walked to the side door and let himself out. His tethered horse whinnied softly, and he laughed. "Take that, Darcy. There is more than one way to get your family's fortune."

DARCY ARRIVED in London three days later. After a brief bath and meal, he made haste to Northampton Place where he asked to see the housekeeper.

"Hutchins, so good to see you again. Will you see to this?" He indicated the crate his coachman was carrying.

"Of course." She motioned to one of the footmen to take the narrow box and remove its contents. When they were alone, she said. "It is good to see you, sir. It has been too long."

"Indeed, and I thank you. Your sister sends her regards." His lips curved at the delight in the housekeeper's eyes. "When Reynolds learned I was bringing Grandmother Darcy to Northampton Place, she would not allow me to leave without extracting a promise to deliver this directly into your hands." He pulled a letter from his pocket. "Errand boy to a duke, so why not postman to the Gwyneth sisters?"

"Oh, Mr Darcy. Thank you." Mrs Hutchins took the letter with a smile. When the favourite nephew of the house bent to kiss her cheek, the old woman blushed. "Mr Darcy!"

"You never complained before, Hutchins. Why now?"

"Oh you…"

"So, tell me"—Darcy straightened and put on his loftiest airs —"why the sudden need for Grandmother Darcy?"

"Big doings, sir. Grand days, indeed." Darcy looked at the woman, noting the absolute joy on her countenance.

"Truly?" he voiced his surprise. "Of what cause?"

"Not my tale to tell, sir. Be assured, though, that Their Graces will share the good tidings with you. Now, let me see you to them."

"YOU!" Darcy stared at Elizabeth, her hand firmly ensconced in her companion's powerful one.

"Darcy." The duke regarded him warily.

Unsettled to his core, Darcy approached, eyes wild with emotion and focused on her as she recovered from his accusatory declaration.

"Yes, it is I."

"How dare you...insinuate yourself." Darcy eyed his uncle as if recognising him for the first time. "And you—bringing her here to my aunt's home. How could you?"

Elizabeth stood less than a foot from her accuser. "Before you impugn another innocent in your twisted concept of relations between a young woman and a man old enough—"

"—to be her father." The duke rose, seeming to tower over Darcy.

"Father," Darcy scoffed.

Father and daughter cocked identical brows, the self-same glower shaping their lips.

"Father." Elizabeth threw down the word like a gauntlet, arms crossed and glaring.

Darcy stared into her eyes, caught in their intense hold. "But—" He broke from her gaze, looking between the two and noting the similarity in their noses, the shape of their brows. "But your eyes—"

"—are from me, I do believe." The duchess appeared beside her daughter, taking her arm.

Darcy gasped, seeing the comforting features of his aunt mirrored in Elizabeth's expressive eyes, her full lips, her lustrous curls of Darcy mahogany, and the alluring shape of her face. "But how?" He swayed as if wavering between stepping back and reaching for her...for them.

Seeing his genuine distress, the duchess took Darcy's hand and led him to the portrait awaiting its unveiling. "Look, Darcy. Look, and tell me what you see."

He lifted the linen cover, and all thought fled. Looking back at him from a decades-old canvas sat Elizabeth Bennet, eyes dancing, her lush lips curved in a wry smile. Darcy whipped his head from the painting to its live subject, now standing beside him. Elizabeth's mouth opened as she stared at what could be her own reflection. The duchess's head turned from Elizabeth to her husband. She regained hold of Elizabeth's arm with great care.

"Elizabeth, dearest?" she asked noting her daughter's tears. The duke replaced Darcy at her side.

Darcy gaped at his grandmother and his grandmother's double. *How could I have missed this?* "But how...?"

The duke replied, "As you know, our daughter, Elizabeth, was taken a little over fifteen years ago, and was left alone…"

"…through a night of bitter cold and rain." The duchess's voice choked.

"In Hertfordshire," the duke continued. "By God's grace, a Mr Edwin Bennet found her. That is why Elizabeth is alive. A country gentleman, whom I can never thank, did what neither your father nor I could do." He looked at his daughter. "He kept you safe, Elizabeth." He kissed her hand. "And I promise you I shall continue his work." Seeing his uncle struggling, Darcy placed a hand on his shoulder.

Elizabeth's whisper stopped them all. "Catty…"

Darcy looked from his aunt to his uncle, who returned his questioning gaze with their steady ones. "Catherine?" he whispered, but it was enough that Elizabeth heard and backed away.

Alarmed at her panic, the duchess cajoled her. "Elizabeth, dear, come. It is time to dress for dinner." Leading her daughter to the door, she commanded, "Darcy, you will stay."

"Darcy." The duke interrupted his staring.

"Yes, Your Grace?"

"My study."

"Of course." Grimacing, Darcy threw back his shoulders to face the inevitable.

nine

THE DUKE OF NORTHAMPTON LED DARCY TO A CHAIR BEFORE HEADING to the sideboard for a drink. After watching him pour a second glass, the younger man observed the duke move directly in front of him.

"Darcy." He glared. "Would you care to explain your…unfathomable accusations against my daughter?"

Darcy hung his head.

Allowing Darcy his shame, the duke sat. "Your aunt informed me of your *first* offence."

Darcy winced at the disgust in his uncle's voice.

"While it was disgraceful enough when she was Raleigh's niece, it is nigh unpardonable to reiterate such an abomination to *my daughter*!"

Perspiration prickled Darcy's brow, and he tugged at his cravat.

Placing both glasses on the side table between their chairs, the duke rose. Darcy watched from downcast eyes as his uncle paced, hands restrained but twitching behind his back.

"I know the duchess and I have left you to your own devices these last years, but I had no idea you had sunk so low." He paused. "It is hard enough to bear knowing you would accuse two different men old enough to be her father of compromising an innocent—but that I should be one of those men! That you believe *I* would dishonour my home and name with such conduct? What were you thinking?"

The young man looked up, red-faced and silent.

"I demand an explanation. You have dishonoured not one but two great houses. Admiral Raleigh is a *highly* respected member of the admiralty. Your reckless speculation has besmirched a war hero, *boy*. Had you considered that? And there is the matter of your accusing *me*! Do you honestly think that *I* would take a mistress? That I have *need* of one? That in another lifetime, another world, I would denigrate myself in such a callous manner by bringing the poor creature into my home— the home my father and *his* father made for me?"

Darcy sank further into his chair.

"I am not Matlock! Do not ever confuse me with that reprehensible excuse for a man. Ever! I held great admiration for your father. His approach to childrearing was my guide in raising Julian." He poured a fresh glass and drank. "It disturbs me greatly to hear that *you* would contemplate making such an offer to a woman—*any* woman! That you would willingly take advantage of a woman you believed to be defenceless!

"I admit it is difficult not to think less of you. It is a struggle. I shall not spare you knowing my feelings on learning that the woman to whom you made an improper proposal is my *daughter*! That she was out there in the world, and that *you* of all people…I swear on all that is holy, if things were one iota different, I would run you through!"

"I want to marry her," Darcy managed to utter.

"What?"

Clearing his throat, Darcy repeated. "I wish to marry Elizabeth."

"And *this* is how you express your undying devotion? By an indecent proposal? Offering to make her a woman whom you could never receive in your home? Never introduce to your family—to her own mother? Never acknowledge her children? Forgive me for wishing to spare *my* daughter that fate."

"Please, sir, let me explain."

The duke gave Darcy an incredulous glare, but sat. "Go on."

"I have been under a great strain of late. Matlock and Lady Catherine have combined forces, pressuring me to marry Anne."

The duke leaned forward at the mention of Lady Catherine.

"More so than usual? While we have not been vocal, you know we have been involved in your fate. I am aware of both Georgiana's near disaster and the source of her sorrow. Are they using that to force your hand?"

Darcy nodded.

"Catherine was sloppy in that." The duke rose and paced the room, unaware of Darcy's shock. "But, why now?"

"It was my dance with…your daughter…that ignited Lady Catherine's interest. I am not in the habit of making such a spectacle of myself at a ball."

"No, you save that for morning walks in the park," his uncle grunted, and Darcy winced. "Continue."

"They came to Darcy House not long after the Montridge ball. My aunt claimed that I had humiliated Anne, and to make amends, I must unite Rosings and Pemberley."

"Old business." The duke waived his hand. "Why was Matlock there? It is unusual for him to be present for her demands, am I right?"

"You are, sir." Darcy shook his head, amazed at how well informed the duke was. "Lady Catherine spoke first, then he sent her away to speak with Georgiana. He, too, demanded I marry Anne, explaining that, should I so desire, I could make a different kind of offer to Miss Bennet—"

"And you decided that *this* was the time to listen to him?" The duke was incredulous. "After all the years he has been after you to invest here or to back a candidate there? You refused *those* ludicrous proposals. And now, in *this* you heed his advice?"

"You do not understand."

"I agree—I do not. Enlighten me." The duke held up his hand. "On second thought—no. I do not want to know."

"She made me laugh, sir. Truly, she is amazing. She is perfection. Her grace is undeniable, her beauty astounding."

Darcy glanced at his uncle who still scrutinised his nephew.

"But it is more than that. Her mind is keen and precise, much like your own. She is charming and witty but never unkind. It is absurdity she abuses, not the person afflicted with it."

He ran his hand through his hair. "I wish to be nearer to her than is possible. When I am not, I am exiled from hope, joy. The thought that she had taken…the admiral…" He hung his head. "It drove me past reason. I went mad in a way."

"What made you think Elizabeth was…was *with* Raleigh?" the duke asked.

"Miss Caroline Bingley." Darcy groaned and rose, going to the window. "I am a fool."

"People in love are rarely rational." Northampton refilled their glasses and joined him at the window. "Here.

"I wish to learn how your *baser* feelings purified into a desire for marriage." Giving Darcy a significant look, the duke returned to a chair by the hearth.

Tasting the smooth liquid, Darcy ordered his thoughts. "I left London for Pemberley to avoid running into Elizabeth…Miss Benn… Lady Elizabeth—your daughter. Lady Elizabeth was in London, and that our paths might cross was insupportable, not when she had so adamantly refused me. It was more than I could bear."

"So you beat a hasty retreat to Derbyshire?"

"Yes."

"I must know," the duke asked. "Is it that Elizabeth now has the social standing—"

"No!" Darcy cried. "No—I could not stand my behaviour, and I was ashamed of the man I had become. The duchess's visit, then your letter regarding Grandmother Darcy's portrait, and being at Pemberley —all gave me the strength to fight *myself* for Elizabeth, if that makes any sense. I brought Mother's engagement ring with me."

The duke's head snapped back.

"I was determined to seek out Miss Bennet…your daughter…to rectify my standing in her eyes."

"Well I am glad of *that* at least, although I believe this morning's exhibition only increases the distance you must travel."

The two men finished their drinks in silence.

ALEXANDRA WAVED off the maid's help as she brought Elizabeth to her chamber. "A glass of wine, please."

"Yes, ma'am." Markum glanced at her mistress, who was pale and shaking.

The duchess sat her daughter on the chaise, bending to place her slippered feet on the cushions. *Oh dear. In all the rush and excitement, I forgot that it was Darcy who… I will tan his hide and hang it in the conservatory!*

Hearing Elizabeth sob, the duchess took her in her arms.

"I am so ashamed! That he should find me here and think such things." She looked into her mother's eyes. "How could he *say* such things."

"Elizabeth, it is not *you* who should be ashamed. You have done nothing wrong. *He* is wrong. Your father and I shall take care of him."

Elizabeth turned away, her lower lip between her teeth. Insight flooded the duchess, but she kept her own counsel. "We are here for you—*with* you, Elizabeth. This shall *not* go unanswered."

"What will you do to him?"

Her mother brushed a stray curl flirting with Elizabeth's eyelashes. "Your father will not call him out if that is your concern. But Darcy *will* apologise and explain himself to Philip's and my satisfaction."

"And what of mine?" Elizabeth asked, strength swelling in her eyes.

The duchess looked at her daughter. "Oh, my darling, you *shall* have your say to that wayward cousin of yours."

"Cousin!" Elizabeth gasped at this new understanding. "I had not… that is…" Emotion rolled over her countenance. "This is all so new. Shall I ever adjust to it?"

"Of course you will, my dear. Look how far we have come since finding each other. This is a great tumult for us all. Your return brings up a painful part of our past, one that never healed. But, as in every healing, there is some pain at first, but with you here with us, we *will* recover. As in everything, *we* shall only get better."

She reached for her child. "You are my daughter, Elizabeth. Flesh of my flesh, blood of my blood. All that matters is that you are home with your mother and father and Julian."

"Julian," Elizabeth pondered. "My brother."

DINNER WAS A STRAINED AFFAIR. The duchess returned downstairs after Elizabeth was safely asleep. The trio ate in a heavy silence, their quick, clever minds processing the afternoon. Alexandra made no pretence of hiding the scowls she aimed at her nephew. Elizabeth's abbreviated account of his first proposal, coupled with what she witnessed in her own parlour, rankled. *Yet, there is what Darcy confided at Pemberley. Why not speak of that rather than jumping from one false conclusion to another. He is still that young lad, so sweet underneath but so sure of his own counsel.*

Alexandra was less certain of her daughter's response to everything. Concern surged in her heart, and she scowled at Darcy. *Perhaps Mrs Raleigh was right. The poor child has been through so much, and we have only added to her burden.*

Catching her eye, the duke smiled.

No matter how difficult it is in this period of adjustment, we are family. We belong, and we are strongest together.

Northampton was struggling with emotions of his own. *How stupid can the boy be? Elizabeth is a lady even if she was raised far from London! He says he knows her, loves her, and yet he accuses her... twice!* The duke groaned, and Darcy grimaced. *I swear I should take a switch to him till he cannot think straight, but I guess that is already the case.* He shook his head. *Of all the love stories ever, this must be the most unusual.* Glancing at the empty seat, he recalled Elizabeth's crumbled retreat. *He is unworthy of her. All men are unworthy of her. If he touches her, I shall string him up by his thumbs.*

Darcy's mortification intensified at each scowl and glare. He had shown his worst to the people who had shown him love, *insulting—no, humiliating—the woman I love. Twice!* Looking at the empty seat, his spirit fell again. *She is distraught by my words, my jealous rage.* He laid down his spoon.

"Pray forgive me, ma'am, sir, but I think it best I return to Darcy House."

"Nonsense, Darcy." Putting down her own spoon, the duchess lifted her chin. "While it is true that this afternoon's performance is regrettable, you *shall* apologise to my daughter."

He looked down, repentant.

"We *are* family, and we know that you are prone to speak in haste on occasion. I fear it is a trait inherited from my dear brother."

The duke chuckled.

"No running away this time I am afraid. You must make things right with her."

TWO DAYS LATER, Lady Catherine crossed Madam LeSage's threshold, dragging her sallow daughter behind her.

"Madam LeSage." Lady Catherine pushed aside the inconsequential patron who was speaking with the owner of the shop. "I am Lady Catherine de Bourgh, and I am told you are the best, so I have selected you to create my daughter's trousseau."

Madam LeSage quirked her brow but remained silent.

"She will be married soon. There is no one in England with such taste as I, and as such, I shall oversee your designs.

"I see. This way, please." Madam LeSage ushered the interlopers to a side room.

"Do you have any idea who I am?" Taking umbrage at being pushed aside, she stamped her foot. "I am Lady Catherine Fitzwilliam de Bourgh! My patronage will *make* your reputation. See to it that you keep this in mind while sewing my daughter's gowns."

"One of my assistants will be with you momentarily, your ladyship. I am attending—"

"Nonsense!" Lady Catherine boomed. Advancing, she narrowed her eyes. "It is not every day you have such a vision to adorn. My daughter is to be married to Mr Fitzwilliam Darcy of Pemberley. Do you know who *that* is? They shall be married anon, and her gown must be made post-haste."

"I heard you the first time, madam, but as I said, I have other ladies who have waited patiently—"

"If they are patient, they can wait a bit longer." Lady Catherine stood in front of the dressmaker, eyes flaring and lips twitching.

"Lady Catherine." The Duchess of Northampton stepped through the doorway.

Lady Catherine's nostrils flared, her eyes and lips sneering. Turning, all colour drained from her face. "Alexandra…"

"I have never given you leave to address me with such informality, *Lady* Catherine," a steely calm replied. "My enemies know better than to cross my path."

Lady Catherine let out a hollow laugh, eyes darting to Anne.

"To what does London owe the *pleasure* of your presence? Are the halls of Rosings overwhelmed with the lamentations of those you have wronged?"

Lady Catherine growled. Then, standing tall, she sniffed. "My daughter—you remember Anne, do you not?—is to wed *my* nephew Darcy."

"Did not Matlock finally bring you to your senses and make you see that you will never have Darcy?" The duchess sashayed nearer.

"My daughter will be the next mistress of Pemberley, Duchess, you mark my words."

"And you mark *my* words, Cathcrine. That sacrilege will never happen."

Lady Catherine laughed. "Because you think *your* daughter will be his bride?" Her eyes glittered with maliciousness. "Your daughter is *dead*."

A feral smirk on her lips, Alexandra looked Lady Catherine dead in the eyes. "My daughter lives."

Lady Catherine faltered, and the Duchess of Northampton turned, leaving the sputtering old woman.

The sound of a body falling broke her stupor as Lady Catherine screamed, "Anne!"

ten

THE EARL OF MATLOCK STORMED INTO DARCY'S STUDY, THE MORNING paper in his grasp and sons Viscount Braddleton and Colonel Fitzwilliam on his heels. "Darcy, is this true? She has been recovered?"

"Does she remember anything?" the colonel demanded.

"Is she as beautiful as her mother?" Braddleton leered.

Ignoring them, Darcy remained seated, surveying his relations with new understanding. The earl's face was mottled with fury. Concern with a trace of guilt stretched across the colonel's face. And Braddleton, the cagiest of the lot, simply observed Darcy with the deliberation of a predator. Seeing Darcy shudder, the viscount smirked.

Darcy tented his fingers beneath his chin, assessing each of his relations. "I am unable to offer any more information than you have already." He indicated the paper.

"I am your nearest relation, and I demand you answer me," the earl bellowed.

"No, sir, you are not. The duchess is my father's sister—on that score you are equal—and *she* and her husband, the *duke*, have requested I remain silent on the matter."

"Then answer this—Will they take legal action?" Braddleton pushed away from the wall against which he was leaning.

"I am not privy to His Grace's counsel on that matter. It would be inappropriate for me to place myself between the two sides of my family." *Although at the moment, I would allow the physician to leech my blood if I could disengage from you.* "Now, if this is the sole reason for your unplanned visit, I ask that you leave. I am inundated with work."

"Darcy!" The door flew open, and Lady Catherine stormed through. "So, this is the *family* business that keeps you from Rosings?"

She shook a copy of the paper at him. "These...lies must be retracted *immediately!*"

"Enough, Catherine. I shall handle this," the earl said.

She advanced on her brother. "Just as, I suppose, you handled his engagement to my daughter? No, it is time I take matters into my own hands. If you had listened to me, this would have been concluded years ago."

Darcy's mind reeled as they continued arguing. "I beg your pardon. What are you two going on about?"

Lady Catherine spat, "Pay attention, boy. This is serious."

"Yes, I agree." He glared back.

"What my father, brother, and aunt are so *ineffectually* prattling on about—" Braddleton began.

Lady Catherine slapped her outspoken nephew.

"Madam, you forget yourself." Braddleton barely controlled his rage.

"How dare you?" Lady Catherine hissed. "Matlock, do something about this whelp."

"What would you have me do, Catherine. He is right." The earl's smirk fuelled his sister's grimace.

Darcy caught the disgust Braddleton held for his father. *How could I ever have contemplated that these people cared for me—or held the idea of sacrificing myself to serve their whims?* He shuddered.

"The salient point," Braddleton interjected, "is that the duke *has* claimed this upstart and will present her as his own."

Catherine scoffed, and Braddleton turned on her. "You forget,

Aunt, that the *Duke* of Northampton is a distant member of the royal family. He and this Lady Elizabeth *are* of the blood royal."

"A remote cousin," Matlock said dismissively.

"I am always amazed at your ability to blather on about the Matlock lineage, using the Darcy name as it suits you, yet you hold my family in contempt!" Darcy rose to his feet. "What is it you want?"

"You must announce your engagement to Anne, immediately," Lady Catherine demanded. "That will protect her."

Darcy filed away that last morsel for later review. "That, Aunt, shall never happen. Anne is the last woman I would *ever* consider marrying."

Lady Catherine gasped. "You ungrateful wretch! After all I have done—" She marched towards Darcy, anger pulsing in the veins of her temple.

"That is on *your* head, as I truly doubt you have a heart!" Darcy turned to his uncle. "And you—what do you want?"

"I..." the earl sputtered.

"*I* want this to go away." The colonel looked at Darcy. "I want no mention of the alleged doings of any member of this family to be made public in any way."

Braddleton laughed, and Darcy sent him a withering glance. "That is unlikely, Richard. The duke is enraged as the family that saved Elizabeth's life has recounted the *condition* in which she was found." He noted Lady Catherine's tremor with satisfaction.

"Recollections over a decade old are not unimpeachable," the earl thought aloud.

Darcy's head thrummed with disgust. Hearing Lady Catherine snort, he turned in surprise as the fingers on her right hand twitched. "Aunt, are you unwell?"

"Her existence was insupportable," she spat.

"I beg your pardon?"

"Her *living* was a pox on this family, boy. You should be thank—"

"Catherine!" the earl shouted. "Silence."

Shaking with controlled rage, Darcy boomed. "Enough! I am done. Leave! All of you!"

As no one obeyed his wishes, he began again. "Shall I call Winters and have you forcibly removed?"

"You would not dare!" Lady Catherine shouted.

"No?" Darcy stared her down.

"Aunt, Father"—Braddleton addressed each in turn—"I believe that it would not be wise to try Darcy's temper further."

"That, Braddleton, is the wisest thing you have *ever* said," Darcy added. "Now, out! All of you."

Darcy slumped against the window of the front hall and watched them board their carriages. *Mother, how could one as good as you come from that den of vipers?* Tugging the cuffs of his sleeves, he returned to his study.

IT WAS THUS that Georgiana found her brother later that afternoon. "What has happened? Please tell me!"

"The Matlocks were here and—"

"No!" She hugged him.

Allowing himself a moment of her comfort, Darcy led them to a sofa. "Lady Catherine as much as confessed her guilt regarding Elizabeth."

"Lady Catherine was here as well?" Georgiana's mouth dropped open at their audacity. "Oh, Brother. It must have been horrible."

He stroked her hands as they sat in silence.

"There was no remorse, Georgiana—none. Their concern is with the impact of Elizabeth's reappearance on *their* reputation—the damage of the scandal on *their* name, *their* place in society."

She shook her head, lips pursed. He embraced her until she mastered her emotions.

"We must impart to the duke what I have learned." He tucked a stray curl behind her ear. "I need you with me, for this will not be pleasant."

"Then let us go. I am rarely given the privilege to see the duchess twice in one day."

"And Elizabeth."

"Oh yes, she is wonderful, brother. She is everything I could ever wish for in a cousin."

"A cousin?" He smiled for the first time that day. "What about a sister?"

A wide smile spread across her lips, and her eyes lit with excitement. "Are you...? Do you mean you...?"

He ran a hand through his hair till his curls bounced back around his face, one falling errantly into his eye. "I—that is to say—I have, ah...Miss Elizabeth Bennet and I have..."

She watched with wonder as he turned away.

"Before, when I ran and hid at Pemberley, it was because I...I made her an offer..."

"You are to be married? Oh, and now she is our cousin!"

"Ah, no. Miss Elizabeth..."

"*Lady* Elizabeth..."

"She rightly refused my offer. It was not an offer of marriage."

"Not of marriage?" Her eyes widened, then narrowed. "You offered to make her your...*mistress*?

Darcy rubbed his hands together. "At that point in time, I was contemplating offering for Anne. Matlock was persistent, and at the time, I believed I owed him my allegiance. And Lady Catherine ranted at every opportunity...and there was no other who touched me..."

"Until Elizabeth," Georgiana's voice held understanding.

He nodded, unable to speak. Mastering his shame, he continued. "I felt I could not offer marriage to Miss Bennet. She was an orphan of uncertain birth. I am ashamed, grievously ashamed of myself, but I cannot retake my steps, no matter how much I wish to."

"Yes, yes of course." Darcy heard her shift in her seat, her silence deafening. When she rose to go, he tugged at her hand. "There is more, is there not?"

"Yes. The Northamptons know of my disastrous attempt to secure her."

Darcy gaped as Georgiana's unrestrained laughter rolled though the room. It was several minutes before she could control herself.

"I can only imagine your face when the duke informed you of that!" Beginning with giggles, she again convulsed in laughter.

Darcy huffed and crossed his arms over his chest.

"Oh, do not take that tone with me, dear brother. Not now and perhaps not ever again." Her brow arched, but there was a sparkle in her eyes. She tapped his knee. "But let us go to Northampton Place."

He took her hand. "You know this will be difficult and could bring our family down."

"We are Darcys, and *we* have done nothing wrong…well almost nothing." She glared at him, and he blushed. "The Matlocks have brought this upon themselves. Even I knew of the rumour that Lady Catherine was responsible for Elizabeth's disap—her abduction. Never once have they expressed regret at our loss, of the damage for which I believe she is responsible. Never! All I have ever heard is their not-so-veiled disdain for our Northampton relations even though our uncle is a duke. It has never made sense to me. I know there are political and philosophical differences, but the Matlocks have acted in a base manner and are, perhaps unconsciously, ashamed."

She fell silent. "I believe in opening the sore so we may all heal from this wound."

Darcy looked at the last member of his immediate family and brought her hand to his lips. "Have you always been this wise, little one?"

"No, but life is willing to teach me."

WHEN THE DARCYS arrived at Northampton Place, Georgiana went in search of her aunt and cousin. Darcy walked to the study where he found the duke in his chair, staring at a sheaf of papers stacked neatly on his desk. As he failed to respond to the first knock, Darcy opened the door, peeking his head around. "Your Grace? Are you…? Forgive me for disturbing you, sir." He stood at his full height.

"Darcy! What brings you to Northampton Place?" Shaken from his intense mental focus, he was a bit disoriented. "Not that you are unwelcome, but I was unaware of a previous engagement."

"No, there was none. Georgiana and I have come unexpectedly."

The duke smiled, his outstretched arm indicating a seat across the wide expanse of his desk. "Take a seat and tell me what is on your mind."

Darcy did and, once comfortable, leaned forward. "Matlock and Lady Catherine paid me a visit this morning."

"I imagined they would." He looked at the morning's paper on his desk. "Tell me. How did it go?"

"They wished to know about Elizabeth." Darcy's hands clutched into fists. "Lady Catherine...she as much as admitted..."

Northampton's eyes flashed, his entire being jolted alert.

"...that *she* was responsible for Elizabeth's abduction."

The duke's eyes widened.

"From what I gather, her design was to kill Elizabeth."

Darcy gathered his courage to face Northampton. Though consumed in private thoughts, his body hummed with energy, and Darcy sat back, watching the duke's brilliant mind untangle the facts to the path they would all soon follow. He nearly jumped out of his seat when the duke next spoke.

"What stopped her from carrying out her hellish plan?"

"As strange as it may seem, it was my uncle Matlock."

The duke snorted. "So, murder is too much, even for him?" Pushing away from his desk, he stood and paced then headed to the sideboard, pouring two snifters. He handed one to Darcy then placed his own glass on a side table before pulling a mid-sized chest from behind his desk.

"Mrs Raleigh let it be known that her sister, Gloria—the former Mrs Edwin Bennet—kept a hope chest for each of her daughters. Elizabeth and Jane..."

"...Mrs Bingley."

"Yes, that is right. I take it this is the family of the Miss Bingley who has fostered the rumours being spread about town?"

Darcy nodded.

"Curious. But then, you are on good terms with Mr Bingley, are you not?"

"Yes, sir. He is one of my oldest friends and one of the best men of my acquaintance."

"Good." The duke nodded. "And this Miss Bingley? Elizabeth has shared her experiences with *that* woman. Where does she fit in the scheme of things?"

"Collateral damage, I would have to say."

"Of course. But where were we?" The duke looked at Darcy, his eyes saddened as he took in the wooden box at his feet. "Ah, the chest —Elizabeth's cornucopia of memories sequestered in the attics of Longbourn. Its current mistress never appreciated Elizabeth. Seems she felt a *foundling* was beneath the notice of a country gentleman's wife and made her displeasure known."

The duke smirked as his commanding nephew squirmed. "Fortunately for our Elizabeth, Mrs Bennet's predecessor was made of nobler stuff and accepted Elizabeth as she would her own flesh and blood. She made Elizabeth's first years in Hertfordshire as pleasant and loving as possible. Mrs Raleigh is one of the most intelligent females aside from my family circle, so I am not surprised that her sister was just as insightful."

Bending forward, the duke opened the chest. "Mr Edwin and then Thomas Bennet, the current master, maintained a journal of sorts, chronicling the significant events of Elizabeth's life." The duke leaned back in his chair, his perceptive eyes locked on the contents of the chest. Darcy followed his lead, curious as to its contents. Beneath a young child's dress, he saw journals, too numerous to count.

"When Elizabeth returned from her recent *walk in the park*"— Northampton held Darcy's eyes as the young man realised what his arrogance cost the woman he loved—"Elizabeth's dreams intensified, returning to her abduction."

The duke leaned forward, steel in his words. "The admiral sent an express to Mr Bennet, requesting this chest be sent here."

Bending, he extracted a child's gown, handing it to Darcy. "This is what Elizabeth wore the day she was *taken*."

Darcy took it with great reverence.

"Note the Darcy roses. *Your* mother made this for Elizabeth. It was right before Georgiana's birth, and Anne was so hopeful she would soon have her own little girl. You know, Elizabeth's abduction gave great fear to your mother when Georgiana was born. She thought if it could happen at Pemberley…"

Darcy stroked the gown. Bringing it to his nose, he searched for the long-ago scent of autumn, the leaves crisp and crackling in the air. He and Julian had had a scuffle, and Elizabeth had intervened, *always on the side of her brother*. When the adults had marched them to the house, Elizabeth had dropped her baby doll, Maisey. It was this irreplaceable doll that had consoled her through her scrapes and sorrows and had drawn her out of the nursery later that afternoon—the afternoon she failed to return.

Darcy turned to his uncle. Relaxing his fierce grip on the gown, he turned it to complete his examination. Seeing the faint brown stains on the back, he looked up at his uncle, who waited for his response.

Lifting the journal, the duke read from the faded pages.

November 20, 1794

Although it is nigh midnight, I cannot sleep. Soon it will be my turn to watch over Elizabeth. It has been three days since I found her huddled near Netherfield Road. As horrific as it was to see this beautiful child—shivering, alone, wet, and terrified —that was not the worst of it.

He took a deep breath with a slight tremor.

The worst was lifting her to my horse. I moved as gently as my dear Jane had taught me that little girls must be lifted, but being placed on the saddle sent Elizabeth into paroxysms of panic. Placing my arm around her back, her panic turned to pain, and she screamed in physical agony. Once at Longbourn, I discovered the reason. Gloria, my excellent wife, and our devoted Hill tried to remove her gown, only to find it bonded to her back by her own, caked blood. Her back…

The duke paused, his hand shaking to reach his brandy.

Foreboding ran through Darcy.

The duke continued.

Her back was covered in open, bleeding stripes where she had been struck without mercy. My blood boils even at the recounting of the horror. Who inflicts such violence upon a defenceless child? For even though I had the pleasure of hearing her sweet voice one time, I saw her beautiful eyes only that once before exhaustion and, I fear, fever closed them. We all—Gloria, Hill, and I—understand what a unique and wondrous child Elizabeth must be.

Darcy leapt to his feet, pacing till his emotions settled into turmoil. His uncle stared, lost in torment, eyes reflecting his unendurable pain. Returning to his chair, Darcy picked up the gown from where he had dropped it, holding it like a holy relic.

The duke cleared his throat. "This entry is from three weeks hence…"

Elizabeth again suffered through the night. Her screams roused us at the third bell. Glory and I heard the name of the one who must be responsible for Elizabeth's agony. To hear the terror in her voice, the pleading! Though not a man of violence, I swear upon my father's grave that, should I ever meet them, I will exact my revenge. May God forgive me should I ever meet the one called Catty.

Visceral shock jolted Darcy, and he nearly dropped the gown again. Northampton refilled their snifters, and they drank in silence.

Darcy spoke when the glasses were nearly empty. "There are no words to convey my horror…my shame for what my relations and I have done. I loved Elizabeth. I…I still do."

Speaking from a well of silence, the duke's response was measured. "I did not read from Bennet's journals—books that Alexandra and I shall cherish for the rest of our days— to hear your pitiful claim of love for either Lady Elizabeth Elliston or Miss Elizabeth Bennet. I read so you will understand when I bring your aunt to the bar for *treason*."

"Treason?"

"You and your Matlock relations have always underrated the Northampton nature. Your aunt, in her mania to control Pemberley, forgot that the dukedom was created by a British monarch. An attack on me or mine is an attack against the crown. And in the year of this particular crime, we were at war. She shall hang, Darcy, and all in her confidence. Tell your uncle he will hear from me."

"Sir, they are my—"

"*She* is my *daughter*! My blood and your own runs in her veins. What would you do if Georgiana were taken that day and one of *my* ancestors committed the sacrilege?"

He was lost in a whirlwind of images; memories swarmed in his mind of the Matlocks comforting him while little Elizabeth endured their villainy. Images of Matlock's calculating avarice contrasted with the impish child and the enchanting woman who returned. The duke watched, of no mind to ease his struggle.

The arrival of Hutchins beckoned them to the duchess. Standing, Darcy placed his hand on his elder's arm. "I *will* do what you ask, and know I stand with you."

LADY ELIZABETH LOOKED out into the starry night sky from her new bedchamber, her conversation with Georgiana repeating in her mind. *Such a sweet girl. So different from my Bennet cousins.* Thoughts of her former life with Jane flooded her mind: the boisterous summer days wandering through fields, creating plays and songs, and dancing on the shores of Noah's Puddle. Tales of fairies, knights, shared thoughts of love, and the men who would take them from their home.

But never have I thought it would be my own father to rescue me. Elizabeth leaned into the silk drapes of her window. *And Darcy. Everyone wishes to explain his behaviour as aberrant to his true nature. And yet with me? I bring out his worst, it seems.*

"Georgiana and Mama were very clear they did not agree with him nor excuse his behaviour"—she smiled—"and neither do I. But which is he—rake or reserved man? Can these two, opposing currents run in one person?" She thought of the Darcy chastised by her mother, and the man submersed in grief as she walked away after his disastrous insult. "His eyes are so beautiful," she said leaning against the window. "He is so lost…"

She thought back to her conversation with Georgiana.

"Lady Elizabeth, forgive me for being so presumptuous, please. I learned only this afternoon of my brother's…insult." Georgiana's eyes pleaded with Elizabeth. "He…he has been under such pressure this last year. I nearly ruined my life—not only my life but also my family's reputation. I came so very close to eloping with a man who loved only my fortune."

There were tears in her eyes, and Elizabeth hugged the young woman as she continued. "Fitzwilliam rescued me—saved me, really. Then Lord Matlock and Lady Catherine..."

Elizabeth stiffened, pulling back with fear and suspicion in her eyes. "They spoke to Darcy?"

"They demanded he marry Anne to save me."

"You?"

"Yes—" Georgiana stopped as Elizabeth pressed her arm. "Lady Catherine threatened that unless Fitzwilliam married Anne, she would reveal my...shame."

Elizabeth gasped. "But my parents..."

"I know not how, but after my father died...your father was away for so long in Austria, and then your mother...well there was your father's fall from his horse. She was so very worried about him."

Seeing Elizabeth's surprise, she rushed to finish. "He is well now, but there was a time when he would not awaken. The duchess was distraught. She would not leave the duke's side, and Fitzwilliam could not leave Pemberley for such great lengths of time—"

"And the Matlocks came to your aid."

"He carries so much. I know how it feels to shoulder the weight of the world. It colours one's reason, makes one suspicious." *Change is upon us, but it will not always be so. Do not give up hope; do not judge. Not yet.* Agreeing that it was too early to pass a final judgment on either her cousin or herself, she pushed away from the window and took herself to bed.

eleven

DARCY HAD BARELY HANDED HIS COAT TO CUMMINGS WHEN THE DOOR opened again and the duke entered. "Ah, Darcy, I am glad you are here." He shrugged out of his coat and ushered Darcy into his study.

Passing the parlour, Darcy sighed. *It seems I shall again be denied the opportunity to apologise this afternoon.* Seeing the urgency in his uncle's demeanour, Darcy cleared his head and followed the duke into his study. Northampton poured hefty brandies for himself and his nephew, looking him in the eye. Darcy refused to back down.

His uncle nodded, and they sat. "I have just come from a meeting, a highly confidential meeting at the Exchequer. Some information has come to my attention regarding your uncle Matlock."

Darcy became uneasy.

Hesitating, the duke assessed him. "Matlock and Braddleton are heavily invested in a number of *speculative* endeavours abroad."

"How speculative?"

Northampton crossed his legs. "Enough to be worrying, at least for Matlock's financial, and perhaps social, well-being. Matlock and Braddleton—"

"I am aware that Braddleton favours the gaming tables."

"And Matlock favours unsavoury investments with unscrupulous men. The combination has driven him into a nasty alliance." The duke watched the emotion roiling over Darcy's face.

"The cur! He would sell me, sell Anne, to redeem his incompetence! Why could he not just come and ask…?"

"I shall not excuse nor pardon his behaviour, but your uncle—the entire Matlock clan—are a stubborn, proud lot. They had an illustrious run fifty or so years ago but let it slip through their fingers."

"And now they covet the *Darcy* fortune, dragging me down with them!" Darcy sputtered. "Like a sheep being led to the slaughter."

"So it would seem."

"Thank you, sir," Darcy grasped his hands together. "I have informed them that I shall never marry Anne."

"That went over well, I am sure," the duke replied drily. "I fear this will make them all more desperate, and therefore—"

"—more dangerous. What will you do?" the young man asked.

"Darcy, you are aware…that is…"

"What is it?" Darcy asked the decidedly ill-at-ease duke.

"I wish you to announce your engagement to Elizabeth—as soon as may be."

"What? Lady Elizabeth will surely not look favourably on this."

"I am not sure *I* look favourably on it." The duke smirked at the shock on Darcy's face. "Nor can I vouchsafe that your aunt or Mrs Raleigh will either. However, it is the only way I see—at the moment —to protect her, and *that i*s more important to me. Marrying you will stir them, and in their agitation, they will stumble. We shall be waiting to catch them. *That* will fulfil the wishes of both fathers."

"So, it is true then? You did…?"

"Yes, well, not legally. Your father and I signed a note attesting to our wishes for the union. It was that conversation that incited Lady Catherine—"

"And if I had asked Anne to marry me?" Darcy asked

"If you loved her, I would have supported you. If not? I would have supported you."

"Could you have?"

"If Alexandra and I agreed there was no love in the union you proposed, we would have intervened, yes."

Darcy blinked at the emotion rushing through him. *I was never alone. They were looking out for me.* With a choked voice, Darcy whispered, "Thank you, sir. This means more to me than I can say."

Northampton rose. "Come, let us speak to your aunt and cousin."

"THERE YOU ARE, MY DEARS," His Grace greeted the women. "Georgiana, it is good to see you."

"It is good to see you, sir. Brother…?" Georgiana arched her brow. At his slight nod, she relaxed and smiled.

"Lady Elizabeth." Darcy bowed. Elizabeth's breath caught at the naked humility in his eyes. "I am honoured you would remain and not flee my presence."

"Mr Darcy," she stammered. "Please sit."

Darcy retreated to a solitary chair.

"Ladies. I have news of some import." The duke took Elizabeth's hand. "You know the details of the Matlocks' visit to Darcy?"

The ladies nodded.

"Lady Catherine all but admitted that she is responsible for your kidnapping, Elizabeth."

The duchess gasped, and Elizabeth clutched her father's hand. "Even before this…disclosure…I requested a unit of royal guards be placed around the house and a personal guard for you. However, there is more."

Her mother held on to Elizabeth's arm, and Darcy moved closer to Georgiana.

The duke cleared his throat. "I believe the surest way to ensure your safety is…" The duke hesitated, glancing at his wife and then Elizabeth. "…is for you and Darcy to announce your engagement."

Elizabeth's eyes widened in shock. "But…but…" She looked at Darcy, whose eyes pleaded.

"We shall make the announcement. That should suffice for now. We shall not rush you beyond this."

"But—" Elizabeth stood. "This is…it is as bad as"—her eyes darted to Georgiana—"before." Rising, Elizabeth rushed towards the door.

"Elizabeth!" her mother cried out. "Wait!"

Elizabeth turned, misery in her bearing and eyes. "I was so happy to have found you, so happy." Tears crested in her eyes. "Now I find it was an illusion. You, too, wish me gone. Promising me to a man who only thinks of me for…for his pleasure…"

"No, Elizabeth!" Darcy rushed to her side.

"Do not touch me!" she cried. Looking at them, she clutched her gown. "I have my Bennet dowry. I shall live on my own."

"Elizabeth!" The duke leapt forward. His wife restrained him.

"If you would call a carriage, I would be most grateful." Elizabeth left the salon.

Darcy followed her as far as the stairwell. "Elizabeth, please wait. Please. We—none of us would do anything to harm you."

"No?" Whipping around, she faced him. "I beg to differ. That *any* of you would believe I would agree to this is ludicrous—truly beyond the pale. Excuse me."

"Where will you go?"

"To my family."

"*We* are your family, Elizabeth."

"You may be my blood, but you have no love for me. You love the little girl you lost. I am a grown woman with experiences vastly unlike yours. I see things differently, and being sold to you is *not* my idea of future happiness." She left Darcy at the foot of the stairs.

He shook as the front door closed.

THAT NIGHT, the Earl of Matlock, leaving his mistress, found an unmarked carriage waiting. Trying to place the unfamiliar vehicle, he startled when two broad-chested men emerged. The earl quaked from his knees to his teeth.

"*Lord* Matlock," the first spoke.

"His lordship would have a word," said the second.

"Now?" Matlock whined. The first man turned to the waiting carriage. Matlock complied as the other took his arm.

The earl was unsurprised when his escorts did not follow him into the conveyance. Eyes adjusting to the light, he shook at the black-clad figure of the notorious Lord Delaboix, head of an ancient family that traded in respectability to organise the underbelly of

English society. A rap with his cane, and the carriage moved forward.

"The *Celestine* was raided two days ago," the criminal rumbled.

Matlock cringed. "I had nothing to do with—"

"I understood you were to *prevent* that from ever occurring! You failed, Matlock." Delaboix relaxed against the squabs. "I have told you on numerous occasions that keeping my trust is paramount to your...*livelihood*. Your word is your bond, Matlock. And *yours* is broken."

"But you must understand, the seizure—"

"Seizure! They will keep the ship?" Fury blasted across the carriage.

Matlock swallowed, a frigid sweat soaking his shirt. "I believe so."

Delaboix placed both hands on the tip of his walking cane. "That changes things. Now I must replace the *Celestine*. Shall we add another five thousand pounds to what your son has lost to me?"

"Five thousand?"

"Yes."

Again, Matlock gasped, tugging at his neck cloth.

"I *will* be satisfied, Matlock." Delaboix leaned forward. "Either you have the *Celestine* returned to me, with reimbursement for my lost cargo, or the cash."

Matlock stammered, "When?"

Delaboix relaxed with a controlled grin. "The middle of next month." His cane signalled for the carriage to stop, and his lieutenants reached in for the earl, hoisting him onto the street. The door slammed, leaving Matlock on the edge of the theatre district where he would not be out of place. Gaining his wits, he stumbled home.

THE NEXT MORNING, Mrs Raleigh knocked softly on Elizabeth's chamber door, opening it a crack. "Elizabeth?" Mrs Raleigh asked softly. "May I come in?"

"Of course, Aunt," Elizabeth said from the bed in which she had taken refuge after surprising her relations the evening before.

Mrs Raleigh entered, coming to sit on the edge of the bed. With kind eyes, she surveyed the young woman who had been her niece. She took her hand in her own and, with the other, tucked a curl behind Elizabeth's ear.

"What happened?" Mrs Raleigh asked. "Was someone unkind?"

Elizabeth looked down. "They want to send me away."

"But why?"

"My safety! That his majesty's guards would not be enough to protect me! No. They wish me gone."

Mrs Raleigh took up Elizabeth's hand again. "I am sure that is not the case, Lizzy. Surely you see that?"

"No, I do not." Tears welled in her eyes.

"What are you thinking?" Mrs Raleigh asked with great care.

She lifted her head in defiance. "They want me gone? Then I shall go. But I shall go on my own terms."

"Elizabeth!"

Twisting her handkerchief, Elizabeth continued. "It is too much! I do not know who I am anymore! I am a Bennet no more, but am I an Elliston? My world has unravelled. Jane is gone. Longbourn is lost to me. If not for you, I would be utterly and completely lost."

"Oh, my dear," Mrs Raleigh said, squeezing Elizabeth's hand.

"I do love them, Aunt. I feel they are mine and I am theirs. I understand, from their perspective, but it is not a solution for me. My thoughts, wishes, and ambitions lie in another direction entirely."

Mrs Raleigh cocked her head. "And they are…?"

"To live where I am wanted. I care not whether it is on a grand estate. I have enough to establish myself somewhere…" Her voice cracked.

"But what of safety? Your physical safety?"

"If I remove myself entirely from the situation, I shall not be a threat."

Mrs Raleigh drew a deep breath. "I do not believe that is true."

"But—"

"Hear me out. Lady Catherine will not rest until her point is carried. You are the daughter of the Duke of Northampton. If, as you say, you move to an estate of your own, you would still be a target—whether for your fortune or a connexion to the royal line."

"But I am not—"

"Yes, you are. Regardless of whether or not you wish this, it is your destiny. This is not something you can escape."

"But that is what they want…to push me away…from here…from them." She fell silent.

"And Mr Darcy? Have you spoken with him at all?"

Elizabeth shook her head.

"No? Well then, you must."

"But what would I say?"

"The duchess has always spoken of her shy nephew. His life taught him to be wary of strangers, especially women. While not excusing his behaviour, I believe it indicates deep feelings for you—feelings that have overwhelmed his taciturn demeanour.

"Yes, that he wished to *use* me!"

"Again, I cannot countenance what he has done. However, he has repented, and I would not tell you this, save that I believe it may help you. Your mother went to visit him after I told her of his impropriety—though at the time, I thought I spoke of his cousin Braddleton. Upon her return to London, she informed me that Mr Darcy intended to propose to you."

"Propose…marriage?"

Mrs Raleigh nodded her head.

"I do not understand. If he…" Elizabeth paused. "How could he make such a horrid mistake?"

"Because he is human, and humans make mistakes. Again, I do not approve of his choice, but he intended to make amends before all the clamour of finding your family."

Seeing Elizabeth about to interrupt, Mrs Raleigh continued, pressing her niece's hand. "Yes, I know we are your family, and nothing will alter that, but the commotion and perhaps"—she smiled —"a note of embarrassment and humility have developed in your Mr Darcy?"

"He is not *my* Mr Darcy."

"I believe he is and shall be until you chase him away again."

"What man would risk being rejected twice by the same woman?"

"Would you reject him out of hand again?"

"I already have. Yesterday, he was in the room when I informed my family I would not acquiesce to their plan."

"I am sure he will not hold that against you." Mrs Raleigh thought for a moment. "But before you do, you must ask yourself what you truly desire. Only then should you speak with him to discover the truth you need."

A knock on the door interrupted their tête-à-tête.

"Elizabeth?" the duchess's voice began, unsure and soft. "May I come in, please?"

Turning to the mother she barely knew, Elizabeth saw that dark circles had formed under her eyes. Those eyes were not certain but timid, and they melted her own uncertainty. "Of course."

Mrs Raleigh rose.

"Mrs Raleigh, please do not leave," she said as she replaced her on the bed.

As she passed her friend, Mrs Raleigh squeezed her arm, causing the duchess to offer a weary smile.

"Elizabeth, Mrs Raleigh, I thank you for letting me come this morning. Philip and I are grieved for all that occurred yesterday. Your father should have prefaced his statement with an explanation."

Elizabeth's eyes widened.

"The…announcement will be made to rouse Matlock and that woman to act, but we would never force you to do anything you do not wish to do. This is so new to all of us."

"Then I may stay here?"

The duchess shook her head. "No, Elizabeth. It is not safe for you here. You, Darcy, and Georgiana will go to Pemberley. All we can offer at this time is to delay your journey by a few days. But with Matlock and Lady Catherine enflamed as we hope they will be, the danger to you increases."

"Mr Darcy and Georgiana will come with me?"

"Of course. They insist on accompanying you."

"Is it true that Mr Darcy intended to seek my hand in marriage?"

"Yes, he did—before I knew who you were. At that time, you were the Raleighs' niece, which was enough for me to seek him out and lay into him for what I believed to be Braddleton's insult. When I learned Darcy was the culprit, I thrashed him soundly—verbally of course."

The duchess took Elizabeth's hands in hers and looked into her eyes. "He admitted his love for you—of his need for your laughter, for your eyes, and for the way you engaged his mind. In the brief time he knew you, you lifted the darkness from his soul."

"He said that?"

"Yes, he did. I demanded of him the reasons he would disgrace himself in such an ignoble manner." She patted her daughter's hand. "I am afraid you will find your mother an indomitable force when needs must."

"Aye," Mrs Raleigh agreed.

"I cannot fix what is wrong between you, but I truly believe Darcy's feelings are sincere and profound, overwhelming his rather reserved nature." Alexandra looked at her daughter. "I shall not ask what you feel for him today, Elizabeth. I *do* ask that you speak with him and hear his reasons for yourself."

Elizabeth nodded.

"Thank you. I hope you will come home. Please. Perhaps not today," she said at the lack of enthusiasm around her. "But soon, my darling? Please."

"I shall. Perhaps in a day or two."

"Thank you, Elizabeth, thank you."

Darcy House

"I WILL *NOT*!" Darcy's fist slammed the mantle in his study.

The duchess rolled her eyes in exaggerated exasperation. "But Elizabeth is willing to receive you."

"She walked out on me. Is that not a precise indication of her feelings? And now, you ask me to return and...and what, exactly?"

"Speak with her. That is all," she said to his pacing frame. "She knows now that you returned to find her—to ask for her hand in marriage."

"She what?" He stopped, gasping in shock. "You...you *told* her? You—our conversation at Pemberley was private!"

The duchess sighed and waved away his concern.

"You told her what I said—about her?"

"Of course I did." She faced him, amused by the utter stupefaction on his handsome face. "Nephew dear, please take hold of yourself. You know as well as I that honesty is essential in situations such as these."

"Revealing my innermost thoughts and desires—"

"Let us leave your *desires* out of this conversation. She is my daughter who has had her entire life upended…" Her voice cracked.

He paused, his head bowed. "It was not fair to reveal my…heart when she holds me in such disdain. I am grieved you would act so cavalierly when so much is at stake."

"That is precisely why I *did* act so 'cavalierly.'" She looked long and hard at her nephew. "You are fixed on your course?"

"Immovable." His lips were pressed in defiance.

"Pity. It seems to me that her heart has softened to your cause."

"Truly?" He spun towards her chair.

His aunt nodded. "My dear nephew, for a man of such sense and education who has lived so well in the world, you truly know nothing of women and the workings of the heart."

Looking away, he blushed. "Tell me all. Leave out nothing."

The duchess laughed. "All I shall say is that she knows you *were* properly humbled in the park, and your *own* counsel decided to return and make a *proper* offer. What she needs to understand is *why*—"

Darcy blinked, stupefied.

"—why you made the offer you made, why you changed your mind, why you love her. Be a man. Open your heart to her. She cares about you as more than a cousin. Remember, she knew you first as a man and danced with you as one. She was insulted by you as a man, not a relation. Now, as a *man*, talk to her and win her."

"You make it sound so easy. You know I am not my best when speaking—"

"I disagree. Perhaps not in an assembly or when you feel yourself on display. But when you are with us, you are eloquent. Please, you must make the effort. Your happiness and my daughter's depend on it."

"Not that there is any pressure…"

The duchess lost her levity. "You have the opportunity to begin this union with love and understanding. It is a rare gift. Do not waste it."

She forced the weight of her words upon him. "Elizabeth returns to Northampton Place the day after tomorrow." She rose. "I expect you soon thereafter." Giving him a peck on the cheek, the duchess left a stunned Darcy to ruminate on the unsettling new developments in his life.

twelve

Darcy entered the library and stopped as Elizabeth looked up from her book. His heart rejoiced till, recognising him, her expression changed, and that wonderful, expansive feeling disintegrated into a guarded mask. "I beg your pardon, Lady Elizabeth."

"Wait please, Mr Darcy." She rose with a blush. "Please." She indicated the seat next to hers.

Darcy's heart reignited as he came to her side. "Lady Elizabeth, you must allow—"

"Again?" She rolled her eyes. "Must I spend our entire acquaintance *allowing* you, sir?" Elizabeth laughed at his widened eyes and gaping mouth.

"I…"

"Only a moment ago, you had much to say to me." Her eyes twinkled, increasing and diminishing his distress.

"Lady Elizabeth, I am truly sorry, both for what I said and for what was left unsaid…before. I humbly beg your forgiveness."

She looked long and hard at him, finding his remorse. "I shall take this into consideration, sir. But first, you must tell me whether your remorse is for making such an offer to me as a gentleman's daughter or for doing so to your cousin? And secondly, why? What possible need would *you* have for a mistress? I am sure there are many women of your circle who would welcome a *respectable* offer from you."

"Elizabeth...Lady Elizabeth," he self-corrected. "I shall answer your first question, although there are really two, before proceeding to the sorry state of my affairs."

She is family, and as my father said, one must always be honest with family, no matter what. "I...from our first dance that evening, all my senses ignited at your touch. Conversing with you was as easy and satisfying as conversing with my uncle or aunt Northampton, your parents. I felt different and still feel with you more than I have with any other woman." He looked at his feet. "I did not, at that time, consider that you could be related to me. For so long, I—we, our family—have been without you. That I would find you on that particular night in that particular place was not in my realm of possibilities."

"And yet it was."

"And yet it was." Gathering his courage, he forged ahead. "Elizabeth, you must forgive me, but Miss Bingley was very vocal in presenting your history."

Elizabeth gasped.

"After...you rightly slapped and refused me, I hied to Pemberley. It was there I decided to return and seek you out again—as Miss Bennet." He started to reach her but quickly stopped and clasped his hands together. "I vowed to find you, to court you, to see...what we could become, to see how my family would respond to you and you to them."

"My parents are that class conscious?" Elizabeth looked caught unawares.

"No, not the Northamptons! They know the value of *all* members of society. Your disappearance exposed them to a wider circle of acquaintances than my...other relations."

"The Matlocks?"

He nodded. "At first I was horrified at your rejection—a girl of no consequence, no fortune, no protection..."

"That was not true! The admiral—"

"Yes, but I was under the impression that the *nature* of your relationship was of a different kind." He blushed.

"How—?"

He looked miserable.

"Miss Bingley?"

Darcy nodded.

Elizabeth turned, eyes narrowed in fury.

There is absolutely no doubt that she is Northampton's daughter. Oh, my good lord. He tugged at his cravat. *When Julian learns of this, it will be pistols at dawn.*

"Mr Darcy?" Blinking, he found the fire in her eyes had melted into concern. "Are you unwell?"

"I—I was just thinking of your brother. He will…suffice it to say that he will not take kindly to this bit of family history."

She laughed, but he heard no malice in her merriment. "You know what you did was wrong, do you not?"

He nodded.

"Hearing such an improper overture is a crushing experience." She clasped her hands tightly. "It makes a woman doubt her worth. I wondered what I had done wrong to be so singled out."

"No, it was not that! I wanted you—"

"I have no doubt of that. You were very clear on *that* particular subject. But for what? To use me—body and soul? Not a very flattering prospect, sir."

"To use me—body and soul." This turned Darcy's perspective on its head. *I thought I was offering her something of value! To be with me…but all I was suggesting was degradation.* His heart spasmed in pain. "Please, Lady Elizabeth. Tell your father I must speak with him at his earliest convenience on a matter of the utmost urgency, but…at present…I must return home."

"You would leave without answering my second question?"

"I—I believe it best that I return to Darcy House. I do not deserve your forgiveness, madam. I am ashamed of my actions and the careless way I would degrade a woman I have come to…admire." He turned to leave.

"No, wait, please. Come." She reached for him.

He hesitated.

"You did agree to satisfy me on *two* points, Mr Darcy."

He looked up and took heart.

"I am tenacious, surely, but I truly believe that, while painful, it is best to muddle our way through this." She looked into his eyes. "My father—Mr Bennet, my *other* father—always stressed that the best way to handle a difficult situation was to face it head on." Her voice turned soft. "He was very wise."

"Indeed, he must have been," he said. "And now, your second question?"

"Why? Why did you offer…that…to me?"

He realised she deserved the entire truth. "For as long as I can remember, my aunt Lady Catherine decreed her daughter and I would wed. My uncle Matlock agreed, citing it as payback for services"—he raked his left hand through his hair—"services I have only recently learned were never performed by them. They only claimed the credit."

Sensing the rise of his self-loathing, she reached to caress his arm. He covered her hand with his. "Over the last few years, their entreaties have been more strident. And, as no *other* ladies of my acquaintance lifted my heart or garnered my attention, I considered…acquiescing to their demands and having done with it."

She waited for him to look her in the eye. "Mr Darcy?"

"I thought, with you by my side—even in *that* manner—I stood a chance." He inhaled, and Elizabeth pursed her lips. "To maintain my humanity—to keep something warm, a light in my darkening world. I am so very sorry. You were…you *are*…this shining, beautiful being, and I so want to be near you. In my deluded state, I could see no other way to have you close by, and so I…disgraced us both." He hung his head. "There, I am done."

Hearing footsteps in the passageway, Darcy looked up. His eyes, full of fear and shame, touched her heart, and she took his hand with a tentative smile. Darcy's courage soared as the Northamptons entered the chamber.

"THANK YOU, SIMMONS." Bingley shrugged out of his greatcoat as he and his bride returned to their town house. Making their way towards the parlour, they startled as a surprised Caroline was leaving his study.

"Charles!" she squeaked, her smile an imposter.

"Caroline!" Startled that his sister knew the location of, let alone had business in, his private domain, Bingley narrowed his eyes in suspicion.

"I was unaware that you were expected today. I thought your honeymoon was for another three weeks at least."

"Elizabeth sent an express."

"And you came running back for that...*tramp*?" she spat, incredulous.

"Caroline!" Bingley stepped forward, cheeks reddening.

Jane stood stunned. *Lizzy was right! She is a vicious creature. I shall keep a close eye on her.* "Elizabeth needs our counsel. She and the admiral requested our precipitate return."

"And being *family,* we came." Bingley's bearing was a warning to tread carefully.

Heedless, Caroline continued, revulsion on her tongue. "I can only imagine." Huffing, she turned her chin to the sky. "It is *your* wedding journey, and if you see fit to shorten it, so be it. I shall have Mrs Nattles make up your rooms."

"Jane will see to it. *She* is the lady of the house."

Caroline cringed, nodding. "As you wish."

"Jane, dearest, while you speak to Mrs Nattles, I shall be in my study."

Caroline spoke quickly. "Charles, you...you have just arrived. Would you not rather wash the dust from—"

"I find a need to reacquaint myself with my affairs, Caroline," he snapped. "Unless you care to explain what you were doing, sister. Really—my study? Until now, you have never willingly entered that chamber." He searched her eyes while cataloguing what could possibly be of interest to her. *I left everything in order. All business matters are filed at the solicitor's except the transfer of Elizabeth's inheritance.*

He dragged her into his study. Thrusting her onto an overstuffed leather chair, he strode to his desk where his papers lay, disordered.

"Explain, Caroline. You went through my *private* papers?" He dropped into his chair.

"Why would I go through your affairs?" she waffled.

Cocking his brow, he scanned the pages, ire blooming when he removed the lease to Netherfield from the top, revealing an unsealed packet. Anger flushed his cheeks, and he glared at her as she tenuously maintained her defiant posture. Reading the pages, his eyes hardened on finding there the transfer of Elizabeth's financial future. Pounding his fist on the polished wood, he spoke, low and deadly. "You have done things in the past of which I have been ashamed"—Caroline winced—"but *this* borders on criminal."

His sister rose. "What is criminal is defending that…that *whore!*"

"Caroline!" Bingley stood and glared at the hatred in her eyes.

"She is a *kept* woman, Charles. Surely you see you must distance yourself—and our family—from that…that…!" Inhaling, she straightened her shoulders. "I have written Aunt Clarissa to find a suitable hovel where she can spend the rest of her days. Once she is gone, we shall resume our lives."

"It is obvious that I must distance myself from *someone*, but it is most certainly *not* Elizabeth Bennet." He leaned over his desk, fists clenched as he and his sister met eye to eye across the narrow stretch of wood.

Scrutinising the unrepentant fury in his sister's eyes, he sat, prompting Caroline to smugly settle in her chair as Charles, taking a clean sheet of parchment, quill, and ink, began to write. She examined her nails, smile widening at the scratching nib. Letter complete, he rang for Simmons.

"Caroline"—his voice remained even and calm—"I am advising Mayesworth to release your dowry from my control. I suggest you reach Louisa and Hurst to finalise living arrangements for yourself and the location he may reach you to review your alternatives. As of today—this very minute—we are through. You have always followed your own counsel. Now we shall see where it takes you. As of today, it is official."

"You cannot be serious!" She scurried around the desk, but he simply looked up at her.

"My tolerance for your histrionics is limited. I simply no longer desire your disruptive presence in my house."

"You! You choose *her*? That…that *thing* over your own flesh and blood?" Her eyes flashed.

"I choose to live in a house where my affairs remain private." He stood. "This is repulsive, even for you, and I shall no longer tolerate such chicanery, such deceit. You have till tomorrow to remove your belongings. And these"—he scooped up the papers—"shall remain sequestered in my chambers until you do!"

Immobile, Caroline watched Bingley walk away till his hand sought the doorknob. Heels clacking across the hardwood floor, she grabbed his arm, turning him to look at her. He sighed at her customary qualities: a vindictive gleam in her eyes, almost predatory. But, after time away from her pettiness, he saw something else: fear.

"Then I disown you! I have learned something at father's knee, and I know what I am entitled to do. I shall not let your association with that—that *woman*—taint *my* good name!" She straightened. "I know how to act, and I *will* disown you and sever all connexions, once and for all time, between me and the name of Bennet."

With one last glare, Caroline brushed past her brother and out the door. With the handle in her hand, she turned. "I shall have my trunks packed and be rid of you as soon as may be."

Closing his open mouth, Charles Bingley watched his sister climb the stairs, and he sent a guilty prayer that, for once, Caroline was better than her word.

As the carriage ambled along the busy streets, Darcy was apprehensive. Fingers tapping one knee while the other hand patted his lips, he was unmindful of Georgiana's spreading grin.

"Fitzwilliam, fear not. All will be well. I have spent more time than you have in Elizabeth's company, and she is delightful. She is not a vengeful woman who will hold your…transgression against you. Once you grovel appropriately!"

He groaned, fuelling her chuckles till the carriage jolted to a stop in front of their aunt's home.

"Darcy, welcome." The duke gave his wife a knowing look as Darcy looked at Elizabeth. "Darcy?"

"Thank you, Your Grace," he said. "We are pleased to be here."

"Shall we? The Raleighs await, and Hutchins has prepared a feast!"

Kissing his aunt's hand, Darcy turned to Elizabeth. Her eyes met his, and the rest of his family faded away. *Is it possible? Can she welcome me?* "Lady Elizabeth." He took her hand.

"Mr Darcy." Her whisper sent a quiver to his heart. He looked up, and her eyes held no malice. He smiled, and she returned it.

"Nephew, Elizabeth," the duchess called. "Come."

The duke offered his free arm to Georgiana. Darcy and Elizabeth followed not too closely behind.

"Lady Elizabeth," he began. "I am still overwhelmed that you…I am so very grateful that you are willing to receive me at all."

"Mr Darcy, please."

His fingers covered her hand where it rested on his arm. "No, let me just say, I am humbled by this chance to demonstrate that I am more than I have shown before. I shall not squander this opportunity to earn your good opinion. I beg of you—tell me that your good opinion, once lost, is not lost forever."

"It is not. What are we if we cannot forgive each other?"

"Thank you." He touched his lips to her hand.

"Nephew! I shall not ask you again," the duchess called. "Hutchins waits for no man."

thirteen

"DARCY!" BINGLEY EXCLAIMED. "WHAT ON EARTH BRINGS YOU OUT so early this fine morning?"

"I surmise the same that carries you from your happy home. Good morning, Mrs Bingley. It is a pleasure to see you looking so well. May I introduce my sister?"

"Oh, please forgive me," Charles blustered. "Miss Georgiana Darcy, my wife"—he beamed—"Mrs Jane Bingley."

"It is a pleasure to meet you, Mrs Bingley," Georgiana stammered shyly. "May I wish you great joy?"

"Thank you, Miss Darcy," Jane replied.

Darcy noted her impatience. "Shall we continue this indoors?"

"Of course." Bingley took his wife's arm.

"Welcome!" Admiral Raleigh beamed. "Mrs Bingley. It is good to see you." With a wide sweep of his arm, he ushered his guests to the parlour where sat Elizabeth and two persons wholly unknown to the Bingleys.

"Lizzy!" Jane ran to her sister. "Are you well?" She buried her head in Elizabeth's hair. "Oh, Lizzy, I have been beside myself with worry."

The unknown couple exchanged warm glances before focusing on Bingley.

Entering the room, Mrs Raleigh interrupted the *mise en scène*, followed by Ketchum, her housekeeper. "Jane!" She turned to Charles. "Mr Bingley. Let me welcome you to the family again, sir. I am so happy for you both."

"Thank you, Mrs Raleigh." Bingley took his eyes from the sisters' reunion.

Looking from her husband to her guests, Mrs Raleigh went to Jane. "Jane dear, please come and sit, and we shall explain our reasons for sending for you." Jane brought Elizabeth, wiping her own tears. Darcy and Georgiana seated themselves after greeting their relations.

"Now then," Mrs Raleigh began as the admiral sat beside her. "Let me first assure you again that all is well. No one has contracted a fatal illness or anything of that nature." She chuckled at Mr Bingley's widened eyes and, leaning over, patted his knee. "I should not tease so…"

"At least wait until Mr Bingley acclimates to your humour, Aunt, Uncle…" Elizabeth's eyes twinkled. Finding Darcy's intense gaze focused on her, she squeezed Jane's hand, cocked her brow, and sent him a saucy smile that spread a crimson blush across his cheeks. Satisfied, she returned her attention to her aunt.

"Please, forgive my negligence. Jane, Mr Bingley, these good people are Philip and Alexandra Elliston, the Duke and Duchess of Northampton."

The couple dipped their heads, as did the surprised Bingleys.

"They are Mr and Miss Darcy's paternal aunt and uncle. The duchess is the sister of Mr George Darcy, your friend's late father."

Jane and Charles exchanged astonished glances then turned to Darcy for an explanation of their presence at this *family* reunion.

"Mrs Bingley, for so long I have prayed for you, and in these last few weeks, I have so wished to make your acquaintance. And to thank you," said the duchess.

"I beg your pardon? Thank me? For what, may I ask?"

"For loving my daughter."

Jane gasped, looking at Elizabeth who waited with a hopeful smile. "Is this true, Lizzy? Can it be?"

Elizabeth nodded. "Jane, I have my family back! Is it not marvellous?"

At her sister's hesitation, she paused. The older women did not. Mrs Raleigh tilted her head to the covered portrait, and the duchess nudged her husband, indicating it was time.

The duke rose, and Mrs Raleigh spoke. "Jane dearest, perhaps this shall help you see the truth of the matter." As the veil lifted, Jane gasped, drawn to the woman in the frame. Bingley followed, mouth agape in wonder.

"It is you, Elizabeth," he whispered.

"No, Mr Bingley. It is a portrait of *my* mother," the duchess stated. "The grandmother of Darcy, Georgiana, and Elizabeth."

Jane spun from her sister to the painting; the right brow of the young woman in the frame was raised as her own sister's had been thousands of times before. "Oh, Lizzy." She wiped away a tear, and Elizabeth retook her hand. Mrs Raleigh came to her other side, embracing her.

"And Jane," she whispered. "It seems that little *mark*"— she cast her eyes towards Elizabeth's bottom, and both girls blushed—"is a mark *all* Darcy women bear."

While the others gave the sisters time to adjust, the topic of Miss Bingley was addressed.

"Caroline has agreed to remove herself from my home. She will stay with my sister and Hurst. Louisa is in a *delicate* condition." Bingley cleared his throat. "Her assistance will be most welcome, I am sure."

Darcy doubted anyone would welcome Miss Bingley's 'assistance,' but the conversation moved to safer topics.

"Mrs Bingley?" the duchess asked as they walked to the dining room. "I cannot thank you enough. You and your family took in my precious girl after *our* family failed her. She was taken from us, you see, by one of our own."

Jane, reversing the order of things, took the older woman's hand into her gentle clasp.

"I know not how to thank you...or your mother and father. I know they are deceased. But I swear to you, in my heart, I shall pray for you all till the day I die for everything you have done for us. You loved

Elizabeth when we were unable to care for her. You saved her and brought her back to life. We have read the journals your father and mother kept. The duke and I wish you to know that you and Mr Bingley are members of our family. We shall never keep you from Elizabeth or her from you. We only ask that you share her with us. And forgive us if we are greedy. We have so much to make up for."

Jane gave her a warm smile. "Thank you."

Mrs Raleigh returned to the parlour, hesitating as her friend and niece embraced. "Come, Duchess, Jane. We wait upon you."

Sharing a smile, they linked arms, rejoining their family.

ELIZABETH TOOK Jane's hand between her own. "Are you unwell?" The two were ensconced in Elizabeth's room in the Raleigh household.

"I…no, I am well, Elizabeth. This is just so…" She looked at their interlocking hands. "When I read your letter, I do not recall precisely what came to mind, but it was most definitely not this."

"You are not happy for me?"

Hearing the despondency reminiscent of their adolescent years, Jane knew Elizabeth still needed her. "Oh no, Lizzy—may I still call you Lizzy?"

"Of course. Nothing changes between you and me."

Jane threw her arms around her sister. "Oh, thank heavens, Lizzy, I was so afraid."

"Afraid? You? Never. I could never lose you. I would die inside— simply die."

After more hugs, they unlocked their arms and wiped their tears.

"Lizzy, tell me all. Every detail!"

And Elizabeth did, from their initial meeting to relocating to Northampton Place. "Jane?" Elizabeth bit her lower lip.

"Yes, Lizzy," Jane snacked on another delicacy.

"Caroline…"

Placing the apricot tart on her plate, she faced her sister. "What has she done *now*?"

"She was the source of the rumours…"

"Regarding you and Uncle Raleigh?" Jane enunciated each word with precision.

Elizabeth nodded as colour drained from Jane's face. Her fingers curled around the pink silk of her gown. "That shrew!" Jane turned to Elizabeth. "I tried, Lizzy, I did. For myself, for Charles…but this! This is beyond the pale." Jane headed for the door.

"Where are you going?" Elizabeth rose to catch up. Jane waited as she had throughout their childhood.

"I must speak with Charles. She is no longer welcome in my home. Not now. Not ever!"

"But—"

"No. For God's sake, you are my sister. That vile incarnation of evil spread vicious lies about my sister! And the admiral!" She stopped, stricken. "The shame! My happiness has brought misery upon my family. Oh, Lizzy! Can you forgive me?"

"Forgive you? For what?

"For leaving you to face her alone." Jane looked miserable. "For bringing her into our world."

"I am stronger than Caroline Bingley, and I was never alone."

"To think she is so unkind. Why would she attack you—?" Jane paused.

"What is it?"

"Charles told me that Caroline…harbours a tendre for Mr Darcy."

"That would explain a great deal."

"Well, not for *him*, precisely."

"Not for him, *precisely*?" Elizabeth repeated.

"Charles says it is his fortune she desires."

"The poor man! First his own relatives conspire against him, and then Miss Bingley hunts him."

"And she is not alone. Charles says Mr Darcy is sought after by all the ladies of society, unmarried or not!"

"What a world we have entered. Thank heavens you have your Mr Bingley."

"Yes, he is mine, but Elizabeth, we stand with you. As do the Raleighs, and of course, your parents."

"And my brother."

"You have a brother?" Jane gaped.

"It appears I do. He is on a diplomatic mission of some sort but shall return anon. Is it not exciting? It is like a continual birthday with unending presents." She bit her lower lip. "Jane?"

Jane gave Elizabeth her full attention. "Yes?"

"Mama *insists* that Caroline will have her due."

"I have no doubt Caroline will rue the day she opened her spiteful mouth."

Elizabeth laughed. "That is the most uncivil thing I have heard from you—ever."

"You may not have heard me *speak* my wicked thoughts, but that does not signify I do not have them."

BINGLEY PULLED DARCY ASIDE.

"Darcy, did you have any inkling of this? That Elizabeth was your…"

"*Is* my cousin, Bingley. No."

"But that portrait? Was it not at Pemberley?"

"It was removed years ago."

"I don't understand."

"Mrs Reynolds said it upset the duchess."

"Upset her? But it was her mother…"

"You saw the painting. It is as if they are the same person."

"But Elizabeth, she was a little girl…"

"The eyes, Bingley." Darcy pointed to his own. "They are identical. And it upset *her.* So to calm his sister, who had just lost her child—and shortly after, their mother—my father removed it. As for the resemblance, truly I was not looking for a connexion. I had not seen the painting in nigh on ten years." He dropped his voice in remorse. "If only I had…"

"Darcy, this is all so upsetting. Jane says she is well, but I can only wonder how she truly feels."

"You do not think she begrudges Elizabeth her true family, do you?"

"I do not know."

Darcy became restive.

"Oh, not in that way. It is just…in some ways, Elizabeth is the only family Jane has left."

"Apart from you, now."

"Yes, apart from me and my family." He ran a hand through his hair. "Look, you cannot take Elizabeth away from Jane. It would be too cruel."

"It would. And my aunt and uncle understand the pain of separation."

Charles nodded. "Speaking of separation, I had an *interesting* conversation with Caroline the other day upon our return. She had rummaged through my papers. She even opened and read Elizabeth's settlement."

"Settlement?"

"From Mr Bennet—Jane's father, not her uncle."

"Ah." Darcy frowned at the notion of Caroline reading private, legal documents relating to Elizabeth. "Bingley…"

"I know, I know. She and I had words. It is why I threw her out."

"So it was not sisterly affection that called her to the Hursts?"

Bingley chuckled. "I wrote my solicitor, and it is done. Caroline controls her fortune and is out of my domain." They exchanged smiles.

"Shall we?"

"Yes, yes of course."

"Where will she go?" Darcy asked.

"Do you care?" Bingley teased.

"It is good to know where one's enemies are at all times."

"For now, she will stay with Louisa and Hurst. Louisa *is* with child and feels Caroline will be of assistance. As she is out of my hair, I did not ask too many questions."

"That is something." They arrived at the duke's study, and Darcy knocked. "Jane *has* made a man out of you." They entered the chamber, finding the duke and admiral.

"There you are, Darcy, Bingley." The duke offered a waiting glass to each. "Here you are. What were you two discussing so intensely?" he asked.

"Sisters," Bingley offered. "The loss of one who, I admit, holds a warm place in my heart and that of my wife."

Walking over to Bingley, the duke put his hand on his shoulder. "Bingley, we *hope* you and Mrs Bingley remain close to Elizabeth. She needs you, and *we* need you to help us move through all this."

"Thank you. I know it would destroy Jane if Elizabeth were out of our lives altogether."

"This is overwhelming still, and we have had a few weeks to adjust," Northampton said.

"It is an adjustment for all of us," Raleigh added.

Beginning with a chuckle, Bingley's mirth grew to a full-blown laugh. The disbelieving and somewhat censuring astonishment of his companions only fuelled his amusement. "Pardon my outburst, but I pictured my sister's response to this bit of news."

"Your sister?" The duke straightened, his voice cutting like steel.

"When Caroline hears this, it will be a moment to treasure."

"Your sister, Miss Caroline Bingley? Whom you recently removed from your residence?" the duke stated.

"Yes. How? Why?" Bingley turned to Darcy. "What has she done now?"

Darcy began. "She has been spreading rumours."

"Caroline is an unrepentant gossip, but no one of sense pays her any mind."

"Your sister," the admiral said, "has spread vile rumours through society that *I* am Elizabeth's...*protector.*"

"That Raleigh took *my* daughter," the duke said angrily, "as his mistress."

Bingley staggered with horror. "I will kill her! Poor Elizabeth! What do I say to Jane? Your Grace, Admiral, I am beyond sorry..."

"A bit late for that, man." The admiral's voice hard and cold.

DARCY SPENT the next morning with Elizabeth in the Northampton library, perusing the morning papers. Their tentative truce still held, and they surreptitiously studied each other without pretence or interference.

"*The Morning Chronicle* says you are a vision and that the court will gleam all the brighter when you take your rightful place."

"I shall not be asked to court, shall I? I mean, I was presented to some royals. I still cannot believe that I, Elizabeth Bennet of Longbourn, dined with the Prince Regent." She shook her head, missing the storm in Darcy's eyes.

"What was it like for Miss Elizabeth Bennet of Longbourn?" he asked.

His breath hitched at her eyes sparkling with mirth. "Oh, it was an *experience*, and I am glad Papa says we do not have an active acquaintance with the Regent. He was most judicious in keeping me well away from his roving hands."

Darcy's spine stiffened, and Elizabeth watched the storm break upon his face. She laughed. "Mr Darcy! I was in a room with thirty people. No harm could come to me."

"Not there, Elizabeth. But…"

"I do not think my father…"

"Or I," he muttered.

"Or you"—she laughed—"would allow me to fall prey to the likes of him."

Darcy glared, but as that only spurred her on, he surrendered with a shrug and a sly smile. Elizabeth's laughter intensified, and she looked at him with amazement.

"You are so handsome when you smile," she whispered. "It becomes you."

So he smiled again. Their interlude was interrupted when the door flew open and Georgiana skidded to a halt before them. "Fitzwilliam! Elizabeth! Come quickly!" Georgiana urged the startled couple.

"What is it?" Darcy was both concerned and upset at the interruption.

"My mother and father are well, are they not? No harm has come to them?"

"No, silly. Nothing of that sort. But do come quickly." She pulled them out the door.

"Calm down, Georgiana. You can hardly expect Elizabeth to run, and neither shall I." Eyes twinkling, Darcy straightened his waistcoat. "It would not be dignified."

Snorting, Georgiana and Elizabeth headed for the door. Risking being left behind, Darcy caught Elizabeth by the arm, escorting her as Georgiana nearly danced ahead. "Is my cousin always this excitable, Mr Darcy?"

"No, she is not." He forced his eyes from her. *Those eyes will be my undoing.*

"There must be something truly inspiring around the corner." Elizabeth smiled as Georgiana darted through the door. Darcy's heart fluttered at the curiosity sparkling in her eyes.

The duke and duchess stood alongside a handsome man of eight and twenty.

"Julian!" Darcy exclaimed. "When did you get back into town?"

"Today, Darcy. I made land this morning and came as quickly as possible." Julian Elliston, Marquess of Glascomb, turned to the woman who, since hearing of her return, had held his every thought. "Who have we here?" He strode to Elizabeth, taking her hand to his lips and smiling into her full-wide, surprised eyes.

His eyes. They are so familiar. Like someone I used to know and love. "Ju—lian," she whispered.

Julian's eyes lit, and he enveloped her in his strong embrace. "Elizabeth," he whispered. "I dared not believe you are truly here."

Relishing his strong arms around her, Elizabeth had flashes of memory: strong arms comforting her when she fell or scraped her knees, or being carried on his back. Memories of his gentle voice reading adventure stories or tales of King Arthur and his knights. She hugged him, and he responded. She knew instinctively that she would always be safe with him.

He released her, and she smiled. "You would sing to me when I was sad, and I remember your smile. You stayed with me for years…" she whispered so only he would hear.

Amazed, the marquess grabbed her, humming a song he had created over a decade ago. Elizabeth's eyes opened as wide as wheels before she surrendered to the bliss of being held by her big brother.

fourteen

"Elizabeth," Julian called as she headed for her chamber. "I was hoping, if you are not too weary, for a word or two."

"Of course." She took his offered arm. Walking in silence, Elizabeth was bombarded by emotion. She pressed his arm. *My brother, my very own brother.* Lifting her eyes, she saw that his were looking at her, and they smiled, shyly.

"'Tis a bit strange, is it not?" He leaned towards her.

"It is. And yet I choose to dwell on the happiness, Julian. I have heard so much of you from Mother and Father and am eager to know the man who grew from the boy I knew." She stopped them both on the stairs. "I so wish to remember."

Julian caressed her cheek with the pad of his thumb. "You will."

He led her up the stairs. "I shall regale you with stories of my bravado! Bizarre adventures of crushing the pirates of Green Haven and almost single-handedly overrunning the marauding frogs that had the nerve to invade the ponds of Pemberley—with Darcy, of course." His eyes darted quickly to assess her response. Catching the hint of her blush, he opened her chamber door and nodded to her maid, looking at the new face in his home.

Following a quick introduction, Elizabeth dismissed her maid. Julian dropped into a chair in front of the fire in her sitting room. When Elizabeth sat next to him, he leapt from his seat.

Julian grabbed hold of the wine decanter and a glass. "Do you mind?" He raised the bottle.

"Help yourself."

"If you are very nice to me, I shall share," he teased.

"I am *always* nice—well, nearly so."

Careful not to spill a drop of wine, Julian returned to his chair. "Now tell me all." He took a sip, a look of expectancy on his handsome face.

Taking in her adult brother, Elizabeth smiled. Julian was over six feet tall with clear brown eyes that sparkled with intelligence. His hair, like hers, was chocolate brown, and it curled every which way, giving him a look simultaneously roguish and boyish. His chin was strong, his cheekbones high, and his skin clear. His physique was impressive with strong arms, a broad chest, and firm legs that well filled his breeches.

Elizabeth swallowed. "Where would you have me begin?"

Leaning forward, his forearms resting on his legs, he spoke gently. "I want to know all about you and all you have endured—not from morbid curiosity but because I want to *know* you, your life, and how it has brought you back to us."

He gazed down at his hands solemnly. "For so long—too long—there was heaviness and darkness in this house. You became a hole in our hearts that never healed." He lifted his eyes to her. "And now, here you sit, and I find myself catapulted from all that I knew. I barely know…anything."

"Now I know you are my brother." She reached across to squeeze his hand. "For you have put into words what I have felt all my life."

Looking into each other's eyes, they smiled. "The Bennets, Papa, my other father…my second father…" Elizabeth's eyes clouded, and she looked up desperately at Julian. "You must understand, they were wonderful to me. And Jane…"

"They are gone now, are they not?"

She lowered her head. "And I still miss them greatly."

"Father said that your time with the current—"

"Uncle Bennet is a good man."

"But Mrs Bennet…?"

"She is…" Elizabeth sighed at an unwelcome sorrow welling in her heart. Turning her head, she tried to shield her brother from that particular pain till her strength returned and she returned her clear gaze to him. "Mrs Bennet could not embrace me as Mama Gloria did. I was made to feel my worth acutely…as a foundling."

Seeing her brother become anxious, she took his hand. "Do not fret, Julian. I had Jane and Mr Bennet and my cousins—Mary, especially. They…all of them rallied around me, protecting me as much as they could. And I found solace walking about the estate. And Mr Bennet made sure that I always had paper and paints."

She shrugged, taking a moment to form her thoughts. "When I needed it, I escaped into my drawing."

Julian watched a profound disquiet overtake his sister. "Father showed me some of your sketch books. They were in the chest sent from Longshore."

"Bourn, Long*bourn*."

"Of course." He sipped his wine then pointed at her with his wine-glass. "You are really good."

"You seem surprised!"

He smiled. "I have no such talent."

"And so, neither should I?"

He shrugged. "It *is* a woman's art…"

Elizabeth laughed outright, and Julian joined her.

"Father mentioned the rumours about town at the moment…and that Caroline Bingley is involved."

Her anger rose. "That woman has disliked me from the moment we met. And Aunt Bennet had no compunction about announcing my *obscure* origins to any and all within five minutes of making their acquaintance." A hidden bitterness seized her, and Elizabeth shook herself to break its hold.

Julian took her hand.

"It was bad enough from the first, but as Jane and Mr Bingley's relationship deepened, Caroline's attacks became sharper. She disdained any association with a Bennet, but she and Aunt Franny were allied in their dislike of me. When Darcy came for the wedding, Miss Bingley's venom erupted."

"Darcy?" Julian straightened. "How so?"

"Jane recently revealed that Miss Bingley carries a tendre for Mr Darcy…"

"For Pemberley, you mean," Julian said as he refilled his glass. "Not that she is alone, but her avarice is acute."

"To her, I was an obstacle to her objective."

"Were you an obstacle?"

Elizabeth looked at her hands. "We danced together at the wedding...and he laughed."

Julian startled, spewing wine over his breeches.

"Julian!" Elizabeth gaped at her choking brother, pounding his back till he came under regulation.

"Darcy?" Julian coughed. "Laughed? In public?"

"In public. More than one person witnessed the event." Elizabeth smiled.

"No wonder Miss Bingley had her talons out." He shook his head. "Father has informed me of..."

"Mr Darcy's improper suggestion?"

"Yes!" Julian's voice rose, so Elizabeth took his hand.

"Do not, Julian. Mr Darcy and I have made our peace with everything. We are working our way through this. No matter what, we are all family. *That* is what matters."

Looking into her eyes, he saw his family's strength. "I cannot promise I shall not speak with him about this. It is my place—as your brother and Darcy's friend."

They locked eyes, and Elizabeth nodded.

"But I promise, I shall leave something of the scamp for your satisfaction."

Elizabeth held out her hand for the now empty glass. He smiled as, instead of setting it down, she re-filled it.

"Then you are well? With travelling to Pemberley?"

"I..." Elizabeth looked around. "I understand that Father believes it is best...for my safety."

"Until Lady Catherine shows her hand, it is." Julian watched her. "If there were any other way, I would—"

"No, no, it is well." She gave him a tender look. "I—it will be good for me to spend time with Fitzwilliam and Georgiana. But I do wish you were coming with us. I do not like leaving when we are only just reunited."

Returning her grip, he kissed the back of her hand. "I wish it could be otherwise, but there is danger here, and until it is safe—or safer for you—I agree with Father. Pemberley is better defended."

"But…"

He stroked her hand. "I understand your reticence. Pemberley is no longer a place I feel comfortable. But at this particular moment, it is our best hope. Darcy's servants are extraordinarily loyal and at far enough a distance from—"

"—Lady Catherine," Elizabeth finished for him. He nodded. "But why not Green Haven?"

Julian was pleased with her logic. "That would mean a retreat by either Father or me. And it *is* best we remain here."

He leaned forward. "There is much afoot, Elizabeth. The Matlock relations of Darcy's mother are involved in a dark business with ruthless men and no mercy. Father is better able to watch and respond to… developments from here than from Green Haven."

"Could you not come?"

Pleased at her request, he smiled. "I wish I could. But I…have connexions of use to Father, connexions unseemly for a duke…"

"But acceptable for a marquess?"

He shrugged with a smirk. "Now, sister, is there anything else you would like to know about me?"

Eyes gleaming with expectation, she squealed, "Oh yes, please!"

"Ask away."

He was happy just to be with her, and throughout the night they discussed the lost years and their hopes, ambitions, and pleasures. As the sun rose, the bleary-eyed brother and sister parted, having made progress in restoring their faith and healing their hearts.

JULIAN TETHERED his horse after a twenty-mile ride and scanned the darkening horizon. Following the explicit instructions of his friend, Winston Hornsby, he easily found the secluded cottage. *For once Hornsby's fastidiousness served. It was tedious of him to go on about 'third oak' and 'second elm,' but without those directions, I would still be riding through the night.* He headed to the back door. *And the area is thick with thieves. But that is the point, is it not?*

Rapping lightly on the door in the predetermined pattern, Julian waited, then knocked again in a second, distinct pattern. *Hornsby was adamant. Knock man. Knock or you shall not see the light of day again.* As the door creaked open, Julian entered. One pistol was cocked in his ear while another was pressed into his back.

"Keep your eyes straight ahead," a gruff voice ordered as a hand searched for weapons. "Onward."

Julian stepped into the unknown. *Odd. Hornsby forgot to mention this.* They headed towards a faint light spilling into the dark. As he entered, Julian found Hornsby waiting with a nervous smile.

"Glascomb." Hornsby then nodded to the gunman, who removed the weapon from Julian's back. Hornsby rose, leaning towards Julian. "Do not speak unless spoken to, understood?"

"Yes, Mama," Julian whispered back.

"These are not men to trifle with."

Julian nodded, and they proceeded through another door to a neat room with a cosy fire.

"Your tardy friend has arrived," a deep baritone spoke from the shadows.

Hornsby replied before Julian could. "Yes, señor. He never was good at following directions."

Their host chuckled. "Then we have something else in common, Lord Glascomb." The man stepped forward, and Julian assessed the compact body of pure muscle. He had a direct gaze both ruthless and intelligent. "My wife, Señora *Natalia* Catervaux, speaks highly of you, sir. *She* is the reason you are here. That, and she does *not* speak highly of Lord Matlock."

Julian nodded.

"You have shown my wife kindness. She is sentimental. You gave her respect, both for her person and her mind. She—*I* respect you for that."

Julian dipped his head.

"I will tell you what I know of the House of Matlock. Let us sit." He pointed to a table with three chairs. Three glasses and a bottle of brandy appeared, and their detailed conversation lasted long into the night.

THE DUKE SETTLED into his favourite armchair while watching his son. "What is it, Julian?"

"There were some things last night that are disconcerting." The son looked at his father. "Matlock is well known in certain quarters."

"For what—gaming? Debauchery? Cruelty?"

"As the politician to go to for protection."

Northampton remained silent.

"*Political* protection for blockade runners."

The duke found his tongue. "Do you mean…?"

"Not only brandy was bought into the kingdom, sir—"

"Are you implying that Matlock aided…?"

Julian shrugged. "I have no proof that he knew what—or should I say *who*—was ferried in, but French sympathisers were on those ships under his…protection of sorts…"

Northampton's shoulders slouched.

"There were rumours in Copenhagen—a well-known secret if you know who to ask."

Northampton rose, heading to the sideboard. Turning, he silently asked his son to join him. "Any other of our fine, upstanding members of Parliament connected to this?"

"No, none that I heard of." Julian rubbed his hands together.

"Good. That is good. Lord Ballington sends his regards." He filled a glass for each of them.

"What is it, Father?"

"Your information conforms with mine." He gave his son a significant look. "Matlock *is* beholden to Lord Delaboix."

"The *lord* of crime?"

Unbuttoning his waistcoat, the duke replied, "One and the same."

"But how?"

"This is all conjecture as Delaboix keeps his business very close to the vest. 'Tis no secret Braddleton *frequents* Delaboix's gaming hells, and Delaboix never loses." A wry smile played upon the duke's lips. "Although he need not employ any deceit to beat Braddleton. He is abysmal at cards."

Julian took another sip.

"So, Delaboix leans on Matlock, and Matlock leans on Darcy." The duke lapsed into a brief silence. "Did you know he was blackmailing Darcy?"

Julian spat out his scotch. He wiped his mouth and clothes. "Blackmailing? How? The debts *we* purchased?" Julian was bemused. "You mean Matlock claims that he…?"

Northampton swirled his glass. "Worse. Darcy never received our letter, and *Matlock* offered for a small monthly fee to keep Wickham at bay."

Julian shook his head. "What happened to our letter?"

"I know not. Darcy was distraught at the time, and we were consumed with…"

"Your health."

Nodding, the duke emptied his snifter. "Thinking we had abandoned him, Darcy allowed Matlock and his motley crew into his affairs."

"So *our* letter, with the Northampton crest proudly embossed, *happens* to go missing and *then* Matlock extorts money from his own sister's son."

"So it seems."

"It may not be the elder Matlock," Julian opined thoughtfully.

"No?"

"Matlock has been more detached of late, even for him. Braddleton is a more likely candidate. Matlock is a Lothario, but Braddleton is vicious."

"It is strange. Darcy would commit to a life of misery to protect his sister, and yet we all know of her near calamity. If we know, who else truly matters? He must know we stand with him."

"But how could Darcy consider marrying that girl…" Julian scrunched his brows.

"She is a woman, lad, remember that. Darcy is eight and twenty, you nine and such. The de Bourgh girl must be five and twenty. She *should* be married by now."

"They would marry him to Rosings to…?"

"Gain access to his fortune. Not only is Matlock in financial straits, but with Perceval's assassination, the government is in disarray. I have a…*friend*, highly placed in the Exchequer, who knows of my interest in Lady Catherine. There are papers attesting to the extent that she and her brother have emptied their coffers and what they have done about it." The duke shook his head. "Matlock is so sure of his plans. Word is he intends to use the disarray to petition a title for Darcy."

Julian nearly choked on his brandy.

"Kill two birds with one stone. Matlock could pay his debts and gain another vote against any maritime reforms."

"Brilliant." Julian sat back. "Diabolical, but you must admit, brilliant."

"I agree. *And* I agree that it might be Braddleton's doing. I know of his financial schemes that, while well thought out, were poorly executed. He sees what needs to be done, but he just cannot deliver."

"Thank heaven for small miracles."

Elliston refilled their glasses. "And you are right, Julian. Matlock *has* been a bit adrift. His last few speeches have been barely comprehensible."

"And at White's…"

"Go on."

Blushing, Julian continued. "Word is, his mistress…you do know he has a mistress?"

"The latest of several these last five years or so…"

Julian's eyes darkened. "This one—I have met her. She was invaluable to us last year. And she has impeccable taste in selecting men nose-deep in turmoil."

"As long as it is in service to the Crown," the duke half jested. "Just see that it stays that way."

"Yes, sir. My *associates* at White's have commented on how *tired* the old boy is. He has been found stumbling and mumbling about the place."

The duke looked sharply at Julian.

"It is true. I have heard it from a number of dependable sources—"

"The girl, boy…?"

"Ah. Well, it is *said* by most that *she* is the root of his distress."

"Is this plausible?"

"He nears three score, am I right?"

"There about." Northampton slapped his knees. "So, the old goat indulges his passions while the young heathen is in the devil's pocket!"

"That about sums it up." Julian took a final sip. "There is more, Father."

"More? What could top this?"

"Miss Natalia is a woman of hidden…attributes. She also keeps company with a certain smuggler."

"Matlock has absolutely the worst taste in women." The duke clapped his hands. "I do not care how attractive a woman may be, son. When a smuggler enters the picture, abandon ship—unless, of course it is your mother, sister, or wife. The lady is either insatiable, greedy, or a fool. Matlock has always paid well for their company."

"I believe they have earned whatever he gave them."

"I have heard the rumours. He has been linked with many a broken woman. So, this Madam Natalia has taken a smuggler, has she?"

"He was there first."

Northampton was surprised. "My, what a tangled web. As a matter of course, how did you come by all this information?"

"Hornsby, my friend from Cambridge, is with the Maritime Ministry. His office inspects trafficking of all kinds."

"Matlock deals in contraband? Enough to gain the notice of the Ministry? On top of everything else?"

"No. But they have a *man* who, when he returned to London three or so months ago, found his *wife* badly bruised," Julian emphasised. "Since then, he has limited his activities to shorter-range raids. To keep an eye on her."

"Is it a good thing or not?"

"Not. Their man is a *patriotic* smuggler—carries an agent or two and informs the Ministry of movements along the coast of France, Spain, and Portugal."

"I see."

"Should we tell Darcy?" Julian asked.

"Heavens, no. Darcy is at a very delicate point, as are we. You know things have not been easy between us ever since your uncle died. We were in the Netherlands, then my blasted accident, and now Elizabeth. While we did what we could, we were not *with* him when he needed us. They, the Matlocks, were. While their influence is nothing *but* pernicious, he is only beginning to see them for what—I mean, who—they are. But they are still blood to him."

"But what if they convince him to…"

"That is not a possibility, or probability, I suppose. And for that I believe we must thank your mother and Elizabeth."

"You still believe their marriage…is best?" His unease grew.

"Yes."

"Even if they do not love each other?"

"Has Elizabeth revealed her feelings to you?"

"No. I was thinking of Darcy. I mean…"

"That lovesick mooncalf?" The duke laughed. "When he is within fifty feet of her, he hangs on her every move. No, I do not believe Darcy is the one with objections. If it were up to him alone, they would marry yesterday. Elizabeth has made—*is* making—her peace with Darcy."

Julian's eyes twitched.

"I, too, have difficulty with Darcy's apparent…inclination…to continue the Matlock tradition…"

Julian's fists clenched, opened, and clenched up again. "I could kill him!"

"A popular response." The duke smiled sadly. "However, you shall do no such thing. He is to be a groom, not a corpse. Their time at Pemberley will give them time to ease into their…relationship."

"For how long?"

"Till right before the ball."

"You think that wise?"

The duke shrugged. "It is necessary."

"Necessary?" Julian sputtered.

"Julian," the duke said, "whoever took your sister is still at large. *You* will see that rumours of the engagement of Elizabeth and Darcy are circulated. Then, while they are safe at Pemberley, we shall smoke that she-devil and her legion out of whatever hole they hide in." He was adamant. "We *shall* be ready for them."

"I hope you are right, Father. It has been many years since I have felt safe at Pemberley."

"I know of no other way to draw these rats from their lair *and* protect your sister."

"Do you…I mean to say…when this is over, will you…will you hold Elizabeth to this engagement?"

His father nodded.

"But, how…after such an insult…?"

"He has made a decent beginning to make amends, and she has… well, not exactly forgiven him…but has accepted he made a mistake. They are working through the rest." The duke's eyes twinkled. "A few weeks on their own, away from prying eyes, offers their best chance to begin anew. It does my heart good to see him unbend a bit. She knocked the arrogant stuffing right out of him, and as a country miss, mind you. With the Northampton name behind her…well, let us just say that the boy is in for a wonderful life."

"Darcy admitted to a mistake?"

"Without hesitation."

"I wish I had witnessed that." Julian chuckled. "First he laughs, now you say he has admitted an error. What next?"

THIS IS HER HOME, HER PERMANENT HOME. DARCY WATCHED ELIZABETH begin her early morning ramble on their first day at Pemberley, a duo of Pemberley's footmen following her. Glancing at the clock, he hurried through the door to catch her as she headed towards a wooded path.

"Elizabeth!" He sped forward as she turned from her habitual path towards the orchard. "Elizabeth! Elizabeth, please wait!"

She did not.

Boots crushing the dewy grass, he searched the rows of trees. "Elizabeth!" Where are you?" Desperation pulsed in his heart, and he searched each direction till a sound from above split the silence. Dangling feet hung down from a tree in the next row. "Elizabeth," he sighed, swinging his tall frame to her branch. She turned from him, and he handed her a handkerchief.

She turned back, her smile faltering. "How did you know where to find me?"

"I heard you."

"All the way from the house?" she challenged.

"No, I saw you depart and…I hope you do not think I…"

"Followed me? No." She smiled, looking at the nearby pond rippled by the breeze. "You have James for that. Or Martin."

He swung his leg. "I had hoped they were not so...obvious."

She laughed, and he smiled.

"It is just—"

"You fear for me, returning." Her eyes darted to the meadow beyond the trees. She looked back, and he nodded.

"It was there." She pointed to the water's edge. "I dropped Maisey there. They came from over there."

She stretched her arm to the left, her breath quickening and growing ragged. "I had just found her when I heard horses. There were two, riding so fast. I ran because I was afraid they would trample me. They swooped down, one on each side, and pulled me up. I remember screaming. One let go, and the other yanked me onto his saddle." She stopped, wrapping an arm around her waist.

Darcy struggled against his fury. *I want to throttle Lady Catherine till she tastes fear.*

"We rode until it was dark. There was a carriage in a forest, waiting. I don't know where or how far away. Catty was there, waiting in the carriage. The lantern had a single candle, and she was not happy. She screamed the entire night." Elizabeth grew silent.

"She struck you, did she not?" Darcy asked in a hush.

Elizabeth nodded.

He gripped the branch above him till he was in command of his anger. Elizabeth sat, eyes unfocused, tears trickling onto her gown.

Darcy clasped her hand, and she pulled away at first but then relented, accepting his comfort. They sat—in what he would thereafter refer to as *their* tree—until the gardeners returned from their rounds.

ELIZABETH SLID her weary body into the steaming tub of water, sighing as the tension in her neck and shoulders eased. Though her time at Pemberley had been healing on many levels, she could feel a danger swirling around her. Dragging the washcloth across her arm, she thought of Darcy. *Who would have thought that Fitzwilliam Darcy and Elizabeth Bennet would ever sit on a tree limb?* She leaned her head back against the rim. *But then again, I am no longer Elizabeth Bennet, am I? That is the point, is it not? I am Lady Elizabeth Aubrey Rose Elliston, a grand lady.* The tension returned. *Daughter to a duke, about to be handed to the wolves and hunted...* Her breath was laboured. *They are out there*—she *is out there.* Water splashed as she jerked up, one hand on each side, panting. Gone was the dressing room of the luxurious bedchamber. She felt the oppressive, damp carriage and saw her attacker's brutal face emerging as from a fog. Fear gripped her heart.

Markum took one look at her mistress and, throwing her bundle of clean towels to the floor, flew to her. "Lady Elizabeth? Lady Elizabeth!" She put her hands on Elizabeth's shoulders, avoiding her scars. Elizabeth shivered, unresponsive. Grabbing one of the dropped towels, she flung it over Elizabeth's shoulders, gently rubbing circles across her the back, singing her lullaby. Markum sighed with relief as Elizabeth's breathing returned to its usual cadence.

Elizabeth's eyes refocused. "Thank you, Markum. Thank you."

"Think nothing of it, my lady."

"I was so afraid. So afraid."

"You? Afraid? Lady Elizabeth, you are one of the bravest women I know." Pulling back to look her in the eye, she continued. "You are here, and that is something. Being here is half the battle."

WICKHAM EMERGED from the Lamb's Inn of Meryton in fine form. *It is almost too easy.* He fingered his night's winnings. *That ought to hold those vultures for another week...* He thought of Kent then gasped as he felt a cold steel blade pressed into the middle of his back. An arm grabbed his throat, and a guttural voice hissed, "The maestro wants a word."

"Tomorrow..." Wickham croaked.

"Tonight," the voice rumbled, pressing harder.

Unable to identify his assailant, he moved towards a dark carriage, door open. Wickham stumbled into the coach to face the most powerful man in London. "Lord Delaboix. Good evening, sir."

The man nodded, and the carriage rolled, unsettling what was left of Wickham's composure. "I have my—"

"Money, señor?" the middle-aged man smiled indulgently.

"Half."

"Half? Did you not tell my man that last week and the week before and the week before that…"

"Yes, sir. About that…"

"Was Marcel wrong, Wickham?" Delaboix nodded to the man at his right who flexed his arm.

"No, no." Wickham flinched. "You are, of course, correct. I just need a bit more time…"

"For what?" Delaboix waited.

"I have something in the works."

Delaboix folded his arms. "I have been patient, yet you withhold information, Wickham? Most uncivil."

"It is not like that." Wickham swallowed.

"What is it then?"

"Things are at a *delicate* stage."

The older man assessed his 'associate.' "How long before they become *less* delicate?"

"Another month? Or two?"

Delaboix rubbed his chin. "How profitable?"

"Enough to pay you in full."

"See that you do. You cease to amuse, Wickham." Delaboix nodded to his muscular cohort who rapped on the roof. The carriage came to a halt. "You have become irritating, and I do not tolerate *irritants*. I thought you understood that."

Marcel grabbed Wickham, tossing him from the coach.

THWACK!

Raising his hand against the afternoon sun, Darcy watched his pall-mall ball roll into the untamed fringes of the meadow. Turning, he smiled at Elizabeth's mixture of chagrin and glee at his disbelief.

"I told you—*I* am the Longbourn pall-mall champion, but you refused to believe me. Now, go retrieve your ball so I may add the honour of Pemberley's championship to my long list of accomplishments." She curtseyed.

Darcy's heart pounded as she stepped closer. Looking, his eyes darted between her lips and the laughing sparkle of her eyes.

"The ball? Our game, sir?"

He remained transfixed. *She is so enticing, so close.* He blinked. "Of course. I shall be but a minute." Darcy strolled towards the tall grass, mumbling about women who only appear to be light and pleasing. Georgiana came towards Elizabeth, and giggling, they watched Darcy search for the errant sphere. The approaching butler caught their attention.

"Miss Darcy?" Stacy, the head butler, announced. "A carriage."

Looking first at Elizabeth, she called out. "Fitzwilliam! Guests!"

Darcy emerged, tossing the errant ball. Seeing his butler, he hurried to them. "What is it?"

"A carriage, sir," he said as he took Darcy's ball and mallet.

Darcy ran a hand through his hair. "Whose?"

"The Matlock crest was visible, sir."

Elizabeth paled and swayed, and Darcy took her arm before she stumbled. "Let us make haste. Georgiana, take Lady Elizabeth to her chambers."

He turned to Stacy. "Instruct Reynolds that rooms should be prepared in the guest wing—*not* the family wing."

Stacy raised his brow.

"Say there are renovations in progress…anything, I care not. But under *no* circumstance place them anywhere near Lady Elizabeth, do you understand?"

"Yes, sir."

"Now go, man. I shall accompany the ladies and return as soon as may be. See to it that our guests are watered, fed, and *kept* in the parlour."

Stacy bowed, rushing to complete his tasks.

"Elizabeth, I know not why they are here, or even who is in that carriage, but I promise I shall do all in my power to make their stay as short as possible. Their visit is unexpected. How do they know I am not in London?"

"Perhaps they do *not* know that."

"What are you saying?" Darcy faced his sister.

"Richard—and sometimes Braddleton—stay at Pemberley while you are in town."

"What? I find out about this now?"

"I am sorry. You always said they are welcome at all times—that they have free rein of the house. Reynolds wished to tell you, but I said not to bother you."

"I did…I had…but I did not know they were frequent visitors. How often do they avail themselves of my home?"

"Often."

"I see. Hurry. I must speak with the guards, and I wish to be downstairs when they arrive."

JULIAN FOLLOWED his father and the Exchequer's undersecretary to Lord Eldridge Riverton's office.

"This way, Your Grace, Lord Glascomb." Riverton led his friend to his private office past an array of men scrambling about the chamber. "You must forgive the lads. Ever since the prime minister—" He shook his head. "We are all a little lost."

"I understand they have caught the villain, have they not?" Julian asked.

"Yes, they have. But…well, it is no small feat. I admired the prime minister as a fiscal genius, but also he had the right of it…" Riverton glanced at the portraits of the King and the Prince of Wales. "Now? Well, it is anyone's guess who will take up the mantle."

"I feel"—Riverton looked out the window—"an *undercurrent* of instability running through the realm. Speculation is rampant about who will lead the nation should another war erupt." He gave the duke a significant look. "Perceval kept Prinny in line. Matlock was—*is*—an associate of Prinny…"

The duke watched his friend.

"…and a confounded foe of Perceval."

The Northamptons looked at each other.

"Is there any information you are able to share?" The duke clasped his hands together.

Riverton pushed back from his desk, tapping his fingers under his chin. "Yes and no." He smirked at the hopeful looks of his guests. He tucked his chin on the tips of his fingers. "Perceval was one of the cagiest politicians I have ever known." He nodded at their sceptical looks. "He sent you as ambassador, Duke, and then you, Glascomb. Even you must admit that shows sagacity. Or insanity."

His guests chuckled.

"And, he had an uncanny ability to make plans. Unfortunately, he was able only to *present* his plans for economic recovery."

Riverton looked away for a moment, lost in his thoughts. At length, he said, "And, or rather, he shared these with his closest advisors—regarding methods that could keep certain factions in check."

The Northamptons shared a quick glance before turning intent eyes to their friend.

"And this is how he would have brought the house of Matlock to its knees…"

Colonel Richard Fitzwilliam stepped out of the carriage, turning to hand out his companion. Pretty blonde curls bobbed as a young woman descended from the carriage. Satisfied and with a proprietary gleam, Richard led her up the stairs, faltering when Darcy strode through the door.

"Richard! How *fortunate* it is I am here to welcome you and…"

"Miss Beverly Windham, Mr…?" the coquette simpered.

"Mr Fitzwilliam Darcy, my dear." Richard bristled. "Fortunate indeed, cousin."

"Why did you not write of your visit? We would have had rooms prepared."

Miss Windham glared at Richard.

"I thought you to be in London—what with the Northampton business and all…"

"How kind of you to recall my cousin," Darcy pressed. "But, please, come in and break your journey. How long will you remain in Derbyshire?"

"A day or two."

Miss Windham's eyes flared. Darcy vacillated between anger and amusement till he recalled his legitimate guest.

"How is Lady Elizabeth?" Richard asked after refreshing himself as the cousins waited for Miss Windham.

"She was well when last I saw her." Darcy crossed his right leg over his left.

"And Northampton? Does he still pursue—"

"Her captors? Yes. As any *father* would, the duke works to bring them to justice." Darcy watched his cousin flinch. "Does the notion upset you?"

"No, no—not at all." Richard looked away.

A rustle of silk warned them of Miss Windham's return. Turning, they gasped.

Richard stood, immobile, as Elizabeth entered to sit beside his cousin.

I THOUGHT *Richard was almost engaged to Lady Sedgwick.* Georgiana watched Miss Windham, who kept glancing at Darcy as if he were a prize. Richard focused on Elizabeth, earning glares from Darcy.

Elizabeth sipped her soup, aware the man whose family had attacked her own was making a study of her. *He does not look so terribly troublesome, nearly harmless. A bit of a rake, a touch of vanity, but on the whole, a man who follows orders.* A chill ran in tingles up her spine as echoes of long-ago orders barked in the darkness of a midnight carriage resounded in her head. Her hand shook, and her eyes fled to Darcy, who met her gaze with concern. Elizabeth's courage rose.

Her eyes darted to the colonel, who watched, cataloguing the details of her appearance. Holding her gaze on his eyes, Elizabeth waited until his attention rose to her face, and she cocked her brow. Assessing the man before her, she contrived a plan. *The danger is in his informing his family I am here. I shall write Papa and ask for his guidance.*

She swept the table with her eyes, choking a giggle at the daggers Darcy threw at his guests. She wiped her mouth with the damask napkin. "Tell me, Colonel Fitzwilliam, how fares the situation on the continent?"

"Pardon, madam?" the colonel stuttered.

Elizabeth smiled into her soup. "I was only wondering—since His

Majesty's leading officers have time to holiday in Derbyshire—whether we citizenry may relax our anxiety at imminent invasion."

The colonel blushed. "I believe the good citizens need not fear Bony's advance at the present time."

"Thank heavens." Elizabeth took up her wine glass. "I would hate to think our flanks were exposed."

Both men nearly spat out their soup. Befuddled, Georgiana looked from her brother to her cousin while Miss Windham only lowered her head.

"How long will your party remain here in Derbyshire?" the colonel asked after regaining his composure.

"Our plans are not yet settled." Darcy saved Elizabeth from replying. "We came for a brief respite before Elizabeth's presentation."

"You will be presented this Season?" Miss Windham asked with genuine interest.

"Yes, Miss Windham, I shall," Elizabeth replied as Darcy watched the colonel.

"How lovely. One's entrée into society is such a thrill," Miss Windham enthused.

"I can only imagine," Elizabeth replied.

Darcy glowered at the colonel. "My cousin has only recently been returned to us. The delay in presenting her to society was, it seems, unavoidable."

"Will you play for us, Georgiana?" Elizabeth attempted to lower the tension. "Unless you play, Miss Windham?"

"Regretfully, my education did not include the musical arts."

"Ah," was all Darcy could manage as he counted the minutes till the evening would end.

DARCY WORKED through the morning to keep the previous evening from repeating in his mind. *Damn the man!* He threw his quill on the desk. *What kind of libertine is he? Bringing that Miss Whatever when he is all but engaged to Lady Sedgwick,* then *stares at Elizabeth all the blasted night!* That *will not win him any favours with Miss Winder—whatever. Thank the good Lord that is not my concern.* He rubbed his lips with his index finger thinking of their earlier conversation...

"Now I understand why you have abandoned London, Darcy—taking the cream of the crop with you."

"You are speaking of my cousin." Darcy sipped his brandy, watching and waiting. "What are you about? Truly."

"Nothing, thanks to your untimely return."

"To my home."

Richard chuckled at Darcy's grimace. "I was hoping for a dalliance longer than a carriage ride." He clasped his hands together. "But, be that as it may, your presence here may have done me some good. Your cousin is a beauty. Once she is presented, she will be on the market, eh?"

"No, she will not."

"Northampton has her promised already?" Richard smirked. "I have to hand it to the old man. He works fast. She has only been home—what—a month? Two?"

"Three—and she will not be on the marriage block because she is"—he paused, or will be—*"marrying me."*

"You?" Richard asked incredulously. "But...that is to say, does Lady Catherine know of this? And Father—what of your promise to him?"

Darcy pondered Richard's distress. "I promised a reply only by month's end, and that was before the recovery of my cousin."

"But..."

Darcy took a perverse pleasure in his cousin's disquiet. He wondered whether Richard was fully aware of his uncle's plans and decided it was time to find out. "Why do you *not answer*

Lady Catherine's lament and marry Anne? She will not mind your philandering half as much as the Sedgwicks will."

"I thought you held me in some esteem."

"No more than you hold me." Darcy locked eyes with the colonel until the soldier looked away. Examining his pocket watch, Darcy stood. "Shall we?"

DARCY FINISHED his labours and leaned back in his chair, relieved that his unexpected guests had departed earlier than they had anticipated. From the study's window, he followed Georgiana and Elizabeth's ramble from the formal gardens to the pond. Moving to the green parlour to keep them in his sights, he rested a knee on the window bench, one hand on the glass.

Sitting on the bay window's bench, Darcy grunted in discomfort. Curious about the annoyance, he pulled a leather folio from its hiding place beneath the cushion. Flipping the pages, he marvelled at sketches and watercolours filling three-quarters of the book. There were ink renderings of Jane Bingley as a young girl, of people he assumed were Mr and Mrs Bennet, of Charles Bingley, and a particularly *fanciful* rendition of Caroline Bingley that drew a snort. Working his way through the drawings, each one providing insight into Elizabeth's mind, Darcy admired the delicacy of her brush. He stopped at a maze of long, black-inked slashes across the white page. In the lower right corner was a very young girl's face, eyes brimming with horror, peering out of the mishmash of angry lines. A single eye glared menacingly from the top left of the page, its cruelty palpable.

Darcy recoiled in horror, closing the book. Then, re-opening it, he flipped through the remaining pages, still unsettled by the disturbing image. Another drawing stole his breath. As if looking in the mirror, Darcy saw his own face: cruel, cold, lifeless eyes glared back at him. Slumping against the window, he noticed the portrait's date. "April seventeenth," he whispered. "That was...right after...the park." He forced himself to study her depiction of his own degradation. Overcome by his heartless behaviour, he closed his eyes, rubbing away the stain. When he opened them, the pages flopped to an unfinished composition of Georgiana and him sitting, as they would often do, in the yellow parlour across from Elizabeth's favourite chair.

"She draws these from memory as I have never seen her with pen and paper. She is astounding!" Studying the portrait, he traced Georgiana's delicate features and the kindness in her eyes. He looked at her more recent treatment of his own façade, and his heart quickened when he saw not a cruel brute but his love for Elizabeth unabashedly committed to the page. "Perhaps"—he smiled through his tears —"there is hope after all."

sixteen

JULIAN FOLLOWED HIS FRIEND, SILENTLY CHUCKLING AT THE GILT flourishes on the cornices and bookshelves of Winston Hornsby's study. Taking a furtive glance at Julian, Hornsby plopped into a chair.

"It is rather like this, Glascomb," Hornsby began. "I looked into the *Celestine* as you requested."

"Do get to the point, will you?" Julian wiped a dust speck from his immaculate breeches.

Shooting his friend an irritated glance, Hornsby scooted closer. "The *Celestine* was boarded at Gibraltar a few weeks back." Hornsby rubbed his hands, as if massaging out a deep tension. "Portuguese flagged, we had no right to board her, but we did have a clue about a nasty bit of arms and ammunition smuggling. Featherstone handled this personally."

Seeing the doubt in Julian's eyes, Hornsby added. "Totally dependable. Not one for exaggeration, mind you—stickler for the facts."

"Yes, yes—please continue."

"Right." Hornsby looked away then back at Julian. "We found the arms as expected, but...the *Celestine* had a few surprises in the captain's cabin: documents in the ship's safe." Hornsby lowered his voice. "It seems Bellacroisse, the captain, had a ledger recounting the first leg of his journey as well as a cache of correspondence.

Julian scooted to the edge of his chair. "And in that ledger…?"

"It recorded earlier passages, creating a significant paper trail—and considerable money trail, I might add—that led to—"

"Matlock?" Julian concluded.

Hornsby nodded. "And even though the entire cargo was totally illegal, there was a letter guaranteeing safe passage through British waters, signed by a highly placed member of the admiralty. Thank heavens Captain Crestlewait was able to surprise their captain before he could retrieve it."

Hornsby gave Julian a significant look, and Julian shook his head.

"The *Celestine* had one more surprise for us. As you are aware, we have known of a traitor in the admiralty for some time. However, we had word that this *particular* person sought passage to the Americas. To wit, Crestlewait was charged to board expeditiously in time to find both the *brigand*"—Hornsby smirked at his unflappable friend's response—"as well as evidence in that ledger containing the traitor's moniker."

"That is excellent news."

Hornsby dipped his head. "It was a bit of luck. And with their quick response, our men kept Lord Belmont from jumping ship. The blackguard remains in irons."

Julian guffawed.

"But back to Matlock. Crestlewait was *incensed* at how protected the *Celestine* was, and he nearly threw the entire lot into the sea." Hornsby grew serious. "Their papers had all the correct seals and signatures guaranteeing safe passage through our waters, no matter what they carried."

Hornsby looked directly into Julian's eyes. "It *was* his doing, Glascomb. Matlock. He badgered the ministers into issuing the documents so they were in that *particular* safe for that *particular* voyage. That a respected—"

Julian snorted.

"Come now, Glascomb, no matter what you think of the man, that a peer *facilitated* a traitor's escape shakes one…to the core, I say." Hornsby drew in a deep breath. "I reported in with our *friend*…"

Julian nodded.

"Catervaux knew Matlock requested the papers, relaying that the *owner* of the ship, the real power behind the operation is not happy that his property now belongs to the admiralty."

Julian looked up from studying the floor.

"Are you not curious as to *who* owns the ship?"

"Tell me."

Smiling victoriously, Hornsby uttered one word. "Delaboix."

THE MORNING LIGHT glistened on the dew-laden grass as Elizabeth walked through the park. *Tomorrow we return to London.* She watched the dawn's light crest the rise of a nearby hill, clasping her arms about her waist. "And the business of gowns and bonnets and tea. Endless pots of tea."

I shall miss being here. How dear Pemberley has become. "And Darcy. How dear he has become. Underneath all that bluster, he is a good, kind man. But that cousin of his!"

She shuddered, recalling Colonel Fitzwilliam's eyes raking over her before handing Miss Windham into their carriage. "With an example such as that, it is no wonder Darcy felt no compunction in offering…that…to me." She walked further, her fingers brushing the bushes and trees. "I have forgiven him." She stopped mid-step. "I have. The question becomes, can I forget and move beyond this dilemma? He is my cousin, and he has recanted."

She continued walking. "And, he loves me."

ELIZABETH ESPIED her cousins visiting the family cemetery beyond a second grove of trees, laying flowers on their parents' graves. She made her way towards them, stopping when she heard her name.

"When we return next time, perhaps Elizabeth will join us," Georgiana whispered.

"I think not, Georgiana."

"Why not?"

He ran a hand through his hair. "I intend to end this understanding between us. The engagement, such as it is."

Georgiana's gasp covered Elizabeth's own. "What? Why?"

"I do not want her…to marry me out of obligation or to feel that she has no other choice."

"You will release her?"

He nodded and took her hand. "Come, let us return to the house to see whether Elizabeth has returned. Fear not, little one, I shall stay close by."

Seeing his sister's confusion, he continued. "Georgiana, she deserves to be courted like the lady she is. And she deserves to choose from amongst the best of men our society has to offer. I only hope to be counted in that company."

Georgiana noted a length of blue fluttering behind a bush a short distance from the small cemetery. Stopping, she looked first at the cloth and then the broken branches bending towards the house.

"Oh!" Holding up the blue silk, her eyes grew wide, and her voice flattened. "Elizabeth was here. I wager she heard us."

Reaching for the ribbon, Darcy lifted it to his nose. *Lavender.*

"This cannot be good." Georgiana looked towards the house.

"We must find her." Darcy slipped the ribbon in his waistcoat pocket.

LADY CATHERINE THREW her brother's express on the desk. "That ungrateful girl! She should have remained in the gutter where she belongs. I shall know how to act."

She rummaged for her quill and paper. "Harrison is still workable. I shall call upon him one *last* time. And if he is too old, then Wickham will suffice."

"Madam—" Lady Catherine's long-suffering butler, Banister, interrupted.

She covered her missive with a clean sheet. "Enter!" Seeing he had anticipated his summons, Lady Catherine glowered at the intruder.

"Lady Catherine, begging your pardon, but you asked to be notified when Mr Collins returned from Westminster. He awaits you in the sitting room."

With a fleeting glance at her unfinished correspondence, she said. "Very well. I shall attend him."

A moment later, Mrs Jenkinson entered the study in order to fetch a shawl for her mistress Anne and discovered the unfinished letter. Following her employer's long-standing instructions, she slipped it in her pocket to be sent post haste via special courier.

JULIAN SHUT the door to his father's study. The duke looked up from his correspondence. "Father, I have something that might actually be of use. He sat down, outlining his conversation with Lady Matlock and with Hornsby.

"So, not only has Matlock betrayed his king, but he has Delaboix hot on his tail as well?" The duke shook his head. "He is more a fool than even I imagined. Well done, son, well done. You have exceeded my expectations."

"Thank you, Father." Noting his father's brow still knit in troubled thought, Julian gently asked. "What is it?"

"I received an express." The duke took a moment. "I am satisfied that Matlock not only will face charges of treason but he was a secondary participant in Elizabeth's abduction. It is Lady Catherine who concerns me. We need to focus on her."

"What can she do?"

"*She* is the one who orchestrated Elizabeth's abduction." He slammed his hand on the arm of the chair. "Do not underrate her because she is a woman, or old, and very possibly out of her mind."

The duke rose to pace. "News of Elizabeth's engagement has stirred her to action. Mrs Jenkinson has earned her keep yet again, providing us the name of the man who…" Philip's throat constricted and, helpless, he looked at his son. "…the man who most likely abetted her in abducting Elizabeth."

"What have you done to stop her?"

"Colonel MacTiernan will detain this 'Harrison' until Elizabeth is back home with us."

"This is the first piece of actual proof of Lady Catherine's involvement."

"Darcy is bringing Elizabeth home. We must draw her out *here*, *before* she strikes. You recall George Wickham?"

"I would rather not, but yes, Father, of course."

"He has been to Rosings. I wish to know what his involvement is in all of this."

"I shall see what I can uncover."

"Thank you, Julian."

"When do the lovebirds return?"

"A day or so. There is one more thing." The duke looked at his hands. "Darcy claims he will release Elizabeth from their engagement."

"What!"

"WELL, THERE YOU HAVE IT, DUCHESS." Mrs Raleigh paused. "What I assume is being said…"

"Throughout the *ton* no doubt."

"No doubt." Mrs Raleigh took another sip of tea.

Suddenly, the duchess made her way to her desk. Mrs Raleigh turned to watch the graceful woman pull an elaborate invitation from a niche. She took a quill and inkpot from their drawer. "Where did you say Miss Bingley now resides?"

Surprised, Mrs Raleigh replied, "Jane said that her sister, Mrs Hurst, has taken her in."

A wicked gleam filled the duchess's eyes. "Hurst? Hurst? I do not know a Mrs Hurst."

Mrs Raleigh smiled. "No, I do not believe you would, Your *Grace*." She rose to peer over the duchess's shoulder.

"Do you know the address?" The duchess looked up at Mrs Raleigh.

"Mayfair, I believe."

"Very good." She wrote the invitation in an elegant hand. "I suppose I shall have to include this other sister? And her husband?"

"To what?"

"Why to Elizabeth's ball, of course!" The duchess blew on the ink then wafted the cream-coloured parchment.

Mrs Raleigh looked into the mischievous eyes of her friend and giggled. "Oh you!"

ELIZABETH HAD BEEN absent most of the day but as the dinner hour approached, Darcy found her in the rose garden that their mutual grandmother had designed over three decades earlier. She caressed the tender blossoms, lifting her head to watch a passing cloud. A bird's song filled the air as a gentle breeze caught a stray curl dangling along her neck. A thousand thoughts ran through his mind at once beholding her.

Elizabeth, I would have you...if you would have me. That is the most ardent desire of my heart. But I want you to choose me. I cannot —will not—force you. I am afraid—afraid you will choose another, one who is more worthy of you. But I promise, no one loves you more. This love gives me—you give me—the courage to see the man I have become and start on the path towards being the man I wish to be....My every thought is centred on you—on finding ways to ensure your happiness, your safety, and your love. Please, Elizabeth, I beg of you another chance to prove to you and to myself how good a man I may yet be...

I cannot chain her to a life she would not choose. I cannot.

Steeling his courage, he straightened his jacket and moved towards her.

"Elizabeth?"

She turned, eyes full of emotion.

He took her hand, slipping it on his arm. "I would speak with you."

She nodded, looking at him.

Darcy searched her face. Unsure of her feelings, he stumbled, and she clasped his arm with more strength than he had imagined. "I know, with all that has surrounded your return, that...well...that the news of our alliance is...well, it was rather precipitous. Especially when you consider our, that is, *my* abominable behaviour to you...before."

He flushed with shame. "Again, I offer my heartfelt apology. I—"

Elizabeth pulled away. "I know you wish to be freed from our...the understanding our fathers..."

He was alarmed when she stepped further away. "No, it is not that! I...no! Wait, Elizabeth!" He hurried to her side. "You must know I wish nothing more than for you to be...for me to be...your husband...but..."

"Then, *why*?" Elizabeth demanded, fists clenched at her sides, confusion in her eyes. "I heard..." Emotion closed her throat.

"If you overheard Georgiana and me, then what do you not understand? How could you run away?" A growing sense of dread crept over his face. "Is it that you do not wish to marry me?"

"*You* do not want to marry *me!* How could I—"

"You misunderstand!"

"Oh! You say one thing and then another! What is the truth?" Anger was replacing dismay. "I have heard all my life I am unworthy, that no man… No more…"

She walked away, muttering. "Insufferable! He humiliates me, then woos like a true lover, then tosses me away like yesterday's scraps! No more, I say!"

Darcy ran after her. "Heard *what* all your life, Elizabeth?" He offered his outstretched arms to her.

She crossed her arms over her stomach, and he fell to his knees on the gravel path. Both winced as the stones pierced the fine weave of his breeches, but his eyes held hers. "I have never felt the joy of existence as fully as I do with you. You have reanimated my heart and my will to live. Nothing would please me more than spending my life with you as your husband."

"Then why send me away?" Her voice trembled.

Darcy composed the most significant words of his life. "I…to have you, knowing it is not by your choice…is insupportable. I would not have you unhappy in an arranged marriage to anyone, even me. I want you to have the freedom to choose…" He exhaled fully and took a deep breath. "Even if it means you choose another."

Feeling vulnerable, he looked away. Hearing no response, Darcy rose unsteadily till—midway between his kneeling and standing positions—her palm slid gently to his cheek. His eyes flew to hers, and his broken heart, finding love, was healed into a glowing, living whole.

Her voice was just above a whisper. "Thank you." They stood, holding hands as if to fuse their lives together, till heavy boots on the gravel warned them of the approach of another.

"Mr Darcy." The buttons of the red coat gleamed in the morning's light. Elizabeth shielded her eyes with both hands, breaking the connexion to Darcy who felt the retreat to his core.

Darcy sighed. "Yes, Lieutenant Greymond?"

Taking in the interrupted scene, Greymond's cheeks were redder than his uniform. "I…that is…my men are ready to depart. We wait upon you and, of course, the ladies."

Darcy looked at Elizabeth. "Very well. We shall leave within the hour—as soon as Lady Elizabeth and Miss Darcy are ready."

"Very good, sir." The lieutenant turned towards the great house.

Darcy had a wide view of the gardens and hills rolling down to the lake. *I want more time.* He looked at his empty hands. *How could the touch of one little hand mean so much?*

Darcy waited as Elizabeth took one last look. "Shall we?"

Nodding, she slipped her hand on his arm, and feeling her squeeze his forearm, he smiled, leading her home.

THEIR ESCORT of royal house guards rode two abreast and flanked the carriage. Another sat atop, alongside Pemberley's coachman.

Looking out the carriage window, she thought of the walks, picnics, and tender moments shared with her cousins when the world was miles away. She smiled at the gentle, thoughtful man hidden from society for so long. Inevitably, her thoughts returned to the great gift he offered. *I am free to choose my fate, my destiny.* She turned to his impressive form as he rode alongside the carriage. *But how am I to know what to choose? And if I choose him? What then?*

His eyes caught hers. Mastering the tumult of her thoughts, she held his gaze. His eyes widened in surprise, and she relaxed, more confident in her future.

seventeen

IN JUNE, WITH ELIZABETH SAFELY RETURNED TO NORTHAMPTON PLACE, preparations for her coming out became frenetic. The *ton* was buzzing with word of her return, insuring that her ball would be the crowning triumph of the season. While their women oversaw the myriad details, Julian and his father escaped to the established male bastion: their study.

The duke poured a generous measure of brandy into a snifter and handed it to his son. He then poured himself an even more liberal dose.

"Father, I met with Colonel MacTiernan as you requested."

"And—?" The duke sat in a comfortable armchair, his feet on the fire grate.

Julian settled across from his father. He leaned forward, fingers intertwined. "The chosen assassin is *detained*—for more than a week now. He cannot hold his liquor, causing a public spectacle in South-wick—and had to be incarcerated."

The duke smiled, nodding. He leaned against the back of his chair, closed his eyes, and sighed. "What a damnable business."

Julian nodded.

"To try...not once, but twice?"

Julian nodded, his eyes deeply disturbed. "How can one live with that on his conscience?"

The duke's eyes flew open, enraged. "They have none, Julian."

"Surely, all men have a conscience somewhere buried in their hearts."

He must know that some men are beyond redemption— The duke stopped mid-thought at the depravity of his own thinking and its implications. *And yet we are all accountable on some level—in some way— for our actions, are we not?* He blinked, stunned at this test of his own understanding. *Which means if every man is accountable and in possession of a conscience, a soul, then every man has the possibility of redemption, of forgiveness.*

Unhappy with his thoughts, he looked at his son, a grown man who, despite living in the world, held on to the beliefs he and Alexandra had instilled in him as a child. Even the loss of Elizabeth had not shaken his faith in the inherent nobility of man—every man.

"Yes, each and every one of us contains the Divine spark though, in some, it is a flicker. And I thank you for reminding me of that." The duke wiped his hands over his eyes. "Elizabeth's return has brought the balm of kindness and the bitterness of the wicked to the fore, and I admit to being blinded by the darkness. You have helped me recall that, no matter how base, we all possess the potential to repent and receive forgiveness."

"I am not so noble, Father." Julian blushed and took a sip of brandy. "I have only recently seen a wider array of human behaviour... remnants of the war being over."

Shaking off the heavy silence, Julian straightened. "But back to this business with Matlock. He will soon be detained. Not only has word been spread that Delaboix has called in all of Matlock's debts, but charges of treason are being...processed. With Lady Catherine's henchman detained, will not her frustration increase—?"

"—their pressure on Darcy to marry his cousin Anne?"

Julian nodded.

With a gaze full of determination, the duke smirked before closing his eyes. "Then marry his cousin, he shall."

ANNE DE BOURGH had never been a healthy woman, so the daily upending of her stomach was no cause for undue concern. Accustomed to frequent nausea, she only ordered more ginger tea and biscuits. Therefore, she was surprised when the ball gowns she ordered were unsuitable when delivered.

"Such incompetence! That seamstress cannot even take simple measurements. Mother is right!" She gyrated in the mirror, failing to notice the wide-eyed stares of her maid. "Breeding wins out, every time."

Anne stepped closer to the mirror. Pressing the gown across her stomach, she felt for the pelvic bones habitually protruding from her bony frame. "I have a belly! How can that be?" Her eyes rose to her chest that ached as the fitted bodice pressed against her. She felt her bosom, and her knees weakened as each palm was amply filled with a plump breast.

"I am a woman," she whispered. "Darcy will be so pleased."

JULIAN MADE his way to his chamber in the family wing of Northampton Place. *Just a few more days and then we can all relax.* Hearing voices from his sister's apartment, he stood just outside the partially open door.

"And then he said, 'to have you, knowing it is not by your choice, is insupportable. I would not have you unhappy in an arranged marriage to anyone, even me.'"

Julian frowned at the tearful quiver in her voice.

"'I want you to have the freedom to choose,' he said, but before I could respond, the guards announced it was time to go."

Julian gritted his teeth as his sister sniffled.

There was a rustle of silk and his mother's voice. "Choice is a magnificent thing, my dear."

"I am not so certain."

"No?"

Julian could imagine his mother pushing that annoying curl from Elizabeth's cheek.

"Is it not better to be the master of your own fate, Elizabeth?"

"Yes, Mama, but why does it have to hurt so?"

Julian nodded.

"What else did he say?"

"He said"—she squirmed in her chair—"'I have never felt the joy of existence as fully as I do with you.'"

Julian frowned at the emotion in her voice.

"'You have reanimated my heart and my will to live. Without my true, full consent,' he said he 'would never force me into anything...'"

The room fell silent. "And you, my dear? What do you wish?"

"I am uncertain."

"Elizabeth. He *is* in love with you, of that I am certain. The question is—What is *your* desire? You like Darcy, do you not?"

Julian could only guess his sister's response was a nod of her curly head. He leaned as close to the door as he dared.

"He is an attractive man..."

"Yes, very handsome."

Julian snorted, pinching his side to regain control of a snort as Darcy's 'handsome' face filled his mind, and his attention shifted to vigilance as the room grew silent. He relaxed and leaned against the door as his mother continued.

"He is kind."

"And intelligent," Elizabeth added. There was another hesitation while Julian held his breath, releasing it only when his sister said, "But, Mama, I do not wish to force him into anything. He is such a good man."

Suddenly, the door flew open, and Julian bolted backwards, sending him scrambling for his balance; he teetered for a moment before falling to the floor with a crash.

"And so much more mature than my brother!"

Raucous laughter greeted the startled marquess, who sighed. Elizabeth offered him her hand. With a mischievous grin, he pulled her down rather than hoisting himself up. She shrieked, and as Alexandra bent to pull her back to an upright position, Julian tugged at his sister's waist, causing his mother to tumble on top of her as Elizabeth sprawled across his lap.

Moments later, Philip encountered them on his way to his chambers. Rather than helping his wife and children to their feet, he rolled his eyes and uttered a droll, "Carry on," before continuing on his way.

His nearest and dearest erupted again in peals of laughter. Only when he had rounded the corner did their father allow his lips to twitch upward in delight.

"Miss Mary Bennet comes to town." Elizabeth drew a line in her sketchpad perched atop her knees. Her brother, sitting opposite, attempted to scratch his nose. Elizabeth swatted his hand. "Julian, you must be still."

"You are one to speak. You get to scratch on that parchment while I must remain…*august*."

Elizabeth smirked, making a wide sweep with her charcoal.

"What is this Miss Bennet like?" their mother asked.

"Mary is a serious young woman." Elizabeth focused on capturing her brother's full lips and frowned at her effort. "I believe she feels the need to protect me especially, but Jane as well."

"Protect you?" This piqued Julian's interest.

"Yes," Elizabeth drawled. "Hold steady, Jules." Elizabeth moved her graphite stylus quickly, recording Julian's intelligent eyes to paper.

"How so?" Philip asked.

"She is a serious young lady but not without her own particular sense of humour." Elizabeth smiled at her father, which he reciprocated. "It is just that Lydia and Kitty, the youngest, are such flighty, silly creatures. Mrs Bennet took such a dislike to me, especially after Papa Bennet passed. Mary orchestrated my rescue many, many times."

The duchess forced her heart to calm. "Rescue? Why would you need rescuing?"

Elizabeth paused, eyes downcast. "Nothing, truly. It is just…Mrs Bennet could be harsh. She never took to me, 'tis all."

Her parents' eyes met, their concern noted by their son. Elizabeth frayed the edges of her sketch.

Julian shook his head. "If you keep that up, you will have to start again, and I am unsure I can maintain a dignified posture for such an extended length of time."

A heartfelt smile transformed her face. He laid his hand on hers.

"Elizabeth," the duke began, "I do not wish to distress you. However, I must ask, how do you wish to inform the Bennets?"

"Pardon?" Elizabeth gave him her full attention.

He coughed. "I mean to say…that is…Raleigh indicated that you and Mr Bennet are on good terms."

"Yes, sir, we are."

He shifted in his seat while the duchess observed their daughter. "Then, with the notice in the papers, do you not think it wise that I write to them—or at least to him? Perhaps invite them to the ball?"

"Oh." Elizabeth's mind conjured images of Mrs Bennet's nerves among the *ton*. "I…" Her mind flew to Jane, wondering what she would do in that situation.

"Surely, Admiral Raleigh and Mrs Raleigh will see to it, Father."

"I think not." her mother spoke emphatically. "Mrs Raleigh has never looked kindly on the current Mrs Bennet. I see no reason to invite them, Philip. Why do you?"

The duke turned to his wife. "They were responsible for Elizabeth's well-being for a time, and it is only proper."

"Can we not just have them to dinner the next time they are in town?" The duchess smiled as Elizabeth relaxed. Julian only looked from one to the other.

The duke addressed his wife. "The Bennets are infrequently in town."

"Precisely," the duchess replied in as regal a tone as she could muster.

LADY CATHERINE WALKED the night halls of de Bourgh Manor, one of the stately, if not dated, mansions of Mayfair. For years, the deep sleep of the innocent had eluded her, and she was long accustomed to her lonely vigil. With the dawn's light streaking the sky, she hobbled past her daughter's apartment as two maids emerged with a chamber pot she could smell from a distance of five feet. "You there, bring that to me."

The startled maid turned. With a frightened look, the maid walked towards her employer. "Yes, ma'am."

Lady Catherine lifted the linen covering and spoke with narrowed eyes. "Miss de Bourgh is ill again? And no one saw fit to inform me?"

The second maid responded. "Miss Anne asked that we say nothing, seeing as how she would always regain herself by mid-morn. We made her promise that, if it continued, you would be notified."

"I see." Lady Catherine's mind whirled with possibilities. Dismissing the girls, she stormed into her daughter's chamber.

MARY BENNET'S eyes widened as the Bingleys' coach pulled up to a stately mansion on Grosvenor Square, rather than Raleigh House. "Jane, why have we stopped here? I thought we were to see Lizzy today."

"And so we shall." Jane smiled at her cousin's confusion.

"I do not understand. One cannot simply impose upon her acquaintances…"

"No, Mary." Charles looked at Jane. "We are to visit your cousin at her new home."

Jane reached across to take Mary's hand. "With her family."

"Family?" Mary leaned back, overcome. "She found them? Here? In London?"

"Yes." Jane smiled.

"But how?" She looked out at the grand edifice. "Who are they?"

The carriage stopped and, giving one last look to his wife, Charles exited, turning to hand out his companions. Mary seemed unable to move, and Jane looked back into the coach. "Come, Mary. All will be explained. There is nothing to fear."

Taking a hesitant glance out the window, Mary swallowed and took the strong hand of her cousin. Saying a prayer, she rose to meet her sweet Lizzy.

DRAWING BACK HIS HAND, the earl let it fly across the young woman's cheek. "How dare you?" he growled, poised to strike again.

Struggling to stand, she remained defiant against another attack. "I dare so much more, your *lordship*. I know you—who you are and what you have done."

"Why, you little…whore!"

"If I am, what does that make you?" she spat. "I, at least, am honest with myself in what I do. But you? You are so proper, yet you return time after time."

The next blow sent her reeling. With a rush of adrenaline coursing through his blood, Matlock advanced as she braced herself against the nearest wall. Pinning her with his body, he ripped her gown.

Viscount Braddleton threw open the unlocked door. "Father!" For all his personal debauchery, even he startled at the purple bruise blooming across the woman's cheek. He shook off the degree to which his father's brutality unnerved him. "I believe the *lady* has made her feelings known."

Sparing only a glance at his eldest, the earl ripped more of Natalia's gown as she struggled to get away. "Shows what little you know of women, son. Leave me."

"Father, get hold of yourself. There are more important matters…"

Matlock, in the full throes of lust, turned on his son. Braddleton cowered, darting his eyes to the frightened woman. Taking a deep breath, Braddleton hurtled himself against the considerable bulk of his father, stunning the older man, who stumbled. Fear replaced Matlock's anger as a tingling sensation crept down his right side and he fell onto a backless stool that provided no purchase. Braddleton rushed to his father, screaming for help, while the woman scrambled to a corner, clutching her gown, unaware that they were no longer alone.

A dark-haired man had entered the chamber. Assessing the situation, he retrieved a long, jagged blade from his coat's inner pocket and, with two steps, thrust it between Braddleton's ribs. With a strangled cry, the viscount turned, eyes widening with fearful recognition before he crumpled to the floor, a gurgle of blood heralding his demise.

Watching his son fall, the earl's heart squeezed tightly, and his vision grew fuzzy. He struggled to sit upright, arms outstretched as his mistress collapsed into the arms of the assassin. Bewildered by his condition, they rushed to the door. Matlock's heart raced, and he called out. Natalia turned, and with a sneer of contempt, she spat at him before rushing through the door. A jolt of tight pain flared in his chest, and uttering one last, incomprehensible groan, the Earl of Matlock collapsed on the floor.

MARY LOOKED up as the massive front door revealed a brilliantly happy Elizabeth rushing down the stairs. Seeing her open arms, Mary's face lit up, and she met Elizabeth's embrace.

"Lizzy!" Mary held her favourite cousin tightly.

"Mary, I have missed you!"

"And I you." Mary searched Elizabeth's face and shook her head. "Oh, Lizzy." She looked at the door, blocked by one of the most handsome men she had ever seen. "But how? Who are you?"

Elizabeth laughed at her honest curiosity. "As difficult as it may be to believe, I am Lady Elizabeth Aubrey Rose Elliston, daughter of the Duke and Duchess of Northampton."

"No!" Mary tugged Elizabeth to a halt. "Not that I do not believe you, but this is so fantastical!"

"It is, yet it is so, Miss Bennet," a man's sonorous voice addressed her. "Julian Robert Elliston, Marquess of Glascomb, at your service."

"Oh my!" Mary blushed.

"Mrs Bingley, please come in. Bingley." Julian bowed to each. "Lady Elizabeth, my charming hostess of a sister, has laid in provisions." He spread his arm in the direction of the parlour. "Shall we retire to the salon?"

"Julian!" Elizabeth decried. "Behave."

"Always, Elizabeth."

"You must forgive my brother." Elizabeth took her cousin's arm. "My mother and father are at a meeting with my cousin Darcy"—she gave a knowing glance to the surprised Mary—"and he feels his responsibility as 'master of the manor' a bit too significantly."

Cheerful chatter followed them from the parlour to the dining room as they revealed the details of their lives since Elizabeth's departure. "Mary, you must come to the ball. I do so long for a familiar face— beyond Julian's. And we know that Jane will only have eyes for her dear Bingley." The cousins chuckled at Jane's blush. Seeing Bingley's flaming cheeks, they burst into laughter.

"I see how it is," Julian proclaimed. He nodded at Mary. "You must not encourage her."

"Oh, for that I believe you are a few years too late," Jane said, then appeared repentant as a flash of pain crossed Julian's face and he looked away.

Elizabeth pressed her hand against his arm. When he looked at her, she smiled, her eyes filled with love.

"Please, Lord Glascomb, forgive my thoughtlessness," Jane pleaded immediately.

"No, no." Julian looked around the table. "It is something we must all come to terms with. It is…at times, it is more difficult. I miss those years with you, Elizabeth."

"As do I."

Taking a deep breath, Mary spoke. "One of my first memories of Elizabeth was her showing us, myself and my two sisters, Kitty and Lydia, all the best places in which to forage."

A brilliant smile illuminated Julian's face as he squeezed his sister's hand, leaning forward to hear more. The remainder of the afternoon revealed Elizabeth's adventures of pirate expeditions across Noah's Puddle, building tree houses in the orchards, or collecting stray animals that made their way to the kitchen and, on occasion, the dining room, which sent Aunt Bennet's nerves atwitter.

WHEN THE STUDY door slammed open, Darcy rose from where he had been writing a letter to Pemberley's steward. "I beg your pardon."

"Are you deaf as well as daft, boy?" the imperious woman spat.

Darcy cocked his brow, praying that the duke and duchess, who had called earlier, remained in the drawing room where they had retired while he attended to his correspondence—*and to face an enraged madwoman*, he thought wryly.

"This slander must stop!"

"Slander, Aunt?" Darcy asked calmly.

"You *must* denounce these rumours of your being engaged to that…chit…and marry Anne! Immediately!"

"I shall do no such thing. Elizabeth is—"

"Elizabeth Elliston is dead!" Lady Catherine pronounced. "That woman is an imposter, a charlatan insinuating herself into the first circles—"

"How would you know that?"

Caught unawares, she retorted. "How could a small child survive such an ordeal? She was terrified!" A malevolent smile contorted her lips. "The tears, the pleas for mercy."

Lady Catherine took another step forward, her features animated by her evil tale. "When I struck her, her pain was exquisite. The urchin would *not* be still, crying for her *Mama* and *dear* Papa. Oh, she was weak, Darcy. Too weak for you."

She swished her skirts, taking another step. "She would drag you down! Your Matlock blood would be diluted even more with Darcy blood."

Darcy fought to control his disgust, needing to hear the full confession.

"She *cried*, boy. Incessant wails as I struck her with my crop, but it was not enough. She *cowered* in the corner when I struck again and again, but she would not stop." Catherine narrowed her eyes at him. "The blood was disgusting. It took *weeks* to remove it from the squabs. But it was her eyes, Darcy, the utter terror as she begged for mercy."

She crossed her arms with a smug smile. "But I am not weak, boy. I carry through with my purpose. She had to be eliminated, and eliminated she was! Thrown from my coach like trash. No one stops Lady Catherine Fitzwilliam de Bourgh. I am not to be gainsaid."

At the sound of a pistol being cocked, they saw Northampton step forward. "You are, as always, mistaken, Catherine. God Almighty has already thwarted you. Elizabeth lives."

"Impossible!"

"But she does—and takes her *rightful* place in the world. As for you—!" Without turning his eyes from his captive, he called out, "Alex, send for Colonel MacTiernan. Tell him to bring an armed escort."

Shaking with fury, the duchess marched through the door with a withering scowl at Lady Catherine.

Lady Catherine scoffed. "Are you going somewhere?"

"No. You, however, are." The duke kept his gun aimed at her heart. "Darcy, do you have something to bind her?"

Darcy settled on the curtain ties.

"You would not dare!" Lady Catherine sputtered as he wrenched her hands behind her back. Panic seeped into her voice as Darcy tightened the knot. "Stop this nonsense! I am your blood!"

"I take no pride in that, madam. I am thoroughly disgusted with you, and I am mortified that we share anything whatsoever." Darcy roughly shoved her into a chair. "You showed no mercy to my cousin, a *child* with no defences."

He knelt at her feet, wrapping another cord around her ankles as she kicked out. "You are no lady. You are barely human."

"You and Anne were formed for each other. Matlock and I agreed."

Northampton advanced. "Your brother had a part in this?"

"He had no stomach for it. It took a while, but I convinced him of the necessity of removing her expeditiously—"

The duke's slap stopped her venomous words.

"You beast!" Lady Catherine screeched.

"Never in all my years have I encountered a monster such as you." Northampton looked at Darcy. "I apologise, Darcy, for my unseemly display."

The duchess re-entered, moving towards her nemesis. "Lady Catherine, I shall not rest until you are skewered on the altar of justice. I intend to enjoy watching you endure the fruits of your labour. Elizabeth *shall* marry Darcy."

With demonic fury, Lady Catherine turned on the duchess. "You! All of this is *your* fault."

The duchess smirked. "How is it *my* fault?"

"For marrying *him*." Lady Catherine jerked her head towards the duke. "My sister was to secure him, but no, I could not catch them together. Otherwise, I would have—"

The duchess gasped, and her husband looked shaken.

"So, we settled for the Darcy fortune, binding it to Matlock. It gave us dominance until *you* came back to Pemberley for that…to *court* that girl." Lady Catherine glared at the duchess. "You! A wild, rambling *thing*! Anne tried to civilise you, but no, you had to have your way, your man." She turned to Darcy. "What else could I do? Your father's devotion to her was *unseemly!*"

Her deranged eyes returned to the duchess. "And you, flouting every dictate of society! What did you mean by traipsing about Pemberley like some washerwoman? Petticoats six inches in mud! A disgrace through and through."

She returned her glare to Darcy. "You should be on your knees, thanking me for saving you from marrying that…that—"

"Enough!" The duke stuffed his handkerchief into Lady Catherine's mouth. "No more. Darcy, a parchment and a pen if you please." Northampton sat at the vacated desk.

"Of course." Darcy gathered the necessary supplies then stood at his uncle's side.

Nodding his thanks, the duke wrote and, when finished, handed it to Darcy.

"Uncle?" Darcy asked. "What does this mean?"

"That the inquiry into my daughter's abduction is now open."

"But that was a decade ago. Has not the time limit expired to try such a crime?"

"Elizabeth is of the royal house."

Lady Catherine's eyes went wild, increasing her struggle against her bonds.

"True, only a *distant* cousin, but still within the legal limits. Your house will be ruined, Catherine. Matlock will be fortunate if he retains his title." He leaned back in his chair. "His reach for power is over." He leaned down, looking her directly in the eye. "It is over. All over. The politics, protecting the smugglers, and"—his eyes narrowed—"treason. I am sorry, Darcy. I had hoped to keep that from you."

"Mr Darcy?" Winters opened the door. "A Colonel MacTiernan is at the door…with a contingent of armed guards." The loyal butler's curiosity increased on seeing Lady Catherine bound and gagged.

"Good, good. See them in, Winters." Darcy strode towards his man to assure him.

"Very good, sir." Winters exited, returning moments later with Colonel MacTiernan and a gathering of five red coats.

"MacTiernan," the duke addressed the officer, "thank you for coming so quickly."

"Of course. Is that…?" The man nodded towards Lady Catherine.

"Yes," Philip replied. "Lady Catherine de Bourgh."

A cold gleam filled the colonel's eyes. With a wave of his hand, the soldiers claimed their prisoner.

Northampton looked at his feet. "Regardless of her guilt, she is an old woman and…"

"I shall see what may be done," MacTiernan assured him. "Although it is more than she or her kin deserve."

"Thank you, Mac. I am in your debt."

The officer nodded, and with Lady Catherine in the custody of his troops, he bowed to the duchess and to Darcy, then departed.

Darcy walked to the sideboard, pouring three glasses of brandy. Handing one to each of his relations, he claimed his own. Raising his glass, he shook his head, noting the duchess had drained hers and was holding it out for another.

eighteen

THE MERRY REUNION OF MARY AND HER BENNET COUSINS WAS interrupted by the return of the duke and duchess, accompanied by Darcy.

"Mother," Elizabeth said, rising to greet her parents. "I would like to—"

Her introductions were cut short by the evident distress of her relations.

"What is it?" she asked, her eyes scrutinising each in their turn.

Her father took hold of her hand, and taking his wife's arm, the quartet joined the rest of Elizabeth's party. Julian, taking stock of their demeanour, supported his mother to the sofa. He looked to Darcy for answers.

The duchess began. "We were at Darcy House when Lady Catherine arrived."

His father took up the story. "She has confessed to her part in your kidnapping, Elizabeth."

"No!" Elizabeth felt her knees weaken, but Darcy was there immediately, escorting her to a nearby loveseat.

Jane, Bingley, and Mary exchanged worried glances but held their tongues.

"What happened?" Julian asked, his agitation apparent in his voice.

"She is in custody," Darcy said.

"And will likely be sent to Bedlam, post haste," the duke added.

The duchess turned to address her daughter. "Until this day, I had believed that only Newgate or the gallows befitted that woman, but she is mad."

"Most likely has always been so," the duke said. "Forgive me, Elizabeth, but I agree with your mother."

"Why would you seek my pardon?" Elizabeth asked. Her parents looked at each other, trying to explain their reasoning.

"Our parents have, all these years, sought justice for the crime committed against you." Julian offered.

"Is not Bedlam punishment enough?" Elizabeth asked with surprise. "If she is ill, then it makes the most sense." She turned then, moving away from the conversation and hoping they would see her need to digest the extraordinary circumstances laid before her.

The duchess turned to Jane. "And who do we have here?"

Jane blushed. "Forgive me, Your Grace. May I present my cousin Miss Mary Bennet, soon to be Mrs Michael Waverly."

"A pleasure, Miss Bennet. My daughter"—here, the duchess cast a concerned glance at Elizabeth, who had retreated to a corner of the room—"has shared some of your wonderful adventures."

Elizabeth looked back on the gathering, a smile breaking through the tension, and the room relaxed. Returning to sit next to her mother and Jane, Elizabeth allowed them to carry the conversation as she surveyed those surrounding her.

They are concerned for me. How shall I respond to this latest bit of news? Catty is gone.

She sighed, her arms involuntarily coming to hug herself, and she settled deeper into the cushions. "I can scarce believe it." Her whisper was heard, but her companions steeled themselves not to respond nor draw too much attention to her.

Feeling Darcy's eyes upon her, Elizabeth looked up. She smiled at him, and to her relief, he smiled back. Nodding to him, she reached for the tea her mother had called for, and for the rest of the afternoon, as if by silent agreement, their conversation remained light, focusing on nothing more challenging than the shopping expeditions planned for the next week and the final fittings of Elizabeth's gown for the forthcoming gala.

CAROLINE PRANCED about her chambers in Mayfair, pure satisfaction filling her pinched heart as she held her invitation to the Northamptons' ball. *I shall open the evening with Mr Darcy, of course. And then, perhaps, allowing him to dance with his cousin, the marquess will come to me and ask for the second...*

A notion that the marquess would ask his mother to dance crossed her mind, but she dismissed it.

Her mind drifted to the brief introduction she had enjoyed one evening a year prior before Charles's grand error and Mr Darcy's unexplained absence. But soon her mind tired of thought, and Caroline sat in a chair in front of her mirror, examining her face and the facial expressions she had honed to perfection. A delicious thought crossed her mind. *How I shall enjoy the looks of Lady Chatterlawn and Miss Heatherton. I hope their gowns coordinate with the colour green, for thus they will be with envy!* The thought of gowns drew a shriek as Caroline realised there was no time to procure a new one.

Dashing to her closet, she tore open the doors, her eyes scanning the gowns hanging there. *Perhaps the past few weeks have not been so harsh, indeed. Half of these have not seen the light of day since they arrived.* Caroline rang for her maid and spent the rest of the afternoon selecting the perfect gown to mark her grand re-entry into society.

Longbourn, Hertfordshire

THOMAS BENNET LOOKED out the window of the room that had been his refuge for years—and now even more so since his two favourite nieces had left his care. Lying across his desk was a packet of letters from his brother's brother-in-law, Admiral Raleigh, informing him of Elizabeth's reunion with her true family. *Oh, Edwin,* he sighed, thinking of the devotion his brother had for the little girl who had captured both their hearts. *She is home with her own, and happiness is in her grasp.* Tears welled in his eyes as his mind cascaded through the years of her impish grins and turn of phrase or the expression of her emotions through those riveting eyes. *I miss you, Lizzy. I always knew you were special, Lady Elizabeth, and now the world shall know the same.*

Thomas Bennet sat contentedly, thinking of the dazzling splash Elizabeth—no, Lady Elizabeth—would make. *Oh, how Franny will sputter and quake when she hears of it.* But this notion stilled Mr Bennet's rumination as images came to mind of Franny's treatment of Elizabeth over the years.

If I tell her now, that will give her time to twist this into a perceived advantage. She might even... Bennet's quick mind thought of her grasping nature and his three daughters. *She might interfere with Mary's...*

He turned to the parchment once again. *Better to tell her that business dictates we hasten our journey to town.* Thomas Bennet drained his glass of port then rose to face what was left of his family.

LATER THAT NIGHT, Wickham made his way from the Windham town house after a rather pleasant interlude with his latest conquest. *Ah yes, when I make Lady Catherine aware of her daughter's condition, I shall use the fortune Darcy denied me to set up Miss Windham to my liking.* As he was about to mount his horse, the appearance of two able-bodied men halted his progress.

"Wickham," the first said, his Irish brogue unmistakable.

"Yes?"

"Lord Delaboix is anxious for a meeting," said the second, his Scottish brogue a clever way of distinguishing the two.

"Delaboix?" Wickham gulped.

"Aye, laddie. And the man is in no humour to tarry."

"Right then—I shall mount and meet him anon."

"Ah, no," said the Irishman, taking control of the reins while his companion took Wickham by the arm into a waiting carriage. Pushing Wickham in, both men entered the coach and slid a deadbolt across the door. With a knock on the roof, the vehicle took off at a hurried pace.

"What necessitates a call at this hour?"

His companions maintained their stony silence. After twenty minutes of the same, the carriage came to a stop. With no chance of escape, Wickham exited the coach. Silently, they entered a warehouse, Wickham noticing its unnerving proximity to the Thames.

Inside, the cavernous room was lit sparingly, allowing great swaths of shadow. As they walked through the room, Wickham noted his companions were joined by others, all of whom formed a semicircle with him at the midpoint. From above, an iron chandelier cast a circle of light surrounded by a sea of shadow. Lord Delaboix stepped to its edge, a cigar in his hand. "Wickham," he began, taking a long puff, the lit end flaming red against the background of darkness.

"Lord Delaboix, sir," Wickham replied, having the good sense to drop all pretence.

"How good of you to join me this evening."

Wickham tugged at his cravat and nodded.

"It seems the time has come for you to account…for your sins." A fleck of ash fell to the floor. Turning to Wickham, Delaboix advanced. "I believe fifteen thousand is what your pound of flesh is worth these days."

Wickham gulped. "If you could but wait, sir, I am in line for a sizeable windfall."

"Really?" The cigar end flared again.

"Yes. I um…I am in possession of information that a certain family will be well pleased to keep quiet."

"Which family?"

"Matlock." Wickham was confused by the snorts of derision behind him.

"Matlock would be concerned were he not so near death's door himself!" Delaboix turned on Wickham, his anger palpable. Wickham's hope fell.

"What?" Wickham felt his heart constrict. "Then Lady Catherine will—"

"I am sure Lady Catherine would be interested in the information"—Delaboix regained his calm as he circled Wickham, who felt the beads of sweat trickle down his spine—"if she were not on her way to Bedlam."

"Bedlam?" Wickham gulped as desperation bubbled in his blood.

"Yes. It seems there was a confrontation at Darcy House only hours ago." Wickham turned to keep his eyes on Delaboix. "After which the grand lady was seen being escorted away. A few coins changed hands, and her destination was revealed. Bedlam. It is certain."

"Braddleton?" Even to his own ears, Wickham's pleas sounded feeble.

"Is dead."

"Dead?" Wickham's brow now felt warm and clammy simultaneously.

"Not by *my* doing," Delaboix said, disappointment ringing in his voice. "Catervaux."

Wickham gulped—again. Delaboix continued. "So it seems your resources have evaporated."

"My duties...I have not been able—"

"The time for excuses is gone. You have outlived your usefulness to me. If you were trustworthy, I could have found occupation for you, but you are too much a rogue. Pity you were not more willing to follow directions, Wickham. And for that..."

He walked out of the light, the red tip of his cigar the only indication of his course.

When a door slammed at the end of the cavernous room, Wickham knew his life was drawing to a close. He felt only the first thirty blows before his body collapsed and consciousness seeped out of his body along with his blood. As from a great distance, he heard a splash and felt the water's embrace. There was a moment of struggle, then nothing.

THE DUKE OF NORTHAMPTON and his son were shown into the study where they found Darcy staring into space. As they approached the desk, he stirred and looked at them as if they had appeared out of thin air.

He greeted them without emotion. "Uncle, Julian."

"Sorry for your loss. I know Braddleton was—"

Darcy raised his hand to silence his relations. "They were not what I thought. I know that now." Turning, Darcy addressed them directly. "I am relieved they can no longer harm me or Elizabeth. In any case, to what do I owe this call?"

"Your aunt wishes to know whether you would like us to postpone the ball," said the duke.

In truth, I would like to cancel it. Darcy grimaced. "No, I think it best to carry on. Do you not agree?"

"Very well, then," the duke said. "How is Matlock?"

Darcy shrugged. "His doctors do not hold out much hope for a recovery that resembles anything near his former life."

"Unfortunate." The other two gentlemen nodded, rising to take their leave. "Shall we see you tomorrow?"

"You may depend upon it."

And with that, Darcy was left alone to sort through the disorder left by his family.

An overburdened carriage turned the corner onto Gracechurch Street, and within minutes its door opened and a tired looking gentleman emerged. Looking with resignation upon the well-kept façade of the building, Mr Bennet turned and handed out his wife, Frances, and his youngest daughters, Catherine and Lydia. The girls almost ran up the stairs to the now-opened front door. There stood the lady of the house, her hands clasped at her waist. By her side stood her husband, Mr Gardiner, who took in the chaos advancing towards him.

"Brother, how good of you to invite us," Frances Bennet said, appraising the tidy flower boxes on each of the front windows.

"Frances," Mrs Gardiner said. "Come, you must be tired from the journey."

"Oh, the roads, they were miserable what with all the rain the other day. Dreadful, simply dreadful. I was telling the girls I had not seen such conditions since I was a youth myself."

As Mrs Gardiner led her sister indoors, Edward Gardiner waited for Thomas Bennet to finish instructing his coachman and head towards the stairs. He stretched out his hand. "Come, Thomas, I have just the thing waiting in my study."

With a raised brow, Mr Bennet smiled at his brother. "Lead on."

AT ANOTHER HOME, miles away from Darcy House, Anne de Bourgh looked out of her window. *It has been weeks since he has come.* Anne de Bourgh pulled away from her watch and sighed.

"What a waste. I shall have to procure more laudanum. Everyone says I am looking so much better."

I suppose it is for the best. In a matter of weeks, I shall be wed, and Darcy is not fond of my Wickham.

She pulled on the silk ribbon fastening her chiffon robe. *I wonder whether I can convince him to keep separate residences. He is not excessively enamoured of Rosings. I could keep Wickham there, Darcy could keep that Bennet chit for his pleasure, and all will be well.*

Taking one last look out the window, Anne blew out the lone candle and slipped between her silk sheets.

ELIZABETH TOOK a last sip from the wine her mother had left with her. *Such a week!* Rising, she went to her sketchbook, and taking hold of her stylus, she drew. As she had since she was a little girl, Elizabeth allowed her inner self to reveal the workings of her heart and mind in the nearly unconscious drawings.

She began by sketching the lines of the trees of Pemberley near the spot where it had all begun. Her pencil drew as her mind revisited different points in her life: being lifted off the ground by two strange men, seeing Lady Catherine in the carriage, hearing the sound of the riding crop slice the air, the dark and the cold once they were through with her. She wept as her mind travelled through the years of Franny Bennet's verbal abuse, and her fear that no man would want her— could ever love her.

These last thoughts turned to Darcy, and thoughts of him stopped her tears. Her mind stilled, and her heart calmed. She took up her stylus and pencil and continued with her drawing, allowing his eyes and his recent expressions of love to soothe her.

An hour after she had begun, Elizabeth looked at the drawing she had produced. There on the page was a portrait of Lady Catherine de Bourgh, but in *this* drawing, her eyes were full of fear.

RICHARD PUSHED AWAY from his late father's desk. *Who knew so much work was involved in carrying the title? If I had known, I would not have wasted so much time envying my brother.*

"Bills, bills! All of them!" Richard Fitzwilliam, the newly raised Earl of Matlock, grabbed his brandy, draining it in one gulp. "How did Father do it?" He ran his free hand through his sandy curls and again glanced at the open ledger. "Every time it seems we are beyond the pale, he receives an infusion of cash with no record of whence it came —or how to duplicate it!"

Unceremoniously, the study door opened, and three men were shown in by Dorset. Standing at attention, Richard felt for the sword no longer at his side. The shortest of the men—flanked by two large and, Richard thought, insensible men—began.

"Pardon us, Lord Matlock. May I?" The man indicated the chair.

Richard nodded, waiting until his unexpected guest sat.

"My sincere condolences on the recent loss of your brother and father."

"You know?"

The man smiled, his lips recognisable as a sneer. "Best to say we are…were…business associates of a particular nature."

Richard snorted. "Then you were no friend. Neither my father nor my brother had a head for business."

"Alas, that is true." The man steepled his fingers, looking at his host. "Unfortunately, due to the nature of the association, I feel unable to continue the relationship."

Richard thought of the mysterious source of funds sitting before him. "Why not?"

"I am well aware of your skills on the field of battle. In fact, I am aware of the entirety of your particular skill set. And"—he gestured towards the men flanking him—"I have no need for more…soldiers."

"What exactly, sir—if you do not mind my asking—were the skills my father and brother brought to your association?"

"Your father, for all his other qualities was a consummate politician."

"And my brother?"

The man lifted his hand in the air. "Matlock's apprentice."

"And would I not become that?"

"Your father's alliances and influence fade away with him. You are an unknown quantity, and I need a veteran of the political field of battle, Colonel. I am sorry, but that, as they say, is business. Nothing personal, you understand."

"Of course." Richard's mind scrambled as that mysterious well of revenue closed to him. The man rose to leave.

Before he reached the door, the still-unknown guest turned. "If you are short of funds—which, knowing the habits of your father and brother, I am most certain you are or will be—you may turn to the House of de Bourgh for succour."

"Rosings?"

"Yes." There was a sly leer on the man's face. "I understand that one of the ladies is in a delicate condition, and the root of that undesirable event is...*inaccessible* to make amends. And with the lady of the house away, you should go and condole with the young Miss de Bourgh."

Richard stumbled backwards at this disclosure. The man smirked and turned back to the door.

"Sir?" Richard asked, his voice strained.

The man turned. "Yes, Colonel?"

"To whom have I had the pleasure of speaking?"

The man chuckled. "Delaboix."

As the door closed, Richard fell into the nearest chair. Recognising the notorious name, he found his legs were no longer able to support him.

nineteen

ELIZABETH SAT IN HER DRESSING CHAMBER, CORSET AND PETTICOATS all in place, her fingers gently touching the pearl pins her mother had sent for her to wear 'as a special request.' She smiled, thinking how lovely it was to have a mother who made special requests of her, requests that existed only for her benefit. It had taken Markum some time to readjust her hair, making room between the fragrant golden roses received earlier from Darcy's greenhouse. After what felt like hours, she had sent her maid away, needing a moment to collect her equanimity before her presentation to the best families of English society.

"Lizzy of Longbourn?" she asked her reflection. "Is that really you?" She touched her cheek, feeling the flush of excitement. So much had happened in such a short time…London, her newly discovered family…and then Darcy.

Leaning her elbows on the dressing table, she allowed her mind to wander to the flowers he had sent, blossoms pinned in her hair along with her mother's pearls. Her mind then turned to the glances he sent her way, the gentleness in his hands as he took hers to hold, and all their conversations, whether at Pemberley, at Darcy House, or here at Northampton Place.

"He has changed," she said, wondering what these changes would bring. "I have changed, and I—" She sat up, no longer dreaming.

"I shall not release him from his"—she gave a sly smile —"obligations."

DINNER AT RIDGEDALE, the Matlock town house, was a dismal affair. The recently elevated earl and his even more recently created countess faced each other across the long, dimly lit table. *What does one say to such a hastily gained wife?* Richard wondered.

He fell back on *ton* gossip as an easy subject. "The Duke of Northampton is hosting a ball for his daughter this evening."

The lady of the house froze with her soup spoon midway from her bowl to her mouth. "Where did you hear that, husband?"

"One hears things, Anne," he said, continuing to enjoy his soup.

His new wife lifted the spoon to her lips. As the liquid filled her mouth, she choked as if a new thought had entered her head. "You must have heard it from the lips of your mistress between her screams of pleasure."

Stunned by her outburst, Richard could only say, "Of one thing I am certain—the duchess would never send an invitation to this house. For Darcy's sake, I do wish we could go."

"Why would you cross that family's threshold?" Anne sneered. "After what they have done to our family."

Richard clenched his jaw. "Because, wife, my estate is in tatters, and I need Darcy's aid."

"His purse, no doubt." She wiped her lips with her napkin. "Then let us go. While you are bowing and scraping to Darcy—"

His nostrils flared.

"—I shall do as I must to begin Matlock's restoration."

Richard stared warily at his wife. "It would be wholly improper for us to go. Besides being uninvited, we are in mourning."

"Mourning? We had a wedding did we not?" Anne reached over and tore off her husband's black armband. "I am going with or without you."

"You cannot!"

"I should very much like to see *you* stop me," she said, rising.

"Anne," he warned, as she left to dress, leaving him to mull the wisdom of his hasty decision to wed for the sake of wealth and reputation.

ALEXANDRA ALLOWED her husband to hand her out of their shared bath. "Hurry, my love. It will not do to have the hosts for this evening's festivities arrive later than the guests."

"And let the gossip mongers conjecture on the cause?" he teased. "I believe it could only raise the interest in our son, coming from such good, strong, lasting stock." He puffed his chest becomingly.

With a raised brow she replied, "And of our daughter."

He slouched atop the tub rim. "Alex, is she ready?" She turned to him. "I mean are we being fair to her—foisting our society upon her?"

Fear curled around the duchess's heart. "What do you suggest? That we farm her out to one of our estates like some bastard child?" She stood Darcy-proud.

"No, no, my love, never that." He came and, taking hold of her arms, calmed her. "I only wonder whether this"—he looked around—"is all too much, too soon. Next year—"

"You know why we chose to act."

"But now the threat is over."

She wrapped her arms about him. "It is done. Elizabeth is our daughter, and tonight all of society will know her face. She will no longer be subject to the rumours that have plagued her until now."

"The attention will only increase. And as for the rumours…"

"Those who spread their malicious lies will at least know they attack the house of Northampton and not some poor young woman who was ripped from her family."

Philip brought his brow to hers. "As always, my love, you are right. Come. Let us dress that we may see Lady Elizabeth. Do you think she will like your mother's pearls?"

"She *is* part Darcy, darling."

"And Darcys always admire quality."

Feeling that her husband's impertinent lips needed silencing, Alexandra used her own to do just that.

ELIZABETH SMOOTHED her hands over the champagne silk of her gown, disbelieving that the young lady reflected back had climbed trees in the orchards of Longbourn and skipped stones across Noah's Puddle. Swirling to the right then left, she smiled to see her skirts floating about her.

Now, all I need is my prince. She thought of Darcy and of all the women who would crowd around him, releasing the fears she had corralled to a corner of her mind. "Who will he partner for the first and second?"

Old doubt and fear clouded her mind, and again she wondered why he had chosen to back away from their arrangement and whether another incentive had induced him to release her from their engagement. "He says he wants me, but...now that he is free, will he seek another?"

Seeing her stricken visage in the mirror, Elizabeth straightened, courage and determination rising as she looked herself directly in the eye. "I am Lady Elizabeth Aubrey Rose Elliston. I have survived—defeated Lady Catherine and Frances Bennet. I was loved by Edwin and Gloria Bennet, and I am loved by my mother, father, and brother. I have the world open before me. I may not know my place in it, but I know who I am. I am a good person—a strong woman with a modicum of wit. And I shall win him back no matter who else he dances with."

As remnants of doubt from her years with Frances Bennet pushed against her confidence, she pushed back. She was still Elizabeth Bennet—survivor. And she was determined to thrive.

MARY SMOOTHED HER GOWN, gazing at her reflection. "Can this truly be me?" For the first time in her young life, she saw a glimmer of her mother's beauty, and she smiled. "I shall be a beautiful bride!" With wonder and a surge of assurance, she reached for the earbobs her beloved had gifted her before she left Longbourn.

"I may not be the belle of the ball, but I shall not disgrace Lizzy."

Mary giggled and headed to meet Jane and Charles and the thrill of the night.

ACROSS TOWN, the bustle of four adults and two boisterous young ladies completed the preparations for their evening. "I do not understand why all this secrecy is necessary, Mr Bennet," Mrs Bennet exclaimed. "I swear my brother becomes more and more peculiar."

"Be that as it may, my dear"—Mr Bennet placed his hands on her shoulders—"shall we not simply enjoy the evening and all the surprises it may hold in store?" He looked at her in that particular way that, at one time, would have sent her heart aflutter.

Two rooms away, Catherine and Lydia scuffled for the remaining hairpins. Although her uncle had told them they were too young for London society, they still had hopes of working their wiles on him to change his mind.

twenty

THE NIGHT WAS ABLAZE WITH FASHION AND FLOWERS. NORTHAMPTON Place was polished, and it shone like the jewel it was. The air was heady with the scent of gardenia, Elizabeth's favourite flower. Silk and satin rustled in every petticoat and waistcoat while jewels glistened on every neck, ear, and finger. The men were handsome, the women beautiful, and the room was awash in the twittering chatter of individuals hoping to spot Lady Elizabeth and see whether or not she would live up to her extraordinary reputation.

Darcy was pleased to see Mr and Mrs Gardiner among the arriving guests. "How good of you to come," he said, extending his hand to his new acquaintances.

Once the Bennets and Gardiners had made their way into the crowded hall, Julian welcomed the gentlemen behind them. "Ah, Withersby, Clarington, how good to see you." Darcy noticed Julian giving him a sidelong glance as he spoke to them. "I hope you have brought your dancing shoes as I have asked Lady Elizabeth to reserve a set for each of you."

Surprise apparent on their faces, both men turned to their friend, looking very pleased with their situation. "Thank you, Glascomb, exceedingly good of you."

To Darcy he whispered, "Surely you do not mind, old man? I mean, you have made your wishes known, have you not?"

Darcy favoured him with a glare that could have frozen Dante's inferno, but Julian, having received more than one dose of that particular scowl in his life, simply smirked and turned to greet the newest arrival.

"Miss Bingley?" Julian gulped. "How good of you to come."

"Thank you, Lord Glascomb. I am so pleased to be here," she simpered. Turning her beady eyes upon Darcy, she lurched towards him, extending her hand. "Mr Darcy, it has been an age, has it not?"

"Indeed." He bowed stiffly. "I hope you have a pleasant evening."

Miss Bingley lingered, no doubt hoping that one of the two men would ask for a set, but at length was forced to move on. "I hope to speak with you at greater length before the evening is out, sir," she said, bobbing a slight curtsey.

Not ten minutes later, the grand doors of Northampton Place were opened again, and another announcement was made. Although no one who truly cared took note, the evening was enhanced by the addition of the newly wed Richard and Anne Fitzwilliam, Lord and Lady Matlock.

UPSTAIRS, Elizabeth was—with the fine coaching of her mother, Mrs Raleigh, and Jane—taking deep breaths to marshal her courage. Georgiana, who was staying at Northampton Place for the night, had convinced her to sneak down a back stair earlier to peek at the gathering commotion. The enormity of what lay in store suddenly threatened to overwhelm her even as she held on to her courage, reminding herself she had survived far greater than this.

Her father entered the parlour with a glass of brandy and, ignoring the raised brows of all save the admiral, offered it to his daughter to taste.

"Just a sip or two."

Elizabeth took the drink and smelled it. "Are you certain?"

The duke laughed then kissed her brow. "Yes, my angel."

Hesitating but a moment, Elizabeth took a healthy sip, her cough threatening to retrieve what she tried to keep down. Her father held her hand, squeezing it tightly, and her cough subsided. "One more, Elizabeth, then that will do."

Looking at her mother, who reluctantly nodded, Elizabeth took another sip, and then handed the glass off to Jane. Elizabeth's eyes opened wide as she spied her always-proper sister take a gulp of the spirits.

IN THE FAMILY PARLOUR, the Duke of Northampton lifted his glass of champagne, and he was joined by the family and friends who had made this night possible. "Thank you all for coming," he said, struggling to keep his emotions in check. "Alexandra and I had nearly given up hope that this evening would ever be."

He looked at his wife and then his daughter. "But you, Elizabeth, are here with us and are well loved by us all. To you, my dear. Live long, love well, and shine bright. I give you Lady Elizabeth!"

"To Lady Elizabeth," was said all around, and as each drank heartily to her success, the lady herself felt her emotions shudder on the edge of her control. When she was mistress of herself once more, she looked around and immediately found the dark eyes of Fitzwilliam Darcy upon her, eyes pouring love and tenderness into her. Suddenly, she felt she could conquer the world.

ONLY A FEW FEET FROM HER, Darcy drank deeply from the glass, grateful for its cool presence in his hand. He tried desperately to control the visceral response that seeing her created. *How shall I ever survive this night? Every man in London will want her.*

Darcy tried to keep his eyes from her but failed utterly. He tried to observe his family, to taste of their happiness, but he could not. His eyes drank her in without reserve until she turned her head and caught him. Instantly, her cheeks flushed, her lids lowered, and she smiled.

Darcy froze, his eyes locked on her—calling, begging her to look up. Seeing her head lift to meet his gaze, his heart sputtered into a staccato, and joy spread from his heart to lift his lips and fill his eyes.

All too soon, it was time to attend to their guests, and each family member in their turn came and kissed Elizabeth on her cheek. Darcy steeled himself not to give or take too much.

"Good night, brother." Georgiana smiled impishly. "Bonne chance," she whispered, kissing his cheek and squeezing his hand. "I wish to hear all tomorrow."

"Elizabeth," Darcy said in a hush. "You are radiant."

"Thank you."

Bending to give his kiss, Darcy's lips touched her cheek, his heart leaping at Elizabeth's gasp. "Elizabeth."

"Well then," the duke said, and Darcy pulled back. "Shall we?"

Offering his arm to Elizabeth, Darcy was startled when Julian came between them. Taking his sister's arm himself, Julian smiled with satisfaction and escorted his sister into the fray.

THE RAP OF A GRAND STAFF, a remnant of medieval processions, cut the din of the crowd to an abrupt hush. Darcy, the Bingleys, and the Raleighs slipped down the stairs to positions in the front of the crowd.

Darcy's anxiety was high. Not only were the doyennes of the *ton* present but every eligible bachelor as well. He scanned the crowd, and his heart beat erratically as gentlemen of both good and poor character eagerly gathered.

"Thank you, Hutchins," His Grace said in a low voice.

The duke turned towards his guests, and the proud butler announced, "Ladies and gentlemen, Julian Elliston, the Marquess of Glascomb and his parents, Philip and Alexandra Elliston, the Duke and Duchess of Northampton."

All eyes focused on the elegant family as they descended the stairs, the duchess between her husband and son. None could doubt the pride and joy spilling from them all as the duke, thanking his long-time ombudsman, addressed the crowd.

"Ladies and gentlemen, friends and family, we are so very pleased and honoured you have graced us with your presence here tonight. Our history has not always been a happy one, but tonight, the past is put to rest. We are proud to introduce to you, our daughter, the Lady Elizabeth Aubrey Rose Elliston."

Every neck craned for a better view of the ravishing beauty

descending the stairs. A communal gasp swept the room as those fortunate enough to catch a first glimpse marvelled at her poise and perfection. Due to the extensive rooms and crush of people, not all were so blessed, but those that were, twittered at the quality of her skin, the style of her hair, the pearls about her neck, and her illuminating smile that gave her presence an aura and the glow of being loved. The men mused on settings that were more intimate while the women conceded that she would be a force to reckon with and emulate.

Miss Bingley, who had been hunting for Mr Darcy at the back of the great hall, scanned the sidelines he favoured during social engagements. As the roar of chatter reached her, she clenched her teeth and eyes, offering a rare prayer that it was due to some hideous deformity of the prodigal child.

As the musicians sounded their clarion call, the duke claimed his daughter for the first set. With the duchess and Julian making up the second pair, Elizabeth used the moment to take in her environs. Her lips spread in a wide and amazed smile as she looked up into the eyes of her father, beaming at her. *I am here with my family.* Feeling her heart as light as it had ever felt, Elizabeth began the first steps of the dance.

Involuntarily, her eyes sought Darcy as she was curious about whom he would partner for the first. To her surprise, he did not dance; rather, he was looking at her, eyes filled with such longing that Elizabeth nearly stepped wrongly. Her father noticed this, as well as the direction of her gaze, and seemed to repress a chuckle.

The two dances went by in a trice, and soon her brother was at her side. "Elizabeth? I believe the next set is ours?"

Nodding, the lady of the hour took up her handsome brother's hand and once again regained the floor. She watched as Darcy approached Jane, escorting her to the floor moments later.

Frances Bennet's shriek was fortunately overpowered by the din of the crowd and the music initiating the dancing portion of the evening. Her husband, well aware of the nature of the celebration and their inclusion, handed her a waiting glass of champagne. Leaning towards her, he whispered, "Calm yourself, my dear."

She looked at him as if he were mad.

He took hold of her arm and squeezed, gaining her attention. "Yes, Mrs Bennet, it is Lizzy."

"But how can this be? She is—"

"Returned to her rightful place," Mr Bennet said with a forceful look. Seeing the envy festering in his wife's eyes, he shuffled her to a vacant balcony.

"Mrs Bennet," he said coldly, "this unreasonable stance has continued far too long. Say even one word that might embarrass Lady Elizabeth, and I shall have you packing back to Hertfordshire so fast your head will swim."

His eyes held hers, pinning them as she searched his for a sign of weakness—any sign, like a caged animal testing the strength of its bars.

"But this is impossible," Mrs Bennet protested weakly.

"The duke and duchess lost their young child, and my brother was blessed to find her," Mr Bennet began. "She has brought our family nothing but joy and good sense, befriending our silly daughters while you have done nothing but create misery for her. You should fall on your knees to the Lord above that she is merciful."

Mrs Bennet cringed, knowing the power and influence of the Northampton name.

"One word from her would mean ruination for our daughters, our family, and your brother's family."

"I understand."

Searching for the truth in her eyes, Mr Bennet relinquished his grip on her hand. "Very well then. Would you care to dance, madam?"

Mrs Bennet could only stand mute, so great was her surprise. As his eyes questioned, she nodded. When the music called the next round of dancers to the fore, Jane, Charles, Mary, and Elizabeth all experienced shock at seeing the restrained Mr Bennet dancing with his equally surprised wife.

THE MATLOCKS KEPT smiles on their faces, but the strain of the last few weeks showed in their eyes. They finally found Darcy, and they were moving towards him when Julian noticed and quickly made his way to his father.

Catching Julian's response, Richard hurried Anne towards Darcy, who tracked them with his steely gaze. Anne, however, brightened, and the mooncalf look she sent Darcy turned his stomach.

Despite the desire to flee, Darcy continued towards them. "What on earth possessed you to come to Northampton Place, tonight of all nights?"

"To show there are no hard feelings."

Darcy blanched, seriously doubting his cousin's sanity. "I am afraid there *are* hard feelings, Richard, and your uninvited appearance tonight shall do nothing to dissipate them."

"Darcy." Anne took his arm and rubbed herself against it.

Repulsed, Darcy shivered at the covetous, carnal delight in her eyes. "Anne, restrain yourself."

"I would rather restrain you, Fitz," she whispered in a low voice. "Throughout the night…"

Darcy's disgust made him flush, and he unceremoniously removed her hand from his arm.

"Lord Matlock." The duke's voice cut through their stilted conversation.

"Your Grace." The younger man bowed. "As the new head of the family, I would like to make peace. May I introduce my new wife, Lady Matlock."

All eyes turned in shock as the countess's gaze freely embraced the bounty of handsome men in her proximity. "A pleasure." She curtseyed, pushing her developing assets forward.

Darcy looked at Richard, who looked away, barely masking his indifference and disgust.

"Be that as it may," the duke continued, "this is a private affair and, considering the part your family—"

"Our family," Lady Matlock interrupted imperiously, "has every right to be here. Darcy is here, and we are his closest relations. As such, we shall be here too."

The duke looked at Darcy, who was more deeply mortified than ever before. A crowd had begun to gather and whisper, eager to observe the latest scandal.

The duke straightened his spine and stepped closer. "If you two have not the decency to stay away from where you are most decidedly not welcome, so be it. But I promise you, the perfidy of your family shall be known."

"You would not dare." Lady Matlock stepped forward and swayed, crumpling to the floor.

There was a cry for water and air as the newly elevated earl scooped her up "She is unwell."

Julian muttered, "Undoubtedly," coming forward to watch the Matlocks being led to a small anteroom. Not wishing to create a greater stir, Darcy followed to stand guard against prying eyes. Not five minutes later, the duchess, Mrs Raleigh, Jane, and Elizabeth came hurrying towards him.

"Darcy," his aunt began. "Is it true?"

Darcy looked like a deer caught in the sights of a hunter's bow. "Is what true?"

"That Lady Matlock lies on my couch in that room?"

He nodded, and Elizabeth struggled to keep from laughing.

"Has she no shame?" the duchess demanded.

"Apparently not," Darcy agreed.

"Well, there is nothing to be done about it now. Ladies, into the breach." Alexandra Elliston, the Duchess of Northampton, led her contingent to attend the daughter of her worst enemy. Before Elizabeth could enter, Darcy took her hand, eyes pleading.

"Fitzwilliam?" she asked gently.

"Elizabeth"—he looked up at her—"Lady Elizabeth, I—" He paused to gather his courage. Hanging his head, Darcy's head snapped up as she took hold of his hand.

"My years with the Bennets taught me that one is helpless to choose one's relations, Fitzwilliam."

Darcy placed his free hand atop of hers as she continued. "They are your blood, but they are not you."

He nodded.

"You are an honourable man." He smiled, and she continued, her eyes sparkling with a tease. "Not a perfect man, but then again, I am not a perfect woman."

About to speak, Darcy scowled as Mrs Raleigh's head emerged from the room. "Elizabeth, your mother awaits."

Resigned to another separation, Darcy brought her hand to his lips then let go, taking courage from her gentle blush. As the door closed, Darcy turned and, crossing his arms over his chest, tried to school his features into a disconcerting scowl, but it was a ruse. His heart was too full of hope.

WHEN THE DOCTOR ARRIVED, the ladies left the room after being assured that all that could be done would be done for the Matlocks. Darcy, the admiral, Charles Bingley, and both Elliston men waited, curious at the ladies' grins.

"Well,"—the duchess rubbed her hands together in glee—"it seems that Lady Matlock is in a delicate condition."

"What?" Darcy asked. "They cannot be married but a week."

"Three at the most!"

A steady silence followed as all pondered the goings-on at Rosings Park. Darcy's shock showed on his face. He looked at his aunt, her eyes sparkling.

"The lady spoke as she rose from her delirium."

"And...?" The duke's impatience grew.

"And the name she calls is Wickham's!"

twenty-one

DARCY'S PATIENCE WAS FRAYED TILL HE COULD CLAIM ELIZABETH FOR the supper set. Julian made sure to introduce her to every eligible bachelor while he stood at her side. Darcy's mood darkened with jealousy.

"There you are, Mr Darcy."

"Miss Bingley." He pulled himself from his souring mood. "Good evening. I trust you are well?"

"Yes, I am, sir. Louisa, although invited, was unable to attend. My dear friend Lady Catterval was good enough to accompany me."

Darcy shuddered, learning that the most notorious society gossip was in attendance.

"How do you find your cousin, sir?"

"I beg your pardon?"

"It must be such a shock for the dear girl, being introduced to society at such an advanced age."

"Perhaps. However, El...Lady Elizabeth is extraordin—"

"Caroline!" Miss Herrington called out, hoping to engage Mr Darcy, but before their tête-à-tête could proceed any further, Darcy was surrounded by eager and accessible women. For the first time in his life, Darcy was relieved as it precluded any further private conversation with Miss Bingley.

AFTER WHAT FELT LIKE HOURS, Darcy claimed Elizabeth's hand for the first of their two dances.

"My lady," he bowed over her hand.

"Mr Darcy," she said as her heart began to race. Raising her eyes, she found his gaze locked on hers. Heat rose across her cheeks till he smiled and she was able to create some semblance of order in her mind.

With the first note, he took her hand, and she shook at the fiery response running up her arm. They turned towards each other, and their eyes held as they began to move. When the music brought them close, Elizabeth felt her breath leave her body, not sure it would return, nor sure she cared.

He smiled. "You are a great success, my lady."

"Thank you," she said quietly. "I am very pleased, indeed."

"You should be. You deserve to be celebrated." He added softly, "And so much more."

Unsure of what she was hearing, Elizabeth marvelled and wondered at the awkward nature of their conversation. "Perhaps it is best, then—"

"Pardon?" he asked.

"That…" She found she could not say the words.

"Elizabeth?"

"Our conversation has become strained again."

The dance separated them. Darcy watched as another man turned her about and she smiled sweetly. When she returned to him, his eyes grew stormy.

"You wish to smile and flirt with all the gentlemen clamouring for your acquaintance, *cousin*?"

She looked up, frowning at his rebuke. "Better to dance than stand about speaking to the chosen few."

"Forgive me. I do not wish to quarrel."

She nodded, and again the dance required her to take the arm of another. When she came back to him, he said, "It is hard enough to watch you dance with other men. I beg you, let me have this one dance where you smile at me—me alone."

To this, she smiled and nodded.

When their set was over and the music ceased, Julian was there immediately, leading her to the family table for supper.

"Julian," Elizabeth hissed. "Must you drag me off like that?"

He shrugged then laughed.

"Brothers," she said with an exaggerated sigh as she allowed him to lead her into the banquet hall.

CAROLINE HAD ENJOYED A BITTER SUPPER, seated two rooms from the host family. After the meal, she went in search of her brother, who was speaking with Miss Elizabeth Bennet. *How in God's creation did that thing come by an invitation? Surely her admiral could not have brought her!* Seeing familiar and celebrated personages looking at and twittering about her brother's cosy tête-à-tête, Caroline's fury detonated.

When Admiral Raleigh replaced Charles, Caroline followed her brother onto an unoccupied balcony, but before she could reach him, the Duchess of Northampton and Mrs Raleigh blocked her path.

"Miss Bingley?" the duchess intoned in her most imperious manner.

"Yes, Your Grace." Miss Bingley dipped deeply into a curtsey.

"I am impressed." The duchess took in her guest from head to toe as Miss Bingley brimmed with pride. "Do you know who this august woman is?"

Miss Bingley shot the unknown woman a glance. "No, Your Grace."

"This is the woman you slandered."

"I beg your pardon? I do not even know this person."

"And yet you insinuated that her husband"—the duchess inhaled —"was keeping a woman as his mistress."

"I never—"

"And yet you did. And it is a lie."

"I—"

"And"—Mrs Raleigh joined the fray—"the woman you accused, based on nothing, is…"

"…my daughter."

"No…" Miss Bingley shrank at the hateful look in her accusers' eyes.

"Miss Bingley"—the duchess stepped closer—"you have gone too far. Not only have you slandered a war hero but you also have impugned the house of Northampton. And as such, you are liable to face charges of treason."

"Treason…" Miss Bingley shuddered, her shoulders curling inward

"Lady Elizabeth is a member of the royal house, Miss Bingley," Mrs Raleigh stated.

"It is only—only!—because of the great love I hold for my dear, dear friends, Admiral and Mrs Raleigh, and their niece, Mrs Bingley, that I shall not inform my husband of your cruelty."

Miss Bingley shuddered in relief.

"But if I ever hear of your entering society again, you will leave me no choice."

"Entering society?" Miss Bingley gasped.

"How can I possibly allow anyone as undependable as you to pollute the society my daughter and I shall enjoy?"

Miss Bingley shook her head, seeing the crowd gathering behind the duchess already gossiping, sending her cruel and pitiless snarls. Looking to those who were once nearest and dearest to her, she recoiled. *Even Jane has turned against me.*

Shaking, Caroline walked through the throng without another word, embellishments of her humiliation already multiplying, closing the door of society to her forever.

ONCE THE THRILL of Caroline's departure faded, the ball resumed its rightful cadence, and Elizabeth danced with another of her brother's friends. After enduring three more dances, she wiped a curl from her brow. Feeling overheated, she sought an unoccupied balcony. Walking through the open doors and into the moonlight, she inhaled the jasmine-scented air.

One night, and I am already sick of the insincere flattery—too

many men and women either currying my favour or sharpening their knives to stab me in the back. She leaned against the balustrade.

Reviewing the past half hour's entertainment, Elizabeth smiled at the memory of her family standing with her, surrounding her with love and acceptance. Even there, sitting alone and in the dark, she felt their support and knew they would never abandon her. Jane and Charles, Aunt and Uncle Raleigh…Elizabeth's heart warmed. And Georgiana, Julian, Mama and Papa, and…Darcy…

As if her thoughts had summoned him, Fitzwilliam Darcy appeared at the open door. When the door latch clicked, she turned. With only a moment's hesitation, he stood before her. She rose, and he brushed his fingertips along her cheek.

"Elizabeth," he whispered as his lips gently met hers. They stood perfectly still, their lips barely touching, yet the connexion was made.

Eventually, she stepped back, eyes locked on his. They said not a word as they regarded each other from behind the barricades of their fear.

"I…I should go in," she whispered but did not move.

"Yes, no, please!" He put his hands on her arms. "Do not go," he said, his eyes pleading.

"There you are, Elizabeth." Julian opened the door, and seeing her companion, he stepped onto the portico, shutting the door behind him. "I say, this is cosy, is it not?

"Stand down, Darcy. And you, little miss, your next partner is searching for you."

Julian's tone was commanding. Elizabeth glared, but he held steady. "Lord Hillendale is waiting, and regardless of any feelings you may have for this oaf here, you promised to dance with my friend. Surely, you can bear such an indignity for your dear brother?"

His eyes sparkled in the moonlight, and Elizabeth relented. She looked up at Darcy, whose eyes had darkened, and smiled. Seeing her attention focused on him, he relented, allowing the smallest of smiles to bloom. He nodded, and she headed for the door.

Passing her brother, she slammed her right shoulder into his arm. "Brute!"

Julian chuckled, watching as she found Lord Hillendale. Taking a deep breath, he faced his cousin, who was staring back at him.

Holding his hand up to squelch Darcy's rejoinder, Julian again took the offensive. "Darcy, while I see you advance your cause, and while I have my doubts about that, it *is* Elizabeth's choice. You do realise this night is critical for her. I cannot stand by and let you impose yourself upon her time."

His hand rose again to forestall Darcy's defence. "Not tonight. Not when I remain unsure of your intent."

"Julian?" Darcy gasped. "Surely…"

"Surely what, Darcy? You insult her, launch a half-hearted wooing, at best"—he advanced with menace—"then withdraw, leaving her unsettled at a time when everything, *everything* is unsettled. You, who claim to love her, toy with her. Perhaps we were wrong and you are more *Fitzwilliam* than Darcy." He turned away.

Darcy was immobile, stunned at the outburst. "I…Julian, you cannot believe that of me."

"No? Why ever not?" He glared, unrelenting. "Your moods vary by the hour. Why would I support this for my sister? My—sister—only just returned to me. And you want me to endorse this kind of treatment of her?"

"Julian…I love her and…"

"Love? You call this love?" he scoffed.

"I want her to choose…to have the right, the experience of choosing. Of course I want her to choose me, but it must be *her* choice—not mine."

"So you confuse her with this half-hearted courtship?"

"I am not versed in the ways of romance, Julian. You know that. My abilities to communicate my heart's desires are ill conceived at best. And then, the catastrophe of my relations…" Sorrowful eyes looked at the marquess. "How can I truly ask her…and yet, how can I not?"

Julian, arms folded, looked at Darcy, images of him as a young lad, shy even with his family but loyal and honourable beyond question. "Speak with her. Resolve this…uncertainty." He looked out at the gardens. "She is unhappy…in this confusion. Be a man, Darcy. Decide your course, and lay it at her feet. You want her to choose? Then let her know her choices. Now? She vacillates between knowing your affection and doubting it. Rectify this. Now."

He turned and left Darcy dumbfounded and alone.

ELIZABETH WAS DANCING with yet another aristocratic rake while Darcy watched her graceful figure. Her bouncing curls enticed him from keeping her partner under surveillance. "Willoughby," he muttered. Turning, Elizabeth's eyes caught his, and his heart stuttered.

Recognising the question in her eyes, he shrugged and glared at John Willoughby. Before she turned in time to the dance, her eyes sparkled, and his discomfort melted. He stepped closer, positioning himself to receive her when the music ended.

"Lady Elizabeth, I can barely recall when a dance has given me such pleasure." Willoughby retained her hand as Darcy approached.

"Lady Elizabeth, a word if I may?"

Elizabeth smiled at Darcy's scowl and the shock of her former dance partner.

"Of course. I thank you for our dance, Mr Willoughby." She curtseyed to him.

"The pleasure was mine, one I hope to repeat often."

"Not if I have anything to say about it," Darcy mumbled as he led his fair cousin to the same balcony he had only recently fled.

Smiling while her heart raced, Elizabeth leaned her head towards him. "But will you, sir?"

"Pardon?"

"Will you have anything to say about it?"

Darcy stopped for a moment, turning to face her. Her breath caught, and hearing it, Darcy placed his hand on the small of her back to return them both to the deserted balcony. He turned, shut the glass doors, and gained her side in two steps.

"Elizabeth," he whispered. "I love you. I have loved you for so long now. I cannot imagine my life without you beside me."

"Then why say that you did not intend to pursue our engagement?"

"I am a vain creature—vain enough to want you to come to me on your own, not because your father and mine wished it." He clasped her hands in his. "I want you to want me…as I want you. You are the first thought—my only thought—from morning to beyond my last at night. The threat of losing you has given me not only the strength to acknowledge the man I was but the determination to be better—not only *for* you but *because* of you."

He kissed her hand, rubbing it against his cheek as he looked directly into her eyes. "You, more than any other, are my definition of dignity, integrity."

He slowly lowered her hand to his chest. "I have tried, Elizabeth, to be a better man—to face my failings like a man and return to the principles my parents tried to instil in me all those years ago. But mainly, I have tried to improve myself because the idea of living my life without you is impossible. I cannot. You are more essential to me than the beating of my heart. Your beauty attracts me, your wit enchants me, and your ire enflames my heart to burn brighter, stronger, and more open to life. I love you more than I ever imagined possible, and I want you to choose me because I am the man you love."

"I do love you. And I have for so long now. I can scarcely conceive of my life without you."

He smiled at her repeating his vow to her. "Will you…?" His voice was soft and tender, and he pulled her hands to his lips. "Will you marry me, Elizabeth? Will you be my wife to love forever? Please?"

"Yes, I shall."

His arms encircled her, and he heard her happiness in the sigh she breathed into him. "I love you," Elizabeth said into his chest. "I have loved you for so long now." She raised her eyes to his. "You have tested me and found my strength. You brought me to the brink of my fear and stood with me, allowing me to face it, as I must, while holding me safe. You gave me time to find myself in the midst of all this."

When Elizabeth licked her lips and swallowed, Darcy thought he would faint with desire.

"Your presence awakens my heart, and while it has taken me a while to accomplish, you have allowed me the time to find and test and trust my love for you."

She could say no more, for her beloved swept her into his arms and kissed her with the full force of his passion. Their bodies met, fully feeling the length and breadth of the other, and in a collective sigh, they relaxed, each knowing that all would be well. Nearly twenty minutes later, they returned through the French doors. Hearing the latch open, Julian turned his head, but when he saw the swollen lips of his sister, he turned full face, warning his father that the new lovers were rejoining the world.

"THERE YOU ARE, DARCY." The duke calmly extended his arm to his daughter, pulling her to his side. "I shall expect you by noon tomorrow, Darcy. Understood?"

"Understood, sir," Darcy said, unable to wipe the grin from his face. Seeing his smile, the duke looked at his daughter, whose lips had unmistakably been kissed—and thoroughly.

He gave her his best fatherly glare. "Yes, Papa?" Elizabeth asked innocently, and seeing her joy, the duke softened.

"You look very happy, my dear."

"I am, Papa. I am."

"Very well, then. Perhaps you wish to find your mother?"

Giving Darcy a quick glance and seeing his nod, she went in search of her mother, aunt, and sister.

As Darcy moved to find Bingley, Northampton stopped him. "A word—?"

Obediently, Darcy turned, and avoiding the smirk on his cousin's face, he returned to stand between the two men. "Yes, sir? Cousin?"

"All is well, then?" the duke asked.

"Aye, sir."

"And Elizabeth's tears?"

Darcy's retort died on his lips, seeing the true concern in his uncle and cousin. "I pledge I shall do my best, sir."

Julian clapped him on the back. "Well then, I believe I shall have a bit of explaining to do to my friends who expressed great interest in knowing Elizabeth better."

"Tell your friends I shall have my duelling pistols cleaned and at the ready."

"No doubt you will," added Julian. "No doubt at all."

twenty-two

THE NEXT MORNING WAS QUIET AS THE INHABITANTS OF THE GREAT house were still recuperating from the festivities that lasted until dawn.

Elizabeth met her parents as they emerged from the master's chambers just before noon. Alexandra reached out to her daughter. "How are you this morning?"

"Truly wonderful." She embraced them both. "I want to thank you again for such an incredible evening."

"I am glad you enjoyed yourself." The duke smiled. "Your feet managed to survive Livingston's assault?"

She returned his smile. "Indeed."

They made their way to break their fast. "Elizabeth, I have discussed with your mother your cousin's declaration, and we wish to hear your thoughts on the matter."

Elizabeth turned to her father "Now?" she gulped.

"Well, I did tell your ardent suitor to be here by noon. If I know one thing of young Darcy, it is his punctuality. He likely awaits us even now."

"Oh." Elizabeth stopped to prepare her reply. "Our relationship has not run an expected course, it is true, but he has changed—I have changed. We have both grown and now…" She lowered her head and voice. "Now my heart soars when he is near. Knowing he is in my life calms me when fear beckons."

She looked at her parents, and her father embraced her. Several minutes later, he reluctantly released her and then ushered her into their breakfast room.

Replacing his coffee cup on its saucer, Darcy rose quickly, his napkin sliding to the floor. Standing, Georgiana quelled her sudden desire to giggle at his look of anticipation.

"Elizabeth," he said in a low tone as the two lovers gazed at one another, a faint blush rising in Elizabeth's cheeks.

Breaking the mood entirely, the duke said, drily, "Enough of that, young man—at least until I have some food in my stomach."

Darcy sprung into action, pulling a chair out for his beloved.

The duke also held out a chair for his daughter. "Elizabeth is still mine, at least until after breakfast when you and I shall retire to my study. Until then, let us break our fast together and relive the merriment of the night's festivities, shall we?"

He turned towards his niece. "Georgiana, it is good to see you this morning. I hope you have injected some semblance of humour into your brother?"

Georgiana giggled. "I have tried, sir."

Darcy retook his seat just as Julian entered, rubbing his hands in anticipation. "I have not missed anything, have I? What a surprise, Darcy, to see you here so early. Did you sleep in one of our guest rooms?"

The duchess joined in the teasing banter. "My nephew slept under his own roof, Julian, and has returned to Northampton Place to join us and his sister to recount the many memorable moments of last evening."

Smirking at the rising blush on Darcy's cheeks, Julian continued. "Ah yes, the sight of Willoughby and then Cavendale dancing with my sister was a sight, was it not, Darcy?"

"It is a sight I pray remains a unique occurrence."

"Julian?" Georgiana interjected. "Pray tell, who were the ladies you most favoured last night?" She looked innocently at her cousin, now gaping at her quick rejoinder.

"Being new to society, I am unsure of *all* their names, Georgiana," Elizabeth said with a tart sweetness. "But there was"—she placed her teacup on the table, freeing her hands to tick off the names on her long, elegant fingers—"Lady Gracewell, Miss Simpson, Miss Chatsmith, Lady Stanton-Hope, and Mrs Churchill."

Darcy sat, spellbound.

Julian blushed and abruptly went to the sideboard to fill a plate. As he passed, Darcy leaned back giving him a smug grin.

Elizabeth continued, "There were more, but as I said, I am unfamiliar with all the ladies of society who clamoured for the attention of my brother. It was a shame that you spent so much time hiding behind your fraternal duties to me!"

Julian glared at her until Georgiana's gentle giggle caught his notice. Turning to glare her into submission, he caught the bloom of Darcy's satisfied smirk, and looking around at the table now turned, his chuckle soon turned into a full-out laugh.

"Oh, so that is what the Countess Elisberg meant when she said you were popping about like a popinjay?" his mother asked benignly as she lifted her teacup to her lips. Her eyes twinkled, first at her son and then his father.

"Well, that is enough." Julian caught his breath and raised his hands. "I concede defeat."

"Good move, my boy." The duke's eyes sparkled as he leaned back in his chair, drinking in the contentment. "It is good for us all to be together, although"—he cast his eyes upon Darcy and then Elizabeth, where they remained—"I fear it will not be so for much longer." Elizabeth looked at Darcy, as did the rest of the family, and his cheeks again reddened.

"Sir?" Darcy asked.

"It is a formality, but one we must follow. Shall we?" the duke asked, rising from his chair. Darcy was instantly on his feet, his eyes locked on Elizabeth, who took a moment to compose herself before looking up at him. Finding his eyes upon her, she smiled lovingly. He relaxed his uncertainty and bowed briefly before following his uncle from the room.

ACROSS TOWN, THE GARDINERS' home was a bustle of activity as Kitty and Lydia clamoured for details of the ball from their aunt. Mrs Bennet secreted herself in her chamber. Arranging her writing implements and humming one of the musical numbers of the previous evening, she settled in to her task.

> *My dear, dear Mrs Bingley,*
> *How sweet that still sounds. You can imagine my great surprise when not only were my brother and I invited to a social event of the first order, but to then find that none other than my dearest Lizzy was the guest of honour! I am sure Their Graces must have many questions regarding dear Lizzy's upbringing, those only a mother could answer, and I am more than willing to share with them my memories of our tender years together. Do be a good girl and arrange a time for your Uncle Bennet and me to join them for tea while we are in London.*
>
> *You looked lovely as always, my dear. I knew you could not be so beautiful for nothing.*
>
> *Your dearest aunt,*
> *Frances Bennet*

"There, that will do." Mrs Bennet sanded and sealed her letter. She continued to hum as she addressed the envelope: Grosvenor Square, London.

THE DUKE SETTLED behind his desk, leaving his fidgety nephew to find his seat. Bringing his fingers to tent before his mouth, the duke enjoyed Darcy's nervous display. When he had adjusted his cravat for the fourth time, the duke's compassion took over, and he addressed the young, eager suitor.

"Have you something to say to me as head of this family?"

Darcy coughed. "I do, sir."

"Well, then you had best go to it."

"Your Grace, sir, you know how I esteem your daughter."

"Continue," Northampton said.

"As you know"—Darcy sat straighter in his chair—"my feelings have grown…" Seeing the duke's growing resistance, Darcy's foot shook, and he sighed.

"I love Elizabeth, and I shall until the day I die. I know I do not deserve her regard or your consideration, but I pray you will judge my mistakes—my earlier behaviour when she first came to London—an aberration."

Darcy forced himself to look straight at the father of his beloved and endure whatever he wished to say.

"Yes, there is that." The duke looked long and hard at the nephew sitting before him. He could see the boy of their shared past, the confounded young man who took on Pemberley, and the earnest man who sat before him, his heart so easily discerned in his unsteady manner and the vulnerability in his eyes. Taking pity on him, the duke continued. "But that is in the past, is it not, Darcy?"

"It is, sir."

"What I wish to know is what you intend for the future."

"Lady Elizabeth has agreed to be my wife." Darcy could not help but smile. "And I have come to ask your permission and your blessing for us to marry."

There was a terrible, prolonged moment before his uncle spoke. "You must forgive me. For so long, I never thought I would have this discussion with anyone. And yet, here we are—you asking to take my daughter from the home to which she has only recently returned."

He looked away at the curtains billowing in the open window. "Obviously, we know your parentage and your connexions, and while I have my suspicions on half of that score, I can only approve the other.

"And as it seems that you favour your father's side of things…you have my consent. And my blessing." Sadness darkened his eyes; then suddenly the fierce intellect for which Northampton was known returned, and his eyes bored into those of the younger man. "Do not give me reason to regret this decision, Darcy, or I shall come after you with all that I have."

"I shall cherish and love Elizabeth with all my strength and ability."

"See that you do."

A knock on the door made both men turn as Julian poked his head around it. "Is everything concluded in here?" He entered, shutting the door behind him. With an air of mischief, he took the chair next to Darcy, his smile broadening as Darcy's scowl deepened. He looked at his father, head tilted with an air of expectancy. "Any news?"

The duke replied, "Well now that you mention it, yes, I suppose there is a bit of news. Your mother told me that Lady Abersham is due for tea."

The duke twirled a quill that lay in precise order across his desk. Julian looked stunned as his mind whirled.

Darcy could not contain the snort of laughter as Julian's face blanched. The duke continued. "And she brings her daughter, Millicent."

Julian gulped. When Darcy's mirth receded and Julian's colour returned, Philip added, "And congratulations are to be had. Darcy has finally come to his senses and asked for Elizabeth's hand."

Darcy looked at his cousin for his approval. He found Julian's eyes upon him, and he held his gaze. With a slight nod, it was done, and both smiled. Taking the hand offered, Darcy shook it, his smile the widest it had been since Elizabeth's agreeing to be his wife only hours before.

"Congratulations. You will make Elizabeth happy. I know it." Julian leaned in and spoke in a lower tone. "And if you do not…"

"I know, I know. Your father has already warned me."

"Let me add, I know an even more unsavoury array of characters."

"They concern me not, for I shall never forsake Elizabeth's happiness—not for anything in the world."

"Now that that is settled, shall we join the ladies?"

THREE DAYS AFTER THE BALL, Caroline sat after breakfast in the Hursts' home, the morning's papers scattered about the table. *It was all to be so simple. Charles would marry Miss Darcy, and Mr Darcy would marry me.* She turned her head. *Everything was in place until Charles took that dreadful Netherfield.* She clutched the paper closest to her, shredding it in her grasp.

"Caroline!" Mrs Hurst waddled into the room.

Caroline remained immobile.

"Lady Vestlewick, Mr Hurst's cousin, just left." Louisa lowered her burgeoning frame into the chair. She placed her hand on Caroline's arm.

"Caroline," she hissed. "How could you?" Her sister remained inert, incensing the heavily pregnant Mrs Hurst.

"We are ruined!"

Caroline turned and blinked.

"How convenient to fail mentioning your insult of the Duchess of Northampton? In her own home? In the presence of the first circles? What on earth possessed you?"

"Darcy is engaged," Caroline droned.

"Yes, I know, to Lady Elizabeth."

Caroline's eyes fired before sinking into coldness. "Lady Elizabeth Elliston is none other than Elizabeth Bennet."

Horror gripped Louisa Hurst, her mouth opening and closing. "Impossible."

"Impossible, but true, Louisa." Caroline rose to leave the room. "I shall have my bags packed."

"Where shall you go?"

"Scarborough—the home of every Bingley embarrassment."

Caroline left the room as Mrs Hurst cried out, a searing pain ripping through her. "Caro"—she bellowed—"line." After calling for help, Caroline returned to her panting sister, who pulled her down, holding steadfastly onto her hand.

"Caroline! Hurst will know." Her eyes were wild with fear as another pain shot through her. "This baby is too early to be his."

Caroline's eyes widened, and she recalled fragments of the servants' gossip at Netherfield.

"There will be another to join you in Scarborough," Louisa cried, no longer able to curb her emotions. With uncharacteristic efficiency, Caroline helped her sister reach her chambers.

ELIZABETH, wishing to share her joy with her sister, descended upon the Bingley town house with her mother, Georgiana, and Mrs. Raleigh. Jane was overjoyed for Lizzy's happiness, and she expressed it in words, bright eyes, and an abundance of hugs and teasing.

"Oh, Lizzy, you will be such a happy bride. Mr Darcy is such a good man…and so handsome too," Jane teased gently, smiling at her sister's blush.

"He truly is a good man," the duchess offered. She looked Elizabeth directly in the eye. "Fitzwilliam has always been morally upright. His transgression was a mistake he made at an extremely vulnerable time for him. He was alone and in distress. He has seen the error of his ways and repented."

Elizabeth nodded her head then looked down at her mother's hand that held her own, taking great comfort and strength from her presence.

"Neither your father nor I would ever give our blessing to a man unworthy of you, your love, and your beautiful spirit. You are a gift to be treasured, and we truly believe he loves you with all his heart."

"He does, Elizabeth, I know it," Georgiana added, sincerity unmistakable in her voice.

Elizabeth wiped a tear from her eye and smiled at her relations surrounding her.

Jane smiled at her sister. "Charles said Mr Darcy was a bundle of nerves this morning on the way to speak with His Grace." She saw the questioning surprise on the duchess's face. "Charles was waiting in the carriage when Mr Darcy called. He was…unsure of his reception from the duke—and your son."

"Brothers!" Elizabeth sighed, smiling. "Who knew they could be so bothersome?"

Catching Georgiana's disbelief, Elizabeth laughed. "You know my brother, Georgiana. Surely, you can see my point. All night long he interrupted Darcy when—"

"When what, my dear?" asked Mrs Raleigh as the duchess looked on with a raised brow.

"Yes, Lizzy, what exactly did Julian interrupt out there on the balcony?" Jane asked.

"Balcony?" the duchess asked.

"Nothing at all," Elizabeth said with a glare in Jane's direction. "Darcy was a perfect gentleman. Julian blundered into a conversation; that is all. A private—"

"Intimate," Jane teased.

"Proper," Elizabeth countered.

"A proper, private, intimate conversation," Mrs Raleigh added, unable to stop the giggles that soon overcame all except Elizabeth, who sat there, cheeks scarlet and eyes flashing with indignation.

"If I had known the cruel treatment I would receive at your hands, ladies, I would not have encouraged this conversation." Elizabeth crossed her arms over her chest, a response that all save Georgiana had witnessed at some point in their lives. The duchess was the first to make the connexion with the toddler's tantrum she had witnessed more than a decade before. A sudden wave of emotion welled up in her, and putting her cup on the table, she took Elizabeth in her arms and hugged her, whispering, "I love you so much."

Taken by surprise, Elizabeth uncrossed her arms to embrace her mother.

Giving the Elliston ladies a moment, Jane leaned towards Mrs Raleigh and spoke in a low voice. "I received a letter this morning from Mrs Bennet. She wishes an introduction to the Northamptons. She feels they owe her some recognition for the years of care she provided for Lizzy."

Mrs Raleigh's jaw dropped. "I cannot believe that woman's insolence," she said. Carefully, she looked at Elizabeth, who pulled away from her mother, her eyes curiously aimed at Jane and their aunt.

"Jane?" Elizabeth asked, now fully disengaged from her mother, who like her daughter sat with an identically arched brow. "What is it?" She looked at Mrs Raleigh. "I can only surmise by Aunt Raleigh's response that it has to do with Mrs Bennet?"

Jane nodded, and Elizabeth waited patiently for her sister to overcome her natural hesitation to speak an unkindness.

"Jane?" Elizabeth sighed with exaggerated exasperation. "You know I shall wheedle it out of you, so you might as well tell us all." Both she and her mother tilted their head to the right.

Seeing Jane's hesitation, Mrs Raleigh took pity on her and gave her hand a quick squeeze. "Mrs Bennet sent over a note this morning, requesting an introduction to your parents, Elizabeth. She feels she is owed some recognition for her years of tending to—"

"No!" Elizabeth turned to her mother.

The duchess took hold of her hand, bringing it up for a kiss. "Fear not, Elizabeth. That shall not happen."

"Jane, you cannot expect this of Elizabeth," Mrs Raleigh said, understanding the dilemma her elder niece was enduring. "Surely you see that will not happen."

"Lizzy?" Jane pleaded.

Elizabeth shook her head and turned to her sister. "I am sorry, Jane, but I...I cannot." She looked at Jane and was stunned by the relief flooding through her as she nodded.

"I understand, Lizzy. While I was amazed at her...composure at your ball, I, too, would not wish to hear her exclamations upon seeing you reunited with your true family."

Reaching across the small table, Elizabeth took Jane's hand, giving it a comforting squeeze. "Thank you. I was afraid you would think me unkind or unforgiving."

"No, never." Jane's eyes grew fierce. "I have learned in these last few days that there are those who are so...consumed with their own self-interest that they are unable to consider anyone else. And in their blindness, they trample over all that is good and kind in this world."

Knowing the source of this understanding, both Elizabeth and Mrs Raleigh sighed and comforted Jane as best they could.

In a voice barely audible, Jane continued. "I would like to apologise once again for the reprehensible actions of Miss Bingley."

Elizabeth and Mrs Raleigh looked at each other and then at the duchess, who took up one of the hands Jane firmly clasped in her lap. "The blame and responsibility for her actions rests solely with Miss Bingley, Jane. No one blames you or Mr Bingley. We know he separated her from your house for what she alone did. And remember, we know enough of her previous audacious claims to know that reality rarely intruded upon her conception of her place in the world." The duchess looked at Elizabeth, who nodded.

"Until she apologises and is sincerely contrite, she shall not be welcome here," Jane said with conviction. Her emotion returned as she said, "Charles is beyond mortified over her actions. Not only did she violate his trust, but he is stunned by her behaviour the other night. She was so vicious."

"Come, now," the duchess said, attempting to lighten the mood of the gathering. "Let us leave the past behind." She looked at her daughter. "We have a wedding to plan!"

"Jane, I hope you will agree to stand up with me?" Elizabeth asked.

"Oh, Lizzy, yes! Of course I shall!" Jane crossed the distance to embrace her sister. As they held each other, she whispered, "I am so happy for you!"

The mood lifted as the conversation turned to lace and flowers and where the couple would take their vows. The parlour door opened, and Bingley entered, heading directly towards Jane.

Seeing his unusual seriousness, Jane and her guests stood.

"Charles?" Jane began. "What is it?"

Bingley strode to the sofa and seated himself without ceremony. He held out a letter. "It is from Caroline," he said, his voice devoid of emotion. "Louisa…"

Alarm was raised immediately, the ladies knowing Mrs Hurst was well into the eighth month of her pregnancy. "She, she…" His voice fell, and the foreboding in the room was palpable. "She is gone."

Gasps of horror filled the room as Jane put her gentle arm around her husband and allowed him to release his emotion with her.

twenty-three

Gently, Mrs Raleigh took up the note, scanning for the pertinent information. When done, she folded it in half, looked up at the duchess, and sighed. Handing her the note, she turned to Elizabeth and Georgiana. "Neither Mrs Hurst nor her son survived the birth. Miss Bingley wishes Charles's help in locating Mr Hurst and instruction on how to proceed."

Composing himself, Charles looked up and addressed the women although his hand never left the sanctuary of Jane's clasp. "I shall go to her immediately and...see what may be done. I have sent word to the...clubs I know Hurst frequents."

"You must bring Caroline back with you, Charles."

"Jane!" Elizabeth and Mrs Raleigh exclaimed at once.

Meeting their pleading looks with resigned determination, she said. "She cannot remain with Mr Hurst. It is unseemly. And I shall not let her wallow in more degradation, no matter how self-imposed it may be."

Bingley brought her hand to his lips to kiss it in gratitude. "Thank you, Jane." Replacing her hand on his lap, he continued. "I promise it shall not be a visit of long duration. Knowing how things stood in the

Hursts' marriage, I should probably return Louisa to Scarborough. I shall accompany her and see Caroline settled in the north."

"I shall join you," Jane said with determination." To her family, she added, "Come, let us see what we may arrange while Charles attends to the things only he can do."

Of one mind, the women left the parlour, heading towards Jane's study to tackle the particulars of arranging a suitable funeral for a woman who had never been kind to any of them. By the time of the evening meal, not only had the details of the next few days been arranged, their men folk had come for them and together offered comfort to each other. Only Mrs Raleigh remained with Jane to welcome Charles and his unrepentant sister back to their home.

JULIAN ENTERED the dressing room that Angelo reserved for him when he was in town. Wiping the sweat from his face, he thought, *Darcy has improved since last we fenced. I shall have to resume a more rigorous practice schedule if that lovesick pup poses such a challenge.*

He stripped the linen from his back. Splashing water over his face and chest, the marquess reviewed the thirty-minute match, his hands resting on the catch basin, and smiled. *The move that van Miepsdorf showed me is neat and precise, very precise. Darcy nearly soiled himself when I launched that sequence!*

Julian walked to the cupboard where his clothes were neatly folded. Stripping off his sweat-stained breeches, he reached for the crisp linen of his waiting shirt. As he pulled the shirt from the pile of clothes, a sealed note fell to the floor. Looking around, Julian picked it up. Recognising the cryptic seal, he frowned. After again ensuring his privacy, Julian slid his finger under the flap and broke the seal.

"Hornsby," he said as he read the hastily scribbled missive.

Person of interest received pouch two nights ago, now missing. All are gone. Still trying to ascertain where.

Hastily donning his remaining clothes, Julian left Angelo's and headed for the Maritime Ministry.

BY THE TIME Bingley returned that evening, the ornaments of death and mourning were apparent, within and without his home. Wearily, he handed his hat and walking stick to Simmons.

"Sir?" the middle-aged man asked. "On behalf of all your dependents, sir, I extend my deepest condolences."

"Thank you, Simmons, and please extend my appreciation and that of my wife to everyone for the sentiment, and"—he looked at the black-draped mirrors—"for seeing to…everything so expeditiously. You always take such good care of us."

"A pleasure, sir, to be of service, especially in this time of sorrow."

"Yes, of sorrow," Charles said as he made his way to his chambers where he hoped to find his wife. "Oh, Simmons," Charles said turning, back to the man who had gathered Bingley's things. "My sister, Miss Bingley, will be returning here once Hurst is found and returns to his home." Noting the momentary look of shock on his implacable butler, Charles quickly added, "On a temporary basis. Until we can arrange transport of my sister's body."

With just a hint of resignation, Simmons replied, "Very good, sir. Good night, sir."

"Good night, Simmons," Charles said before heading up the stairs to find Jane and relate the events of his day. Climbing the stairs, he combed through his rust-coloured curls with his hand.

"Temporary—a temporary sojourn, that is all."

THE NEXT MORNING ELIZABETH, the duchess, and the Raleighs descended upon the Bingley town house along with Georgiana and Darcy to support the grieving family. After an exchange of greetings and hugs, there was a natural separation of the sexes as Jane employed the women in sending letters, declining invitations, and preparing the house for their departure on what promised to be a lengthy and difficult journey north.

While the women busied themselves in the details of death, the men gathered in Bingley's study.

"And there has been no word from your brother?" Admiral Raleigh asked.

Taking the glass of port Darcy offered him, Bingley shook his head. "No, and I have tried every one of his favourite haunts here in town and sent two riders to his estate in Cheshire."

"He never mentioned their...plans?" Raleigh asked again.

"No, at least not to me. I mean, who discusses these things when one is in health?" Charles replied morosely.

Clearing his throat and hoping to pacify the umbrage the admiral took at Bingley's last remark, Darcy interjected, "I believe the admiral has, in light of his life at sea..."

"Oh, sir, please, I meant no disrespect."

"None taken, my boy, none taken. I sometimes forget that my experience is not shared by all. But it is a good idea to acquaint one's wife with the particulars—the where and how and perhaps the why of one's last wishes." He gave each younger man a significant look. "Communication is always best in these situations."

Before anything else could be said, there was a knock on the door.

"Come," Bingley called out.

Simmons entered, handing Bingley a letter. "It is from Hurst." Bingley scanned it, his eyes opening wide, and his mouth hanging open. When he had read it three times, he staggered to sit on the edge of the desk.

"Bingley!" Darcy said, reaching his friend before he could slump to the ground. "What is it?"

"He will not come." Charles looked from one man to the other. "And denies permission to bury her in his family's vault."

His guests gaped in shock.

Charles let the missive fall onto his desk. "I had thought as much." His free hand ran over his eyes then pinched the bridge of his nose. "Jane had mentioned Louisa's...rapid expansion. Louisa mentioned the possibility of twins..."

"Twins?"

"Yes, it seems she was rather large early on, or so we were led to believe. I called on them when we returned from our wedding trip. I came upon Hurst in an unguarded moment, and he confessed his suspicions regarding the...um...lineage of the child. He went into rather exacting detail about the schedule of his conjugal visits, and none coincided with the delicate condition his wife presented daily." Bingley's voice was hoarse. "He said that, if he had one shred of proof, it would be finished. He would send her back to me, no matter that they had been married nearly seven years."

And they had the audacity to disparage Elizabeth! Darcy thought angrily.

"It seems we are for Scarborough," Bingley said, collecting himself. "I must write my aunt and inform her, and have the Reverend Baxter prepare a suitable service." He rose and searched his desk for quill, parchment, and inkpot.

"Allow me," Darcy offered. "Your writing is difficult to read under the best of circumstances."

Darcy exchanged places with his friend at the desk. "I shall write the basics, and you can add your salutation and closing."

Bingley thanked him, adding, "I must go and speak with Jane and let her know the change in our destination. Admiral, if I may?—I meant to speak with you earlier. Mrs Bennet wrote to Jane yesterday, twice. She insists that Jane keep Kitty and Lydia in town."

Raleigh snorted.

"Further, she was rather…vocal…in her desire to be introduced to the Northamptons. She is displeased at being kept ignorant of Elizabeth's identity."

"Oh, she is, is she?" Admiral Raleigh had become rigid as his ire flared. "As if she ever cared about Elizabeth before! Leave Mrs Bennet to me, son. I shall see that she leaves Jane in peace."

"And Elizabeth?" Bingley asked.

"Surely she would not dare!" Darcy said.

Raleigh sat on the edge of the nearest chair. "I would put nothing past Franny Bennet." The admiral placed his hand on Bingley's shoulder. "But as I said, leave her to Mrs Raleigh and me."

"Thank you, sir."

"'Uncle,' Charles."

Nodding, Bingley repeated, "Uncle."

CAROLINE LOOKED around the entrance hall of the house she had once ruled, noting with distaste that it looked well indeed. As Simmons oversaw the unloading of her trunks, Caroline turned to her former servant, a note of imperiousness in her voice. "Simmons, I shall take my old chamber," she said before dismissing him with a wave of her hand.

Bingley interrupted immediately. "No, Simmons, the guest wing as Mrs Bingley instructed you earlier this morning. Caroline, come to my study. You do remember where that is located?" He waited, watching her eyes narrow and her lips curl into a pout.

As they walked down the passageway, Caroline asked, "Shall we have time, before we depart, to see Mr Darcy?"

"You cannot be serious. We are in mourning!"

Caroline lifted her chin. "Mr Darcy is one of our oldest and dearest friends. It would be unseemly to leave town without saying goodbye."

"Listen to me, Caroline, and listen well," he said, his voice low and dangerous. "It is by the grace of the good Lord, and Darcy's impeccable loyalty, that he and I have retained our friendship after all you have done to defame our family's name."

"Charles?" Jane's voice cut through the tension. "An express has arrived for you from Scarborough. I believe it is from your aunt."

He gave a curt look to his sister before approaching his wife. Jane took hold of his hand, and he leaned in to kiss her gently on the cheek. "Thank you, my angel," he spoke in a low voice for her ears only.

Caroline, unable to endure the intimacy, sneered. "How becoming, Jane dear, to take on the responsibilities of the steward. Tell me, are you allowed into the master's study?"

"Yes, Caroline. It is a wife's duty to see to the ease and comfort of her husband."

"Yes, you Bennet chi…girls are well versed in comforting your men…" And she added in a venomous tone, "Especially that sister of yours." Caroline's sneer delivered her implied insult.

Jane was a patient woman, willing to forgive nearly anyone for anything save an unwarranted, unprovoked attack upon her family, Lizzy in particular. The drama and anguish churned up by the woman standing before her played through Jane's mind, and something snapped in her heart. Smiling sweetly, she advanced upon her unsuspecting prey. "You asked about Darcy? I dare say he will have little time to spare for you, Caroline, as he is too pre-occupied with my sister, Lady Elizabeth, his intended wife.

"I am particularly delighted, not only for my sister's joy but also because, while on our wedding trip, Charles and I found our home, not thirty miles from Pemberley. So my dear Lady Elizabeth Darcy and I shall be neighbours. Such fun we shall have!" Miss Bingley shrank, her hand flying to her lips.

"I shall take my leave of you, Caroline, in Scarborough. While I accompany your brother, it is only to give him comfort. After that, you shall be dead to me, for we do reap what we sow. Thank you for showing me the true meaning of that proverb." And with that, Jane left her sister to gather the shreds of her sanity that Jane had trod beneath her feet.

THREE DAYS LATER, a frenetic Franny Bennet emerged from her coach. Bustling up the stairs, she called out and nearly barged past the incredulous butler who stood gaping, barely able to close the door before the irascible woman began speaking. "Where is my niece, Mrs Bingley?" Adding, "My, how good that sounds."

Then, as if recalling her environs, she again enquired, "And my nephew?"

Simmons replied, "They are not at home presently, madam."

Momentarily confused, the matronly woman shook her head. "But where can they have gone? It is not yet ten!"

"They left town yesterday, ma'am."

"Left town? Without leaving word?"

"Word was sent to your husband at your brother's residence in Cheapside."

"I see." Mrs Bennet considered this a moment.

While eager to be rid of the dervish before him, Simmons had enough experience with Miss Bingley to suspect the gleam in this unexpected woman's eyes. When she spoke again, he snapped to attention. "Very good. Please summon my carriage."

ELIZABETH SIGHED as she squeezed the arm of her betrothed. Noting her distress, he gently stroked her hand. "What preoccupies you, my love? Have we walked too far?"

Elizabeth turned, and Darcy was happy to see her relax when she looked into his eyes. "No, no." She turned away. "It is not that." Darcy counted three long, full breaths before Elizabeth spoke again. "My thoughts were with Jane."

Darcy sighed as well. "Ah yes…Miss Bingley."

"And Mrs Hurst." Elizabeth stepped towards the willows draping their graceful boughs at the water's edge.

Darcy followed. Midway to the pond, he slowed. *What an unmitigated disaster those shrews have created. First, the one cannot keep her desires to the marriage bed, and the other…* A shudder ran through his body.

"Elizabeth," he called softly, smiling when she turned with a brief lifting of the corners of her mouth.

"I am well." She extended her hand to him, which he took, bringing it to his lips. He stepped as close as he dared in public.

How beautiful she is when she blushes. I hope I shall always bring a flush to her cheeks.

He smiled unreservedly, tucking a curled lock from her forehead back to the rim of her bonnet. "They will be well, Charles and Jane."

He watched as Elizabeth looked up quickly into his eyes. *Kiss her!* —his heart and body screamed.

He took a deep breath. "Truly, they will." He rubbed his hand over her small one, still in his. "We shall see to it. We shall do our best to protect her and the Bingleys from the—"

"—destruction of their name?" Elizabeth replied with a bleak snort.

Darcy could only nod in agreement, waiting for her to continue. Elizabeth looked away at the water reflecting diamond shards of the morning sun and sighed. "Thank you." She turned to her lover again. "In the midst of all this, it is good—so very good—to realise that I am not alone. That Jane is not alone in all of this."

Darcy was about to speak, but she continued.

"That we have family around us who love us and will protect us to the best of their abilities." She brought her hand to his cheek. Darcy locked his eyes with hers. "And is that not truly what matters most?"

Unable to resist her further, he led them through the green curtain of overhanging willow branches to take her in his arms. Darcy thrilled when, pressing his lips to hers, he felt her relax into his tightened embrace. It was more than a sensual delight, it was as if their hearts fused into one. In the cocoon of delicate green leaves sheltering them, their love melded the one heart to the other, their essence intermingled and strengthened by the exchange. When their lungs demanded air, their lips parted, and stepping back, they regained the external world. Darcy was overjoyed to see his happiness and surprise reflected in Elizabeth's eyes.

Stepping closer, Elizabeth wrapped her arms around his waist, and Darcy's heart soared. Hearing children passing with their nannies, they blushed then headed to the pond's embankment.

He led her to a stone bench on the other side of the willows. "Your cousin Mary marries next month, does she not?"

"Yes, why?"

"We should attend the nuptials."

Elizabeth looked off at the sparkling water, allowing the calls of the ducks and geese to attract her attention. "I would like to," she said, her mind still drinking in the prosaic display of the children's innocent delight at feeding the fowl. "Mary has always been so good to me."

"I shall forever be grateful to her for defending you when you needed a champion."

His eyes clouded momentarily until he, too, heard the squeals of the children. "And for all the stories she shared with us about you." He pointed to the gathering of little ones. "Scampering about, leading your gaggle of young pirates through the wilds of Meryton."

Elizabeth laughed and turned towards him. "I think I shall enjoy being married to you."

Darcy took hold of her hand and placed it on his chest, looking into her eyes. "As will I with you, Elizabeth." He smiled from his heart. "Although I can only imagine what mischief our children will create, traipsing about the ponds of Pemberley and Green Haven. And with Julian as an uncle…"

Darcy laughed seeing Elizabeth's eyes widen at the mention of their future children, then sparkled in delight as she laughed.

"I believe we shall have to restrain Julian from influencing our children, or I know not what they will do."

"I do not think it wise to disparage my character in such an unscrupulous manner, sister dear!" Julian's voice broke through their intimacy. Both lovers turned towards the approaching gentleman.

"Mother told me you two had escaped the house, and I thought I should join you. Shame on you, Darcy, absconding with my sister without a proper chaperone."

"We are engaged," Darcy reminded him.

"All the more reason to keep an eye on you two." He took Darcy's seat, forcing his cousin to stand. Elizabeth shot her brother an irritated look, and Julian leaned in so they were nose to nose. "None of that, Elizabeth."

He pulled back, tapping a finger on her nose, and laughed. "Besides, mother wishes you home. Something about setting a wedding date or some such nonsense."

FRANCES BENNET STEPPED out of the carriage, dumbfounded by the magnificent building. Her resolve momentarily faltered until a couple walking by broke through her trepidation. Mrs Bennet quickly climbed the steps to knock on the door.

"Madam?" the butler asked, appraising the unexpected caller.

Nodding, she gathered her nerve. "Mrs Frances Bennet to see Elizabeth."

"*Lady* Elizabeth is not receiving visitors yet this morning."

"I am family."

The impeccably appointed man looked down on the short woman, his glare flaying her pretensions like dried, lifeless skin. Startled by his examination, she added, a little less confidently. "I am Frances Bennet, Lady Elizabeth's aunt."

"Ah." The man nodded and bowed slightly. Spreading his left arm to indicate a room to the left, he said imperiously, "This way, madam."

Gathering her skirts, she brushed past the butler and a footman, murmuring, "Thank you."

"Go and tell His Grace or the marquess of our unexpected caller." The butler's eyes trailed after the retreating matron. "And be quick about it, man."

Nodding in agreement, the younger man hurried off to the study where the duke was known to spend his mornings.

twenty-four

MR BENNET AWAITED HIS CARRIAGE IN THE COMFORT OF HIS BROTHER'S study. *It has been an age since I have been to town. It will be good to see Briscomb and hear what he's been up to.*

The knock of the Gardiners' butler, Cleary, disturbed his thought. "I beg your pardon, sir. I have taken the liberty of requesting the Gardiner carriage for your transport."

"And why would I have need of your master's conveyance?"

Cleary was obviously flustered. "Mrs Bennet has had your carriage since earlier this morning."

"What! Why was I not informed?"

Cleary reddened. "I believe the house thought you were, sir."

Bennet hurried through the door. "Tell my brother that I appreciate the use of his carriage, and please have my daughter Mary join me immediately! Tell her we have no time to lose."

DURING HIS LIFE, the Duke of Northampton had presided over more onerous conversations than he could count, but as he stood, hand on the doorknob to his study, he was unsure how to proceed. Cummings told him that Frances Bennet awaited, and the only urgency he felt was to dispatch her before either Elizabeth or Alexandra got wind of her presence in their home.

Rubbing his hand over his eyes, he sent a silent supplication to the Divine. *My Lord, please let Alexandra finish reading her novel. Please!*

Steadying himself, he took a deep breath and entered the study.

A woman rushed to stand and greet her illustrious host. "Your Grace." She gave an unpractised curtsey.

"Madam." He nodded slightly. "I presume you are Mrs Bennet?"

"I am."

"Please sit." He indicated a chair and moved to the one opposite her. "To what do I owe your presence? I am unaware of a prior acquaintance."

Startled by his rebuke, she quickly said, "Your Grace, surely you know that it was I, along with my husband, who raised your daughter."

"I am aware of those who offered *true* care and refuge to my child —and I am also aware of those who begrudgingly let fall scraps from their table and their heart. And I believe both of us know which you are. Now, what do you want?"

She blanched and stammered, "I, I came to see Elizabeth. I…I was a mother to her—"

"How dare you!" The duke rose, towering over Mrs Bennet who shrank into the deep chair. "You—you are the reluctant guardian who mistreated her as a child! A child that was given to you to protect."

"I opened my home!"

"Your brother and his wife opened their home, Mrs Bennet, and opened their hearts to Elizabeth. You came along after their deaths to rip apart the little security my daughter enjoyed."

"Papa!" Elizabeth's bright voice called out, floating in on the breeze as she approached the duke's study, followed by her betrothed and her brother. Seeing Mrs Bennet, Elizabeth halted, her fear and disgust plain.

"Elizabeth!" Mrs Bennet rose from her chair, but Darcy and Julian closed ranks in front of her.

Mrs Bennet's eyes shot between the two broad-chested, muscular men who in any other situation would be courted and flattered as potential husbands for Kitty and Lydia. "Mr Darcy! I…I came to…"

"Disturb my daughter's peace of mind?" the duke asked. "That is something I shall never allow."

"No, ask Elizabeth," Mrs Bennet said. "She will tell you."

Elizabeth pushed her way past her brother and her betrothed. "There are many things I wish to tell you, Mrs Bennet, none of which should be spoken before an audience."

Mrs Bennet gasped theatrically. "I cared for you, you little wretch! You sat at my table like a member of the family."

"Only because Uncle Bennet insisted I was a member of his family. You were never welcoming—never civil."

"I fed you! Literally gave you the clothes off my back! The benefit of my experience. And this is the thanks I receive?"

"What did you expect, Mrs Bennet?" The duchess stood in the doorway, her fingers itching for a fight.

"You dare come into this house uninvited, unwelcome, and claiming to be a mother to my child?" She moved to stand beside her husband, who took her hand upon his arm. "You and I, Mrs Bennet, have an entirely different notion of what constitutes a mother's care.

"Is it a mother's love to give a child only hand-me-downs to cover herself?" Her eyes flashed to Mrs Bennet, narrowing as the woman jutted out her chin. "Elizabeth told me of the times Jane would tear a sleeve on purpose, or rip a hem so Elizabeth would not have to wear your cast-off gowns.

"Is keeping my child from your table when entertaining a demonstration of motherly love? Forcing my little girl to rely on your kitchen maid to keep her belly filled? Or perhaps it is delaying a call to the apothecary when she falls ill?"

Darcy clenched his jaw, and he took Elizabeth's arm, slipping it into the crook of his own.

The duchess stepped closer to Mrs Bennet, her voice a growl of fury. "I could strike you for the cruelty you displayed to my daughter. And yet you dare come here! Have you no shame?"

"I think it best you leave, madam," Julian suggested, looking at his father for confirmation. It took a moment for the duke to respond, but he nodded to his son. "Retreat while retreat is still possible."

The bustle of approaching footsteps caught their attention as all six looked at the open doors. Cummings appeared, Mr Bennet and Miss Mary Bennet behind him.

"Mrs Bennet," Thomas Bennet cried, horrified at the spectacle before him. "What possessed you to impose upon this house?"

Mrs Bennet regained her courage. "I am Elizabeth's closest relation! Of course I shall come and speak with her."

Mr Bennet quickly came to stand before his wife. "You are *not*. We are not. And you would best recall that we were only blessed to have Eli—Lady Elizabeth with us by the grace of God. These fine people are her true family."

Mary, having come up to Elizabeth, who still stood within the circle of Darcy's protective arm, gave her cousin's arm a quick squeeze before going to her mother. "Please, Mama, let us return to Aunt Gardiner." She looked earnestly at her mother, taking hold of her arm, and gently but urgently pulling her to the door.

Mrs Bennet began. "What about—"

"No, Mrs Bennet. There is nothing to ask of these good people except, perhaps, their forgiveness." He looked at the duke. "And to promise that we shall not intrude upon their hospitality again."

Mrs Bennet nodded, reluctantly allowing her husband to lead her out of the room. Mary followed them, and as Mr and Mrs Bennet left the room, the five remaining relaxed decidedly. Before she exited the chamber, Mary turned and headed back to Elizabeth who stepped forward to meet her.

"Oh, Lizzy, I am so sorry."

"Mary," Elizabeth took her hand in hers.

"I am so humiliated," Mary cried, "but mostly I am full of sorrow. We shall not meet again. I shall miss you, Lizzy. I love you."

"Oh, Mary," Elizabeth embraced her cousin, holding her tightly to her heart. "Fear not—we shall meet again, perhaps after you have married."

Nodding, Mary wiped the tears from her cheeks and pulled her emotions back into her heart. Smiling through her tears, she took Elizabeth's hand and gave it a squeeze. "Until then, be well." Mary turned to the duke and duchess and curtseyed, then added, "Lord Glascomb, Mr Darcy."

And she left the room.

Julian Elliston walked with his friend Hornsby towards the sitting room of Lord Brisbain where the two were engaged for an evening's dinner and conversation.

"So, I may tell Jenkinson you are out of the running for that little jaunt to Vienna?" the shorter of the two men asked in a hushed manner.

"Please," Julian said as they followed Brisbain's man down the corridor. His eyes scanned the empty hallway as they made their way towards the formal parlour where thirty of their friends, associates, and their ladies awaited. "With Elizabeth's return, and now her engagement…well…family business, you know…"

"Yes," Hornsby sighed, "I do. I recall when my sister wed. You would have thought she was a crown princess or some such rot what with all the lace and frippery. Never thought you were one to go in for all that nonsense."

They turned towards the left and Julian quirked an eyebrow. "I never was interested in all that fluff because I had not a sister who was interested in it. Now that Elizabeth is home, well, I am interested in knowing her and seeing her endure all the nonsense. That and seeing Darcy get all moon-eyed whenever she is near. She has him tied up in knots."

"That would be a sight to see."

The din of people gathering and mingling could be heard, and Julian shook his head. "I should have guessed that a quiet evening at Brisbee's would involve a crowd of fifty."

"Quite." Hornsby's fingers nervously tugged at his cravat.

Julian stopped midway down the passageway, his head leaning close for one final, private word. "From what I hear, the wedding will not be until late fall, December even. If there is a way to get me back…"

"Yes, yes." Hornsby looked around to see if anyone was in hearing distance.

"For just a brief reconnaissance. I must know what happened!" Julian was mortified to hear himself beg.

"Now is neither the place nor time for this discussion!"

Julian nodded, chastised and defeated. Gathering his pride, he continued in a hushed whisper. "I hate leaving unfinished business."

Hornsby nodded and looked towards the salon, indicating they should continue. When the impeccably attired major-domo opened the door, Julian took a deep breath, straightened his spine, and plunged into the crowd.

Julian's eyes were bright and his smile inviting, and they nodded to acquaintances. About to part company, Julian faltered as a light and pleasing laugh danced through the room. Hornsby stepped closer, his hand resting on Julian's arm as the nearly unflappable marquess remained static in the middle of the crowded room.

"Get a hold of yourself, man."

Julian, however, was incapable of responding as the sound for which he had been pining for weeks washed over him. Instinctively, his eyes searched the throng for the woman his mind told him could not possibly be there.

"Glascomb," Hornsby pressed, ushering them to a secluded alcove. There was genuine concern in his voice. "What is it?"

As if coming out of a haze, Julian was finally able to put his jumbled thoughts into words. "Lysetteya," he whispered reverently. Immediately, Hornsby scanned the room for the woman he had met once but had heard of through many a drunken bacchanal.

"Impossible!"

Julian nodded. "Impossible, and yet—" Julian's head lifted and his eyes locked onto a beautiful woman to their right. "She is here." Julian said no more as his eyes cleared, his lips lifting into a true smile. Hornsby could only stare at Glascomb's transformation. As surreptitiously as possible, Hornsby turned to the vision of loveliness that besotted his friend. Fifty feet away, stood a tall, well-proportioned woman, surrounded by men, a shimmering sea-green gown dazzling the eye like a wave in the sun, a brilliant column of intense colour against the jet of her companions' garb. Princess Lysetteya Ninotchka Zakarevskaya was regal in her beauty until her cerulean blue eyes found Julian. Their eyes locked. Hornsby was spellbound as the blonde beauty stilled even further, motionlessly creating distance from her coterie of admirers. Drawn into her power, Hornsby followed behind Julian, who made his way through the crush of people between them.

Conversation stilled as the gentlemen made way for the newcomers. Julian bowed, and their eyes never broke their bond.

DARCY LED Elizabeth through the open doors out to her family's garden. When they were without prior social obligations, the Darcys and Northamptons dined together. While Georgiana relished the attention of her father's family, Darcy was able to steal unguarded moments alone with Elizabeth. They would begin their afternoons together, enjoying their time until the cool breezes of twilight called them to walk the walled sanctuary where fragrant blooms caressed the air.

Gently, he led her to a bench at the far end of the lawn, shielded by an arbour of roses from the lackadaisical chaperonage of the duchess. "Another reason to be grateful to Georgiana," Darcy said as they wandered towards their bench.

"What is that?" Elizabeth asked with a suspicious smile.

"What?" Darcy asked with surprise. "Oh. I had not realised I spoke aloud."

Elizabeth laughed, and Darcy drank in the contentment of being with her in so unguarded a fashion. "I was commenting to myself on how grateful I am to Georgiana for occupying your mother so I may steal you…I mean, to have a moment with you here in the garden."

"In the gathering night?" Elizabeth added, and Darcy smiled and nodded in response. Elizabeth took a step away from him. "You do not have to be so guarded with me you know. I would not crumble or dissolve into tears if you said, 'Steal you away.'"

She quirked her brow. "Especially if you mean to steal me away for this…"

Before Darcy could respond, Elizabeth closed the distance between them, pressing her body to his to kiss him. Taking advantage of the silent 'Oh' he was unable to utter, she slid her tongue along the ridge of his lips then dipped it into his mouth.

As if a floodgate had been opened, he pulled her firmly to his body, arms fully embracing her, lips eager to replicate her actions. When Elizabeth's hands slipped beneath the fabric of his waistcoat, he groaned, redoubling his efforts to feel what he could of her.

Their mouths battled with each other to taste and touch as much as possible. Barely cognisant of their position in the garden, Darcy opened one eye and took a tentative step backwards until he found the refuge of the rose bower. Lowering his heated lips to the soft, tantalising skin of Elizabeth's neck, he revelled in her gasp of desire.

Just as the image of laying Elizabeth in the summer grass was forming in what was left of his thoughts, his sister's voice called out, "Fitzwilliam! Elizabeth!"

"Blast!" whined Darcy taking one more kiss.

"Dinner is ready," Georgiana said with a little laugh.

They heard the silk of her skirts from the other side of the leafy wall, and looking towards the disarray apparent in each other's clothes, they smiled.

"Oh my," Elizabeth said as she patted Darcy's cravat into some semblance of order.

"I am only grateful your brother dines elsewhere," he said, straightening his vest and coat.

"Indeed?" Elizabeth adjusted the top edge of her gown before feeling her curls to test the strength and hold of her pins.

"Indeed. Otherwise, he would know, and I am sure he would announce that you, my love"—he kissed her hand—"have been thoroughly and most delightfully kissed."

"Then, thank heavens he is elsewhere." A note of nerves infested Elizabeth's eyes. "Now we have only to cope with facing my father."

All colour left Darcy's face, and as she dragged her intended back into the house, Elizabeth's delighted laughter floated through the garden on the night air.

June 1812
Town House of Lord Brisbain, London

"PRINCESS," Julian murmured, pressing her hand to his lips. His heart quickened as she trembled. Gooseflesh rose on his neck, and he swallowed hard.

"My lord," she replied in heavily accented English.

"What brings you?" Julian swallowed, trying to form a simple sentence. "I believed you were for Moscow."

"I accompany my cousin, who is here to…for the waters."

Julian raised his brow and asked with a quirked smile, "The waters?"

"Da, in Bath."

"Ah, Bath," he demurred while his mind flooded with images of the bath they had shared in Amsterdam before his summons home had separated them.

"Has *your* business resolved to your satisfaction?"

He led her to an isolated loveseat. He thought back to the reason he had given for his hasty departure only a few months prior. "Yes, in fact it has. My sister—"

"I was unaware you had a sister," she said suspiciously.

"Yes, in fact I do." His eyes bored into her, wanting to pierce them so his heart could once again reach hers. "She was taken as a child." He noted her response with satisfaction. "And only recently returned to us."

"And where is this sister located now?" Princess Lysetteya scanned his face, examining every feature.

Julian laughed at her outright interrogation. "At home, with my mother and father."

Lysetteya's eyes softened, her gaze now a caress. Julian felt the room fill with heat. "It is always a joy when a loved one returns."

Knowing of the recent loss of her brother, he again took her hand to his lips. "Indeed, it is." He kept his eyes on her beautiful face until she looked up at him and gasped. His next words were whispered, husky and low. "Lysetteya, I…"

"I am here in an official capacity, my lord." Her voice was laboured, the lids of her eyes, lowered.

"You do not believe that any more than I do."

"I am not some lovesick girl who chases after the first man who touches her heart. I am a princess of the court of the Tsar!" Her blush belied her words, and Julian held tighter the hand he had yet to return.

"Perhaps. But then again, perhaps not." He smiled at her discomfort. She scowled, pulling her delicate fingers from his grasp. He laughed outright. "My parents are hosting a dinner party in honour of my sister's engagement."

"She works quickly for one only recently returned to you." Lysetteya glared at him.

Relaxed and happy, Julian only laughed. "If you only knew, my dear."

He allowed himself the immense pleasure of drinking in her beauty. *She is here, in the home of my friend, in the same city—my city! It is a miracle. And I shall not allow her to leave so soon.*

"I wish for you to attend. As my guest."

A lovely smile opened her face, and Julian watched her shoulders truly relax. Her eyes sparkled.

"Will you come? Please, say you will?"

"And my cousin?" Lysetteya looked over at the tall, overbearing man glaring at their tête-à-tête.

"Josef Illyonavich Reznokov," Julian muttered, returning his eyes to her. "If I must extend the invitation, I shall."

"Your mother or your sister will not mind?" she asked concerned.

"No. I believe they will be most delighted to have you at our table." A dark thought imposed itself on his mind. "You are still free, are you not?"

Sighing, she said. "Yes. For the time being, I am."

"For the time being? What is this? Please refrain from speaking in riddles. I beg you."

"My mother has…concerns. She has spoken to her sister, Josef's mother."

Julian looked quickly at his rival. "But he…surely he has not consented."

"What care does he have who he marries? It is all for show." The princess sounded resigned to her fate.

"And you?" Julian's tight voice barked at her.

"I was alone, abandoned in Amsterdam—not a word, no promise, no hope to cling to."

"I told you I would return for you."

"And here I am…"

"Have you come for me?"

"I cannot abandon the concerns of my family." She turned away.

"I do not ask you to. Marry me, Lysetteya Vladimirova

Zakarevskaya, princess of the court of the Tsar. I shall take care of you and her."

"It is not that easy."

"What? What does Josef Illyonavich hold over you?" Julian looked with fury at the man dressed in the uniform of the Russian cavalry.

"My mother has habits."

"We shall bring her with us, here to London, and see to her habits. Please, Lysetteya." He looked intently into her eyes and saw the love he had left months before. "Please." He had no desire to wipe the pleading from his voice.

"Yes, Julian," she whispered.

"You will?" he asked, surprised at the ease of her acceptance.

"Yes, I shall come to your dinner."

"And...and to the rest?"

"I shall take it under consideration." She smiled up at him, her eyes remaining locked on his until Hornsby intruded upon their intimacy.

twenty-five

RICHARD FITZWILLIAM, EARL OF MATLOCK, HANDED HIS HAT AND cane to the footman. "Where is Lady Matlock," he asked of the elderly servant.

"Lady Matlock, sir, has not left her chambers today."

Nodding, Richard made his way to his study. *Better still. There is much to do.* Opening the door, Richard took a deep breath. He never had a close relationship with his father, but this room, of all the rooms accessible to him, reminded him of the imposing man his progenitor had been.

How many times was I called to this carpet for some trifling transgression? he asked himself as he slowly made his way to the desk. *All those years believing the old man had our best interests at heart.* A bitter laugh filled the room. "Well, those were well and truly laid to rest this morning now, were they not, lad?" Turning, Richard headed to the sideboard and filled his glass liberally.

"To you, Pater—may you rot in your grave." He lifted the glass and then drained half its contents in one gulp. "You," he continued when his voice regained its strength, "you drained the Matlock coffers, you and Braddleton, and left me!—trained in military, not financial, schemes—to find a way to lead this family and our name back into respectability." He took another hasty drink. "You," he growled, "have reduced me to taking that—" Involuntarily, he shuddered at images of the licentious trollop his wife had become: her belly stretching, an insatiable hunger ever-present in her eyes. "—creature once known as Anne."

He leaned against the furniture that was made before even his father was born. "There was no choice. Darcy is too wrapped up in that vixen of his."

Richard brought the glass to his lips, allowing its smooth coolness to reach his agitation and soothe its raging. "Although I can hardly blame him. Apart from her ample charms"—he smiled appreciatively —"I cannot honestly say he was played fairly. Wickham," he spat and brusquely turned to his desk. "That rapscallion. It is good he has been dispatched, or I would have done the deed myself."

His eyes sought out the unsigned letter that lay among the papers on his desk. A letter sent a week before informed him of the demise of George Wickham. Underneath it lay a clipping from the local papers recounting the finding of a body in a clutch of rocks known to trap large pieces of garbage making their way down the Thames to the sea.

Looking up, Richard was surprised to find his wife of two months enter through the door. "Anne?" he asked suspiciously as he rose to greet her. "To what do I owe the pleasure?"

"I heard you had returned and wished to speak with you."

He held out the chair for his cousin, noting the changes her developing body had wrought.

Despite himself—and his feelings towards her depravity—he could not help his body's response as he admired the revealing cut of her gown. Turning her head, Anne saw the evidence of her appeal and, straining her neck, placed a lingering kiss upon him, chuckling as he shuddered, no doubt assuming he felt pleasure in the act.

"If you would lock the door, husband, I would relieve your present condition to our mutual satisfaction."

"I see you have grown more circumspect. It is a pity you do so with your husband and not the livery boy." He returned to his desk.

A wicked grin spread across Anne's lips. "At Rosings, the servants all know better than to enter a closed door unless bidden."

"I had sent Trosclair to my chambers to retrieve my riding crop. Alas, it was already in service."

"Never mind that. I wish to return to Rosings for the remainder of my confinement."

"So you can cut a swath of seduction from London to Kent? I think not." He returned to stand in front of her. Suddenly, he yanked her to her feet. "You must behave. You are a countess now."

Anne cackled, shrugging out of his grasp. "Rosings and the fortune it generates are still mine, and I shall return to my home and do as I please. You may remain here with your mistresses or focus on the rebuilding of the Matlock name. Truly, I care not. When next we meet, it will be to christen your heir."

She headed for the door. Taking the knob in her hand, she turned to him. "And I take the boy with me. He will be a boon companion during my confinement." And with that, she left a dumbfounded Earl of Matlock staring into space.

JULIAN STOPPED to straighten his cravat before knocking on the door of his mother's study. Although he was a veteran of facing adversaries in the field of honour, society's drawing rooms, and countless political debates, Julian's heart pounded at facing his mother with this singular request. *It is a simple invitation I seek—not the keys to the kingdom.*

Knocking with more confidence than he felt, Julian bolstered himself before calling out, "Mother, may I come in?"

"Come, Julian," his mother called, and he relaxed as he opened the heavy wooden door into the bright, cheerful room.

"Mother—" He stopped mid sentence when he saw she was not alone in her work.

There, sitting alongside her on the golden-coloured couch sat his sister and Mrs Raleigh. In front of them on the long, low table—and various side tables waylaid into service—were stacks of papers and swatches of cloth and lace. His mother resembled a general in charge of outfitting a battalion of soldiers going off on a prolonged campaign.

"I beg your pardon. I was unaware you had company."

"I hardly call your sister 'company,' Julian."

Elizabeth rose and came to him. "Julian, are you well?"

"Of course I am." As she tried to place her hand to his brow, he batted her arm away. "I am well."

"Julian, did you need me?" the duchess asked.

He started to take a seat with the ladies.

"No, Julian, not there!" his mother exclaimed, rising hurriedly to prevent her son's bulk from crushing a particularly lovely swatch of velvet silk. "Over there." She expertly guided him to a hard, plain chair off to the side and kept in reserve for stacks of books to be returned to the library.

Julian harrumphed and took the offered seat. "Thank you for the comfort of your company."

"Julian, a wedding takes tremendous effort to plan."

He turned to his sister. "When is the blessed event to occur?"

"Oh, not for months now."

"And all this?"

Julian looked at Elizabeth, who looked at Mrs Raleigh, who looked at the duchess, who sighed before answering. "There are teas"—her hand pointed to a stack of papers—"dinners"—she indicated another pile and pointed to a third as she continued her litany—"fittings, musicians, bills of fare, gifts…"

She buried her head in her hands. "At least with your wedding, another house will manage all of this."

"I would not care to encourage your aspirations in that regard…"

"At this time?" his mother asked.

"At this time." He looked pointedly at her.

She nodded, and Elizabeth interceded. "So, what brings you to this den of madness then if not to announce your impending nuptials?" She grinned widely as Julian squirmed in his uncomfortable chair.

He coughed and readjusted his seat again. "I, that is, I have recently learned that a…an acquaintance of mine…"

The three women involuntarily leaned in closer to him. He felt the intrusion immediately. "Yes, she is in town, travelling with her cousin."

"I see," his mother said, quickly glancing at her long-time friend who looked back, astonished.

All three women waited for him to continue, and when he realised they were not going to make this easier for him, he shuffled his feet.

"I was hoping, if it is not too much an inconvenience, to include her…"

"Along with her cousin?" Elizabeth asked.

Julian turned to his sister. "Yes, along with her cousin." He returned his gaze to his mother. "To my sister's engagement dinner next week."

"Her cousin is a man?" The duchess assumed the chances of two women travelling alone was nigh impossible.

"Count Josef Illyonavich Reznokov."

"And your other guest…"

Elizabeth completed the thought for her. "Yes. The name of this friend of yours?"

"Acquaintance." Julian shifted in his seat.

"Acquaintance whom you wish me to invite to this family celebration," said his mother. "Of your sister's engagement…?"

"There will be more than simply family, Mama…" His tone was petulant.

Elizabeth quickly took up a sheaf of parchment and her quill. Dipping the tip in the inkpot, she asked, "And the name of this mysterious female acquaintance?"

"Princess Lysetteya Vladimirova Zakarevsky of Russia."

With a sly smile, Elizabeth then asked, "And where, may I ask, shall I send this?" Her eyes sparkled.

Julian straightened his waistcoat. "If you will be so kind as to write out the invitation, I shall be more than happy to deliver it."

And that is what she did as her mother and aunt howled with laughter and she fought to regulate her hand into some semblance of penmanship.

"WHAT DO you mean we must interrupt our travels?" Bingley asked, his face red in frustration. "Given the current climate, I do not believe that is advisable."

"I am sorry, Charles," Jane said, wringing her hands. "The physician advises that Caroline is unable to travel."

"For how long?"

"Two to three days at least."

Bingley turned his head. "But Louisa!" He closed his eyes, trying to resolve giving justice to the living *and* the dead till a gentle hand caressed his shoulder and he leaned into the arm attached to it. Opening his eyes, he watched Jane kneel alongside him, her eyes pools of kindness and concern.

"Oh, Jane, my love." He brought both her hands to his lips. "What am I to do? How shall we"—he choked on his emotions—"bury one sister while tending to the maladies of the other?"

Jane laid her hands on his knees, knowing he would stroke her golden locks and hoping it would soothe him. Gently, she sighed and took a deep breath. "I shall remain here with Caroline."

He gasped. "No!"

Jane placed a finger to his lips. "Louisa must be interred…and then later, perhaps after Mary's wedding, we can bring Caroline…"

Charles thought for a moment. "I shall leave Wilkes and Booth with you to guard her."

"I would like to send an express to Aunt Raleigh." He smiled and brightened. Jane continued formulating her plans. "Perhaps we, Caroline and I, could stay with the Raleighs until you return?"

He smiled. "Jane, you are as brilliant as you are beautiful. I shall arrange for a carriage to carry me to Yorkshire, and ours will return you to town. And I shall write Darcy and inform him of our change in plans. And to be on guard."

"You see, Charles. All will be well."

ALTHOUGH APPROACHING her second phase of pregnancy, Anne de Bourgh Fitzwilliam refused to follow her physician's recommendations, continuing on as she saw fit. As her belly grew with her lover's child, she became consumed with the desire to visit her mother before returning to Rosings.

"Lord Matlock will be occupied with his affairs throughout the day." Anne walked slowly to her desk. Sitting, she flipped through the papers of her predecessor.

"That imposter," she sneered. "She certainly abandoned the honourable house of Matlock soon enough."

She closed the book with her thin fingers. "Smart woman," she said softly. *For how could she compare her rule here with my own? Not yet a full month into my marriage and already I fulfil my duty*—she patted her belly—*the heir of Matlock and Rosings.*

Anne sat in the sumptuous leather chair, smiling. *I shall have this room redecorated while my confinement comes to a close. Then, what parties we shall have! What gaiety!* A wild, uncontrollable laugh echoed about the chamber until a knock announced her footman.

Seeing her solace broken by his unwanted presence, she barked, "What do you want?"

"Your carriage, madam."

"What? Oh yes." Anne made her way to the door. Without a word, she began her journey to Bedlam.

DARCY LET the last sheet of parchment slip from his hand, sighing with contentment. *That is the last of it. Finally!* He rubbed his eyes with his hand. "And now, for something entirely more pleasant." Leaping from his chair, he headed towards the door; instead, it opened when he was midway across the room, and Winters entered, followed closely by the new Lord Matlock.

"Richard?" Darcy could not mask his surprise.

"Darcy." Richard bowed.

"To what do I owe this visit?" Darcy regained his composure and beckoned his cousin to a seat.

"I apologise for my unanticipated call. I…" Richard ran a hand through his sandy hair before looking up at his well-to-do relative. "I have need of your counsel."

"What is it?"

"You know I have trained my entire adult life for battle, only to find myself loosed upon the world of ledgers and figures, invoices and expenditures. And it is all Greek to me."

"And I well recall how you took to the language of the ancients!" Darcy said, a slight smile lifting the unease in the room. "Taking command of an estate is daunting, even when one is prepared and schooled for it."

Richard again smiled and nodded. Darcy entwined his hands together. "I can only imagine in what state your father—"

Richard winced and glanced away.

"Forgive me, I only meant—"

"No no, you are right. From what I can decipher from the books father did leave, we are not yet destitute but very close."

"What about Anne's fortune?"

Richard snorted. "She keeps tight control of the coffers at Rosings."

"But how?"

"Some maniacal legal doggerel established by Lady Catherine. Each expenditure must be countersigned by a member of the female line."

"And you cannot convince her to your will?"

Richard nearly spit out his reply. "Have you tried speaking with Anne? Recently?"

"No, not if I can help it."

Richard smiled wryly. "Always knew you were a smart sod."

He looked away then returned to Darcy. "Her confinement increases her bad humour. She is unreasonable, even more than usual."

Both sat in silence for a moment.

"How can I be of help?"

"I was hoping we could make a plan, a way to address the situation."

"Without Anne's involvement?"

"Precisely."

Darcy nodded. "The town house?"

"Is sound. The estate brings in enough to cover expenses, but only just. The manor is in need of a great many repairs."

"Map out those of the greatest need, and we shall work out a schedule of renovations for the house. And the tenants?"

"I am afraid they are also in great need."

Darcy nodded. "I thought so." Gathering his thoughts, he continued. "You amaze me."

"How so?"

Darcy sighed. "Fate has dealt you a bad hand, and you rise to the difficulty. I am grateful that you took on Anne to give her and her child a name—a name that one day he or she will be proud of."

"I am afraid that day is an age away." He looked at his hands. "I have heard that, if not for father's untimely demise, he would have been tried…for treason."

Darcy's eyes widened.

"How am I to remove that blemish?"

"Of that, I know not." Again, silence reigned between them, but it was an easier one. "I should like to present this to my uncle."

Richard was truly shocked. "Are you mad?"

Darcy stiffened in his chair. "The duke is not a vengeful man."

"No?"

"No. If we are to move forward, you must realise that the infamy you now face was created by your father and our aunt."

"While you face a life with the delectable Lady Elizabeth…"

"I warn you—"

"Do not worry. I am shackled to that…to Anne."

Darcy comprehended the enormity of his cousin's fate. "For that, Richard, I am truly sorry and eternally grateful."

JULIAN STRODE into the parlour of the town house Princess Zakarevsky had taken for her sojourn in London.

"Princess." He bowed, taking her slender hand to his lips.

"Julian." She rose to greet him. "I am honoured you have come."

"I have"—he pulled out the sealed invitation from the inner pocket of his jacket—"the invitation to my sister's engagement dinner."

Her eyes widening in surprise, Lysetteya Vladimirova took the heavy parchment in her trembling hand. Running her fingers along the front of the envelope, she tried to compose herself.

She kept her eyes on her name written in a precise, even hand. "Julian, I…" She closed her mouth as if unsure what to say next.

Hoping to calm her, Julian took hold of her hand. "My darling, what is it?"

Unable to turn her eyes, Julian reached across the divide between them to take hold of her chin, gently leading it towards him. "Tell me what bothers you."

Silence.

"I know your mother needs help, but we shall find that help for her. I have read of a theory or two for curing one's addiction to opiates."

The princess brought her hand to her mouth, turning her head and her amazingly blue eyes from him.

"Please! There is nothing we cannot overcome."

"You do not understand." Her voice cracked with emotion.

"Then you must help me understand."

"Julian, my country is at war!"

"As is mine, but that should have no bearing on you and me."

"But it does."

"I do not understand, Lyse. We were at war yesterday and last week. What has changed?"

"Josef has received word. Napoleon's armies are marching towards the border. My estate is close by. Within a month they will take my home."

Struck speechless by this report, Julian sat for a moment in silence. "When did you learn this?"

"Just this morning," she said, tears audible in her voice. "I shall be penniless. We know what the Tsar's troops will do. They have orders to destroy it all, to burn it so Napoleon will find no refuge there."

Again, she looked into Julian's eyes, searching for the answer to her questions. "I shall have nothing."

No longer caring for the strictures of propriety, Julian took her in his arms, and the woman he admired for her courage and intellect crumbled. While his heart broke for her sorrow, he revelled in the liberty of being the one she turned to for comfort.

As the princess's tears soaked his coat, Julian kept his arms about her until the drawing room doors were thrown open and Count Josef Illyonavich Reznokov stormed through. Seeing his cousin in the arms of her lover, he stopped and announced brusquely. "Glascomb, good of you to come."

Slowly, Julian rose, tenderly disengaging his love from his embrace. "Reznokov."

The count glanced over at the woman who was pulling her

emotions back into place. "I believe Lysetteya Vladimirova has spoken of our...situation?"

"Yes, she told me."

"Good."

"What are your plans now?" Julian demanded.

Reznokov turned to face the Englishman. "I am an officer in the Tsar's army. I shall return and take my place in service to my country."

"And Lysetteya?"

"The princess will return with me."

"No." Julian took a step towards his imposing rival, who stood, continuing to stare at him.

"No? Why would I leave my intended wife here in a time of war when our country needs us?"

"She is not yours!"

A sardonic smile crossed the face of the not-quite-handsome man. "No? I have the permission of her mother and the Tsar."

"But not from her!" Julian exploded.

Again Reznokov baited his rival. "No?"

Josef Illyonavich Reznokov quirked his eyebrow then turned his gaze to the woman who had begun to whimper. "I believe your lady has been keeping secrets from you, Lord Glascomb. I shall leave you for your goodbyes." With that, the count turned and vacated the room.

Julian stared at the now-empty space, his mind a whirl of emotions. Before he could prepare a coherent thought, he turned on his heels, and in one full stride, he returned to stand before the princess.

"Lyse, tell me." Despite his best attempts, he could not keep the helplessness from his voice.

Wringing her hands, the princess took a moment before straightening her back to look at him. "My place is in Russia. I am promised to Josef Illyonavich, and I shall meet my family's obligation."

"What about us?" he asked, unable to believe what his ears were hearing.

Lysetteya took a deep breath. "You...you have been the joy of my heart, the shining moment of my life." Suddenly, her eyes turned to steel. "But, my place, my duty lies elsewhere. Goodbye, Julian. I shall never forget you." Lysetteya placed the gentlest of kisses on his cheek, her hand pressing his arm slightly. Then, she stepped back and walked out of the room.

Stunned, Julian could only look around the room until one of the liveried footmen entered.

"Sir?" he asked deferentially. Julian turned and looked at him as if he were speaking a foreign language.

"Your horse is ready." Julian snatched the invitation abandoned on the seat, leaving the room—and his hope—empty.

twenty-six

CAROLINE BINGLEY PACED THE CONFINES OF THE SMALL CHAMBER, HER thoughts matching the cadence of her steps. *I must escape—I must!* Nearing the window, she peered through the glass, searching for an unseen alternative. *If only Charles had not left Wilkes and Booth!* She wrung her hands and paced back to the hearth. *I can manage any of the others, but those two?* She shivered. *Who knew that...that chit was the sister to one and wife to the other?*

The door opening interrupted her thoughts as Jane entered, followed by a serving girl carrying a tray of tea. Caroline watched as Jane's eyes appraised her demeanour, and she straightened to her full height.

"I see you are remarkably recovered, Caroline," Jane said evenly. Caroline's eyes darted to the open door, but the bulky frames of her guards blocked the entrance, and Caroline slumped in the chair to hide her disappointment. Jane nodded to the girl, who placed the tea service on the table. She then offered Caroline the solitary cup.

"You will not join me even for tea?" Caroline asked

"No, I thank you," Jane responded, taking a step closer. "Please, drink."

"Why? Is there some poison you wish me to imbibe?"

Seeing Jane's eyes narrow, she tossed back her head and said with false assuredness, "I fear I am not yet thirsty."

Jane raised her hand, and the two men entered the room and shut the door.

"There is no escape, Caroline. This is a hole you have dug for too long. If we were to allow you back into society, you would be the ruin of us all. You have brought shame to the Bingley name." Caroline winced as though Jane had struck her. "And I shall not allow your vile behaviour to harm Charles any further."

"Why, you! How dare you speak so to me!" Caroline lashed out at her sister.

Jane laughed. "If you behave, perhaps you will be able to return in a few years. That is up to you."

Caroline felt Jane's gaze press into her.

"Now, drink."

Deciding it was in her best interest to comply for the present, Caroline daintily picked up the cup and, keeping her eyes on Jane, drained the cup to the last drop. Noting the strange taste, she set the cup back in the saucer, and the two women—with their relentless escorts—remained in the room until Caroline felt her head swoon and strong hands roughly carry her to her bed.

RALEIGH WAS a man who had faced numerous adversaries throughout his years at sea, difficulties testing every ounce of courage and fortitude he possessed. But as he read the hastily written express sent by his niece, the admiral felt true fear. "Into the breach once again, fair lads." He scooped the parchment off his desk. With a last look at the bottle of port sitting idly on his sideboard, Raleigh chuckled. *No, a clear head is best, I think. Mrs Raleigh will make mincemeat of me in any case, but it would be wise to keep my wits about me.*

The admiral found the duchess and her daughter with his wife in Mrs Raleigh's private sitting room. "Ladies," he said by way of greeting them. They looked up, startled that he would invade their feminine domain. "Please, forgive my intrusion, but I have just received an express from Mrs Bingley."

"Jane!" Elizabeth said in alarm.

"All is well?" Mrs Raleigh asked, rising to greet her husband.

"Admiral, what does she say?" the duchess asked

"Jane is well," the admiral assured them, taking his seat and settling his wife on the sofa facing their guests. "It is Miss Bingley."

"Of course," Mrs Raleigh said with a scowl. "Who else could it be?"

"What has she done now?" the duchess asked.

Mrs Raleigh took the parchment from his hands. "Oh, my goodness." She dropped her hands along with the express into her lap, turning her attention to her guests. "Miss Bingley claims a fever and a tremor. The doctor recommends complete rest. Jane remains at the inn while Charles has left to see to his other sister's burial."

"Poor Jane," Elizabeth said. "To be so far from home, alone, with Miss Bingley."

The admiral retrieved the missive. "Charles adds that he has left two of his best, burliest men to aid his wife in caring for their sister."

"Stephen, should we…?"

"I have sent word to Ketchum to begin packing our things, my dear." Admiral Raleigh smiled when his wife kissed his cheek. When Elizabeth came over and kissed the opposite cheek, he blushed.

Mrs Raleigh spoke next. "Charles should return within the week, so there will still be time to visit the exhibit before you leave town."

"Unless Caroline creates a stir."

"I believe the admiral and his superior"—the duchess nodded to her friend—"shall have the lady firmly in hand, Elizabeth."

She rose, and her daughter followed suit. "I believe even Bonaparte himself would quake in facing the combined efforts of these two."

And now"—she turned to her daughter—"I believe we should return to Northampton Place and leave you dear people to your travel arrangements. You will keep us informed?"

"Indubitably," rejoined both the admiral and Mrs Raleigh as they clasped their hands together.

DARCY MADE his way through the smoky rooms of Lady Hatfield's. Seeing the familiar face, he navigated the crush of men and women feeding the voracious appetites of the gaming tables. Only nearly missing an inebriated woman storming away from a particularly heavy loss, he wiped away the droplets of spirits she left in her wake and made his way to the beleaguered man.

"Hornsby?" he asked, hopeful for some sense of reason in this den of lunacy.

"Darcy?"

Darcy nodded.

"Come, he is in here." Hornsby led Darcy towards the back of the building to a fair-sized chamber. Looking about, he knocked three times, and upon hearing the lock turn, they entered.

Darcy was stunned to find Julian unconscious on a chaise longue. A dark-haired, buxom woman applied wet compresses to his forehead while a swarthy man kept watch. They spoke in lowered voices in a foreign tongue until, noticing the new arrivals, he approached Hornsby.

"This is Mr Darcy, Glascomb's cousin."

The woman gasped, and the man stepped between her and the new arrivals.

Hornsby continued. "Darcy has been just as wronged by the Matlocks as you have."

"But he is one of them." The woman moved behind the man who now had a short pistol pointed at Darcy's chest."

"No, yes, I…they are my relations, but I am not like them."

"You are the nephew, are you not?" the woman asked, and the man relaxed a bit but did not return his weapon to its holster.

"Yes, yes I am."

"You are the cousin of Lord Glascomb?"

"Yes."

The two conversed quietly among themselves in their native tongue, Darcy bristling viscerally when he heard the name 'Wickham.'

Julian moaned, and the woman returned to her nursing duties. The man motioned for them to sit at a table off to the side. He bowed to his lady and indicated the bottle of brandy and glasses. She nodded, and he attended to his guests.

"Salud." The man poured three glasses of some of the finest brandy Darcy would ever see.

Both Darcy and Hornsby lifted their glasses, exchanging dubious glances at each other. Their host turned the bareback chair, straddled it, and began. "Señor Darcy, I am Giancarlo Catervaux. Hornsby is my acquaintance, as is your cousin. You must forgive your reception, but my wife, Natalia, has no fond memories of your Matlock relations." Catervaux looked Darcy directly in the eyes.

Darcy inhaled sharply at the name, having some knowledge of his uncle's last mistress. "Is she well?"

Clearly surprised, Catervaux could only say, "Si."

"And Glascomb?" Hornsby asked.

"He arrived here midday to avail himself of the house's best vintage. It was not until the *ton* gathered that things got out of hand." He chuckled again and took another gulp of the smuggled spirit. "Glascomb is quite entertaining. His repertoire is extensive. Natalia made me aware of his exuberance, recalling his kindness and compassion to her." Catervaux shrugged. "Y cousin knows my wife, but not in that context."

"Official business, Darcy, all on the up-and-up," Hornsby concurred.

"Your cousin has a unique ability to see the man and not the occupation," Catervaux told Darcy, who nodded. "And to return the favour, I invited him here to sample some of my finest stock." He raised his glass.

"Lord Glascomb is a fortunate man," Darcy added.

"Indeed," Hornsby agreed. "But, Catervaux, how did he…" Hornsby looked over to the sedan where Julian now sat upright, aided by Señora Catervaux, who was tending a bruise on his right cheek. When Julian winced, all three chuckled at the scolding she gave him, as a mother would her child.

"Lord Pendergrin interrupted us, and it seems, Glascomb did not like something about his beard. He said it looked too Russian for his taste."

Catervaux remained confused even in the retelling. "One thing led to another, Pendergrin called in his friend, and the next thing I know, one of Delaboix's best customers is pinned against the wall. I had your cousin pulled off and brought here. But before we reached the door, Pendergrin's friend threw a punch and..." They all looked at the chaise. "That was that."

"Pendergrin's man?"

"Friend," Catervaux said with a knowing glance at Hornsby.

"Friend," Hornsby replied with a nod. "How did this 'friend' look after Glascomb hit him back?"

"He was not hit, señor." Catervaux took another sip from his snifter.

"No?" Darcy asked surprised. "That does not sound like Glascomb..."

"Your cousin was already restrained by my men. The guttersnipe hit a man whose arms were pinned down." The three exchanged glances, and slamming his glass down, Darcy went to his cousin's side.

"Can you stand?"

Julian looked up at his cousin. "Darcy? Is that you? Elizabeth will have somewhat of a fit knowing you frequent Lady Hatfield's." Julian's delivery warned the men that his injury had not cut through the fog of inebriation.

"I do not frequent Lady Hatfield's—no offence intended, ma'am," Darcy said apologetically.

"None is taken, sir," the señora replied with a smile.

Darcy bent to grab Julian's shoulder. "Hornsby, help me."

"Right you are, Darcy." The shorter man came, and between the two of them, they hoisted Julian to his feet.

"Where to, old boy?" Julian asked, looking between his mates.

"I believe your night of carousing is at an end," Darcy said. To his host, he bowed his head. "Thank you, Señor Catervaux, Señora Catervaux. We are indebted to your quick thinking and your discretion."

"I only ask you take care of him."

Again, Darcy nodded. "That we shall."

The three were shown to a back exit where their carriage stood waiting. After a prolonged effort, they were able to usher Julian into the carriage. As he began to feel the damage to his cheek, Hornsby asked. "Where to, old man?"

Swatting Julian's elbow away, Darcy said. "I believe even I am not cruel enough to let Julian face his mother in this condition. Or Elizabeth." Rapping on the roof of the coach, he called out, "To Darcy House, and make it bumpy."

LADY MATLOCK ADJUSTED the belt of her dressing gown as she languidly looked at the drawn bedclothes tussled around the boy, formerly in the service of her husband. *Now, he is in service to me. And what a service he provides,* she thought.

Hearing the commotion beyond the boundaries of her chambers at the travelling inn, Anne spoke sharply to her latest conquest.

"Brandon." She shook his leg, toying with the idea of drawing the rough cotton down his beautiful body. "Wake up—we must soon depart. Hurry!"

Slowly, the male who had only recently entered manhood lifted his eyelids to find his mistress looking at him with hunger. Quickly, he pulled the sheet to himself as protection then rose from the bed.

Sensing his withdrawal, Anne cackled. "None of that, my pretty. You are mine, at least until we return to Rosings. Then we shall see what to do with you."

This brought his attention to the danger before him. "Yes, Lady Matlock."

"That is a good boy." She kissed him roughly. "Now, prepare yourself. We complete our journey today."

The lad scurried off, picking up the clothes she had tossed away the night before, and made his way to the door of the adjoining room. His hand on the latch, he was surprised when Lady Matlock's maid opened the door, nearly spilling the contents of her tray. Seeing the embarrassed looks exchanged between her servants, Lady Matlock howled with laughter.

WITH MORE STRENGTH and enthusiasm than was entirely necessary, Darcy barged through the door to the bedchamber housing his errant cousin. "Julian," he bellowed, striding happily over to the windows where he threw open the curtains. When his greeting was met with only a low, keening moan, Darcy threw back his head and laughed.

Clapping his hands together and rubbing them, Darcy pulled back the duvet cover, exposing Julian as he lay on his back, his hands rushing to his eyes and protecting them from the sudden onslaught of light. "Please, I beg of you—mercy!"

"How is your face?"

Julian lowered his hands and opened one eye. "My face? What happened to my face?"

"Let me just say: it will be a while before you are presentable to any ladies besides our family circle."

Seeing his cousin's true dismay, Darcy walked to the washstand where he poured some clear, fresh water over a cloth and then some into a glass as well. "Here." He laid the cool, wet cloth across his cousin's brow.

"And when you are able, sit up and drink this."

Suddenly, Julian was gripped by true pain. His shoulders slouched, and he turned away, the mirth draining from him before Darcy's eyes. Darcy watched his cousin confront what must be some painful truth he came upon yesterday. Taking a deep breath, he began.

"Should you need a confidant, I am at the ready."

"I shall keep your offer in mind." Silence again stretched between them. "It is…it is still too new." Julian's hand repositioned the cloth to block out all the room's light. "The pain…overpowers. Please, I beg you, a moment of my own."

Darcy looked at his cousin, agony evident in the way Julian drew his body into a curled position, his back now fully turned towards his host.

What more can I do? What would I wish for? he asked himself. *Privacy*, he quickly realised, and so he pushed himself off the bed. "I shall send up a tray for you, Julian. And I will be in my study when you are ready."

Darcy could see Julian's head nod in acknowledgment, so he turned and left the room, barely able to hear the whispered, "Thank you, Darcy. For everything."

ANNE LOOKED out of the carriage door that opened before her and viewed the impressive façade of the institution whose name had come to chill the heart of all England. The Hospital of Saint Mary of Bethlehem, known as Bedlam, had a formal air to it as if order was of the utmost importance.

Mother must like that, she thought as she noted her hand trembled. With a sharp intake of breath, she descended from the carriage.

She headed down the well-groomed path to the entrance of this fortress of insanity. Each step created a unique sensation as the cries of birds caught her ear. *Must be the crows at the refuse heap,* she thought. *I am surprised Mama has not given them her remedy for chasing that nuisance away. Rosings never had such an outcry.*

"Madam?" A black-coated man approached Lady Matlock, and as her eyes raked over his frame, she smiled salaciously. *Perhaps we can have a private discussion of Mama's accommodations.*

Recalling the need to respond to him, Anne spoke. "I am Lady Matlock, here to see Lady Catherine de Bourgh."

"Are you a relation?"

"Her daughter."

"Ah." The man spread his arm towards the front door. "This way, your ladyship. I shall escort you, personally."

"And you are?"

"Stone. I have the dubious distinction of being the second in command here as well as the physician overseeing the general health and sanitation of our patients."

The two walked through the main corridor, and the wailing of the birds increased.

"As overseer of the sanitation, you must do something regarding your population…"

"Madam?" he asked with surprise.

"The birds, sir. The birds."

"Birds?" His face reflected his confusion.

When another wail reverberated through the hall, Anne inclined her head towards the long chamber beyond the iron gate before which they now stood. "The birds. Their raucous cawing must be a source of ire to your patients."

The man rose from his stupor, raising his hand to halt the unlocking of the gate by the guard. "Madam, those are not birds."

"Of course they are, sir. I have heard them in London."

"Those are the wails of the people living here."

As another plaintive wail grew from within the building, Anne's face drained of what little colour it possessed. She looked with horror-filled eyes at her companion. "Within? Here? From those who live here?"

Dr Stone nodded.

"I see," she said weakly.

"Are you sure you wish to continue? Most of our visitors are unrelated to those unfortunates who reside in our care. And in your delicate state…" He glanced at her extended abdomen.

Anne threw back her shoulders and lifted her chin. "Proceed."

The physician nodded to the guard, who unlocked the door and swung the gate on its hinges. Anne kept her eyes straight ahead, and with a shrug of his shoulders, the doctor left his employee, quickening his step to match his guest's pace.

THE RALEIGHS BEGAN their second day of travels in concerned silence. Although they took enough books and busy work to occupy their time, neither was able to control their agitation to stay with anything, even conversation, for very long. Mrs Raleigh watched her husband, his eyes casting about the country passing by their window. As he did at sea when commanding his fleet, the admiral was always scanning for trouble. Mrs Raleigh sighed, wondering who could have predicted this bit of turbulence brewing on the horizon. *After all, she was to attend her sister's funeral, for heaven's sake!* Mrs Raleigh tightened the grip she had on her book of poems. *The nerve of that woman! I know she is up to something. I can just feel it.* Mrs Raleigh felt the eyes of her husband upon her, questioning the strained look that had taken hold of her.

"Mrs Raleigh, are you well?" he asked with concern.

"My thoughts were on Miss Bingley."

The admiral nodded in reply. "As were my own."

"What can she mean by this?"

"There is the possibility she is truly ill…"

"Yes, but that type of illness…"

"My dear, she had to fool a physician."

"A country doctor who may be blinded by her charms."

The admiral considered that. "Perhaps…"

"I put nothing past that woman."

"A wise position—but is she quick enough to devise a plan of attack in so short a time?"

Mrs Raleigh considered this then nodded. "I believe she is."

"But what is her aim?" Raleigh crossed his arms over his chest. "If she does mean to escape her present circumstances, where would she go? Bingley has closed his home to her, and Hurst will not admit her."

Mrs Raleigh categorised Caroline's alternatives. "Her aunt, I hear, is strict but not unfair."

"But not the coddling type?"

"No, I believe that, like most who live on their own, she will not suffer the simpering demands of her niece."

"And Miss Bingley appears to undervalue the strength Jane hides beneath her sweetness."

Mrs Raleigh harrumphed. "You would think one as observant as Miss Bingley would realise that one must have a source of strength to survive Franny Bennet."

"It will be to our advantage, then, if she does not realise Jane's ability. It is a foolish foe who underrates one's opponent."

Mrs Raleigh reached across the cabin to pat her husband's knees. "Always the strategist, my love?"

He smiled completely, taking her hand and pulling her to his side of the bench. "One of my more endearing traits."

After a few minutes of listening to the wheels roll beneath them, he said, "Do not fear, my dear. We shall stand by Jane at all costs. And our resources stretch far beyond those to which Miss Bingley can lay claim. She will be found. And we, as a family, shall decide what is to be done with her."

Mrs Raleigh gifted him with a look full of love and admiration for the man who had always been her hero.

WHEN THE PAIR arrived at the cell, Anne was horrified beyond her worst dreams. There, in a five foot square cell was Lady Catherine, chained and plainly visible through a wide-grill row of thick, iron bars. In front of the bars was a well-dressed couple, twitting her mother behind the woman's fan, which occasionally poked between the bars as if to instigate a response.

"You there!" Anne called out, walking as fast as she could. "Stop that this instant! That is my mother! How dare you mock Lady Catherine de Bourgh!" The pair turned towards the intruder and stared. Anne recoiled as the familiar faces of Lord and Lady Harriman sneered at her; with a huff, they turned and walked away.

Sagging against the bars, Anne breathed deeply, utterly mortified. *I know those people!* She turned to her mother cowering in the corner. With shame, Anne took in her mother's appearance, noting the haggard and frightened look in her eyes. Her gown was dishevelled and soiled, the sleeves frayed at the edges where, even now, Lady Catherine plucked at the threads. It was an action that seemed to soothe her.

"Mama?" she whispered as hot tears splashed against her cheek. Dr Stone's hand gently guided her to the other side of the corridor where he pulled a chair for her comfort.

"Are you well, milady?" he asked with true concern. She nodded.

"Anne?" Lady Catherine's voice was weak and more frail than Anne could recall.

"Mama?"

"Sister!" Lady Catherine staggered towards the front of the cell, only to be halted three feet away by a heavy metal chain. Stretching her arms towards the bars, she called again. "Anne? Go find Mama! Tell her to tell Papa I will not marry Philip. I will not. He cannot force me."

Anne gasped and looked up at the physician. He took her hand and pulled at it gently to help her back to her feet. Leading her from the chamber, Anne noted the armed guards and, as she looked back at her insensible parent, heard her mother's wails increase to screams for the Earl and Countess of Matlock to come and bring her home.

twenty-seven

CHARLES BINGLEY WEARILY REMOVED HIS HAT FROM HIS BOWED HEAD, handing it to his aunt Clarissa Bingley Stemple's housekeeper. With kind eyes, Mrs Littleton took his things then turned to lead her favourite Bingley to the mistress of the house. As the doors opened, the elderly Mrs Stemple struggled to stand and, opening her arms to her nephew, received his embrace.

"Is it done?" she whispered.

He replied, "Yes. All is arranged. Tomorrow."

She led him to a chair. "Charles, you are a good man, a fine man. You have done your duty to your sister and your parents."

He turned away, but she continued. "You are not to blame for the wickedness of your sisters. Those girls were both on the path to ruin, always after more than they deserved."

Charles looked at her sharply, and Mrs Stemple held his gaze. "I do not mean that their father and his honest work held them back, but you know they never thought beyond their own pleasure or gain."

Charles hung his head, and she reached up, lifting his chin so he would meet her eyes. "You were always there to lead them back, but one man can only do so much." The older woman's knees buckled, and instantly Charles gently aided her return to the chaise she favoured.

"What if I fail so with my own children?"

Mrs Stemple's eyes opened wide, her smile expectant.

Seeing she had mistaken his meaning, he quickly added. "Not yet. I mean, in the future. When Jane and I are so blessed."

She patted his hand. "From what you tell me of your Mrs Bingley, I believe your children will be well loved and guided gently but firmly on the path to righteousness."

Charles smiled indulgently at her. "But Jane is as kind and forgiving as I. And look how well that worked with Louisa and Caroline…"

"Your Jane seems able to take care of herself. I would put my faith in her. She loves you?" He nodded with great enthusiasm. "Then she will see that you and your family are well served. You must have faith, boy."

"I shall try, Aunt." He looked at her with tears in his eyes. "I shall try."

JULIAN LET THE CURTAIN FALL, his head still not receptive to the light. Leaning against the window, he sighed, knowing that by now the princess and the count were across the channel, heading to an uncertain fate. He knew from his Foreign Office work that Napoleon would attack in the near future, if not already in progress. His time in Amsterdam, spent with diplomats and Cossack officers, gave him valuable insight into the scorch and burn methods of the Russian Tsar's army. He lifted the sheer fabric, looking out onto the park one more time and recalling the fertile fields of the Ukraine.

Napoleon lives off the land to feed his men and fuel his advance. Bogdanovich is wise to leave nothing to feed Bony's beast. But Lysetteya!

His heart clenched in pain, and he staggered, grateful for the window's sill. *Raz…has won,* his mind cried. *He will re-establish her family's honour at court while I…? I could only bring her here, away from her home. At least now, she will have the chance to rebuild.*

After a long sojourn through an internal struggle, Julian pulled himself back to the present. Straightening, he adjusted his cravat, ran a hand through his hair—a trait he shared with his sister—and left to find his cousin.

Entering the breakfast room, Julian was surprised to find the master of the house leaning with his head bent towards his betrothed, his own father at the opposite side of the table with the morning's papers strewn in front of him across the table. All three looked towards him as he bounded into the room.

"Father!" Julian watched the older man search his countenance for clues to his well-being.

"Julian," Northampton replied. After a moment, his eyes cut back to his daughter and nephew.

Darcy helped Elizabeth to her feet, and as they passed the marquess, Elizabeth gently kissed his cheek while Darcy gripped his shoulder. In a moment, father and son remained alone in the room. Talking a brief look at the departing couple, Julian began. "I take it—"

"Darcy informed me of both where you were found and in what condition."

"Does Mama…?" Julian could not help but wince.

"She knows you were at Lady Hatfield's." The duke resumed his seat. "They can piece together the reasons you were brought here rather than home." Julian was now at the sideboard, filling a most welcome cup with coffee.

The duke waited until his son was seated before speaking. "What I wish to know is why."

Julian's eyes fell, his throat tightening.

"Your mother informed me of your lady friend. I assume she has something to do with this?"

Julian only nodded.

The duke sighed into the silence of the rooms, a hundred questions filling his mind. Dismissing them all save one, he asked. "Is there any hope?"

Julian shook his head.

"You are sure?"

"She is on a ship bound for a Russia that is either under siege as we speak, or will be by summer's end." Julian's fist hit the table. "By the time I could find her, she would be shackled to a man who loves no woman but will re-establish her family at court."

He looked at his father. "She has chosen another. I offered her my hand, my name, my heart, but she chose another." His fingers curled around the fork he held. "And her country above all."

IT HAD COST Caroline two gold pendants, but she was able to convince the serving girl at the inn to steal the case containing Dr Clements's potions. Another ring—the topaz—and she was able to purchase the girl's cooperation in doctoring the tea offered to all three of Caroline's companions.

As the bustle of the day began, two large bodies and one graceful figure slumped to the floor, and Caroline slunk out of her rooms and onto the streets of Nottingham. Breathing deeply the air of freedom, she pondered, with a smirk and a wary eye, her next move.

To London I must go! She headed towards where she could secure passage on the next coach south.

Uncharacteristically, another thought entered her head, and pain ripped through her heart. "Louisa!" Her mind recalled the still and silent figure of her sister as she last saw her. She thought of Charles, standing alone at the grave. A scream threatened to overwhelm her, and she stumbled backwards against a nearby building, falling into a void of misery.

DARCY LED Elizabeth along the passageway to his study where he hoped to enjoy an uninterrupted visit with her. Leaning against the closed door, he gave himself the pleasure of watching her move through one of his most private, intimate spaces. While concerned for Julian and all too cognisant of the pain of unrequited love and missed opportunities, Darcy could not but feel his heart's joy in having Elizabeth finally at Darcy House.

"Elizabeth." He approached, arms outstretched to receive her. Turning, she stopped her perusal of Darcy's private domain to smile brilliantly at his open greeting. They met in the middle of the chamber, arms instantly around each other's waists.

She pulled back to look into his eyes as if searching for answers. "He looks so despondent."

Darcy could see concern fill her. He took a deep breath, amazed at the raw pain suddenly filling his own heart. "He has lost his love." Sensing he spoke of more than her brother's feelings, Elizabeth redoubled her grip on him. Lifting onto her toes, she showered his face and neck with kisses and words of endearment. Darcy held her, drinking in her love with every pore of his body.

"Elizabeth," he moaned, answering every one of her kisses with two of his own. "How I love you. If you were to go away now, I believe I would die. My heart would simply stop, broken under the yoke of sadness. I want to marry you."

She laughed. "Yes, that is the general conclusion of an engagement, my darling."

He gave her a lopsided grin and took her hands to hold against his heart. "I mean now." He kissed her nose. "As soon as may be."

She broke away, slowly making her way to the sofa where she sat down. He came and sat near her, his leg pressed against the silk of her gown. Gently, he took her hand, eyes transfixed on the workings of her mind as they played across her lovely features.

Coming out of her internal reverie, Elizabeth turned to him. "I believe I may convince Mama of the beauty of September."

"September?" he asked, nibbling the knuckles of the hand he held to his lips. His eyes twinkled as her response was wiped out by his ministrations. "September," he repeated. "What will happen in September, my love?"

Dazed, Elizabeth looked up at him, snapping to attention as he lowered her hand. "We shall wed. You must stop that! We must focus, and I...that is not possible when you do that!"

"No? I find my focusing powers"—he leaned in to her lips, speaking softly, his breath caressing her skin—"incredibly heightened by the activity." Before she could respond, her lips were sealed by his, and he leaned ever more into her, forcing her to recline against the cushions of the sofa.

His hands now upon her waist, his lips at her ear, he whispered, "September." He pulled on her lobe. "Sounds like a magnificent month in which to wed." He slid his hand along her left side, rising until it caressed her neck. He smiled, feeling her shiver in response, his heart rejoicing as she pressed herself to him, pulling him onto her reclining form.

"Is it September yet?" He ran his tongue along the hollow of her neck.

"Soon, my love. Soon," she answered before their lips locked again and speech was rendered redundant as their bodies effortlessly communicated their desire.

CAROLINE'S EYES fluttered as her mind comprehended that she was in a moving vehicle.

"Madam?" came a reedy voice as Caroline closed her eyelids against the unknown. "Are you ill?"

She sat up, straightening her gown. She took in a nearly handsome man and a woman old enough to be Methuselah before she replied, "No, I am well."

The man released her but kept his eyes alert for another spell. He tipped his hat. "Mr Ambrose McDonald, ma'am. At your service." The man looked to his left. "And this is my mother, Lady Sara Bingham McDonald."

"Caroline—" She hesitated, thinking quickly. *I cannot use my true identity. Charles may be simple, but he is as tenacious as a bull. No, best to think of something else—something that will throw my dim-witted brother off my trail.*

She smiled coyly at the gentleman who was staring openly at her. The carriage hit a bump, and involuntarily, all eyes skittered to the countryside rolling past the window, giving Caroline a moment to think. *Meryton is where this all began...*

"Meryton, Miss Caroline Meryton," she said with a demure smile.

"May we see you to your destination?" The older woman smiled at Caroline, whose head turned between the kindly looking woman and her son. Giving her rescuers a half-smile, she was about to speak when she realised she knew not where to turn. Her lovely features reflected her distress.

"I am unsure."

Lady McDonald watched the beautiful, haunted-looking woman

intently. "Then, if you would allow me to offer my house as a respite?" Seeing her recoil from the offer, she chuckled. "I shall be happy for your company until you can decide upon your next move."

Caroline hesitated until a carriage rolled past, heading in the opposite direction towards Nottingham. Mrs Raleigh's profile passed before her, deciding Caroline's fate. With a reluctant smile, she nodded. "I thank you, sir, Lady McDonald. That would be most kind."

Allowing his smile to widen, Ambrose McDonald leaned back against the cushions of his carriage, very pleased indeed, as his carriage continued down the road.

twenty-eight

BEFORE LEAVING THE YARD HIS PARENTS HAD FIRST WALKED AS MAN and wife, Bingley took a last look at the newly dug grave. "Louisa. How did you fall so far?"

He bent to touch the freshly dug ground. *Who could have known that this would be the end of your brief life?* After the burial, and seeing the mourners were hosted to a toast at the local inn, Charles had returned to the cemetery for his final farewell to the girl who had helped him learn to read and keep his figures in line. Louisa had played with him, spending hours lying on the floor and arranging his tin soldiers in formation long after his mother had insisted he should have left them in the nursery. In the quiet of the summer's morning, he recalled happier times when Louisa chased him around the park or took him to feed the ducks.

Returning to the home of his youth, Bingley allowed his thoughts to turn to his wife and remaining sister. *I shall not let you bring your shame to Jane's door. Not this time, never again. No more!* With new determination, he unlatched the gate to his aunt's residence, striding up the steps. The door opened as he reached the last step, and nodding, he handed his stick and hat to Stallings.

While taking the young master's gloves, the butler spoke. "Sir, an express came for you nearly half an hour ago from Admiral Raleigh. I left it in your father's old study."

"Very good," Bingley said before heading down the corridor to the room where the elder Bingley had secured their fortune. As soon as he entered the room, he hurried to the desk and opened the express with alacrity.

June 24, 1812

Bingley,
Be not alarmed, son. Jane is well. Mrs Raleigh and I arrived mid-day to find our dear Jane and your men, Wilkes and Booth, unconscious. I know no other way to say this but that your sister has vanished. Jane found that her trunks remain in her chamber, and from what Jane can tell, not much if anything has been taken. Jane knows of no acquaintance your sister may claim in the area, and we are at a loss where to begin our search. I have sent two of the cadets I brought with me to scour the town for her.

Upon our arrival, we spoke with the innkeeper and his employees in hopes of gaining the least bit of information. Lieutenant Shelling has just informed me that the girl who attended your sister during her convalescence did not arrive for work this morning. I shall end this, as I believe a visit to her domicile will be a good place to begin our investigations. Please, come at your earliest convenience—for Jane's sake and so that we may leave this place and return to London. Both Jane and my dear wife agree with me that town would be the logical destination for your sister. We shall discover what we may and reveal all to you upon your return.

Raleigh

"Stallings!" Bingley bellowed as he hurried out of the room. "I must leave as soon as may be."

Stallings promised to notify his man and directed Bingley to the drawing room where his aunt sat.

"There you are," Mrs Stemple said as she rose to greet her nephew. She met him midway through the room. "How was the service?"

"It went very well."

"What is it, dear?" Her eyes scanned him, no doubt seeing his agitation.

"Caroline. Always Caroline."

"What has she done now?"

"She has drugged my wife and footmen to escape."

"No!"

"It seems she used the laudanum Dr Clements gave us for her. In any case, the admiral and Mrs Raleigh need me straightaway."

"I shall pack my bags."

"You, Aunt?"

"Yes." She patted his hand that still held hers. "You and your Jane will need help in tracking Caroline. I know how she thinks."

"As always, dear Aunt Clarissa, you are right."

A KNOCK RESOUNDED in the silence of the duke's study. "Enter," he called without looking from the letter in front of him.

"Papa?" Elizabeth entered the room.

Hesitating, he rose to greet her. "Elizabeth, my love, please come in." He watched her take her seat before him. Her hands trembled as she clasped them together.

He took a seat beside her. "What is it?"

She returned his full smile with a weak one of her own. "Father, I —I have been thinking lately…been consumed really in one fashion or another…"

"With Darcy?" The Duke attempted to tease, only to be surprised by the shaking of her head.

"No…with Lady Catherine."

"Lady Catherine!" Northampton reared back. "My dear, she is gone. We have no need to worry about her."

"No, I mean, yes, I know and understand this. It is just…last night I had a dream, and the vision of it haunts me." Elizabeth took a deep breath. "I wish to go to Bedlam and see her."

"Absolutely not!"

"I assure you I have no morbid curiosity to see her or torment her—"

"It would be absolutely in your rights to do so!" the duke exclaimed.

"Papa!" Elizabeth scolded teasingly. "No. I need to go and… forgive her. It is the only way I shall find peace."

"Out of the question."

"But people go there every day. I have read about it in the papers."

"Yes, I know that some indulge their prurient desires to see…but it is a place of suffering, my dear, great suffering."

He sighed, holding on to the delicate fingers that encased his own. Elizabeth stroked his hand, her eyes kind. *Might this provide a sense of completion for her?* "But to forgive her?" the duke asked aloud.

Elizabeth took a long time to reply. "Yes, Father. I have found in my numerous run-ins with Mrs Bennet that only in forgiving shall I find peace."

This piqued the duke's interest as Elizabeth's eyes began to dance with delight. "And," she added, her lips twitching at the corners. "It is so beautifully confounding when the person you forgive has absolutely no notion of what they are being forgiven for."

Absolutely at a loss to deny her anything as she sat, innocence and determination in her eyes, the duke squeezed his daughter's hands. "Of course."

Elizabeth's eyes lit up even more, and she jumped up to kiss her father on his cheek.

"I shall arrange everything," he said. "But…you will be the one to explain this to your mother!"

DARCY STRODE into the rooms Julian had taken as his own at Darcy House. As the door swung against the wall, Julian startled, the book in his hand falling to the floor. "Julian, I have great need of your assistance."

"If this is some outlandish means to get me to vacate these rooms, I am afraid you are wasting your time and my own." Julian returned to the pages of his book. When Darcy came and unceremoniously pushed his feet off the furniture, he looked up, his brow arched.

"This is no time for your juvenile attempts at humour," said his benefactor.

"What is it? A recalcitrant tenant? Or has one of your prize stallions thrown a shoe?"

"Caroline Bingley has escaped."

"How could Bingley—"

"Bingley was not there."

Julian leapt from the couch and began to pace. "You said he was dependable…"

"Bingley was forced to continue on to Scarborough to bury his other sister."

This stopped Julian in his tracks. "I am sorry. I forgot."

Darcy nodded. "While attending to his duties to one—"

"—the other flew the coop." Julian turned away, his hand caressing his lips as he strode to the window.

"It seems neither Mrs Bingley nor the two guards Bingley left with her believed Miss Bingley capable of laying hands on laudanum and drugging them."

"That would give her perhaps three hours—depending on the dosage, of course." On his cousin's enquiring look, Julian added, "I have had occasion to familiarise myself with various preparations of the medicinal. What is being done to retrieve her?"

"Admiral Raleigh and his wife are headed to Nottingham where the Bingleys parted ways."

"And you wish to continue the search here?"

Darcy nodded.

"I shall be happy to aid you in your quest, my soon-to-be brother."

With an abject look of relief, Darcy asked, "Where should we begin?"

"It has been my experience with one not necessarily accustomed to a life on the run that the subject does not stray very far from the familiar."

"But does that not lessen the chances of maintaining one's escape?"

"Yes and no." Julian re-settled himself in the nearby chair.

"Although Miss Bingley has shown herself to be more resourceful than I would have imagined…" Julian allowed his thoughts to silence him.

"Julian?"

"Ah…right." Julian reclaimed the moment. "A woman of Miss Bingley's reputation and resources would not stray too far into the disreputable."

"At least, we may be grateful for something."

"One must learn to take advantage of all one can." Julian ran his hand along the small table next to him. "What do you know of Miss Bingley's habits?"

"I cannot really say." Darcy thought for a moment. "She plays the pianoforte tolerably enough to amuse. She is not a great reader." Darcy snapped his fingers. "Shopping! I have never met another who is more obsessed with keeping abreast of the latest fashion than she is."

"At the risk of upsetting my father, I shall recommend that my mother and sister visit the shops and perhaps ask a few questions of one of the favourite patrons of the *beau monde*."

Darcy relaxed against the back of a finely appointed chair. *Finally —a plan!*

twenty-nine

CAROLINE BINGLEY COULD NOT BELIEVE HER LUCK. NOT ONLY WAS SHE free from the nuisance of both her brother, his insolent wife, and their dreary aunt, but she was the guest of Lady and Mr McDonald. She cackled at her own brilliance; her story of running away from home to join a mission worked like a charm!

She sat herself contentedly in the fashionable chair. *The man is besotted, it seems—his eyes! I felt like he would devour me if his mother were not in the room.* She kicked up her heels in satisfaction. *And the bit about my going against the wishes of my heathen brother was sheer brilliance!*

With an appraising eye, she surveyed the richly appointed, if somewhat sombre, suite she had been given. *Something worthy of Mr Darcy.* Thinking of Mr Darcy led Caroline's mind to linger on the fit physique of Mr McDonald, and she smiled avariciously. *Perhaps this missionary man would be good for me,* she thought, running her hands over the top of her body. *There is something in his eyes that enthrals me.* She sighed.

A knock on her door stopped her pacing. "Come," she barked as a serving girl entered with a dark gown on one arm and a brush and comb in the other.

Caroline nodded towards the table in the corner then turned, dismissing the servant without a word. "If you please, miss—" the girl shyly began once she had deposited the items as directed.

Caroline turned in a huff.

"The master wishes you to join him and Lady McDonald in the music room once you have refreshed yourself." Her eyes looked towards the sombre gown.

Caroline nodded again and turned. Expecting more, the girl waited a moment then bobbed her curtsey to the lady's back and left the room. Again alone, Caroline examined the gown. It was of the finest muslin, but its colour was deep indigo, nearly black. Holding it up, she shook her head in disgust. *So unfashionable. At least five years out of date.* A wicked thought entered her mind, and she smirked. *No one would ever expect Miss Caroline Bingley to wear such a gown.*

Perhaps it will not be so useless after all.

DARCY PACED about the confines of his uncle's music room. *Where is she?* He nervously fingered the small, square box in his waistcoat pocket. After another three rounds of the room, he stopped before the window overlooking the garden and pulled the box out into the daylight. Opening it, he smiled as the facets of the clear stone cast rainbows about the room. Gently, almost reverently, he traced a long finger around the oval diamond then took up the delicate band of white gold, imagining what it would look like on Elizabeth's hand.

When the door opened, he looked up, so entranced that his fingers let go of the stone. The sound of the ring bouncing against the wood floor stopped him from gaping at his intended. Executing a hasty bow, he bent to his knees hoping to retrieve the errant jewel before it rolled behind the curtain.

Sensing what was happening across the room, Elizabeth came to his side and knelt. "What do you seek?"

Looking up into her sparkling eyes, Darcy paused, sitting back on his heels. He held his breath. *Elizabeth is here, on her hands and knees, gown gaping.* He swallowed hard before continuing his train of thought.

He licked his suddenly dry lips, his stare unabated until her giggle forced his eyes to her face, and he blushed at her mirth. Leaning forward, she kissed him on the lips, and he grabbed hold of her arms, pulling her towards him. His lips sought her cheek and then her neck before he kissed his way up to her ear. "I came bearing a gift for you."

"Fitzwilliam," she gasped before her lips took in the lobe of his ear, her hands pulling his head closer to her own.

Feeling his need for her increase nearly beyond his control, Darcy finally pulled away, marvelling at the desire he saw flashing in her eyes. "We must desist...I...your parents..."

She nodded and, taking deep breaths, retrieved her hands from his hair to rearrange her own.

He smiled and drew his eyes away, catching a gleam of light. Stretching for it, his shoulder collided with her breast, and he moaned at its softness. Instead of falling back, she pushed into him. He snatched the errant ring before wrapping his arms around her. "You do not play fair!"

"Of course not, my love. What would be the fun in that?" Elizabeth pulled Darcy to her, latching her lips to his.

As their tongues touched, footsteps approached. They pulled back, and their eyes held as their panting breaths calmed. Darcy offered to help her to her feet. Gently, he kissed her knuckles, watching as she lowered her eyes to their clasped hands, still held against his chest. Darcy took great pleasure as Elizabeth's eyes grew wide. Following her gaze, he surveyed his pinkie finger where, at the knuckle, sat his... their... grandmother's ring. "This is the ring the last Elizabeth Darcy received from her—"

"—beloved."

Elizabeth smiled at him, and a great joy rushed through him.

He clasped his hand over hers. "Yes—beloved. And as my beloved, it is my desire that you wear this as a token of the love I so dearly have for you." She nodded, and with her hand still in his, he manoeuvred the ring from his finger onto hers. Reverently, he whispered, "With this ring, I pledge thee my life, Elizabeth. You have my heart, my love, my everything." He looked unwaveringly into her eyes. "I love you."

She smiled, and her face radiated her joy. "As I do you."

Their lips reengaged until the duke's aggressive clearing of his throat drew them apart. They looked up with a blush of embarrassment to see Georgiana looking on as they heard the duchess's laughter filling the hall.

ANNE SNUGGLED BACK into the cushion of her open carriage as it rolled along the lanes of Kent. The countryside coming into full bloom was lost to her as she recalled the young man whose blossom she had plucked—repeatedly. *I believe I rather enjoy being with child,* she thought, her hand languidly stroking the protrusion of her belly. *It whets the appetite so.*

As Rosings came into view across the way, Anne's thoughts darkened. *Mama will never again see the sun shine on Rosings, her...our... home.* Her eyes turned downward to the child within. *And you, little one—you shall never know how great is your grandmother.*

Anne's agitation was churning as quickly as the wheels of her carriage. *This is not to be borne!* An idea grew in Lady Matlock's brain.

WHEN THE ELLISTONS and Darcys settled themselves, Elizabeth served tea, and the duke addressed Darcy. "I take it Elizabeth has not informed you of her plans?"

"Plans?" Darcy asked. "What plans?"

The duchess said, "Elizabeth wishes for an audience with Lady Catherine."

Darcy stared silently at Elizabeth, who focused on the teacup in her lap. He remained so fixated that Georgiana reached over and gently shook his hand.

Recovering, Darcy blurted out, "Absolutely not!" He addressed Elizabeth. "Are you out of your mind?"

Elizabeth rolled her eyes then calmly sipped her tea while Darcy continued to glare at her. The others sat back in anticipation.

"Aunt, Uncle?" Darcy continued. "You cannot seriously consider allowing this to happen?"

Before her father could reply, Elizabeth responded. "It is not a request, but yes, he has."

"And you, Aunt?" Darcy could not keep the disapproval or desperation from his voice.

"I have been outnumbered. Perhaps you could convince her not to attempt this folly," the duchess said with earnest hope.

Again, Elizabeth was too quick. "No, he cannot." She turned to Darcy. "I understand your reservations—"

"Do you?" Darcy leapt from his seat to pace about the room. He rounded back on her. "Do you really?" He placed one hand on each arm of her chair and brought his face within inches of her own. "Bedlam is a filthy, horrendous place—full of people who suffer terribly. There is filth…"

"Yes, you mentioned that," Elizabeth said as calmly as possible. When Georgiana giggled nervously, her brother turned his glare on her.

"…and disease."

"Be that as it may," Elizabeth said before taking another sip of tea, "I must." She looked up at Darcy who held her gaze until he could no more and looked away.

"I never thought you to be vindictive, Elizabeth."

Shocked, Elizabeth hastily put her cup on the table and rose, giving her future sister a gentle squeeze on the shoulder before going to him. "It is not for vengeance."

Her eyes searched his. "For as long as I lived with Aunt…Mrs Bennet, she and I would…have disagreements. Papa Bennet told me the only way to move past a situation where I had been wronged was to forgive."

Softly, he asked, "Must you truly go?"

She nodded, and when his lips lifted in the faintest of smiles, she relaxed.

He nodded. "I shall go with you. If you are willing to walk into the lion's den, I shall be brave enough to walk with you."

"That woman does not deserve forgiveness," cried the duchess. There was great pain in her eyes and anguish in her voice. "For what she did to you? To this family? To me?"

Her Grace sobbed. "The hole in my heart your loss created! And you wish to forgive her for tearing my world in two? For ripping my peace—my life—to shreds?"

The duchess rose and paced the room. After a moment, she spoke as if from a dark, desolate place. "For years I could not sleep the night through. My life…was not a life. I existed, for I did not know whether you were alive or dead. I was broken, and nothing made me whole— not until the day I saw you again."

She came and sat again near her daughter. "For fifteen years, I drew breath but felt nothing. And now you ask me to forgive that…that demon from hell?" Her eyes blazed with rage. "Never!"

She rose from her seat, heading for the door. Before she could escape, Elizabeth rose. "I do not ask that *you* forgive her. But it is the only way I know to stop this pain—*my* pain! It is the only way I know to stop her villainy from haunting me. Please!"

The duchess took in the distraught nature of her child. Summoning all her strength—all her will—she forced herself to say, "Do as you wish."

Then, before anyone could breathe, she turned and left the room.

CAROLINE BREEZED INTO THE MCDONALDS' salon at Grantly Hall with the same familiarity as her brother's town house. Like a hawk, she took in her environs, searching for the appropriate place to land and perhaps settle. With a practiced eye, she inventoried the furnishings, the drapery, and the quality of the gilded frames, heedless of the age and quality of the paintings contained therein.

As Mr McDonald rose, she stretched out her hand to him. The swish of her skirts warned Lady McDonald of her presence, and the older woman opened her eyes to see her son take the newcomer's hand to his lips.

"Miss Meryton, thank you for joining us. I see the gown suits you well—very well indeed."

Caroline had the sense to blush and look to the side demurely.

"Come, my dear, come and sit by me," Lady McDonald said, patting the seat next to her on the sofa.

"Thank you, Lady McDonald."

"Miss Meryton," Mr McDonald began, "My mother and I have been discussing your, um, predicament."

Startled, Caroline looked up. "My…my predicament?" she asked with concern.

"Yes, child. Ambrose and I are very attentive to the fate and misfortunes of others."

"Misfortune?" Caroline's colour rose. "I beg your pardon, madam?"

"We mean no harm…"

"Or offence," Mr McDonald added. "However, you are at odds with your brother and I…I find myself in need of a wife. We might be able to help each other."

"A wife?"

"My son was married to Lady Malwina Sedwick…for a time."

"A lovely lady, truly genteel," he added.

"However, she was…unfit for the duties of…" Lady McDonald's hands waved. "…our way of life."

Mr McDonald added with quiet sorrow, "Lady Malwina died of a fever a few years back."

"A fever?" Caroline was not sure whether to be relieved or suspicious.

"Yes," Lady McDonald continued. "A sickness swept through our community, and…she took ill, nearly six months after the wedding. It was ghastly at the end, but at least the good Lord was merciful, and her suffering was of short duration."

Mr McDonald had bowed his head.

"Heavens," Caroline muttered, her hand clutching at the neck of her gown.

Mr McDonald looked up, pointing at the indigo muslin she wore. "That was one of her gowns. It looks so lovely on you, does it not, Mother?"

"Yes, indeed it does, Ambrose. And although it is somewhat sombre, it will well serve as a wedding gown."

"Wedding?" Caroline gasped.

"Yes, my dear. A wedding. Our wedding!" Mr McDonald rose to kneel before her. Taking up her hand, he kissed it again, focusing his blue eyes upon her. "Our marriage answers so many of our difficulties."

"Difficulties?" Caroline's mind ran through the evident advantages of being a part of this new, titled family. The disadvantages of joining a family of which she knew next to nothing were tallied against her present circumstances. She ran her hands along the dark fabric, smoothing out any wrinkles. *I would be free of Charles and that mouse of a wife, and her sister. As if that absurd claim to be an Elliston could bleach the stain from her...* Her lips twisted in disdain, and she looked around the room to collect herself.

Lady McDonald said, "You are in need of a home, and we— Ambrose and I—are in need of a bride."

"A bride?" Caroline's heart pounded with uncertainty, and she clasped her hands more tightly together.

"Yes. My brother, Lord Malcolm, is…sickly and unable to marry."

"No?" Caroline had to fight to focus on anything other than his eyes while her mind absorbed this bit of family history.

"No." Lady McDonald continued. "My eldest, Rodney, Is not well. And our work, the work of the McDonald line must continue."

"Where is the McDonald ancestral home?" Caroline squeaked out.

"In York," Mr McDonald responded, anticipation glowing in his face.

"Ah," Caroline whispered. "And do you get to London very often?" she asked, trying to compose herself in this most unusual set of circumstances.

"Oh yes, my dear. When not on the continent, we travel at least twice a year, and we stay for a good part of the Season."

"You will have every opportunity to fulfil your heart's desire, my dear."

Caroline smiled as she looked upon the older woman.

"My lady," Mr McDonald added, moving closer to her, "I apologise for rushing you and promise I shall not…impose myself upon you before you are ready."

Caroline nodded, understanding the unspoken implication. He coughed self-consciously. "Miss Meryton, Caroline. Will you do me the great honour of becoming my wife?" Mr McDonald pulled out a velvet box, opening it to reveal a substantial emerald surrounded by diamonds. Caroline's eyes widened, and her hesitation fell away.

With difficulty, Caroline turned her attention to the nearly attractive man whose eyes would not release her. "Yes," she whispered. "Yes, yes I shall."

He kissed her hand, and Lady McDonald threw her arms around Caroline as Mr McDonald got to his feet.

"Where are you going?" Caroline asked.

"I have much to arrange if we are to wed tomorrow."

Stunned, Caroline asked, "Tomorrow?"

"The bishop is at hand and is very amenable to my desires." He returned to retake her hand. "We must seize the wind, as it were. Do not worry, my dear. Everything will be as it should. You will see. It will be beautiful."

Mr McDonald then turned and left the room. Caroline stared at the opened door while Lady McDonald gathered herself.

"Would you care for a tour of the house? Now that you will be its mistress, you should become familiar with it."

This reassured Caroline, and she nodded her agreement. The rest of the morning was spent exploring the rooms and preparing for the afternoon's event.

"JANE," Bingley called out as he burst through the chamber's door.

"Charles!" Jane cried, opening her arms to him.

Moving around the embracing couple, Mrs Stemple came forward, her hand outstretched in greeting. "You must be Admiral and Mrs Raleigh."

"And you"—Mrs Raleigh searched for the woman's name—"are Mr Bingley's aunt? Mrs Stemple, I believe?"

"It is a pleasure to see you again. We had so little time at the wedding."

"At least this bit of business will have some good come out of it," the admiral added, retaking his seat when the ladies had settled on the sofa.

Mrs Stemple turned to the admiral. "I understand you interrogated the chamber maid who attended my niece."

"I would like to think it was not exactly an interrogation, madam."

"Oh no, Stephen, that poor girl was terrified of you and your bullies."

"But we did obtain the required information," the admiral noted.

"And what did you learn, Admiral?" Charles asked, interlocking his hand with Jane's.

"Maria admitted to helping Caroline obtain the laudanum, going so far as to help her force the lock of Dr Clements's bag."

"Oh my," Mrs Stemple added with surprise.

"She added it to our morning tea," Jane said. She smiled at her husband. "We had a lovely nap."

Admiral Raleigh cleared his throat. "What we were able to get, besides what we knew from discovering Jane and the two men, is the timing of events…"

"And that Caroline had not truly thought out her plans…" Mrs Raleigh offered.

"Beyond escaping from our company," Jane added.

"For such a self-proclaimed clever girl, Caroline has no sense whatsoever," Mrs Stemple said.

The admiral continued, "We gained more information once we had a better idea as to the time of Miss Bingley's departure. It seems that a Mr Conroy, who owns a notions shop across the square from this inn, was sweeping out his store around the time your sister made her escape. He saw a woman who fits your niece's description."

Mrs Raleigh took up the story. "She encountered a couple called the McDonalds."

"The McDonalds? Who are they? Are the respectable?" Charles asked.

"They have an estate on the edge of town, Grantly Hall. Respectable family, Charles," Raleigh replied. "We have asked around, surreptitiously of course. Lady Sara McDonald and her son Ambrose are in residence at Grantly Hall, one of their estates. Lord Rodney McDonald takes the waters at Bath. Sickly fellow from what I gather."

"And?" Bingley asked.

"And, it seems Caroline swooned a bit," Jane said. "Mr McDonald came to her aid, and they entered the McDonald's carriage.

"Alone?" Bingley exclaimed.

"Lady McDonald was there," Mrs Raleigh reassured them.

"Have you sent word to this McDonald?"

"We were about to when we received your express," Jane added.

"But I have a few of my men scouting the area and making discreet inquiries about the family. Respectable folk, good Christian family." Raleigh ticked off the characteristics he had uncovered.

Mrs Raleigh smiled gleefully. "And they are missionaries. Lord McDonald contracted an illness a number of years ago whilst accompanying his mother and brother in their religious devotion. He now spends the majority of his time in Bath, attending to his failing health. Ambrose, the younger brother, has conducted several expeditions since then."

"Caroline is in the company of missionaries?" Charles was incredulous. "And she has not run away?"

"Not yet," Mrs Raleigh replied.

Mrs Stemple added, "It might be a fit punishment to leave Caroline to them."

And while Jane did not join in the laughter that filled the room, her serene lips did twitch in appreciation.

thirty

RICHARD FITZWILLIAM LIFTED HIS HEAD FROM HIS HANDS, A POSITION he had enjoyed for the last fifteen minutes. *Could it be that simple?* he asked himself again. *Rutherford says it is so once I get the physician's certificate. Is it possible?*

She will join her mother, and I shall be free! A boyish smile lifted his lips, and he leaned back in the chair. "It could make salvaging the estates a bit easier."

A knock on the door disrupted his musings. "Enter," he bellowed, uncrossing his long legs. The door opened, and Robert Stachley was ushered into the room. Fitzwilliam rose to greet him. "Stachley! Good of you to come. How are you?"

"Well, Fitz, well. And you?" After a moment where he must have recalled what he knew of the past six months of Fitzwilliam's life, Stachley quickly added. "I am sorry for your loss, Fitz. To lose both a father and a brother. Too much, even for the best of us."

Nodding, Fitzwilliam looked away.

"And, to marry? Your cousin, was she not?"

Fitzwilliam involuntarily winced. "Lady Matlock was formerly Miss Anne de Bourgh."

The two sat in silence, each contemplating their next move. The earl spoke first. "That is why I wish to speak with you."

"Regarding your wife?" Stachley shifted in his chair. "You have concerns about her health?"

"You might say," Fitzwilliam snorted. "My wife seems to have taken leave of her senses."

Stachley raised his brow. "And this would have nothing to do with your needing control of the assets she brings to the union?"

Fitzwilliam shrugged, locking his hands in front of himself. "I shall not deny that taking command of her fortune is an influencing factor." Silence hung in the air. "However there is more to it."

The air thickened between them.

"Anne is…unseemly in her…appetites."

"Surely, you are not such a hypocrite as to deny a woman her needs? Why not simply allow her to…" Stachley allowed the unspoken to hang in the air.

Fitzwilliam looked at his hands again. "You are aware of the… condition of her mother?"

Stachley nodded.

"Anne shares many of the…qualities that led Lady Catherine, my aunt, into her…predicament. I wish you to examine her."

"And sign commitment papers?"

Fitzwilliam shrugged. "If it leads to that, I would not be disconsolate, but I do want your honest opinion." He took another minute to test his words. "There are times when I fear for my safety."

"Richard—"

"There is a look that comes into my wife's eyes. It is a look I have seen in battle when the shock and gore of war have addled the mind, loosening it from reality. I see it in her."

The two sat in silence. Stachley leaned back in his chair with his legs crossed, evaluating both the words and the manner in which they were conveyed. His hands picked at the crease in his trousers. "I shall have a conversation with her, Fitz. Perhaps you could invite me to dinner?"

Seeing his friend was about to interrupt, he added. "I believe it best that she is unaware of the medical significance of the interview—fewer defences in play, less resistance."

Fitzwilliam nodded. "She returns to town later this week."

"I remain in London for another fortnight."

"I shall send word when it is arranged."

Both men rose, and Stachley took the outstretched hand. "Excellent. I await your invitation."

Once Fitzwilliam had accompanied his friend from the room, Yvette Younge rose from her chair, hidden behind one of the sliding panels of the many secret passageways.

While mindful of the lightless stairs, Miss Younge's mind was anxiously occupied with the text of the letter she would soon compose and send to her mistress.

ELIZABETH SMOOTHED the front of her gown as she stepped off the platform in Madame LeSage's fitting room.

Thank goodness, that is over. She patted her hair and took a deep breath. *I do hope Jane will return in time to attend. It will just not be the same without her. To think Jane may miss my engagement dinner, all due to that...that wretch of a woman!*

"Elizabeth, what is it?"

Trying to compose herself, she replied. "I was thinking of Jane and Miss Bingley."

The duchess paused to form her response. With a weary, slight smile, she led Elizabeth to a chair. "You know that Jane would move heaven and earth to be here with you."

Elizabeth nodded.

"But she must stand by her husband as he recovers his sister." She lifted her daughter's chin. "'Tis what families do for each other."

Elizabeth gave her mother a weak smile.

"Would you wish to postpone the dinner? It is not too late. I am sure all would understand."

Elizabeth took a moment. "I would like to wait a day or two. Perhaps we could send an express? To ascertain when they think they might return?"

"A brilliant suggestion, my dear. I shall send it once we return home." The duchess squeezed Elizabeth's hand.

As if on cue, Madame LeSage entered the room, her arms full of fashion magazines and swatches of fabric. Bustling in, she emptied her arms upon the table between them. "Now then, Lady Elizabeth, your mother mentioned we have a wedding gown to create."

Smiling at her young charge, Madame LeSage opened a few of the magazines and placed the illustrations before her. Elizabeth looked at each one, eyes hopeful and expectant. At the second to last, she stilled, her hands picking an illustration of a simply cut gown overlaid with intricate lace.

Madame LeSage peered over the top of the page. "Oh, that would suit you beautifully, Lady Elizabeth! And I have the perfect thing. If you will excuse me." She rose and hurriedly left the room.

The duchess took the drawing from her daughter's hand. Focusing her attention on the illustration, she smiled. "It is beautiful."

Before they could say another word, Madame LeSage returned, accompanied by two women, each with a bolt of fabric. "This," the proprietress of the shop began, "will serve exquisitely as the underskirt." She unrolled a yard or two for the women to touch.

"So soft." Elizabeth smiled.

"So lovely," her mother agreed.

"And this"—Madame LeSage dropped the silk and unfurled the bolt of lace—"will make your gown the talk of the town."

As the women took the lace into their hands, they gasped then looked at each other. Their eyes met with matching smiles, and they nodded.

The duchess turned towards the seamstress. "Perfect."

AFTER TEA, Bingley and Admiral Raleigh marshalled their troops and headed to Grantly Hall, west of Nottingham. As the carriage left town, their nerves flared. The afternoon sun shone gloriously on the bountiful fields.

After nearly an hour of travel, the carriage turned onto a long, tree-lined alley and both men straightened in their seats. Bingley looked at the seasoned officer who straightened his arms, adjusted his cuffs, and nodded to his companion.

The carriage door was opened, and the men descended the stairs, taking in the well-kept façade of the building. "Fit and trim." Raleigh cast his gaze to the roofline. "New fittings, well tended."

"And this tells you...?" Bingley asked as they ascended the ten steps to the front door.

"That they know their business. No ostentation, but..." He glanced at the flowering shrubs strategically placed to offer both the perfume of their blossoms and shade to the front rooms. "...utilitarian, using what they have to the best advantage." Raleigh looked at his nephew. "None of the frippery and ostentation you so often find in the gentry. Bodes well for us, my boy—very well indeed."

"Gentlemen?" asked the man who opened the door. "How may I be of assistance?"

"Admiral Stephen Raleigh and Mr Charles Bingley, here, to speak with Mr McDonald, if you please." Raleigh passed through the door.

"If you gentlemen would be so kind as to follow me?" He indicated a room off to the left. Charles and Stephen looked at each other and, with a shrug of their shoulders, followed the servant into a well-lit room.

DARCY WALKED his horse in a circle as Julian again interrupted their ride through Hyde Park to speak with a cohort of ladies, giggling and simpering at the marquess.

"Ah, Darcy, there you are." Although there was a smile on Julian's face, his eyes spoke of something else. "I was wondering whether you would see fit to join us."

The ladies twittered politely. Darcy sighed and tipped his hat to the coterie that seemed to grow before his eyes as the ladies of the promenade noticed these eminently eligible gentlemen were entrapped by their numbers.

Miss Herrington sighed with exasperation. "I would be remiss not to congratulate you on your recent engagement to Lady Elizabeth." She fluttered her eyelashes in Julian's direction.

A genuine smile lit Darcy's face as their audience gasped at the unusual sight. Julian snorted. "Thank you, Miss...?"

"Herrington, sir. My dear friend Miss Bingley introduced us last year."

Julian exchanged a significant look with his cousin. "Miss Bingley?" Darcy leaned forward in his saddle.

"Yes, at the Evers ball."

Julian took up the inquiry, giving the young woman his most charming smile. "Darcy and I were just commenting on the lack of Miss Bingley's company. Do you know whether she is in town?"

"I believe she visits with her relations in the north."

"Really?" The marquess calmed his impatient horse. "It would be a shame…" He looked away at a gaggle of ducks that strutted alongside the gathered women.

"A shame…?" Miss Herrington asked with growing interest.

"Yes." Julian beamed. "My mother is hosting a small gathering before we depart for Green Haven, and I was hoping to invite her. I am sure we could include you in the invitation, but if you say she is not in town…"

"No." Miss Herrington's smile fell. "She is not, and as I understand it, there are no plans for her return."

"Perhaps another time." Julian tipped his hat. "Darcy?" His cousin looked up from observing the ladies. "Shall we?"

Darcy kicked his heels, and they left a contingent of dissatisfied females in their wake.

Julian slowed his horse to a sedate walk. When they were two abreast, he spoke. "Well, that was informative."

"Was it?" Darcy asked.

Julian looked at him askance. "I believe that, if Miss Herrington knew of Caroline being in town, she would have mentioned it."

"You believe her incapable of loyalty?"

"Loyalty?"

"What if Miss Bingley asked for her to keep a confidence?"

Julian laughed. "It would be easier for Miss Herrington to keep from breathing than to keep a confidence. She is an even greater gossip than Bingley's sister."

"So, what now?"

Julian looked about the congregating populace taking in the summer breeze, looking for another source of possible information, and frowned. "I think we have done all we may here. What say you to a touch of the foils?"

Darcy's eyes flashed. "You are on!" He kicked his mount to a gallop, and they raced—dodging nannies and their charges—to regain Darcy House and the challenge established as boys.

ANNE HESITATED before the door to her study at the de Bourgh house in London. Uncharacteristically doubtful, she glanced at a portrait of her mother. Seeing the steel in her mother's eyes look down upon her, her resolve stiffened, and taking hold of the door handle, she thrust the impediment open. Immediately, the occupants of her study rose, executing hasty and incomplete bows.

"Mr Denny, Mr Dawson?" She bid them sit.

"Yes, Lady Matlock," they offered, sitting closer to the edge of their seats.

"My companion, Miss Younge, recommends your services highly," Anne began in her most imperious voice. "As well as your discretion regarding our arrangements."

"Of course," Dawson replied. "And our compensation?"

Anne shot him a contemptuous glare. "Why such a hurry for payment, sir?"

Denny, answered for both. "A disagreement with His Majesty's army, my lady, requires a hasty retreat from our shores."

"Very well." Anne turned her attention to the parchment before her. Satisfied, she handed it to Dawson. "This is the direction. You will find all is ready. I shall await you there."

She opened the top drawer of the desk and retrieved a small purse. "This is ample recompense for now. The rest will come at the conclusion of our adventure."

She rose and rang the bell. "I trust you are men of your word?"

"Aye, my lady. And thank you." Dawson bowed.

"My lady." Denny shuffled to his feet. Reston entered, and she nodded in his direction then swept out the door.

GLANCING ABOUT THE ROOM, Admiral Raleigh noted the artwork; Bingley stared out the window. Hearing the approach of boots, both turned, straightening their coats as the door opened. A well-dressed man entered, stretching out his hand to them.

"Admiral Raleigh, I presume."

"Indeed—Mr McDonald?" Raleigh took his host's hand.

"No, I am the Reverend Peter Clarkson, Bishop of Nottingham." The visitors looked uncertainly at him before turning to each other.

Admiral Raleigh continued, "Forgive me, but our business is with Mr McDonald."

"Alas, I have just seen Mr McDonald off—"

"Off?" Bingley interrupted. "To where?"

The bishop seemed irritated to have been interrupted. "Perhaps you should tell me the nature of your call?" he asked, the weight of his office evident in his voice.

"As I stated previously, our business is with McDonald." Raleigh stepped towards the religious man. "It is a private affair, and we wish to discuss this with him. Alone."

"And as I have said, that is impossible." The two men stared at each other.

Bingley tried a more conciliatory manner. "We have come here seeking my sister."

"Miss Meryton?"

"Meryton? No. My sister is Miss Caroline *Bingley*."

The bishop blinked. "Then I cannot help you."

"Miss Bingley was last seen"—Raleigh's temper became threatening—"entering the McDonald carriage yesterday."

"That was Miss Meryton." The bishop studied Bingley's distress. "Your sister, Miss Bingley, she is around this tall?" He brought his hand up to his chin.

Bingley nodded.

"Dark hair?"

Admiral Raleigh nodded.

The bishop turned towards the window. "Oh dear. This woman, your sister, this Miss Bingley, introduced herself as Miss Caroline Meryton. She said she was evading her brother who wished to keep her from serving God on a mission of mercy."

"Where is she now, sir?" Bingley grasped the back of a nearby chair.

"I am sorry, gentlemen," the bishop said with true sympathy. "She wed Mr McDonald this afternoon."

The two visitors gasped. "How? She was gone but a day."

Seeing the incredulous looks on the faces before him, Bishop Clarkson took a chair and indicated that his guests should do the same. "One of the perks of being a bishop," and the chagrined clergyman clasped his hands. Bingley and the admiral glared.

"Mr McDonald is of special value to our work in Africa. He is a linguist and a born diplomat and…with the archbishop's preference for married men to serve on these missions, he—"

"Where is my sister?" Bingley asked with urgency.

"Mr McDonald is one of our best negotiators…invaluable in convincing the Mende and Temne chiefs to desist in capturing their neighbours. He has a way with people, persuading them to see reason when they would rather not."

Admiral Raleigh said, "What has this to do with—"

The bishop lifted his hand to forestall the questioning. "We are in a delicate stage in our relationship with the native leaders of Sierra Leone. McDonald's exceptional sense of diplomacy, his sensitivity to the unspoken meaning in a gesture, a look…it could be a decisive factor in the harmonious continuance of our people in the area."

"Yes, and…?" The admiral was beyond the limits of his patience. "How does this apply to McDonald not being in his home on his wedding day?"

"They left after the ceremony," said the bishop. "Just a toast of champagne and they were off. I was just finishing up the paperwork and seeing to a list of last minute instructions McDonald left with me to close the house here."

Bingley asked, "How long will they be gone?"

The bishop took a moment before answering. "Two years at least —more likely three." He looked at Raleigh, now sporting a large grin.

"And this McDonald is a good man?" Raleigh asked.

"Yes, the finest," the bishop assured his visitors. "And Mrs McDonald seemed to focus on the promise of the future. She smiled somewhat pleasantly when he mentioned this union as the fulfilment of both their life's desires. I know he was thinking of his work for the mission. Perhaps I was wrong, but I—we all—assumed that she was as well."

Bingley looked away, knowing he would find disbelief in Raleigh's eyes.

The bishop sat in the chair before speaking. "We must believe, my son, that the Lord still works in mysterious ways."

THE RETURNING men entered the sitting room attached to the Bingleys' chambers, and Jane, Mrs Stemple, and Mrs Raleigh rose, expectant looks mirrored on all three faces.

Bingley said simply, "Caroline is married."

"No!" Jane cried.

"What?" Mrs Raleigh and Mrs Stemple exchanged suspicious looks.

"This afternoon," he continued.

"As a missionary, McDonald is very close to the Bishop of Nottingham," the admiral added. "He was still at Grantly Hall."

"Still...do you mean that they...that she is not...?" Mrs Stemple was stupefied.

Bingley forestalled further interruptions. "Caroline is of age. She entered this union with her eyes wide open."

"But how?" Mrs Raleigh turned to her husband. "How could this happen in a few days' time?"

The admiral released a heavy sigh. "It seems that Mr McDonald is a very gifted diplomat. His services are needed on the continent—the *African* continent." He allowed his words to sink in. When he saw their comprehension, he continued. "And his presence is required there as soon as may be to negotiate the rights for the Anglican church in Sierra Leone with the tacit approval of the native chiefs and councils..."

"But why does this necessitate such a hasty union—of two people who barely know each other?" Jane asked.

"Caroline framed her desire to escape me," Bingley began, "as the reason for being unescorted on the streets of Nottingham. It seems I am the impediment to her joining a mission..."

"No!" Jane recoiled.

"The archbishop has decreed only married men may undertake

missionary work to allay the legitimate concerns of the local popu-lace," Mrs Stemple added. Responding to their questioning and dumb-founded expressions, she continued. "His decision has been a topic of discussion for weeks among my sewing circle."

Exasperated at their incomprehension Mrs Stemple added, "There are a number of families whose daughters have married second sons sent to replace the single pastors. We felt it best to educate ourselves as best we could on the realities they will face."

"Well?" Bingley asked.

"It will not be easy, but if Caroline can muster the fortitude, she may relish the adventure."

With difficulty, Mrs Raleigh tried to control her snort before it devolved into full-blown laughter.

Jane looked doubtfully at her new aunt. "And they say *I* am naive."

When the laughter subsided, Mrs Stemple asked, "Where are they now? When can we offer our congratulations and welcome this new nephew into the family?"

Bingley looked at the admiral for a way to respond, and he only looked at his boots.

"Charles?" Jane gently asked. "Where is she now?"

He took her hands in his. "They are on their way to Portsmouth."

"Portsmouth?" Mrs Raleigh was surprised. Her husband nodded. "Why?" Her understanding of nautical geography kicked in. "You mean…?"

Her husband nodded sheepishly. "With the tide."

"With the tide?" Mrs Stemple looked from the admiral to her nephew. "That means…" Her hands dropped to her lap, and she stared blankly at her relations.

"Means what…?" Jane asked until her mind linked the information into a coherent sentence. A broad smile graced her beautiful face, and with a lightness in her voice, she proclaimed, "Well, if we take a fast coach ourselves, we shall be back in town for Elizabeth's engagement dinner!"

thirty-one

ON THE EVENING OF HIS ENGAGEMENT DINNER, DARCY KNOCKED ON
the heavy wooden door leading to his sister's chambers.

"Come," Georgiana called.

Darcy crossed to his sister in three steps. "Georgiana—" he began
impatiently, but her flawless beauty stopped him. "You are a beautiful,
grown-up woman," he exclaimed.

She giggled at his look of utter astonishment then leaned forward,
placing a gentle kiss on his cheek. "And you look very well this
evening." She pressed her hands to the lapels of his dinner clothes.
"Elizabeth will be well pleased."

Sheepishly, he grinned. "Are you done here?"

"I am ready."

Darcy made an exaggerated perusal of her gown, indicating with
his hand for her to turn. "Ah, I see you have forgotten something."

"What?" she asked.

"I recently had cause to examine the contents of the family vault
and found this." Darcy pulled out a large, velvet box. Opening it, he
offered it to her, silencing her with its bounty.

"Oh, Fitzwilliam!" Georgiana exclaimed, her hands floating over the tourmaline stones. "They are impeccable!"

"They were Mother's. Father made me promise to give them to you at the appropriate time—when you were ready for them."

Georgiana looked at her brother. "And I am ready?"

He kissed her brow. "You are ready to celebrate my engagement, to help me form my own family, Georgie." Taking her hand, he held it tightly, surprised by the emotion welling in his breast. "For so long you have been my beacon, my one constant source of hope through a long, dark time."

Tears formed in her eyes, and she embraced her brother, who held her desperately to his heart.

"I am so happy you have won Elizabeth, my dearest brother. For I could not lose you to anyone less worthy."

Fighting to regain their composure, the brother and sister nodded and, linking arms, made their way to the waiting coach that would carry them to the loving arms of their family.

MRS CAROLINE MCDONALD, née Bingley, leaned against the banister of the ship, her eyes unmindful of the setting sun's blaze of colour and focused on the unending, unrelenting expanse of churning sea before her. The wind whipped her face as she stood full against it and hoped the threatening tears would be scoured from her cheeks.

The bustle of men around and behind her barely seeped into her consciousness as they fulfilled their required tasks.

Along the port side, Ambrose McDonald and his mother exchanged concerned glances, but Caroline was too absorbed in her inner thoughts to notice.

"Ambrose," Lady McDonald said, her voice barely a whisper.

Quickly looking away from his wife, the new husband turned his eyes briefly to his mother and then out to sea. "Yes, I know, Mama." He hung his head.

"We were deceived," she said cautiously, carefully ignoring what could have been a sob from her son.

"I am a fool, Mother, but what can I do now?" McDonald shrugged his shoulders.

"Come, walk with me." Lady McDonald took his arm, and they walked towards the bow of the ship. "First of all, we must convince Caro…Mrs McDonald of the absolute unfitness of creating the kind of row she did the first night. It is unseemly and will do no one any good."

"You cannot blame her, Mother," Ambrose said, again looking out at the horizon. "She was deceived."

Lady McDonald stopped, pulling her son to a halt as well. "We are the ones aggrieved. Did you not hear her? She thought we were sailing to the *European* continent for your honeymoon! She *never* entertained the idea of serving our Lord. It is beyond her comprehension!"

Her grip on his arm strengthened. "She was escaping her brother, who was sending her away to a relation—to an aunt!"

Lady McDonald took a moment to control her anger. "There are a number of reasons one sends a woman to live with a widowed aunt, the majority of which are not rooted in Christian charity."

Releasing her grip on his arm, she turned to the sea. "What are we to do with her?"

"She is my wife, Mother. She is a McDonald."

"We are fools to have taken her in."

McDonald rested his hands on her arms. "It is done. We can only advance from where we are. We must have faith and believe that our Lord has a purpose in all this…misery."

His mother saw the will in his eyes and stroked his cheek. "You are a good man, Ambrose. A very good man."

"Thank you, Mama." He looked at the woman standing alone at the bow. "Now let us go and make our newest member feel the embrace of our Lord."

"COME," Elizabeth called as her maid placed the last diamond pin in place. Turning, she found her parents.

"Elizabeth, you are a vision!" her mother declared.

Stepping closer, the duke added, "Indeed, child. You are beautiful."

"Darcy will be beside himself." The duchess's wide smile filled her eyes. "And ever so grateful that the engagement is made so no other may lay claim to you."

The duke reached into another pocket, pulling out a long, velvet box. "This belonged to your great-grandmother, the second Duchess of Northampton. It was her express wish that this would go to a daughter of our house. I believe she would agree with both your mother and me that you are well worth the waiting."

Elizabeth rushed into her father's welcoming arms. He nearly crushed her to him. "This is a happy occasion, and yet I cannot seem to dispel a sorrow." She looked sheepishly at both her parents. "I feel I have only just come home, and now…"

Gently, her mother said, "You are not leaving us. You are ours and we are yours—always, no matter what."

Elizabeth nodded.

Northampton opened the box, distracting them. Elizabeth came eagerly to her father, who presented it for Elizabeth's view. Seeing the brilliant gems glinting in the candlelight, Elizabeth swallowed, looking first at her father then her mother. "They are perfect."

"As are you, my daughter." He took the necklace of alternating rubies and emeralds, leading to a central diamond pendant, and placed it around Elizabeth's slender neck.

The duchess admired the deep rose silk of Elizabeth's gown and the similarity to her mother that this daughter of her heart truly was.

AMBROSE LOOKED up into the dark night sky. *My Lord and Creator, what magnificence You are to create such majesty. I beg you, hear my prayer.*

He lowered his head, overwhelmed by the misery his haste had created. Returning his eyes to the heavens, he pleaded, *Hear the words of my heart, oh Lord, and grant me your wisdom. I thought I would serve you best in taking this woman to wife. But I find it was vanity— all vanity.*

His hand knocked hard on the wood of the ship's wall. *She is not suited for this life you have chosen for me, and I would not keep her to her vows, not when she is so manifestly unhappy. I…I am sorry, my Lord, for failing You.*

"Mr McDonald?" the newly familiar voice cut through the night air. Turning, McDonald beheld his wife, a woman who had not spoken to him since discovering, on their first night at sea, their true destination and purpose.

"Mrs McDonald?" He nodded to her.

Caroline hesitated. "I have given this a great deal of thought and I...I believe I have made a mistake. I would like to seek an annulment." His eyes widened, and he nodded again. "I understand how difficult this may be for you, being a man of the cloth and all." Caroline straightened her spine. "But you must see the futility of our trying to create any sort of life together."

"I understand, madam." McDonald made to move away but turned back. "You do realise that we shall not see land for another fortnight?"

"What?"

His nod was barely visible in the low deck lanterns. "Yes, until we reach the mainland."

"That is impossible! I demand you speak with the captain and"—her hands began to gesticulate wildly—"turn this boat around! Immediately!"

Ambrose looked at her, and his heart's hope fell. "It is not for me to countermand the charge of a ship's captain."

"But...but...you must!"

McDonald grabbed hold of her wayward arm. "Mrs McDonald, you will desist from this behaviour. It is embarrassing and unseemly." He was a hair's breadth away from the now-silent woman.

"You do realise, Mrs McDonald, to what you will be returning?" Even in the low light, he saw her panic. "I shall give you your annulment, but even that will drag both our names through the papers. My line is an old and honourable one. While I shall endure this disgrace to right the wrong we have committed, I cannot work miracles. Until I can arrange transport for your return to England, you will comport yourself as a lady befitting the name McDonald. Do I make myself clear?"

Caroline nodded, speechless.

"If you will excuse me." He brushed past her but, before disappearing, added, "You would do best to return to your cabin, madam, as the night hides many dangers for a woman aboard a ship such as this."

Seeing her hauteur in the faint light of the ship's lanterns,

McDonald headed below decks towards his chambers. Alone among the sailors keeping their watch, Caroline shivered.

THE DARCY BROTHER and sister were welcomed by the Northamptons, and Georgiana happily related that she had spent the morning, "reminding my brother that ladies take more care with their appearance and, therefore, need time. Otherwise, we would have been here shortly after breakfast!" Elizabeth's laughter dispelled the retort on Darcy's lips.

The family gradually assembled in the front hall, awaiting their guests. The duchess's uncle, Sir Gregory Darcy, a judge and advisor to the current government in matters of jurisprudence, was a particular favourite of Her Grace, and as their first arrival, she welcomed him and his wife with great delight.

"Sir Gregory," she enthused as he and his wife, Lady Darcy, began the receiving line.

"Your Grace." The judge opened his arms to embrace his favourite niece. "How good to see you." The duke gave his aunt a kiss on the cheek before releasing her to Julian and Darcy.

"Your Grace." Judge Darcy smiled, shaking the duke's hand. "As always, a pleasure." With a beaming smile, the judge turned to Darcy. "My boy, how are you?"

"I am well, sir." Darcy looked at Elizabeth. "Very well indeed."

Judge Darcy followed his nephew's line of vision. "Lady Elizabeth." His smile widened. "Come, child. Give your dear old uncle a sweet kiss."

Shyly, Elizabeth allowed his arms to embrace her, and hearing his whispered words, her resistance melted. "It does this old heart good to see you and your mother so happy."

Pulling back, he looked into his great-niece's eyes. "You are the very image of my sister, Elizabeth. And I know you will not only be a great mistress of Pemberley but will make young Fitzwilliam a happy man."

He kissed her hand and then turned to greet Georgiana, who asked, "Where are Peter and Mary?"

"They are coming, my dear," Lady Darcy offered, giving Georgiana a peck on the cheek. "Abigail arrived the day before yesterday, and she and Mary were having a deuce of a time concocting a suitable ensemble."

Elizabeth turned, and she was struck by her brother's response to the inclusion of Miss Abigail to the evening.

"Why is that?" she asked, noting Julian's increased interest in the cuffs of his evening wear.

"It seems their evening gowns are of the same colour, and apparently that is simply not done."

Trying to defend her daughter-in-law, Mary, Lady Darcy added, "Not only were the colours nearly identical, but the pattern of their gowns as well."

"Great minds do think alike," the duchess offered.

"Was not Miss Abigail…" Elizabeth began.

"Cartwright, my dear," Lady Darcy said kindly.

"Miss Cartwright." Elizabeth gave her brother a quick glance. "Was her arrival unexpected?"

Julian cocked his head ever so slightly.

"Abby simply turned up on our doorstep!" Lady Darcy replied. "Of course she is welcome, seeing as she is Mary's only sister. But the two of them were ensconced in Mary's chambers all afternoon. I believe that is why her children were so peevish this afternoon. They are so very desirous of their mother's attention."

Further discourse on the impromptu visit of Mary Darcy's sister was postponed as Cummings announced the arrival of Admiral and Mrs Raleigh.

As ELIZABETH LEANED FORWARD to embrace Jane, she noted that Julian's attention would drift. He started at Bingley's greeting, as if being pulled from an inner monologue. Throughout the half hour in the receiving line, her intended had caught her focus on his cousin. After promising to join up with Bingley later that evening, Darcy took advantage of a momentary lull. "What is it?"

"I wonder at Julian's behaviour."

"Behaviour?" His lips lifted.

"He has been odd since the mention of this Miss Abigail Cartwright attending our dinner tonight."

Darcy lifted his brow.

"What do you know about her?"

The Earl and Countess of Hemstead appeared before them, and each turned a practiced smile on their guests. When the peer and his wife had been handed down the line, Elizabeth turned back to Darcy.

"She is a beautiful woman." His hand gesticulated about his head. "With wild, red hair." Elizabeth's eyes widened at the quality seeping into her betrothed's voice. She scowled and turned, forced to greet another couple who had come to wish them joy.

"So good to finally meet you, Lady Elizabeth," said Sir Arthur Seaton. "Mother and I are simply over the moon at your return." He leered at Darcy before feeling the tap of his mother's fan.

"Come, my boy," the old, stern-eyed woman said. "So good to meet you, my dear." Lady Seaton peered down her long nose at Elizabeth, to rest first on the prominent diamond at her neck and then the one on her finger. "Ah yes, I see the resemblance now. Cannot be too sure of these things." She huffed then turned on her heel towards the parlour where the rest of the guests were waiting.

Elizabeth stared after the woman with amazement before Darcy took her hand and kissed it. Seeking to divert her, he added, "Abby is a tour de force." His eyes caught the look on his beloved's face and quickly reassured her. "Much like you yourself, Elizabeth. She is the older of the Cartwright sisters, and there was a time, many, many years ago, when there was talk of a union between—"

"You?" she asked aghast.

"No, no." He chuckled, seemingly delighted by her jealousy. "Not with me—with your brother."

Elizabeth looked over at Julian, whose eyes were focused on the front door. "What happened?"

"What happens to most young love?"

"Love?" Elizabeth's concern grew. "They were in love?"

"They were inseparable for a time. The Cartwright estate is near Green Haven. They let me tag along when I would visit. But then we all began to grow and…Julian was feeling his oats. I believe he let loose uncensored remarks of a first kiss or two…"

Elizabeth's eyes widened, and Darcy laughed, holding her hand and arm closer to his body. Finding his aunt and uncle conversing with Julian and giving them a modicum of privacy, he continued. "There was a row or four, and Julian was left with his proverbial tail between his legs while Abigail went off to greener pastures."

"Greener than Julian?" Her eyes went round. "Or do you mean London?"

"Ireland. A great aunt had left her an estate, and she decided to visit. When she returned, Julian was already working with the Foreign Office." Lowering his voice, Darcy continued. "His work kept him from London, often for months at a time."

Elizabeth looked around the gathering crowd. "But she is still *Miss* Cartwright?"

"So it seems. Elizabeth, I can see your mind working already. I do not think Julian would look kindly upon your foray into the field of matchmaking on his behalf. In any case, Miss Cartwright is a handful…"

"And that would preclude her being the one who could make Julian happy? Or are women with a lively spirit unworthy of being loved, sir?"

"No, but a woman like Abby…Miss Cartwright…needs someone who can hold their own against her will."

Pulling her hand free, Elizabeth crossed her arms below her chest. "I see," she said, looking at Darcy. Then she smiled wickedly. "You should be grateful then, sir, that you are blessed with such a reasonable, compliant, soon-to-be wife."

Incredulous, Darcy looked at her, and her full-hearted laughter was brought under regulation only when Cummings's voice caught her attention. "Mr and Mrs Peter Darcy, and Miss Abigail Cartwright."

thirty-two

T<small>HE</small> P<small>ETER</small> D<small>ARCYS</small> <small>WALKED ACROSS THE HALL, GREETING THEIR</small> family.

The striking woman who followed was statuesque; her copper hair gleamed in the candlelight, yet it was her eyes that riveted. They were blue, like sapphires glowing with life, and piercing in their depth of feeling. She moved with grace and confidence.

"Abigail," the duchess called warmly.

"Your Grace," Miss Cartwright replied, her eyes conveying relief at her host's genuine welcome.

They held each other a moment, and then the duchess turned. "Abby...Miss Cartwright, this is Lady Elizabeth, my daughter."

"Lady Elizabeth." Miss Cartwright curtseyed, as did Elizabeth, who could not stop staring at the woman whose name had so unnerved her brother.

"Miss Cartwright," Elizabeth replied.

Miss Cartwright straightened, appraising the woman before her. "I would say you have not changed, but that would be a total falsehood. I am glad for your return. You have been greatly missed."

"Thank you, Miss Cartwright." Emotion coloured her voice. When her eyes darted to her wayward brother, Elizabeth was only half-surprised that he had slipped further down the receiving line to be the last person to greet the lady. Elizabeth smirked with satisfaction that her guest was focused on Julian as well.

"Miss Cartwright." Darcy bowed over her hand. "It is a great pleasure to see you again."

Miss Cartwright looked at her sister who was now in conversation with Julian. "I arrived in town unannounced, and my sister was kind enough to invite me."

"You are family. It is only right that you are here to celebrate my engagement."

Blushing, Miss Cartwright returned her eyes to Elizabeth. "Forgive me…congratulations on your engagement! I have known him for some time, even more so as his cousin married my sister. I trust your good sense and humour will cajole him out of that staid persona he presents to the world."

"I shall do my best, Miss Cartwright, I promise."

"Miss Cartwright!" Georgiana exclaimed. "I am so happy to see you again."

"Thank you, Miss Darcy."

"Miss Cartwright," Julian said, his voice low and rich.

Miss Cartwright looked up, blue eyes matching brown, her hand rising to meet the one he offered her. Rather than a simple bow like the one Darcy gave her, Julian brought her long fingers to his lips to kiss.

"Lord Glascomb." Her voice was low, and their eyes never left each other.

Darcy and Elizabeth exchanged a knowing glance, and his lips twitched upward as he spoke.

"I understand you are only recently returned from Ireland." Miss Cartwright nodded. "Lady Elizabeth and I remain undecided as to our wedding voyage, and we would welcome your opinion." He took Elizabeth's arm, offering his spare to Miss Cartwright. He looked at his cousin. "Julian?"

"Yes?"

"Do escort Georgiana." Darcy's smirk was full blown. "Thanks, old boy." He then returned his attention to the two beauties on his arms, opening a discussion of her travels in Ireland and Scotland.

Lord Matlock greeted his dinner guest in a more subdued atmosphere. "Stachley, thank you for coming on such short notice."

The two men walked to the armchairs settled near the fireplace. Although it was a summer's evening, Richard Fitzwilliam still preferred the warm, comfortable leather of the chairs his grandfather would use in speaking with him. "Anne returned to town unexpectedly a day ago, and I thought—"

"—it would be best to get this over with," said his companion.

Richard nodded.

"So, it shall be just the three of us?"

Richard grimaced. "Anne insists on her companion, Miss Younge—"

"And your stepmother?"

He scowled. "Ran back to her mama," he scoffed, "knowing her father was unable to protest."

"Oh?" Stachley raised an eyebrow.

"Seems he suffered an apoplexy—rendered him mute."

Stachley nodded.

"Damned unsavoury, leaving me with that." He looked at the door. "Dinner conversation is nil and, well"—he shrugged—"it is best not to…upset Anne by denying her. Her temper is…"

"Unpleasant?"

Richard nodded again.

"Then you have made a wise decision."

Beyond the heavy door, the dinner bell rang, and from years of training, the two men rose. With a wave of his hand, Richard led his friend to the business of the night.

"Lords, ladies, and gentlemen." The duke stood with a glass of vintage champagne in his hand. Instantly, footmen presented each guest with the same. "A moment's indulgence, if you would."

He looked around, pleased as all eyes turned towards him. The duke's brow quirked, and he stared at his eldest until Julian turned his eyes from the woman seated next to him. *Ah, Miss Cartwright—perhaps there is hope for Julian after all.*

Catching himself, the duke again surveyed with great satisfaction the friends and family gathered around his table. "Tonight we are gathered to celebrate the engagement of our daughter, Elizabeth Aubrey Rose, to Fitzwilliam Michael Darcy. As you know, our daughter, Lady Elizabeth, has only recently returned to us after years in Hertfordshire with the Bennets of Longbourn."

A murmur went around the table.

"And while our hearts are overjoyed to have her back with us, tonight we are moved beyond joy to celebrate, or commiserate, depending on your point of view." He looked askance at Darcy, whose cheeks flushed red. The duke chuckled when Darcy's stern countenance reappeared. "All that remains is to bless this union, which we earnestly do."

"Elizabeth, your mother and I love you both—more than we have words to express the depth of our devotion. And our wish is that your life with Mr Darcy is full of more joy than sorrow, more health than discomfort. That you turn to each other, trust each other, love each other, and know that we shall be with you every step of the way."

A round of "here, here" went up, and the duke lifted his glass in salute. "We love you and wish you a life together full of good health, good friends, and love."

"And children!" his wife added.

"And children," the duke repeated, enjoying Elizabeth's blush. "To Darcy and Elizabeth!"

"To Darcy and Elizabeth!" Those present rose as one, lifting their glasses to the beaming couple.

"I HOPE," Miss Cartwright said, leaning towards Julian on her right after the lobster bisque was served, "that my sudden appearance did not distress or displease your mother too much."

"My mother is accustomed to a stray at her table every now and then," Julian replied. He took another spoonful of soup.

"I assume these strays were at your invitation, my lord?"

"Miss Cartwright," he began, contrite as he turned to face her.

However, the perfection of her caught Julian unprepared. He gulped, raising his eyes to hers where, rather than the indignation he expected, he found a playful triumph beaming back at him. "I only meant—"

"Yes, brother?" Elizabeth chimed in from his other side. "What exactly did you mean?"

Julian turned to her. "Miss Cartwright and I were engaged in—"

"Engaged?" Lady Seaton asked from across the table, her imperious voice silencing nearby conversations. "But you are both only recently returned to London! When did you two form a—"

"A conversation, your ladyship." Julian was pinker than his soup. "Miss Cartwright and I were en...we were *having* a conversation. That is all."

"For now." Darcy dipped his head to hide the smirk he was enjoying.

"Is that what it is called nowadays? Conversation?" With a huff, Lady Seaton turned to her left to continue conversing with Admiral Raleigh.

When Julian stopped glaring at Darcy, who was still chuckling, he turned to his sister with a growl, and then he refocused his attention on Miss Cartwright, who hid her smile behind her fine linen napkin.

"I suppose I have been away from town too long. I do not recall proposals being put forth in...such a public venue."

"Miss Cartwright," Julian began, looking into her eyes. He froze, seeing the girl he had known, tormented, and played with throughout his youth. Looking back at him through eyes of the clearest blue was the girl who comforted him each time Elizabeth's birthday came around and his mother retired to her chambers, overcome with the emotion of the day. And then that girl, his comforter, would be gone, and the mischievous tomboy who could outride him would return, and he smiled, the growing din of conversation around him returning.

As Miss Cartwright's attention was caught by the companion to her left, Sir Arthur Seaton, Julian released his breath and relaxed. *This is good,* he thought looking at his sister and then across at Darcy. *And if that clod can find the love of a good woman, perhaps there is hope for me after all.*

Miss Cartwright's snort recalled him, and he turned again to his left, listening as Peter Darcy explained to Sir Arthur that "My sister was not in hiding, sir. She was in Ireland, settling her estate."

"How long were you in the papist hinterland, Miss Cartwright?" Sir Arthur asked the copper-haired beauty.

"Nearly four years, Sir Arthur," Miss Cartwright replied, her features hardening at his bigotry.

"Miss Cartwright?" Elizabeth interjected.

"Yes, Lady Elizabeth?"

"Since you are so recently returned, I hazard to guess that you have not recently been to the Royal Academy?" Her question was delivered in a strident tone that would not brook interruption.

"My time has been confined to visits with my family as of yet." Miss Cartwright's eyes darted between Sir Arthur and Elizabeth.

"Excellent." Elizabeth smiled as Miss Cartwright raised her brow. "I hoped you would join our party when we go."

"I would enjoy that greatly."

"As will I," Elizabeth replied.

AFTER FIRST LOOKING into Anne's sitting room and the parlour used before dinner parties, the two gentlemen made their way to the dining room. Expecting a more intimate setting for the small party, Richard gasped at the overdone splendour before him. Catching Stachley's eye, he gave a nearly imperceptible shrug of his shoulders while his friend only raised his brow.

Lifting her spoon to her lips, Anne said. "I thought you would never come, so we began without you."

"So I see."

"Lady Matlock, if you do not mind." Anne turned to her companion, who had locked her gaze on the newcomer. Anne followed suit, smiling as she watched the flip of his tails as he sat. She licked her lips and snapped her fingers. Instantly, two well-formed young men stepped forward, one placing bowls in front of the men, the other ladling a delicious soup into each one.

"I hope, Colonel…"

"Stachley, Anne." Richard could not contain his anger. "This is my great friend, Mr Robert Stachley. If you had waited for us, as is the custom—"

Waving his concerns away with her free hand, she clucked at him.

Reddening with impatience and frustration, Richard continued. "As I was saying, I would have introduced you."

"Of course." Anne's focus never strayed from their guest. "Dr…I mean *Mr* Stachley, what line of business are you in?"

"Now that I am retired from the Army—"

"I do admire a military physique," Anne interrupted. "So virile, do you not agree?" Ignoring her food, she propped her chin upon her hands and stared at the man closest to her.

"I agree. The physical demands the army imposes on its men are conducive to good health and stamina."

"Oh yes, stamina! That is *always* a greatly desired quality in a man."

"And one I appreciate as a physician." Stachley returned her stare, and Anne was aware of a shift in the balance of the conversation.

Needing to regain control, she looked at her husband. *Yes, Richard, sit there and stare. Your friend let the cat out of the bag, a bag I had already examined.* Her eyes darted to Miss Younge, who smiled at her then lifted her spoon to finish her dish.

"Did you travel to France in your service to the king?" she asked languidly.

"No."

"Perhaps this will be a novelty for you?" Her eyes dipped to the soup in front of her guest.

"Madam?" Richard asked from across the table.

"Bouillabaisse, my lord. Miss Younge had the pleasure of acquiring the recipe, which she shared with Cook." Anne turned to Stachley.

"It is good, is it not?" The doctor reluctantly brought a spoonful to his lips.

Anne watched eagerly as he swallowed, her eyes trailing down his neck as he did so.

She smiled. "I understand it may be difficult for you military men to accept something of quality from your…foe…and yet—what is that divine expression? Oh yes. To the victor go the spoils."

THE SEA DASHED waves at the ship as one rolls a ball across a field, and the bow rose again to greet the sky. Winds shrieked and howled, pressing against the hull and causing the passengers to huddle together, some cowering in fear while others gathered to pray for their safe delivery. Caroline woke from her fitful sleep, cringing in her bed without benefit of candle. So great was the pitch of the ship that she dared not risk setting her room ablaze.

Caroline screeched as she fell the three feet from her berth to the floor. "What is happening?"

Fully expecting her complaint to be met by the disapproving condescension of Lady McDonald, Caroline realised she was alone in their shared cabin. "Lady McDonald?" she called out, struggling to mask her rising panic. Nothing but the screaming wind answered her. Caroline sat up, feeling the roll of the waves beneath her and pitching the empty contents of her stomach.

Feeling the overpowering need to find human company and escape the black pitch of her room, Caroline struggled in the dark to find her robe. Instead, she found her gown and hastily pulled it over her head. Rising, she stumbled as the floor realigned itself and she found herself climbing to reach the door. Then, just as suddenly, the balance shifted, and she was thrown against the floor, flat on her stomach.

"My God!" she cried in fear. "Please, help me!" Crawling back to the door, she clutched at the latch, pulling it open. She peeked out of the doorway and began her trek towards the company of fellow travellers, keeping her hand on the solid wall for support. As she carefully made her way towards the communal dining room that was ablaze with light, she attempted to plait her hair as men dashed about in their pursuit to secure the vessel against the brute strength of the sea. Their calls were loud and harsh to be heard over the incessant wail of the wind.

Occasionally, like the rhythm of a pulsing, beating heart, a swell of water would rush through the open passage and down the stairs to the passenger deck. With its strength dissipating, it lapped at her bare feet as would a gentle wave upon the sand. Caroline shivered, hurrying her step into the common room. There, lit by the night lanterns, sat Lady McDonald, Mrs Constance, Mrs Rutledge, and Mrs Slocomb. They sat, hands pressed together, heads bowed.

In a sudden swell, the sea rolled the boat like a toy in a child's bath, leaving Caroline grasping for balance. Mrs Slocomb lifted her head, assessing the state of the room and nodding to Caroline as her eyes scanned the confined quarters. Using the wall to stabilise her progress, she made her way to the table. Mrs Slocomb returned her gaze forward and lowered her head, her hands clasping her sisters' in prayer.

Caroline vainly tried to calm her nerves. "Where is Mr McDonald?"

The women paid no attention to her. *How rude!* "Lady McDonald, where is your son? Why does he not attend you?"

The shrieks heard from without captured the attention of the women, and briefly, when the gales took a breath, they could hear the captain ordering his men about, the heavy footsteps above their heads moving first to one side then the other as they tried to guide the vessel to safety. The rocking continued, and it unnerved Caroline's slender grip on her nerves. When she could stand it no longer, she paced about the chamber, one hand always touching the now-moist wood of the hull.

"Amen," echoed about the table. Caroline looked over at the women, who all appeared calmer than she felt. Mrs Constance held Lady McDonald's hand while one of their companions approached Caroline.

"Mrs McDonald?" Mrs Rutledge asked, her voice gentle. "Mr McDonald is above. The captain requested his assistance to help rein in the sails."

"My husband?! Is working with those...ruffians?"

"My son," Lady McDonald barked indignantly, "is assisting our captain, as would I if I were younger and of sound body."

Caroline's eyes narrowed. "You most certainly do not suggest that I should be...up there helping the men?"

"No, Mrs McDonald." The hostility set the attending women on edge. "I do not mean for you to go upstairs and hamper them in their necessary work."

She took a step closer, breaking away from Mrs Constance's arm. "But I do expect you to assist us when the men are done and the storm has passed."

"We are paying passengers aboard this vessel, madam. Surely, they have other men to attend to their needs."

Mrs Slocomb looked at Caroline as if she were mad. "Even *you* must see the need for their strength in battling this tempest!"

Caroline took a step towards her to put her in her place. "What on earth do you mean by that remark? 'Even *me*'?"

Mrs Slocomb—the effort to rein in her temper evident in her voice —said, "Only that, as a novice sea voyager, you may be unfamiliar with the need for all hands to work together in a storm as dire as this."

"Dire?" Caroline whispered. She clasped and pulled at her hands as if to stretch them. "What do you wish me to do?"

"Can you cook?" Mrs Rutledge asked.

"No," Caroline said.

Seeing her mother-in-law shake her head, she took in the responses of the other women. *Mrs Slocomb looks resigned. Mrs Constance...is that disappointment? Look how that Rutledge woman placates Lady McDonald. As if that would raise her pitiful position as a shopkeeper's wife and daughter! Rutledge is in a rut.*

She smirked. *How Louisa would find that amusing!* The thought of Louisa brought her up short, the pain in her heart cracking and causing her to gasp. *Louisa.* Caroline fought back the tears pushing out from under her lids. *Why must I think of her now?*

The thought that she soon might be joining her sister chilled her, and she bolted from the wall to join the living women before her.

As LADY MATLOCK swallowed the last of her soup, her husband and his friend slouched in their chairs. She rang the bell, and Dorset, the butler, appeared.

"It seems that my husband and his friend have indulged more than is seemly this evening. How utterly like him." She rose, ignoring the hardening of her servant's eyes. "See to it that he is installed in the green guest room. The master's chambers have only been recently cleansed from the stench of that woman, and I shall not endure the inconvenience of having the rooms stripped and redone so soon. I fear my husband will find he cannot stomach his dinner."

The obedient retainer only nodded.

"Then you may return and take Dr Stachley to the yellow guest chamber."

"Very good, madam."

"Come, Yvette. Let us prepare. Have the carriage summoned." She examined the small watch dangling from an ornate brooch on her left shoulder. "We have but a half hour to depart if we are to meet Denny and Dawson."

"Of course, Lady Matlock." Miss Younge bobbed a slight curtsey and left the room.

Anne walked over to the unconscious Stachley. "You and my pitiful husband think you are so clever, but no one outwits a de Bourgh. No one!"

She leaned back, assessing his physique. Pouting, she cocked her head to the left. "Such a shame. Under more conducive circumstances, I could have been much more amiable. But that is a regret I may easily live with."

With a last look at the room, Anne left, laughing hysterically.

CONVERSATION throughout the evening centred on the abbreviated courtship of Lady Elizabeth and Mr Darcy and reuniting her with her Darcy relations. She was pleased to note that, of a piece, they were intelligent, open-minded, and blessed with a dry sense of humour well suited to her disposition.

Just as Elizabeth let out a satisfied sigh, Sir Arthur Seaton pounced, leaning across the table to speak at a volume aimed at informing the diners in general. "I for one cannot fathom how you could stand it, Miss Cartwright."

Instantly, the more astute members of the party straightened in their seats. "Pardon, sir?" Miss Cartwright levelled her intelligent eyes upon him. "Stand for what?"

"Living for so long among those…papists!" He looked around the table to determine the amount of attention he had garnered. "They are savages!"

Elizabeth saw Julian's fist clench upon his thigh. Miss Cartwright replaced her knife and fork on her plate.

"With all those United Irishmen running about. It is no wonder you returned to the bosom"—Sir Arthur again looked significantly at Miss Cartwright—"of your family."

"United Irishmen?" Georgiana asked.

"Yes," Julian answered, all the while watching Miss Cartwright's unusual response to this turn in the conversation.

Quickly, he darted his eyes to Georgiana but flickered back to Miss Cartwright with increasing curiosity. "The United Irishmen is the misguided"—here he chuckled at Miss Cartwright's response—"attempt to repel English rule and spread insubordination among the enlisted men in the Army."

"And Navy," Peter Darcy added.

"Peter, I was unaware you took note of such things," Julian said.

"Miss Cartwright has amazing tales."

Again, Sir Arthur interjected himself into the conversation between forkfuls of veal. "I have heard those rabble-rousers are hard at work"—he banged his knife against the table—"not just in the ranks or at sea but in Ireland itself. In our own backyard, gaining support to strike us in our sleep! The devils!"

"Is that true, Abby?" Mary Darcy asked.

Miss Cartwright smiled. "Do not worry, sweeting. Blaithan is nowhere near Fiddlehead."

"Fiddlehead?" Sir Arthur enquired not willing to cede the floor or his point. "I read that the hotbed of instigation was Cork."

How could she know? Julian wondered, reeling with what Abigail had just revealed. *Hornsby assured me that the location of their base was being kept hugger-mugger.*

Looking up, Julian was caught by the surprise in Abigail's eyes. "O'Reilly and his men were never a threat near Blaithan. They are—"

"Miss Cartwright," Sir Arthur began, condescension contorting his meagre features. "It is common knowledge that the United Irishmen are led by a French ex-patriot, not by one of their own—and certainly not by anyone with as common a name as O'Reilly."

"Another reason," interjected Sir Gregory Darcy, "to advance the professional standards of journalism to better investigate their sources of information so that we, as members of an informed citizenry, may keep abreast of current events with accurate and timely reports. If one is to judge by some of the papers here in town, one can only imagine the level of inaccuracies at play so far afield."

"Indeed, Uncle," Julian agreed all the while keeping an eye on Abigail. *And since when does Sir Gregory support anything to do with the press?*

As the venerable judge turned his head, he caught the insouciant eye of his grand nephew and did the unexpected. He winked.

thirty-three

July 1812
The Devil's Loin, London

LIEUTENANT DENNY STRAIGHTENED HIS COAT PURLOINED FROM THE Royal Guards. "Dawson?" he asked. "Are you sure about this? I mean the money is sufficient, but…this is a criminal offence."

Dawson fastened the last of his coat's buttons. "We are in too deep, with or without this." His hand now brushed the chevron on his mate's shoulders. "The boat leaves in two days. We shall shake the dust of England from our boots and be free."

"This is the last of it, then?" Denny asked, his face serious.

"With the purse milady offers, we shall be well rid of all of it."

"Then, let us spend our last days in Britain in good service to the King."

Four bells rang through the air. Dawson stiffened and, seeing the anxiety rise in his companion, smiled bravely. "Come on then, *Colonel*, we have work to do."

. . .

THE NEED for fresh air forced Caroline to brave the top deck when it seemed the storm had abated. What was it Mrs Constance had said? *"This close to the continent of Africa, one must anticipate the occasional storm."*

"A hurricane," she had called it. "As if this demonic storm could have a name."

Holding on to the lifelines that had been rigged along the breadth of the ship, Caroline made her way onto the open deck.

While the captain discouraged women on deck, he knew the futility of refusing their determined need for air and an escape from the confines of the cabin.

Testing each step of her slippered foot, she reached the deck, breathing in deeply the fresh salt air. She relished the wind whipping about her, pressing her hair first away and then into her cheek. The unabated fury calmed her mind, ripping away her fatigue as it whirled. Gingerly she took the last step, halting as she stood in the open air, and gasped. All around her the invisible swirls of air pulled on the fabric of the rolled sails and tested the resolve of grown men as they pulled themselves along the edge of the boat to attend their duties.

Clutching her shawl both to warm herself and to prevent it from going into the deep, Caroline opened her eyes wide, taking in the great roll of wave after wave lifting the ship to drop it moments later. The breadth and magnitude of each wave thrilled her in a way heretofore unknown, and she stood spellbound as each increasing wave played with the ship.

"Magnificent," she whispered as the wind pushed her back into the wall of the observation deck, breaking her admiration of the pure power of the sea. She looked around the deck, noting the men scurrying about, a certain emotion firing their eyes.

"Watch now," came the coarse call from the far end of the boat. As the wind raged, she heard the wood groan and the ropes snap, and she sent a prayer of gratitude that they remained secure for the moment in their bindings.

"Get below." Mr McDonald's voice cut through the raging storm. "Now, Mrs McDonald!"

Sheltering her from the gusting wind, McDonald roughly ushered her below deck as the moaning and creaking of the wood increased.

Midway down the narrow stairs, a sudden shock pushed against her body as the broad chest of her husband fell upon her, and they both flew through the air as the floor rose to embrace them. The air was rent by a great, resounding crack that Caroline felt shudder through her heart, and then her world turned black.

Their boots crunching on the flat stones beneath their feet, the pretend Colonels Michaels and Turnquist presented themselves and their papers to the guard on duty.

"Sir?" asked the young corporal. "I was unaware a change in venue was ordered."

Denny sighed with exasperation. "I do not think it is normal practice for the Royal Guard to make its plans known to enlisted men, Corporal."

"The Colonel would be informed, sir—"

Denny interrupted. "Prepare Lady Catherine for our immediate departure. That is an order."

Looking from one 'officer' to the other, the corporal could only comply. "You are sure you do not wish to wait until morning? Major White, the colonel's adjutant, will be back on duty by then."

"It is not up to you or me to question the orders of our superiors, is it?" Denny glared at the younger man.

"No, sir." The corporal fumbled for his keys, leading the two officers to Lady Catherine's cell.

"You, boy!" Lady Catherine scuttled to the far wall of her chamber, her hands automatically rising to protect her heart.

"Lady Catherine de Bourgh?" Dawson asked. The old woman straightened, a hint of her iron will returning.

"Who are you?"

"Colonel Michaels, Colonel Turnquist." He nodded in Denny's direction. "We are here to transport you to your new abode."

"Eh?" she queried with a cackle. "You mean to my new *prison*, do you not? Well, I shall not go. And you cannot make me. I am still Lady Catherine de Bourgh."

"Be that as it may, Lady Catherine. You are to travel with these two officers," the corporal added.

"I most certainly shall not."

"Yes, you will, ma'am," the corporal insisted, opening the cage door.

"And be quiet about it," Dawson added for good measure.

The young officer handed Lady Catherine to Colonel Turnquist, hastening to gather her few belongings, which he handed to Denny. Before he could exit the cell, Denny stumbled, and the corporal hastened to support his superior. Denny clapped him on the shoulders as he righted his position before pushing the younger man further into the cell. The guard, immobilised with surprise, gasped upon hearing the lock fall into place, turned by his own key.

The young soldier gaped at the grinning officer.

Holding up the errant ring with keys to each of the corridors, Denny taunted the lad. "Damn careless of you, Corporal. Perhaps an hour or two's confinement will teach you to be more diligent."

When the corporal stepped forward, grasping at the dangling keys, Denny punched him so hard, he fell against the stone floor, rendering him unconscious.

CAROLINE STAGGERED to the galley to replenish the boiling water for the sailors' wounds. A particularly strong wind had caught the mast, snapping the top twenty feet from the rest of the massive pole. As the sails and rigging fell, nearly half a dozen men failed to clear the deck; their injuries included minor concussions, broken limbs, and a slash that ran nearly the length of one man's arm.

Unfit for much else, even before her fall, Caroline was relegated to keeping the ship's doctor well supplied with clean bandages and hot water. Enduring the rolling of the sea, she spent hours manoeuvring between the men clambering up and down the decks and the women who assisted in the less precarious duties, and Caroline was exhausted. *Bone tired. But those hens will not let me rest—not until that dragon of a doctor says the last of the lot are tended.*

So she filled the cast-iron cauldron with water and sighed, shaking as the wind shrieked.

"Caroline!" Mrs Rutledge called from the doorway. "Please hurry! The doctor is in need of clean water!"

"Coming," Caroline lifted the heavy pot into her arms.

ANNE WATCHED her mother enter the cramped parlour. Lady Catherine took in the details of the neglected farm house, her face contorting in disgust. When she turned to her escorts and sneered, Anne had to control a laugh.

"This is where you have the impudence to bring me? Do you know who I am?"

"Lady Catherine de Bourgh." Anne de Bourgh Fitzwilliam pushed through the shadows of the doorway.

"Anne?" Lady Catherine swung around to confront the vision before her. "Is it you? Is it really you?"

"Yes."

"Oh, Anne! I thought I had lost you!" Lady Catherine took quick steps across the room towards her daughter, falling into the younger woman's arms.

Anne gasped as her mother's spindly arms held her tightly. *How frail she has become. I shall make them pay for doing this to her. But first we must gain our safety.*

Pulling away, Lady Catherine clasped her hands to Anne's cheeks. Her eyes took in the protrusion of Anne's belly. "Oh, you sly girl! Just married and already you carry the heir to Pemberley. George will be so pleased."

George? A moment of panic flushed Anne's cheek. *She cannot possibly know of George Wickham!*

"Mr Darcy will be so pleased with you, Anne—as will Mother and Father."

Lady Catherine patted Anne's hand. Taking a step away, she looked around at the unfamiliar setting then looked back at the pregnant woman. "But why are we here, Anne? You and Mr Darcy have not quarrelled, have you? He has not sent you away?"

Her eyes searched Anne's while her daughter quickly pieced together the fragments of her mother's thoughts. "No, he has not," she replied, trying to understand the increasingly uncertain condition of her mother's mind.

"Then what do we do here? With these...men?" Lady Catherine

glanced at the officers. "It was very accommodating of you to provide an escort, but they"—she glanced over at the men—"make me uncomfortable."

"Never mind them. Would you like a cup of tea?"

"Oh yes, that would be lovely."

"Excellent. Miss Younge?"

Her companion came immediately. "Yes, madam?"

"Make my mother a cup of tea and"—she lowered her voice—"add this."

She walked over to a small valise on a side table. Opening it, she removed two bottles. "Give her enough to let her sleep through the night."

Noting that her mother was now seated comfortably by the fire, Anne walked to Denny and Dawson. "Gentlemen, thank you for bringing my mother safely from that place of abomination. Denny, perhaps you should go and refresh yourself. Miss Younge is making her tea, and with a bit of help she should sleep through the night."

Denny nodded and departed. When he left the room, Anne turned to Dawson. "Once my mother is resting, you and I may discuss the events to come."

"And our payment?"

"Yes, Lieutenant Dawson. And your payment."

Dawson gave her a salute and headed up the stairs.

SEEING light under Elizabeth's door, Julian made his way towards her chambers. Roiling from sitting next to Abigail throughout dinner, Julian wished for Elizabeth's companionship to brighten his spirits.

"That was an interesting dinner, was it not?" Julian said as he entered his sister's sitting room.

She looked up, surprised by his visit. "Yes it was."

"May I?" he lifted the cloth from one of the two framed paintings.

Elizabeth watched as he perused the couple staring back at him from the canvas. Reverently, he placed the painting back on the chair and carefully replaced its wrapping.

"This is quite good." Julian looked his sister in the eyes. "You have a true talent."

"It is a wedding gift for Mary."

"I have only met Miss Bennet twice and her betrothed on the night of your ball, but it seems a fine likeness."

"Thank you." Elizabeth's eyes twinkled as she leaned the canvas against the chair leg and sat down. "I shall do a portrait of you when you become engaged."

Julian slumped into the chair nearest his sister. "If I ever become engaged, you mean."

"You seemed rather taken with Miss Cartwright this evening."

"Hmm?" he asked distractedly. "It was a shock seeing her again after all these years."

"How long had it been since you saw her last?"

Julian toyed with the cuff of his shirt. "Four years, perhaps five. I was surprised she was so learned regarding the United Irishmen…but then again, Abigail was never one to sit by."

"Do you think she is involved in their cause?"

Cocking his head, Julian took a moment to prepare his response. "No, but she comes directly from Ireland. It is only natural that she is well informed. They were active in the counties near her estate."

"You kept tabs on her?" Elizabeth asked.

He wagged a finger in front of her. "No, no, no. That I shall not say."

She swatted at his hand.

"I shall admit that when I heard…things, I did enquire as to the precautions the local constables had instituted."

Elizabeth looked satisfied and leaned back in her chair.

"But not due to any exaggerated sense of involvement or responsibility for Miss Cartwright. No matter what happened between us, she is a friend of long standing. I would do the same—have done the same—for other friends who have Irish holdings."

Elizabeth rolled her eyes. "Of course."

He turned his attention to the second covered painting. "What is this one?" He rose to grasp the second frame.

"That was for Michael—Mr Waverly. *This* is for Mary."

Julian lifted the covering and stared at the five Bennet girls as they once were, sitting clustered beneath the canopy of an old oak tree. Jane and Elizabeth flanked Mary, who stood behind two younger women sitting on a stone bench. While a family resemblance could be seen among four of the five, each looked out at him with lively, distinct eyes, sharing a quality of respect and appreciation for each other. Julian looked up from the canvas to his sister who had moved to join him.

Seeing her gentle smile, he said. "You all seem very close—or at least comfortable with each other."

"We are, or were. Jane, of course, you know. She has the strength to be gentle and kind. I was the witty one. Mary was our moral compass. Lydia and Kitty are full young, still. They all loved me and did their best to protect me." Then more quietly, "They made my life bearable after…after Papa Bennet died."

"That is why you return?"

Elizabeth nodded her head. Putting the canvas back in its place, she re-covered it. "I know that you and Mama do not understand why I wish to return to Longbourn. But Mary is like a sister, and she has asked this of me."

"But…Mrs Bennet…?"

Elizabeth laughed. "We shall stay at Netherfield with Jane and Mr Bingley. And I think, with the wedding preparations for Mary, our parents and Darcy will be enough to keep her in line."

He laughed, taking the paintings and placing them in the prepared crates. "I believe Mama is secretly hoping for another go at her."

"Julian!" Elizabeth joined in her brother's laughter, ending as they stood on either side of the narrow crate, looking at each other, guileless and open.

"I only wish you were not going just now. I find myself in need of your good humour."

"We shall be gone less than a fortnight. Surely, you can manage on your own until then?"

He shrugged.

"Then you are welcome at Netherfield. You know that, do you not? Oh, Julian." She smiled indulgently at him. "Come—lift that. I would like them packed so they are ready for our departure tomorrow."

"I hope Darcy understands the forceful nature of his intended wife."

Elizabeth tucked some excess cloth in the top of the crate before fitting the lid on it. "He does—and looks forward to our life together all the more."

"I must have a word with the boy…"

"You may. *After* the wedding."

THE NEXT MORNING, a weary Lady Matlock, Miss Younge, and both 'officers' emerged from the room they had shared. Anne gave each of them their orders. "Miss Younge, go and see what you can find to break our fast. You, Denny, go and see to the horses."

The two younger people descended to their tasks. "Dawson, while I would thoroughly enjoy a rematch of our earlier exploits"—she trailed a lone finger down his chest—"I must ask you to see to our trunks."

Dawson took her hand and, bringing it to his lips, first kissed then nipped at her fingers. "Naughty boy!" She slapped at his chest. "Mustn't bite!"

The door of Lady Catherine's room opened, and the old woman stuck her head out. "You there! Unhand my sister!" Gathering strength, she rounded on the man. "Have you no shame! Do you know who she is—who her husband is?"

Seeing a scene about to unfold, Anne released Dawson and took up the arm of her mother. "Catherine, I was simply playing."

"It is not good to give these men ideas, Anne." Catherine took her arm. "What would Mr Darcy say? You must not bring disgrace to Pemberley with such behaviour."

"No, of course not." She headed towards the stairs. "Let us see if there is any tea."

"None too strong. I had a difficult time sleeping last night."

"Most likely it is from being in a strange room with a strange bed."

"No, it was the wind—howling like a demon all through the night."

JULIAN TOOK his midday meal in his chambers after seeing his sister, parents, and the Darcys off to Hertfordshire. He was feeling a bit sorry for himself in now-quiet Northampton Place. Retreating to the comfort of his private chambers, he settled in to review some of the papers

Hornsby had sent over regarding the United Irishmen. A knock on his door interrupted him.

"Come," he called out, not bothering to stand.

"Forgive the intrusion, my lord, but this just came, and well…" Cummings handed him the damp parchment. Julian took it, noted the seal of the Royal Guards, and looked up at the man who had served his family for as long as Julian could recall. With a curiosity that bordered on alarm, he tore open the seal and read.

"Lord Glascomb, I regret to inform you that last evening two men, impersonating officers of the Royal Guard, aided Lady Catherine…"

"Oh, my good Lord!" Julian tore his eyes away from the express. "Cummings, have my horse saddled and prepare a valise. I must leave immediately, and I know not when I shall return."

"Master Julian, what is it?"

Julian, who was now rushing to his dressing room, turned, his face reflecting the agitation of his mind. "Lady Catherine has escaped Bedlam!"

thirty-four

AFTER A HEARTY BREAKFAST OF EGGS AND COUNTRY BREAD, LADY
Catherine's spirit had returned, and she insisted on overseeing every
detail of their departure. By the time they were ready to begin their
journey, a constant rain had been pounding the roads for hours.

While Catherine fussed with Miss Younge, Anne stood by the front
room window.

"There is nothing for it, milady," Dawson said, trailing a finger
along her arm. "If we are to make the tide, we must be off this day." He
kissed her shoulder.

"But the rain, Dawson. Surely we can wait a day?" She turned to
look at him as he reclined against the window frame.

"We cannot. Denny and I must make Portsmouth by the day after
tomorrow. If you wish our escort until you sail, then we must depart
from here today."

"As soon"—she kissed his lips—"as may be." No more was said
until the rest of their party had gathered in the front room, and the
house became eerily quiet. After nearly four hours of preparations,
packing, and re-packing of the women's trunks, they were ready. In
order to increase the pleasure of the occupants, Lady Catherine's tea

included a double dose of laudanum before she was bundled into the carriage.

They rode for two hours without rest, hoping to regain the time the muddy roads had stolen.

A sudden gust of wind whipped the carriage, and a large tree branch fell across the road. The weary horses reared then began to run in fright, the coach rocking back and forth until, taking a turn, it upended and crashed back to earth. Both axels snapped as the wheels spun off and the coach hit the ground.

Waking from unconsciousness, Dawson picked himself up from what remained of the splintered carriage and looked for his friend.

"Denny? Denny?" he shook him roughly by the shoulders.

"What?" Denny replied groggily.

"Are you well?" Dawson asked.

He rubbed his head and flexed his legs. "Yes, yes, I think so."

"Good. Good. Get up, then."

"Right." Denny rose. "I shall see to the ladies."

"Denny! Do not waste your time."

Denny simply knelt, staring at him. "What?" he asked in disbelief.

Dawson lifted his rucksack from the rubble. "We have no time." He shook the slivers of wood from his leather satchel. "We must make that ship. It is essential that we quit these shores expeditiously." His arms gestured at the wreckage surrounding them. "This has delayed us prodigiously already."

Finding the women, Denny examined Lady Anne for a pulse to no avail. He found his satchel, slipping it over his shoulder, and the two vagrants walked away.

JULIAN ELLISTON, Lord Glascomb, stormed the gates of Bedlam not two hours after receiving notice of Lady Catherine's escape.

"I want to see the officer in charge, and I want to see him now!" he bellowed through the halls. Having studied the architectural drawings with his father to assure themselves it was impenetrable, he knew where the Royal Guard's commanders were quartered. He marched through the door, slamming it against the wall. Colonel Maulbury and his subordinates looked up.

"Lord Glascomb." The ranking officer rose and straightened his jacket.

"How did this happen?" Julian demanded.

"I…I was following orders, sir," stammered Corporal Wrenton.

"What?" Julian rounded on him before assessing the blackened eye of the young man. Taking a moment to regain his composure, Julian asked with a bit more control. "Tell me exactly what happened and what is being done to recover her."

As the Northampton carriage neared Meryton, the mood in the cabin became anxious. The duke took hold of his wife's hand, smiling tentatively when she took her eyes away from Elizabeth, who sat across from them. Their daughter, unaware of the strain her mother endured, continued searching for recognisable landmarks rushing past the window.

"It is amazing," she whispered.

Georgiana was roused from the lethargy of the journey. "What is, Elizabeth?"

"The scenery. Nothing has changed, and yet it all seems so…different." Elizabeth returned to the increasingly familiar landscape. "That lane leads to Lucas Lodge!"

She turned and pointed across Georgiana and Darcy, who grabbed at her hand, chuckling. "And there is Purvis Lodge. It is a fine house, but has very small attics indeed."

Elizabeth laughed. "And now we are near Longbourn."

Silence sprung up among the coach's occupants as the carriage pulled up alongside a thick wood. "Right there."

The duke rapped his fist against the roof, and the coach slowed to a stop. "If my reading of Edwin Bennet's journals are correct, this"—he indicated the edge of the forest—"is where he found you."

Elizabeth, sounding suddenly far away, replied. "Yes. It is."

Julian sat in the solarium, the morning's papers on his knee, his mind miles away, *I should not have listened to Morrison. I should be out there looking for that witch. Although, I shall admit, if it were I who found her...*

Cummings interrupted his musings. "A Miss Cartwright to see you, sir."

Julian rose from his seat. "Please show her in."

Miss Cartwright walked into the room, eyes full of concern. "I came as soon as I heard."

"Heard? How could you...?"

"We have mutual friends in the Foreign Office."

"Ah." Julian nodded then swept his arm as he returned to his chair, indicating she should join him. "Hornsby?"

"Yes."

"May I ask what were you doing at the Office?"

"I thought that would be painfully obvious after the recent discussion."

"The twaddle Sir Arthur was going on about the Uniteds?" Julian sat back in his chair, his fingers dancing along his lip. "I was curious about that."

"I...there was a bit of trouble, and they asked me to look around."

"Ah...right, then."

"Julian." Her voice was earnest and direct. "I came, knowing that you would be chomping at the bit to go out and hunt down Lady Catherine."

He laughed without mirth. "The thought had crossed my mind."

"That is why I am here—to keep you from such foolishness."

He stomped across the expanse of the glassed-in room. "What is foolish about wishing to be of service to those I love? You have no idea what that woman did to my family—to my sister! She deserves death."

Miss Cartwright rose. "But not at your hands, Julian."

Her eyes bored into his. He tried to break away, but she kept pace with him.

"I know what you are capable of. When your temper is so completely engaged, there is no stopping you." Her eyes pleaded. "Let the Guards do their job."

"I did, and look what good it did! That troublemaker is out there." He gesticulated wildly. "God knows what she is doing—what she plans on doing. I cannot—*will* not—sit idly by, waiting for her to strike."

Miss Cartwright took his arm. He stiffened, but she refused to release him. When she spoke, however, her tone was compassionate. "I do not think revenge is on her mind."

He whirled around to look at her. "No? Why not? Lady Catherine de Bourgh seems to live to ruin the peace—the well being of the Elliston family."

"I believe she is intent on escaping the misery of Bedlam. Hornsby made a visit to Matlock House this morning. It seems Lady Matlock is missing as well."

"The earl must be delighted."

"He might be once he recovers from the laudanum."

"Laudanum?"

"It seems that Lord Matlock engaged the services of Dr Robert Stachley."

"Good man, Stachley. Excellent under fire."

"Be that as it may, the good doctor was incapable of noticing that his hostess had doctored the bouillabaisse."

Julian came and sat next to her, a smile tweaking his lips. "Really?"

"Both he and his lordship were laid out until this morning. Hornsby had to have them both doused with water to rouse them from their beds." She smiled impishly.

"I would have paid good money to see that." He took Miss Cartwright's hand. "Thank you for coming and cajoling me out of my foul mood."

"They will find her. Hornsby now believes that it was Lady Catherine's daughter who orchestrated the whole endeavour."

Julian nodded. "What reason did Matlock give for having Stachley for dinner?"

She squeezed his hand. "He admitted to the degradation in Lady Matlock's demeanour and invited Stachley to assess her."

Julian laughed. "Perhaps he thought he could set her up in a chamber adjacent to her mother."

"Precisely."

CAROLINE SLUMPED against the door of the infirmary, a makeshift affair in what once was the first mate's quarters. She had been assisting the surgeon for the last sixteen hours as he bandaged and stitched men's wounds. For her effort at carting the boiling water from the galley to the sickbay, she received a grunt every hour or two.

As she headed towards the upper deck, a bowl of pus and blood in her arms, her tears fell. Unable to wipe them away for fear of spilling the vile contents of her burden, she rubbed her cheek on the gown she had been wearing since the late hours of the day before.

I shall not let them see me cry! I shall not give them the satisfaction of seeing me crumble. Straightening, she shoved away from the door, heading up the banister-less stairs.

Caroline marvelled at the clear blue skies and the brisk, fresh wind spraying a mist of salty air around her body, and despite the fatigue, humiliation, and misery throughout the longest night of her life, she smiled in wonder. The sea rolled with gentle waves, and Caroline, to her surprise, accommodated herself to the shifting floor beneath her. The freshness of the air, after being below decks for so long, renewed her determination to prevail.

With a lighter sense of being than she had felt in a long time, Caroline walked to the banister, balancing the unadorned metal bowl on the smooth wood. As she lifted the coarse linen cloth, her features contorted in disgust. The foul odour of putrescence—even amidst the abundance of fresh, clean air—repulsed her, and she recoiled from it. Looking around to see whether anyone had witnessed her weakness, Caroline dumped the rank contents overboard and walked away.

In West Sussex, Dr Thaddeus Simmons was returning from the lengthy, hard-fought birth of Lady Sorenson's fifth girl, and he was extremely vexed at the harangue Lord Sorenson had given him at his failure to deliver the needed heir. So intense were his internal musings that he was caught unawares by the appearance of bits of carriage littering the road. With the gathering dusk, it was hard for him to see clearly, but what he did see propelled him from the curricle to be of any assistance possible. So quick was his dismount that he had to return to the carriage for his medical supplies.

Making his way through the wreckage, he stepped over bits of cushion, upholstery stuffing, and copious amounts of shattered wood.

He saw the first corpse—a man—below what appeared to be the trail of a quartet of rampant horses.

Formulaically, he felt for a non-existent pulse. "A blessing really, the legs...and the lungs, his entire chest is crushed. Yes, there's the indentation of a hoof." He sighed heavily then whispered a few words of benediction taught to him by the parson of a nearby village.

Looking around. he identified another body in similar livery. Gently, he picked his way over to the unmoving form. Bending down, nearly able to dismiss the repugnance of his proximity to the cold, life-less flesh, he shuddered then heard the moaning of a woman. *No, two women!* he thought and hurried to offer assistance.

"Madam," he called, hoping for a coherent response—any response, actually.

"Over here," came a weak reply.

Simmons moved towards the words murmuring out of the growing shadows. "I am a doctor and may be able to help you."

"Over here!" came the voice again, and Dr Simmons found himself looking down on a woman with fear clearly written on her face. Quickly, he bent down and touched her leg. She gasped, pulling herself to a half-reclining position. She pushed his hands away.

"Madam, I must examine the extent of your injuries." Simmons could see dark patches that had soaked through her dress. "I insist." He saw her nod and gently raised the skirt of her gown, making sure to test the freshness of the blood on the fabric. *Both old and fresh,* he noted. *Not good. A great deal of blood lost already.*

"You must tell me if the pain is too intense. Perhaps you should recline, madam."

She nodded again, and he methodically prodded her leg, using the fabric of the gown to block her view. With growing dismay, he noted her lack of response to his touch until he reached her knee. Holding her foot, he bent the leg and discovered the reason for her lack of sensa-tion. The back of her calf was ripped open, and the bone was visible through the tangle of sinew.

He took a deep breath then examined a superficial cut that accounted for most of the blood loss. Opening his bag, he took a bandage, neatly wrapped her thigh, and ever so gently encased the useless calf in linen as well. With that done, Dr Simmons again looked into his bag, retrieving a small vial of a clear liquid. He then lifted her by the shoulders, putting the vial to her lips. "This will help with the pain, madam."

"Miss," she whispered after taking a healthy dose.

"Miss." Dr Simmons smiled at her ability to think coherently.

"Younge."

"Miss Younge then, it is. How many were in your party? Beyond the coachmen, that is."

Miss Younge closed her eyes, the effort of speaking taking its toll. "Beyond myself, there were Lady Matlock and her mother, Lady Catherine."

"Very good, Miss Younge, very good. Now, I am going to lay you back down and see to your companions. But I shall not leave you, Miss Younge—that I promise." He lowered her back to the ground, pleased that the laudanum was beginning its work. Simmons went in search of the two women she had mentioned, wondering why no men beyond the servants could be found.

The sound of a keening woman led him to an older victim in what was once a fine gown, rocking what appeared to be a lifeless woman in her arms.

"Madam?" he began, softly so as not to startle her.

The woman jerked around, her gaze steady and feral. "Who are you?"

"I am Dr Thaddeus Simmons."

"Providence always provides," she said with an imperious tone in her voice.

Dr Simmons gently knelt beside her, attempting to pry the corpse from her hands.

She growled. "Do not touch me, knave."

"Madam?"

"I am Lady Catherine de Bourgh."

"Ah yes, Lady Catherine. As I said, I am a physician and only wish to examine her." He again placed his hands on the lifeless body.

"Yes, my sister."

Simmons looked from one woman to the other. "Your sister?"

Lady Catherine smoothed back the younger woman's hair from her face. "Lady Anne Darcy." She looked up into the startled eyes of the doctor. "She carries the heir to Pemberley."

The doctor made a visual examination and agreed that the woman had been expecting a child. He also noted the darting eyes and suspicion in the older woman's movements. *Her dress is unlaundered and worn. I wonder...* He put his hand back on Lady Catherine's shoulder, and turning to hiss at him, she revealed her fear. *Ah!*

"Lady Catherine, perhaps we should take your...sister...to my examination room to determine the extent of her injuries."

Catherine looked from him to her beloved relation, her confidence waning. "Yes, perhaps you are right." She loosened her grip on the body. "But I shall attend you!"

"Of course." He smiled then bent and lifted the body in his arms. Rising, he offered his elbow to the older woman. "It will be a bit cramped, but we shall make do."

"I shall be more than happy to report your solicitous care of his wife to Mr Darcy."

"Mr Darcy?" Simmons asked.

"Yes. Mr George Darcy. You, of course, have heard of him?" Lady Catherine was aghast at the blank expression on the doctor's face. "He is one of the most prestigious gentlemen of the realm!"

"Here we are, Lady Catherine. Please wait here a moment. I shall put...Lady Anne...back here." He gently laid the corpse in the rear of the curricle. "She will be able to...rest...until I may examine her in more immaculate conditions."

Catherine fussed over the placement of her beloved sister. "If you think it best...?"

"I do."

Catherine nodded, allowing the doctor to hand her up into the curricle. Simmons then walked towards Miss Younge.

"Doctor? Doctor? Where are you going?" She craned her neck to follow his movements.

"I must get Miss Younge."

"Who is Miss Younge? She is no one. Come, we must make haste, Doctor."

"I cannot leave her, Lady Catherine."

"I insist you return here immediately!" she screamed, panic rising.

Ignoring her, Simmons lifted the nearly unconscious woman. "She was travelling along with you and your sister."

"She must be Anne's maid." Lady Catherine looked from one woman to the other—one wincing as the carriage moved, the other turning blue. "She will be a comfort to Anne when she wakes."

"Indubitably," said the doctor as he led the horses into town.

DARCY EXITED THE CARRIAGE, handing out first his sister then Elizabeth. She peeped out from under the doorway, looking about and then down.

Of course, he thought, taking her hand and placing it in the crook of his elbow. *She has lived here for the majority of her life. The duchess...* Darcy turned to see his usually confident aunt hesitate, a stricken look of dread overtaking her regal features. He watched, his free hand unconsciously covering the hand that held his arm, pulling Elizabeth even closer to his body as the duke spoke comforting words to his wife. A surge of pride swelled through his heart when his aunt nodded once, then again, and then pushed her way free of the carriage. Casting about for his bearings, he looked to his left and found Elizabeth beaming up at him.

"I am proud of her," Elizabeth whispered, leading Darcy to a fallen tree trunk that was nearly decayed. "Let us give them a moment. I believe this is the part of our journey that Mama fears the most."

Darcy patted her arm, leading them to Georgiana, who was examining the log. As if standing around a gravesite, the three waited for the Northamptons to join them.

The duchess focused on Elizabeth. Disengaging from her husband, she opened her arms to her daughter, who ran to her, and the two wept. Georgiana made no pretence of hiding her tears while the duke batted a few drops off his cheek before looking away. He then sat himself on what was left of the log, facing away from the wood and staring at the ground.

"I imagine this"—he poked gently at the ground with his walking stick—"is where you hid?" He looked at—and then away from—his family.

"And was found, Uncle." Georgiana placed a hand on his shoulder as she sat next to him.

The duke looked at her intently then nodded. "She was found." He smiled, and she smiled back at him. "Thank you, Georgiana."

Mother and daughter approached their family. "This is where...?" The duchess clutched her daughter's hand as she, too, sat on the log. Seeing there was no room, her husband pulled her onto his lap, wrapping his arm around her.

"This is where our daughter was rescued by a generous, honourable man. This is where"—he looked into her eyes—"she was saved."

thirty-five

By the time Dr Simmons reached his home in Cuckfield, Constable Wells was just bringing his horse to a halt. "Dr Simmons," the middle-aged man called out as he dismounted his horse. "I have… Oh! Pardon, may I be of service here?"

Simmons handed down Lady Catherine who went immediately to Anne. "If you would escort Lady Catherine de Bourgh inside, I shall bring in my patients."

"Lady Catherine?" Wells looked shocked. "But I only received…"

"Tell me about it later," he snarled. He nodded in Lady Catherine's direction.

"But she…!" Wells hissed back at him. "Bedlam!"

"Bring her inside and then you may send word." He looked over at the older woman arranging Anne's torn gown.

Wells nodded then went to retrieve his captive. "Madam, let us make our way indoors so the doctor may attend the wounded."

Looking at the back of the curricle where Dr Simmons was intently studying Miss Younge, Lady Catherine relented. "Thank you, sir."

Wells escorted Lady Catherine into the doctor's office, and Simmons studied his patient, Miss Younge, who was still unconscious. He glanced at her leg. *I might be able to take the lower leg now. It will save losing the entire limb. She still has feeling at the knee.*

Mrs Simmons came through the door and looked at her husband as he examined the leg. "Lia, please go prepare the surgery."

"Oh, Teddy."

"Hurry, my dear. We have the chance to save a part of the leg if we are quick and careful."

Mrs Simmons turned to precede her husband.

"And tell Marsden to come and fetch the other."

"There is another?" Mrs Simmons asked, horrified by the destruction invading her home.

"Unfortunately, I was too late, although it seems she has been gone for some time."

Mrs Simmons hurried to carry out her husband's orders.

PREPARATIONS FOR MARY BENNET'S wedding monopolised Mrs Bennet's attentions, so Elizabeth was able spend her days visiting with old friends and showing her family the places of importance to her. She took the intrepid peers on a walk up Oakham Mount to marvel at the beauty that had been such a comfort in her youth. These local excursions not only brought the family closer together, it also served as a means to keep the visitors from Netherfield, thus affording privacy to the newly married Bingleys. That it also kept them from the impromptu social visits of Mrs Bennet was a bonus. Elizabeth was pleased when, taking tea at the local inn, she was able to introduce her parents to Lady Lucas.

"Miss Elizabeth!" Lady Lucas called out as she approached the finely set table. As the older woman walked over, another woman was visible, lighting Elizabeth's eyes with a smile. "Charlotte!" She rose to introduce them to her illustrious parents.

After the other introductions were made, Lady Lucas said, "Your Graces, I am so pleased that Elizabeth has found her family." She looked fondly at the young woman. "Not only has she been a true friend to my Charlotte, but she has always been a joy to know. Ever since she was a wee girl, her liveliness and enthusiasm were infectious. When Mr Bennet...Mr Edwin Bennet...was still alive...God rest his soul...Longbourn was so lively. And Elizabeth was always at its heart. And if ever there was sickness or an illness, it was Elizabeth who would come and help me tend them. Either that"—the woman laughed —"or she would have her nose in a book, trying to find a remedy."

Seeing Elizabeth blush, the duchess squeezed her daughter's hand. "Thank you, Lady Lucas. It is wonderful to hear such things of one's child."

"But surely," Darcy asked, "there are other tales to be told of Elizabeth's youth?"

Charlotte Lucas blushed slightly. "Oh, believe me, sir, there are tales to be told."

"Charlotte! You would not dare!" Her family and friends laughed at the outrage in Elizabeth's expression.

"Oh, Lizzy, I knew tagging along with you..."

"As my willing accomplice, I might add."

Charlotte nodded. "...would well be worth it one day." She turned her smiling face from her dearest friend to her audience. "Well, when we were young, Miss Lizzy would commandeer Jane and me, and we would make mud balls."

"Mud balls?" Georgiana asked. "That does not sound so dreadful."

"Not in and of themselves, but if you add in the notion that these mud balls were ammunition aimed at my brothers and their friends..." Charlotte looked at her friend, allowing the tale to dangle enticingly in front of her.

"They had pulled my ribbons and cut my hair!" Elizabeth declared with a pout.

"After you had tucked that rag into the pillow Joseph sat on...at services!"

Lady Lucas could not contain the laugh that had been building. "That was you? Oh, Lizzy."

"A rag?" Darcy quirked his head. "That is all? A rag?"

Charlotte, who was laughing as hard as her mother tried to reply. "That is all?"

"A rag, even a wet rag, is not that bad," Georgiana said, watching the Lucas women convulse in merriment.

Even Elizabeth was losing her battle with the smile playing at her lips. Looking first at her cousins and then at her parents, she added wryly. "Well, it *was* soaked with two bottles of ink!"

The howls of laughter that filled the dining room of the Crescent Hen could be heard at the innkeeper's desk, causing Mr Rivers to poke his head through the door to see what all the fuss was about.

WHEN DR SIMMONS felt it was safe to leave the makeshift operating room alongside his office, he met Mrs Simmons coming towards him, a tray with a beaker and a goblet in her hands.

"Amelia?" he asked nodding to the deputy who stood outside his recovery room. The small room held a cot and served as a retreat when he returned home from a night-time visit to one of his many patients.

Mr Wells's orders," she whispered. "I have given Lady Catherine the usual dose, if a smidgeon on the high end."

Dr Simmons placed one hand on his hip while the other wearily ran through his thinning locks. "I can only imagine. But why the guard?"

"Wells will explain."

Dr Simmons moved towards the door, but his wife called him back. "And the lady?" She looked towards the operating room.

"Infection had set in, and there was no response up to her knee."

"The poor dear." Mrs Simmons lowered her gaze. "I shall unlock another bottle or two of the laudanum, then?" Mrs Simmons left her husband in the hallway.

With a shake of his head, he opened the door to his office.

"How is she, doctor?" The constable rose from the comfortable chair in which he had been reading.

"She will live," he said, sitting in the companion chair to the one his guest had reclaimed. "However, I had to take her leg to the knee." He lowered his head to his hand. "I began the day bringing life into this world, only to end it attending to death and maiming what is left of it."

Silence blanketed the room while the doctor recovered.

"Why the guard?"

"Orders, Dr Simmons, orders. Very highly placed orders." Wells quirked his brow. "The Royal Guard sent riders out in all directions." .

"From where?"

The constable's voice recalled him to the present. "Bedlam."

Simmons nodded.

"I noted earlier that you were not surprised."

"She escaped."

"Her companions engineered her departure."

Simmons again nodded. "When Lady Catherine insisted that the young lady, the deceased…" he clarified for Wells, who nodded.

"Lady Matlock."

"Then who is Darcy?" asked the doctor

"I have not a clue. Why?"

"She mentioned that her sister, Lady Anne Darcy, must be attended to as she carried the heir to Pemberland or some such." Simmons collected his thoughts before he again spoke.

"Her insistence on her fraternal relation to a much younger woman, in addition to a certain passion"—his hands fluttered about his head —"indicated she had taken leave of her senses." He rubbed his eyes. "I thought it was the shock of the accident, but…"

"It seems she was involved in the kidnapping of a child." Wells looked sideways at the doctor, whose head snapped to attention.

"This Lady Matlock?"

"No. The de Bourgh woman. It seems she engineered the kidnapping of a duke's daughter around fifteen years ago. Only recently, the lady was returned and could prove what it seems some had suspected."

Simmons ran his hand over his face. "How did they get her out?"

"Two men in borrowed uniforms presented forged orders and —*voila*—here we are."

"What happens next?"

"An armed escort will return her to Bedlam in the morning. I have taken the liberty of posting guards outside her windows."

"And I saw your man in the passageway. Do you really feel this is necessary? I mean to say, she *has* been drugged."

"In this instance, we should err on the side of caution. I have received two expresses since we sent word of her confinement."

Another silence filled the room until Dr Simmons spoke. "And Miss Younge…?"

"Hard to say what will happen to her, but she is an accomplice— and the only suspect we have."

The doctor made to protest. "No, save your breath, Simmons. You and I know that the chances of a paid lady's companion arranging a scheme such as this is unlikely. But she is all we have. I would wager it was the other one."

"Lady Matlock?"

"She is the woman's daughter. And rich enough to afford such a scheme."

ELIZABETH FOUND herself sandwiched between Mrs Philips and Sir William Lucas during the dinner celebrating her cousin's upcoming nuptials. Fortunately, she was able to steer the discussion away from her own wedding and the anticipated vulgar prying into the cost of everything—along with veiled attempts to gain an invitation.

"Oh, Elizabeth, I mean, Lady Elizabeth…I am so glad you were able to return for Mary's wedding, my dear," Mrs Philips whispered when Elizabeth had exhausted Sir William's soliloquy on improvements he and his sons had made to Lucas Lodge over the winter. "I know it means a great deal to her.

"Since Michael, Mr Waverly, has been courting Mary, she has been spending more time with us in Meryton." She patted Elizabeth's hand. "She has told us of your many adventures and how dull Longbourn is without you."

In a more serious tone, she added, "I am sorry, Lady Elizabeth. I had no idea my sister made things so difficult for you."

Mrs Philips looked around. "I have spoken with my brothers, and we are on guard to keep my sister at bay—or at least contained."

Elizabeth sat immobile, stunned.

"And your young man!" Again the older woman took command of the conversation. "Who knew Mr Darcy could be so charming? He seems so much more pleasant now. And you, Elizabeth—you are luminous."

"Thank you, Aunt," Elizabeth replied cautiously, causing the older woman to beam.

AFTER SEEING that her guests were accommodated in the parlour while the men remained in the dining room for their port and cigars, Mrs Bennet pulled her errant niece aside. "Elizabeth," she began once she had manoeuvred them into the hallway. "How good of you to join us." With a huff she continued. "After being in Meryton for nearly three days, you have deigned to grace us with your presence this evening. I should be ashamed of you. What will the neighbours think of that?"

"That Lady Elizabeth has the good grace to allow Mary her due as a bride," Mrs Philips replied, entering the parlour.

"The way you were crowing about having the duke and duchess at your daughter's wedding. Honestly, Frances! One would think Elizabeth is the bride and not Mary." Lady Lucas joined the chorus of Elizabeth's supporters.

Mrs Bennet stood motionless, her mouth gaping open.

Lady Lucas added, "We know your history with Elizabeth and your miserable treatment of her in the past. We let it go because she could always come to us for a day or two.

"But to sit here and listen to you go on now is an insult to her." Lady Lucas moved her hand to Elizabeth. "Mary, and not Elizabeth, is the reason for our coming together—to wish her well—not to see how well you pretend to be connected. I wish only the best for her, as I do for Jane, but I shall not sit here one moment longer while you brag about Elizabeth after all those years of having to listen to you abuse her.

"Elizabeth deserves her happiness for all she has endured. Now, you go in and be gracious to her and her parents, and not one more word about their position in society. Frances, why will you not focus on your own daughters? The one who is marrying in two days' time and the ones who remain at Longbourn."

"Why, I never—"

"No, you have not, but perhaps you should have." Mrs Philips would have her say. "We have been negligent as your friends and family, allowing you to carry on so for this long."

She raised her hand. "No more. The happiness of too many young people depends on your keeping a civil tongue in your head. These young people deserve all the attention and care we can give them."

Frances Bennet began to speak, but Lady Lucas stopped her. "No, Frances. No more."

She turned and left Frances Bennet where she stood, her eyes darting about as the women returned to the parlour until they focused on the Duchess of Northampton, who stood at the end of the corridor, smiling at her. Then, with a quick arch of her brow and a self-satisfied smirk, she, too, returned to the ladies.

BRINGING Bingley's curricle to a halt at Noah's Puddle, Darcy allowed memories of his visit to Netherfield and his first glimpse of Elizabeth to blossom in his mind.

"This is where we first saw Charles, Jane and I..." Elizabeth's voice cut through his musings. "And this is where..."

Darcy swallowed, and the shimmering image of the past faded as he looked upon the reality of her presence beside him.

"...I first saw you." She smiled as she tilted her head.

"I was first fascinated by you." He looked away to the small lake then back, focusing his darkening eyes upon her. "And I knew that my life was about to change—to become better."

Seeing her complete surprise, Darcy chuckled as he helped her from the curricle and pulled her into his arms, pressing his lips to hers.

"Fitzwilliam," she gasped when her need for air forced her from his lips. But they never left her, moving lower to the line of her jaw, then back and down along her neck to the border of her gown.

As he pulled her body against his own, he paused, scanning the locale for a more protected spot. Watching his eyes search the area, Elizabeth giggled and pushed away without releasing his hand. Leading him behind a large boulder to a stand of birch trees, she clasped the white bark in her hands and moved between the individual trunks, teasing him to follow her further into the grove.

Growling, Darcy quickened his step, grabbing her by the waist and pulling her to him. "I love you."

"And I you," she replied, kissing along his jaw line while her hands ran through his thick curls. No longer able to support his own weight, Darcy sank to his knees, dragging Elizabeth along with him. Their lips parted, and for a moment, they looked at each other, silently asking a thousand questions. Gently, reverently, he put his hand to her cheek. She smiled shyly, and his face lit up. Then she placed her hand on top of his and, running the other through his curls, sighed as the waves glided through her fingers.

Looking into her eyes, Darcy was caught unawares when, in an instant, her lips were upon him, and he could feel her hunger inciting his own anew. His desire spiralled near the edge of control as the folds of his cravat were pulled and untied until the linen strip fluttered away from his body. Then, the delicate breeze of the late afternoon was caressing his chest. They sat, entangled in their embrace, their lips, tongues, and their very breath tantalising and stoking their desire to new heights.

Sometime later, she said, "Fitzwilliam, please look at me." Her voice was kind, gentle, and full of understanding. "Please?"

Hearing the vulnerability in her voice, he relented, taking in her beautiful face as it looked at him so sincerely. Stopping her attempt to remove her hand, Darcy blushed as she giggled.

Then placing her free hand upon his cheek, she smiled lovingly as he put his hand over hers.

"I love you, more than may be seemly, but I would not change one moment, one atom of my sentiment, my feeling for you—for your happiness, your safety, your heart. It is"—she stopped for a moment —"what makes us human, and is that not what is important? Not the estates we are gifted with or the education we pursue, but the depth and fullness we allow our hearts to feel?" Sensing her eyes on him, he nodded.

Just as Darcy felt he was about to burst, the cry of a falcon pierced the air, and they froze, their eyes the only body parts retaining the ability to move. And move they did, searching the skies for the vocal intruder who was answered by a louder, stronger screech.

The flapping of wings filled the air around them as first one bird and then its mate landed on a branch in the tree nearest to them. Cocking their heads, the majestic birds spied the interlopers invading their grove. The pair of hunters kept the humans in their sight, flapping or cawing each time Darcy tried to embrace Elizabeth until her laughter joined the call of the birds, pulling him out of the peevish mood into which he was slipping.

The sound of boots crunching on the pebbles and stones lining the pond made them spring into action. In a frantic sweep of her arms,

Elizabeth examined her gown, and as she began, Darcy helped her to stand, brushing off the leaves and blades of grass that had attached themselves to him until Elizabeth bent, picking up his waistcoat. Darcy hurriedly slipped his arms through, furiously buttoning it, his eyes searching the ground for his cravat. Just as he was about to reach for the cloth that was hanging off a nearby shrub, the smaller of the birds flew down, snatching it away before he could grab it. Caught between the bird, resettling near its mate, and the advancing couple steadily approaching, Darcy shrugged his shoulders and smiled. Taking Elizabeth's hand, he led her back to the curricle.

As he handed her up into the gig, Michael Waverly and his father made the clearing from the opposite side.

"Mr Darcy? Lady Elizabeth?" Michael said in surprise. "What are you—" He stopped, noting the less than formal appearance of his companions.

"And what do you do so far afield?" Elizabeth asked, hurriedly.

"I am afraid I am the reason Michael is here rather than with his intended," the older of the two men replied.

Seeing the confusion on Elizabeth's face, Michael Waverly added. "Lady Elizabeth, may I present my father, Mr David Waverly?"

"Of course," Elizabeth replied. "We met the other night during the dinner at Lucas Lodge."

"I dragged Michael here, out for a bit of birding. I caught sight of a pair of falcons from the inn and…well, followed them here."

Blushing, Darcy coughed. "Yes, well, Elizabeth wished to show me a favourite haunt of hers as a child."

"And there"—Elizabeth pointed to the avian pair still sitting in the tree—"are the couple you seek."

"And we must be on our way," Darcy said, pulling himself into the driver's seat of the curricle.

"It was nice to meet you again, sir." He bowed to Mr Waverly. To the soon-to-be groom, he smiled and said, "Waverly," with a nod of his head and then, taking the reins, spurred the horses on their way.

thirty-six

July 1812
Freetown, Sierra Leone

CAROLINE WAS PLEASANTLY SURPRISED AT HER RECEPTION WHEN THE *Cantata* docked at the bustling port of Freetown. There, bedecked in military regalia, was the dashing Colonel Reginald Richley, filling his uniform to perfection. He was accompanied by a coterie of adjutants and their ladies, the matrons of British colonial society whose sense of propriety gave no licence to the strange, exotic setting of their circumstance.

"Mrs McDonald," came the screeching, shrill voice of Lady Stanton, wife of the head diplomat of the region. "How good to meet you. It is so rare to have a woman of your refined distinction with us."

"Thank you, Lady Stanton." Caroline curtseyed, elated as the younger daughter of one of the most illustrious families in England stretched a hand of friendship to her. *Perhaps living here will not be so bad, after all. There is Lady Clarissa Stendahl, or no, it is Lady Adams now, I believe.*

She nodded at each lady's introduction. *This will work out well, indeed, until I can return to England.* Before the McDonalds were ushered off the docks, they had invitations to a flurry of dinners and balls that, even with their evangelical intent, they could not refuse to attend.

JULIAN LEANED AGAINST THE WALL, completely composed, watching the woman who paced relentlessly in the confined space of her cage.

"It is just like Anne," she muttered, hands twitching as she grabbed hold of them. "So irresponsible, leaving her untidiness to me. She must have danced all night to sleep so late."

She looked out the window and then, drawn to them, calmly walked over to the bars. Slowly, one frail hand grabbed hold of the iron barricade, the other reaching to touch the crackled glass. "We should have been on the road hours ago. Now, we shall not reach Pemberley until after dark." She knocked her hand against the glass, a finger tracing one of the spider web of cracks.

Lady Catherine stopped speaking, her countenance hardening and her mouth pinching into a line. "Perhaps that is her intent!" she spat. "One less day with that horrid Alexandra, indeed."

Lady Catherine's agitation grew as she resumed her pacing. "Trapped there all alone with that woman! If I had succeeded, I would have married her off to the first man, eligible or not. Then she would not be so high and mighty! Then she would know that the Matlocks are not to be trifled with. Aargh!" she groaned, as if in pain. "What I could do with such riches! But that man was blinded by Anne's golden hair and that simpering smile she used so well with Papa. I hate her!"

Lady Catherine turned, pulling her skirts behind her. "She was always first with Mama and Papa. The golden girl who could do no wrong."

Lady Catherine's pacing became furious. "Oh yes, my baby sister…that perfect image of loveliness that everyone admired…she would not have lasted if I had not intervened and done something."

Julian shook his head, and nodding to Colonel Maulbury, they left the cell.

"She has been like that since her return. Dr Stone believes the exuberance of the last few days has hastened her decline."

Julian nodded. "You have doubled the guards?"

"Yes, sir. And Stone has increased her dose of laudanum."

"Good." They exited the building, and Julian took the reins of his stallion that Corporal Wrenton held at the ready. "Keep me posted."

"Of course, sir."

"We were lucky, Colonel."

"But I do not believe anyone else will be so eager to see her escape."

"No—I imagine not." Julian took in the afternoon sun brightening the courtyard as he mounted his horse. "I look forward to your first report."

"Of course, sir."

With a nod, Julian kicked his heels into the sides of his horse and rode back to London.

"CAROLINE." Mr McDonald sighed, leaning against the door to his wife's sitting room. "I cannot just order the captain to refit his boat and return at my will. Colonel Richley told you—the captain must await the arrival of their cargo from the interior."

"And what is so precious about this cargo that it overrules the wishes of people?"

"As sweet and lovely as you are, Mrs McDonald, the merchants of London are more eager for the cotton, gold, and diamonds that are extracted from the natives and the land than they are returning you to society." Seeing her ire rise, McDonald turned on his heel. "We leave for Lady Adams's in half an hour. Please be ready."

Caroline turned back to face her reflection in the mirror. *Oh, I shall be ready, my dear Mr McDonald. Colonel Richley is not one to disobey, and I have no desire to displease such a man as he.*

"WELL, THAT SETTLES IT," Bingley said, clapping his hands together. "Bravestock sounds like the perfect solution to our predicament." He looked hopefully at Jane, who smiled then looked at her sister.

Sensing her hesitation, Elizabeth left her seat beside Georgiana to sit with Jane. Looking carefully at the new bride, she took her hand. "Jane, it will be good to have you close."

Jane chided her. "When you are newly married, I am sure you will be most eager for visitors close by." She laughed outright at Elizabeth's blush.

Coming to her rescue, Darcy sat beside his sister. "Especially guests who live within an easy distance and can return to their own home if necessary."

"Fitzwilliam!" Georgiana and Elizabeth scolded simultaneously, erupting into laughter when he shrugged his shoulders and calmly took up his tea.

Coming around and pulling up a chair, Bingley disregarded their teasing. "Well, if you would not mind guests who will remain with you through the evening, Jane and I would appreciate your hospitality to look at Bravestock and perhaps another property in the area. I am eager to leave Netherfield behind." He looked at Jane, taking the hand he still held to his lips. "As long as Jane is with me, I have no need to remain here among the memories."

Elizabeth turned to Darcy. "Exactly where is Bravestock?"

"Nearly thirty miles from Pemberley and within twenty of Green Haven," he said, his eyes never leaving Elizabeth.

"An ideal situation, then," she said, suddenly breathless. Seeing his smirk, Elizabeth's eyes narrowed, and when he chuckled at her, she huffed, causing the entire room to erupt in laughter.

The parlour door opened, and Mrs Stemple walked in. "How wonderful to see everyone in such a buoyant mood this afternoon," she said with a wide smile. The men rose immediately to their feet, and she walked towards Bingley's outstretched hand.

"Aunt, I have wonderful news. Darcy has invited us all to Pemberley while we investigate an estate in Derbyshire."

"How wonderful. Jane?" She looked at her niece. "Oh, my dear. Change is always difficult, but Derbyshire is a beautiful place. The peaks are nearby, and they are astonishing." She came and sat beside the newest Bingley, patting her hand. She looked at Elizabeth. "And you will be close to your sister. You can discover the joy of your new homes together."

Elizabeth looked at her sister. "Yes, Jane. It will be new for both of us." Her voice reflected her enthusiasm. "We shall share this experience together."

"Oh, Lizzy. I am happy!" Jane said with a tearful smile. "It is just so much. To have Bingley and you!"

The parlour door opened again, and the duke and duchess entered, followed by the Raleighs, their demeanour commanding the attention of their companions.

"Papa, what is it?" Elizabeth looked at the ashen faces of her parents.

"Julian sent an express." The duke's voice caught their attention. "It seems that Lady Catherine had escaped—"

A communal gasp interrupted his speech.

"—but she has since been recaptured."

"Thank heavens," Mrs Stemple said with relief.

"Elizabeth," the duchess said, taking Elizabeth in her arms. "She is being returned to Bedlam. She cannot hurt you—not now, not ever again."

"But how?" Darcy came around and sat beside his sister on the third couch. He leaned forward. "How is this possible? Was she not guarded?"

"Your cousin"—the duke looked at Darcy, who snapped back as if he had been slapped—"the new Lady Matlock arranged everything, from the forged orders to the purloined uniforms. Everything, it seems, except for the carriage accident that took her life."

"Fitzwilliam?" Georgiana said tremulously, forcing Darcy from his thoughts. He pulled her into his embrace "It is too much to bear," she sobbed into his chest.

Jane spoke to Bingley, who left the room. She then went and sat with her aunt.

"Jane," Mrs Raleigh said, "I have ordered our trunks packed. Will you join us?"

Jane looked at the door. "I am not sure yet, Aunt." She turned to look at Elizabeth and then the Darcys. "But I believe that we shall."

"Shall what?" Bingley asked, re-entering the room followed by a servant with a tray of spirits.

Bingley poured drinks for all, aided by Admiral Raleigh, who distributed them to the grateful ladies.

"Join us in town," Mrs Raleigh filled in.

Coming to sit beside his wife, Bingley looked into her eyes, and when she nodded, he added, "Jane and I wish to be near Elizabeth at this time."

"I shall see to it," Mrs Stemple said, rising from her seat. "If you do not mind, I should like to join you."

"Of course," Bingley said, looking at his departing aunt. "And thank you." She nodded before leaving the room.

"I shall go inform Mrs Nattles that dinner will be earlier than expected." Jane straightened her back. "And that we shall all be leaving in the morning."

"And I shall send word to Longbourn."

"And Mary!" Elizabeth called out. "Do not forget Mary."

"Of course not," Bingley said with a smile before leaving for his study.

"WITH HURRICANE SEASON UPON US, my dear, I truly doubt you will see the cliffs of Dover before autumn."

"Aargh!" Caroline kicked a piece of gravel from their chosen pathway.

McDonald cleared his throat and attempted to do the same to his thoughts. Doffing his hat to Lady Aston, who passed by on the arm of Colonel Richley, he devised his response. He looked out among the artfully arranged flower beds. "I was thinking that perhaps, you would consider accompanying us when we depart next week."

Caroline froze, unable to move, her mouth opening before her mind could begin to work.

She laughed cruelly. "You may wish to spend your life out... there...with those savages, but I do not."

McDonald looked away, trying to hide the disappointment that surprised even himself. When he had mastered his emotions, he spoke again. "I have already delayed my departure by a fortnight. I am needed there."

"You said you were needed here in town to help direct the negotia-tions." She stood with her hands on her hips.

Sensing the growing attention to their discussion in the public gardens, McDonald drew his bride off to a stand of palm trees. "Three weeks ago, I was, but that phase is over. I am needed in the interior to speak directly with the Temne chiefs."

"I shall remain here."

"You cannot be serious. This is not London. It would be unseemly for a woman to remain here unescorted." He stared at her. "Let alone, dangerous."

"I am a British subject and, as such, am entitled to the protection of His Majesty's troops. I shall be safe. This way, should the *Cantata* decide to leave these shores, I shall be here, ready."

"You would leave without saying goodbye?" He looked stunned.

Rolling her eyes, she replied. "Mr McDonald. We agreed—"

"Yes, Mrs McDonald. We agreed. Come, I believe we must hurry or we shall be late for tea."

ANOTHER WEEK PASSED, and Caroline was ecstatic. The *Cantata* was leaving in seven days, and she had secured passage back to England. She had instructed her girl, Ngala, to prepare for her imminent departure. *Tonight I dine with Colonel Richley and the trade delegation, and tomorrow, there is that lovely weekend invitation to Lord Castlebridge's plantation. That should do rather nicely to conclude this dismal adventure.*

She turned to look out the window at the imposed order of the English garden forged from the exotic abundance of native flora. The call of a bird cut through the silence of the British quarter, away from the bustle and heat of the commercial square. She sat in a mahogany chair formed in a local style, allowing her eyes to seek the wilderness not fifteen miles away. *Ambrose,* her mind whispered as she mentally envisioned her husband travelling through the thick jungle on his way to the Temne leader's village. *Will I ever see you again?* she wondered as her hand played with the sheer curtain gently billowing before her.

Her morbid thoughts were interrupted by Ngala's entrance with her evening gown. Rising from her musings, Caroline pushed thoughts of her husband and their misguided alliance from her mind, anticipating a night of sparkling conversation and delight.

September 1812
Green Haven's Stable, Northamptonshire

JULIAN WATCHED as rider and horse cleared the stone fence, smiling at Abigail Cartwright's red curls playing with the September wind. *Ah,* he mused. *It must be time for Elizabeth's lesson.* Pressing his heels into the sides of his mount, he turned towards the stables. *I hope I can catch her before they begin. Who knew an Elliston could be so missish about a horse. The look on her face when presented with Delilah was too precious.*

He laughed outright and rode through the trees bordering the great house. *Darcy was about to buckle, but Abby, she held firm. And oh, Darcy! Those puppy dog eyes will not be easily forgotten. What a beleaguered husband he will make. Lizzy will pout, and his resolve will vanish. Like that!* he snapped his fingers. *Just like his father.* He urged his horse into a canter. "It must be the bane of Darcy men to be so helpless in the presence of the women they love."

Julian's horse was galloping. *No, I do not wish to miss one minute. Not one minute at all.*

ELIZABETH, Miss Cartwright, and Darcy were walking towards the stables as Julian ambled towards them.

"Julian!" Georgiana called. Elizabeth and her teacher turned to the left. Miss Cartwright smiled while Elizabeth's eyes flared.

"I do not require an audience, Julian."

"Oh," he chuckled openly. "I believe you do." He returned his sister's scowl, his eyes twinkling with the tease. "You make no similar claims against your other companions?"

Elizabeth spared a glance at her mother and cousins. "They will not be joining me on my lesson."

"Their loss." He shrugged with a smile.

"If you do not object, Elizabeth," Darcy interjected, "I believe I shall accompany Julian. Unless your progress is to remain a surprise?"

"You like surprises, do you not, sir?" Her eyes twinkled.

"I would like anything you would care to surprise me with."

"Then perhaps you should accompany me on my lesson?"

"Georgiana," the duchess said. "It seems we are no longer needed here."

She turned to her nephew, placing a hand on his arm. "Remember, Fitzwilliam," she said in a low voice. "You are not married yet."

"I remember only too well, Aunt."

The approaching grooms brought 'round the horses, and Darcy aided Elizabeth to mount. "You two go on," he said to Miss Cartwright and his intended, who nodded reluctantly. "I shall catch up."

Julian saluted as Elizabeth led her horse to follow Miss Cartwright. The two women cantered off, their laughter ringing through the yard. Shortly, the groom returned with Darcy's horse, and within a breath, the men set off in pursuit.

Waving away the dust of the departing horses, the duchess laughed.

"Aunt?" Georgiana asked.

She pressed a finger to her niece's cheek. "Fitzwilliam and Elizabeth will wed in little more than a fortnight. I give Julian until January."

"Until January? For what?"

The duchess smiled at her niece. "Why, to ask Miss Cartwright to marry him!"

thirty-seven

THE NIGHT BEFORE THE WEDDING, GREEN HAVEN HOSTED A GREAT gathering of invited guests. Notably missing was the remaining Matlock relation still at liberty, although he sent both a congratulatory letter and a crate of fine, French champagne. The ladies were bedecked in gowns of silk and organza, linen and fine muslin, accommodating the warm breezes of the late summer night. Jewels gleamed from ladies' necks and arms as they swirled about the room.

For the first time in his adult life, Fitzwilliam Darcy was enjoying himself in the midst of a crowded ballroom even though he had danced every set. Fortunately for him, the liberty of dancing three sets with Elizabeth and the requisite sets with his aunts, cousins, and friends was enough to keep the smile on his handsome face.

Before the supper set, Darcy took hold of Elizabeth's hand, leading her to a small balcony partially hidden by a gauzy curtain. Before she could calm her racing heart, he wrapped his arms around her, pulled her close, and kissed her. "Your absence was driving me wild. I can scarcely wait until tomorrow. Then this will be a memory and we shall be alone, beginning our life, together."

Her smile lit up the night, and reaching her arms around his neck, she pulled him in for another kiss. The sound of slippers and dancing shoes approaching was lost on them until the music grew louder and the candles glowing in the candelabras moved closer to their hideaway. A persistent cough broke through the haze of their passion.

"Elizabeth?" the duchess called out. "Darcy?"

The couple pulled their heads apart, looking towards their matriarch. Standing beside her with knowing smiles stood Jane Bingley, Mrs Raleigh, Lady Darcy, Mary Darcy, and Miss Cartwright. "I believe the supper set is upon us, and as the guests of honour, your absence would be noted."

After one last kiss, they walked arm in arm back to the dance floor.

COLONEL RICHLEY LEANED back in his chair, one hand rubbing his lips, the other fiddling with the parchment sprawled across his desk. *I hate this part of my commission.* He shoved the offending folio away. *It is difficult enough writing to the families of those taken in battle, but this…?*

He got up, walking to the open door leading to the veranda. Even though it was nearing midnight, his eyes scanned the jungle at the edge of the British settlement. How does one truly convey what happened? *Can anyone who has not experienced the sweltering heat and the primitive conditions comprehend how these things can occur? That such pestilence can descend and devour all in its path without a moment's warning?*

He shuddered even though the humidity plastered his linen shirt to his chest. He looked at the sea, the docks lined with ships engaged in the commerce that fuelled the empire. Lost in the images of the friends and acquaintances recently lost, Richley mastered his whirling emotions to compose the last letter of the twenty he had worked on through the night.

September 1812
Freetown, Sierra Leone

Dear Mr Bingley,
It is with a heavy heart that I must inform you of the death of

both your sister and brother. Caroline, Mrs McDonald, was one of a distinguished party visiting the plantation of Lord Castle-bridge on the outskirts of Freetown. However, as is often the case here in the tropics, a devastating fever swept the area, inflicting horrific and deadly consequences. The entire Castle-bridge family were stricken as all fifteen of their guests, including your sister, succumbed to the scourge.

While overseeing the destruction of the plantation as a health precaution, I received word that the delegation headed by your brother the Reverend Ambrose McDonald was attacked and that they, too, succumbed to their injuries. At least I am able to report that his end was swift and his suffering brief. In addition to your brother, his mother and all of the evangelical contingent were felled in the attack by the Sherbo against their traditional rivals.

Sir, you have my deepest and most sincere condolences. In the brief time I had the privilege of knowing your sister, I was impressed by her confidence and poise. My association with Mr McDonald was of a longer duration. He was a fine man who truly embodied the precepts of our religion in his untenable charge of making and keeping the peace in this foreign land.

Due to health constraints and the unending heat of our clime, it is impossible to return the bodies of any of your family. Mrs McDonald's remains were buried in the effort to contain the epidemic. As for her husband, the remains that were found and identified were interred to avoid putrefaction. Please advise me on the disposal of the McDonalds' personal effects that remained in her quarters here in Freetown. If it is acceptable to you, their belongings could be distributed to the poor and needy among us here.

Sincerely,
Colonel Reginald Richley

SEPTEMBER SEVENTH DAWNED with the promise of sun and a clear sky. Although Elizabeth knew the house had been bustling since long before dawn, she relished the temporary serenity. Flopping on her back, she stretched her arms over her head, allowing her eyes to take in the details of a room she had barely reclaimed but was still happy to abandon to the past. A starling called outside her window, and she turned, her eyes fastening on the gauzy curtain billowing in the gentle breeze. She smiled at the beauty and the promise of the day.

"At last."

JULIAN FUSSED with his cravat for the tenth time in half as many minutes, clearly unfocused as he looked through his looking glass. As if by chance, his eyes took in the delicate green ivy stitched in columns along his waistcoat. His fingers lowered from his neck cloth to the embroidered vine, part and parcel of his family's crest. "Generous in abundance, tenacious in adversity," he recited to himself. "Since William the Conqueror we have so stood."

He looked out the window to the nearest estate, a scattering of miles away. "Will she recall?"

Pulling himself from the delightful images prancing through his mind, he straightened. "And who would want a wife who thinks as I do?" He quickly strode to the window, pushing the obscuring fabric away. *And how dull to have a woman who enjoys all the things I do...* He snorted.

It is not likely that she would select her gown based upon what she thinks I will wear. He paused. "Would she?" This notion pleased Julian, and, running his hands over the cream silk with the green ivy embroidery, he smiled.

IN THE DOWAGER House of Green Haven, Fitzwilliam, Georgiana, the Raleighs, and the Bingleys took an early breakfast.

"The carriages…?" Darcy began.

"Ready and waiting, Darcy. Once we finish here, we shall be ready to leave." Raleigh smiled at the anxious man.

"And then, sit and wait at Green Haven." Bingley took a sip of coffee to hide his smile.

"Although I am sure the company will be more…congenial."

Jane looked at her husband. "Charles, have mercy on your friend. It is not every day one is married."

"Thank heavens for that. I did not sleep a wink last night."

No, brother?" Georgiana teased. "Not having second thoughts, are you?"

He glared at her then looked down at his plate. "No, but I worry I shall not be the best of husbands to Elizabeth."

Georgiana looked contrite. "You are the best of brothers. I am sure you will excel at being a husband."

"As am I," Jane offered kindly. "I have known Elizabeth nearly all her life. You are exactly the man she needs to make her happy."

"And I shall be more than happy to advise you, based on my months of experience," Bingley added, and the entire table laughed at his puffed up chest.

JULIAN PROCEEDED DOWN THE WIDE, sweeping staircase, careful to avoid the array of footmen commandeered by the housekeeper, Mrs Whitcomb, along with Mrs Hutchins, who had travelled from London to assist in preparations for Elizabeth's wedding. Coming to a stop five steps from the bottom, he paused, watching the two women who had indulged his whims from oatmeal biscuits and mulled cider to caviar and imported cognac. Julian smiled as they huddled together over the last-minute deliveries of freshly cut flowers and various touches to elevate the celebration into the realm of perfection. Chuckling, he took the remaining steps, instinctively tugging on the cuffs of his impeccably tailored coat. Dodging a pair of liveried servants carrying a large and delicate-looking spray of flowers, he was about to nip one for himself when he caught Mrs Hutchins staring at him, her mouth agape in horror. Seeing his hand stop mid-air, her green eyes narrowed, and Julian smiled sheepishly before backing away.

"Lord Glascomb," Mrs Whitcomb interjected kindly, but not

mistaking the iron of her will. "You will find your father and cousins in the breakfast room. I am sure they will be able to entertain you."

"And keep you out of mischief," Mrs Hutchins added almost under her breath.

The Green Haven housekeeper smiled at her London counterpart. "Until it is time to leave for the service."

"Thank you, Whitcomb, Hutchins." Julian bowed as the two held his gaze until he complied. Heading towards the breakfast room, he heard them continue as if his interruption was as bothersome and significant as a gnat in summer.

Entering the brightly lit room, he chuckled at his father, Sir Gregory, Peter Darcy, and Admiral Raleigh.

"Ah, Glascomb." Sir Gregory Darcy sipped his coffee. "I see you have been suitably corralled into the male stockade."

Julian gathered a light breakfast. "At least I am in good company." He looked around. "Where is the bridegroom?"

Raleigh replied, "Well, after looking over the rig they will take to Pemberley…"

"For at least the fortieth time this morning!" Peter replied, and they chuckled at the fastidious groom. "I believe Bingley took mercy on us and took him for a walk."

The duke tore a muffin in two. "His pacing was driving me insane!" He popped a half in his mouth. "Between that and your mother insisting he remain far away from Elizabeth…"

"And the parade of women marching up and down…" Sir Gregory chuckled.

"If I did not know better, I would believe we had no one working here, the way Alexandra was asking me—me!—for a tray of tea, or a compress of cucumber. I ask you"—the duke looked around his table —"What is a cucumber compress, and why does one need it?"

Peter laughed. "I have never seen you look so relieved as when Mama and Mary arrived."

"I think I have never been so relieved." The duke sighed. "Thank heavens I have but one daughter to marry off." All eyes turned on Julian, who was enjoying a muffin of his own.

Feeling their gaze upon him, he looked around the table. "What?"

"What have you done now, Glascomb?" Darcy asked as he and

Bingley strode in, much calmer than in their earlier description. Resplendent in his perfectly tailored coats, it was the absolute joy radiating from Darcy's eyes that startled all into silence.

Resting his hands on the back of the chair, he repeated. "Well? What has my almost brother"—his eyes gleamed mischievously —"done now?"

"Nothing!" Julian replied defensively.

"We were simply wondering"—Sir Gregory placed his cup onto the bone china saucer—"when he intends to join the rest of us…"

"…in the blissful state of matrimony." Peter Darcy took up the chorus.

Laughter filled the room as an embarrassed terror blossomed across Julian's handsome features.

After composing himself, Bingley pulled out his pocket watch and clapped Darcy on the back. "Well, Darcy, it is time to get you to the church." All except the groom, the duke, and Julian pulled out their timepieces and, in a nearly synchronised fashion, wiped their mouths. Pushing their chairs out, they headed for the carriages awaiting them.

Darcy looked around the nearly empty room. The duke stood slowly, and taking Darcy's hand in one of his own, he clasped his shoulder with the other. Their eyes locked, and an unspoken emotion passed between them. Darcy looked at Julian and gave a nod before striding from the room.

ONCE THE GROOM and his entourage were safely on their way, the women came downstairs, brilliant smiles lighting their joyous faces. Jane and Mrs Raleigh were followed by Lady Darcy, Mary, and Georgiana, talking excitedly among themselves as they carefully navigated their descent.

With one last look down the corridor, the duchess took a deep breath then glided down the stairs. She moved to stand between her husband and son. As Elizabeth began her descent, the housekeepers gathered alongside their employers, tears watering their eyes as all— family and loyal servants—gazed at the beauty of Lady Elizabeth. Beaming in utter and complete joy, she stretched her hands to her parents and again felt wrapped in their embrace.

THE CHAPEL at Green Haven was decorated with the blooms of the field and greenhouse, specially tended throughout the summer for this auspicious occasion. Bows of silk and organza, ornamented with ivy, and sprays of roses and orchids billowed in the opened windows, bringing the fresh breeze to cool the rush and heat of the crowded pews. Peers and gentry from throughout the land gathered in the family's house of worship in their late-summer finery to share in the joy of the day. The archbishop of Canterbury stood at the altar to officiate. Nestled among the nobility was a small, well-defined contingent of Meryton's prominent citizens. Decidedly missing was the matron of the leading family although her daughters and son-in-law accompanied the patriarch of the Bennet estate.

Lady Darcy and Mary found Abigail saving their place in the Darcy family pew. Looking at her sartorially splendid gown, the Darcy women smiled at each other, endeavouring to suppress their giggles. Abigail's eyes held a moment of terror, her hands running over the sage green gown she wore, fondling the delicate pattern of ivy embroidered in a creamy ivory silk.

With the family party seated, a side door opened, revealing Bingley and the groom who strode to the archbishop's side. An approaching carriage rolled past the open windows, and the more curious in the crowd craned their necks for a first glimpse of the bride. As the soft strings of the duke's favourite trio wafted from the balcony, the shuffle of feet was heard along with the murmuring of women directing the progress of the bride.

"Do not look so green, Father." Julian's jovial laugh filtered through the apex. "You know Fitzwilliam will be good to her." He slapped his father's shoulder.

"Yes." The duchess's voice was then heard. "You said yourself that you could not lose her to a better man."

"And he knows we shall have his hide if she is unhappy."

All hundred heads turned to look at the groom, who tugged at his cravat. Bingley could not contain himself, his smile splitting his face. When the admiral echoed his mirth, the laughter of the older men in the congregation flowed through the church.

The doors of the chapel opened, and Julian Elliston, the Marquess of Glascomb, appeared at the head of the aisle, his mother perfectly poised on his arm, resplendent in a gown of translucent gold. Both beamed as he led her to her seat and took his place beside her. All heads turned as the dazzling Jane Bingley proceeded down the aisle, smiling serenely, but with unmitigated joy. Once she stood at the altar, again heads turned.

With the morning sun streaming behind them, the duke took a moment to survey his environs. Looking down into the expressive eyes of his daughter, he quirked his brow, and whispered, "Ready?"

Nodding, Elizabeth smiled beatifically, eyes shining in joy and unshed tears. He gave the hand on his elbow a squeeze and, with a nod of his own, led her to her fate and her future and her groom.

THE NEWLY WED couple stepped down the stairs of the church with brilliant smiles. "Elizabeth," Darcy took her into his arms and kissed her with an open heart. Their embrace endured the rush of people until Julian clapped Fitzwilliam on the back and Georgiana pulled at the bride's arm.

"Lady Elizabeth!" the young woman called. "How beautiful you are!"

"And even though you are her legal husband, Darcy," Julian spoke calmly, "I would not press your advantage. She is still my sister."

"But she is my wife, Brother," Darcy replied, emphasising their new relationship. Julian only shook his head.

"What on earth were you thinking, Elizabeth?" Julian asked in mock horror.

"Only of my happiness," she replied, beaming at her husband. He responded with a kiss. The arrival of the duke and duchess prevented further intimacies as the throng entered their carriages for the brief return to the manor house for their wedding festivities.

thirty-eight

September 7, 1812
Green Haven, Northamptonshire

JULIAN STOOD IN THE RECEIVING LINE AS THE ENDLESS WELL-WISHERS offered their hopes for joy. He marvelled yet again at the serene but jubilant composure of his new brother. *And the undeniable happiness, not only of my sister, but our parents as well.* This observation took him a moment to digest. *There must be something to this matrimonial madness*—he shrugged—*but I shall be confounded if I can say what it is.* Glancing to his left at the growing congregation, he wondered, not for the first time: *How did they all fit in the chapel? Will not the tail of this beast ever come into sight?*

Turning back to his filial duties, he automatically held out his hand to greet the next guest. Taking in the identity of the person before him, his mouth froze, half-open, midway through a greeting his brain could not complete. There, standing in anticipation, was Miss Cartwright, her lovely red curls fastened with pins of jade and mother-of-pearl.

Her eyes sparkled at his oafish display until they fell to his waist-coat. Her gaze flew back to Julian's, whose own remained stuck on her.

Both stammered when regaining some control, aided by Mary Darcy's giggle as she leaned forward to kiss Julian's cheek. When Mary returned to her husband's side, Miss Cartwright curtseyed to him.

"Abi...I mean Miss Cartwright. It is a pleasure to see you again."

He tried to disregard the titters of his relations. Looking to his right, he nearly choked seeing his sister, new brother, and both his parents staring at him with the most idiotic smiles he had ever seen.

THE DUKE AND Julian took the duchess's arms and, as they had months before, proceeded into the grand hall.

Seizing the moment, Darcy held Elizabeth, eyes boring through her initial surprise. As understanding of his intent bloomed, he took her in his arms and kissed her, his lips possessing hers and his arms enveloping her with a desire full of both need and love. Elizabeth responded to him completely, her lips yielding with demands of her own as her hands began to rake through his hair. Even the footsteps of Cummings were ineffective in stopping them from expressing their love, not until his distinct cough, a mere three feet away, broke through the haze of their desire. Their lips parted, and with tender smiles for each other, they turned to the grinning butler.

"Your absence has been noted, sir, madam."

JULIAN DUCKED behind a festooned column as Lady Darcy, Mary, and Abigail walked by. Unable to stop himself, he followed their progress as they strolled along the promenade.

"Her Grace must be very pleased." Lady Darcy patted Abigail's arm while smiling at Mary. "This is certainly a tribute to the Northamptons' great legacy of hospitality."

"Indeed," Abigail said absentmindedly, taking in the array of flowers simply placed to compliment but not compete with the architectural details of the great room.

"Oh, I remember such fantastic balls they had when I was young." Lady Darcy's voice took on a wistful quality. "The Northamptons have always been such talented hosts." Mary smiled at her sister as her mother-in-law focused on the past.

"I recall Papa's stories." Miss Cartwright's attention went to the full-length balcony windows. From the raised platform, you could see past the vast meadow to the forests. A cool breeze stirred, invigorating the milling guests. Drawing Miss Cartwright to the open spaces, she led her relations in that direction.

"MARY!" Elizabeth embraced her cousin.

"Lizzy!" Mary sighed, happily. "I am so happy for you—for you both!"

"Uncle Bennet!" Elizabeth greeted her former guardian with a warm embrace then leaned over to peck Michael Waverly on the cheek. Turning to look each in their eyes, she said. "I am so glad you are here."

"We would not miss your wedding for the world." Kitty Bennet gave her cousin a hug.

"Thank you, Kitty."

"Lady Elizabeth, how grand you now are," Lydia teased. Hearing her father cough, she smiled and took Elizabeth's hands in her own. "But I add my own best wishes for you and Mr Darcy. Who would have thought the man could have such a smile?"

She giggled, and Elizabeth, unable to maintain a stern façade, joined her until Mrs Whitcomb found them.

"Lady Elizabeth, I hate to take you away from your guests, but...?" Her eyes darted to the side.

"Oh?" Elizabeth looked around. "Of course. Excuse me." The Bennets murmured their consent, and Elizabeth turned with a radiant smile. "Thank you. Thank you all for everything."

She then followed her family's housekeeper to a small room away from the festivities. Opening the door, Elizabeth was surprised to see Jane reclining on a couch, Mrs Stemple kneeling beside her.

"Jane!" Elizabeth called out in panic, rushing into the room.

"Lizzy," Jane replied, holding out a limp hand to her. In an instant, Elizabeth was at her side, her brown eyes searching the blue pools of her sister's. With Elizabeth close by, Jane raised her hand to Elizabeth's cheek. "I am well. I felt faint, that is all."

"It is not normal for you to feel faint."

"But it *is* customary for expectant mothers to feel faint now and again."

"Expectant mothers?"

"Mothers." Jane's smile was beatific. "I had my suspicions but had not wanted to say anything until after your wedding."

The door burst open, and Bingley barged in. "Jane!" Seeing her reclining but all three women wreathed in smiles, he approached, confused. "My love, are you well?"

Jane smiled at her co-conspirators who were inching towards the door. "I am. All is well. Come here, Papa."

As comprehension filtered into the overwrought mind of Charles Bingley, he smiled ardently and, falling to his knees, took his wife in his arms. Exchanging girlish smiles, Elizabeth and Mrs Stemple quietly shut the door behind them.

GEORGIANA STOOD near Mrs Raleigh who was engrossed in conversation with Lady Hampton and Lady Cuthbridge. Paying only cursory attention to their discussion of a new orphanage in town, her eyes perused the crowds stretching their legs after the celebratory feast. The gentleman she had noticed earlier was nowhere to be found. *Probably outside with the other boys,* she thought with a wicked smile.

"Excuse me, Aunt," a decidedly male voice interrupted their conversation. Astonished, Georgiana found the object of her musings standing next to Lady Cuthbridge, his eyes intently focused on her. Lifting her own eyes to his, she noted a defiance, as if he could read her thoughts, for at that moment, he relaxed into a victorious grin.

"Evans Norton!" the startled matron sputtered. "What on earth do you mean sneaking up on me like that?"

"I apologise, madam," the sandy-haired youth replied with a semi-repentant nod. Taking his aunt's hand, he gazed at Georgiana as he bowed to his elder. Georgiana gasped when, as he lifted Lady Cuthbridge's hand, he shifted his eyes to Georgiana and smiled. Blushing, she felt Mrs Raleigh step closer.

"Ladies," Lady Cuthbridge began. "May I introduce my impertinent nephew? My brother's son and heir, God help us," but she smiled with good humour. "Evans Norton, Lord Millbridge." She and her nephew turned to each woman. "Lady Absinthe Hampton, Mrs Raleigh..."

"Admiral Raleigh's wife?" Lord Millbridge asked with evident awe.

Mrs Raleigh replied. "The very one."

"An honour, madam." He became all that was serious and proper. "My brothers both had the privilege of serving with your husband, and they have only the highest regard for him and his ability to navigate any course, defeat any foe..."

"I believe your brothers were exaggerating my husband's talents." Mrs Raleigh smiled indulgently at the young man. "Perhaps to enhance their tales of adventure?"

"I beg your pardon, Mrs Raleigh, but my brothers never lie..."

"Ideal younger brothers, then?" Georgiana asked. Sensing the eyes of all focused on her with various degrees of curiosity, she blushed.

"Indeed," replied Millbridge, seriously.

"Miss Georgiana Darcy," Lady Cuthbridge completed the introductions, her voice full of possibilities. "My nephew, Lord Millbridge. Evans, Miss Darcy is both sister to the groom and cousin to the bride."

"Beauty is a family trait then, I see." He spoke unthinkingly until, feeling the full weight of the women's gaze upon him, he quickly bowed to hide his crimson cheeks before darting away in a hasty retreat.

As the musicians tuned their instruments, Julian continued his clandestine appraisal of his nearest neighbour as she headed for the open patio and the fresh air. *Finally!* He hastened his steps. "Miss Cartwright—a moment?"

Sighing, Miss Cartwright moved slowly to the edge of the patio, her hands nervously rubbing the stone rail of the waist-high barricade. "Forgive me, Lord Glascomb..."

Julian paused. "Forgive you? For what?"

She swept her hands from the rim of her gown down its length. "I did not think—"

"Think of what?" A sweet confusion spread throughout Julian's brain, and he took a step closer.

"I only thought of the softness of this gown. It is one of my favourites."

"Mine as well." He looked out at the field then turned back to her. "It is a beautiful afternoon for a wedding, do you not agree?"

She laughed. "I do, although I doubt the happy couple noticed anything or anyone but each other.

"That is as it should be, is it not?"

Caught in his gaze, she could only nod. Stepping closer, he whispered, "I followed you to solicit your hand for the first set."

"Do you feel that to be wise, sir?"

He kissed the backs of her hands. "Perhaps, perhaps not. Only time will tell, Abigail."

His eyes challenged her to refuse his plea to risk her heart with him once more. She smiled and nodded, and with a spirit almost gleeful, Julian led her to the dance.

DARCY STEPPED from the master's chambers onto the adjoining balcony, crossing quickly to stand beside his bride.

"It is a beautiful night, is it not, my husband?"

"Indeed, beautiful," he whispered, his voice husky.

Elizabeth held her hand up to his cheek, and before the breath was released from her lungs, his arms wrapped around her, his lips capturing hers in a kiss. Elizabeth's power of speech was temporarily unhinged as Fitzwilliam explored her body, laying claim to the skin of her ear and roving down the receptive column of her neck.

Hearing his delight and need ignited a passion she had kept under tenuous regulation. *But now—now we are united.* Her eyes looked up at the stars twinkling their approval. *Surely, I am free now to love my husband!*

Darcy's hands deftly unfastened the sash of her robe before taking the strap of her gown with him as he retreated down her arms. The combination of cool air on her heated skin, combined with the rush of blood to the delta of her womanhood, enflamed her. Again, she said her beloved's name, but this 'Fitzwilliam' was full of her desire. Darcy growled, bending to sweep her into his arms and taking her to his bed. Gently, he laid her on the silken sheets, standing to unleash his own robe and remove his breeches. As he disrobed, his eyes never left her, as she sat up, her gown pooling around her waist. His gaze was riveting, and she was unable to feel embarrassed, to feel anything but the heat of desire radiating from his eyes.

"Elizabeth," he growled. "You are more beautiful than words will ever convey. I look upon you"—he perched upon the bed—"and my desire shatters all attempts to contain it. I touch your skin"—he ran his hand from her cheek down her neck to her shoulders—"and ecstasy beckons." Suddenly his eyes lifted to hers. "I love you, Elizabeth. More than I ever believed possible. You have changed me—made me a better man, made me remember I am better...than I was." He took her hands to his lips.

Sensing the need to recall his thoughts from the past, Elizabeth shifted her legs so she knelt before him, her eyes filled with the desire he had created. "Come, my husband, my Fitzwilliam. Make me your wife. Make me your own." She kissed him, and as his response grew, she pulled back, unleashing the curtain of her curls and the scent of lilacs that filled the room. Again, Darcy growled, his breathing reduced to short, erratic pants.

With a seductive smile, Elizabeth leaned back against the crest of pillows. "Come, my love. Take me. Show me the heaven that only love can know."

March 1813

ELIZABETH STEELED HERSELF AS THE CARRIAGE TURNED INTO THE drive leading to the Hospital of Saint Mary of Bethlehem. Her fingers flicked across her gown, briefly resting on the still-flat plane of her stomach until her father's broad hand caught hers, holding it firmly in his own. She looked up into his warm eyes, a tender and reassuring smile waiting for her. Her lips, so recently caught between her teeth, released into a brilliant smile. Glancing across the carriage, she found Fitzwilliam looking at her anxiously. Seeing her smile return, Darcy relaxed, and she giggled before turning to her brother, arms folded across his chest and observing her gravely. He, too, relaxed into an "Hmm," which only fuelled her mirth.

"Honestly, it is not as if we are attending a funeral," she said. Julian leaned forward, elbows on his knees and ready to continue his lecture —more like a harangue she had endured in triplicate.

"And I know it is not a pleasure jaunt, either. Thanks to you, I am well versed in the filth and anguish that reside within these walls." She cast her eyes out the window at the fast-approaching group of buildings. Each of the four occupants sat in silence, aware of their location and the possible stress they may encounter.

The footman opened the door and unlatched the steps. With a quick glance at his companions, Darcy exited first, then the duke, then Julian. Turning, he reached in his hand to Elizabeth, who was both glad and grateful for his presence beside her.

Stepping out before the sun-kissed group of buildings, Elizabeth noted the details. While barren of the niceties that lift a dwelling from a house to a home, she observed the well-kept grounds. Taking her father's arm, she allowed the men who loved her to lead her towards the imposing façade and the three officials hurrying down the front steps to greet them.

"Your Grace," began the first, a middle-aged man whose coat was well made but worn. "How…good of you to come. I am Walter Ralston, director of this institution. And, this"—he indicated the man to his right—"is Dr Stone, our chief physician."

The duke introduced Julian then said, "My daughter, Lady Elizabeth, and her husband, Mr Darcy."

The men attempted to restrain their curiosity about the child whose torment had been chronicled in excruciating detail in the official record. All three nodded self-consciously. "This way, Your Grace."

The party then headed towards the cell containing Lady Catherine de Bourgh. As she listened to the clank of the men's boots, Elizabeth's hands and neck grew clammy, and for a moment, her determination faltered. Taking a deep breath, she gathered her strength, even though her breath remained laboured. Looking up, she saw the determined eyes of her husband focused on her, and she smiled weakly, holding out her hand to him.

He took it and drew her near, whispering. "Are you sure, dearest?" She nodded, and kissing her hand, he relented, and they turned the corner. The first locked door more resembled the entrance to a medieval dungeon, and she hesitated. Immediately, the party stopped, the duke replacing Darcy in front of his daughter, wrapping his arms around her.

"There, there. We are all here with you—your brother and that pesky husband of yours."

She chuckled and relaxed.

The duke asked, "Do you wish to continue?"

Looking up, she squeezed his arm and smiled. "My courage always rises at every attempt to intimidate me. This day shall be no different." The duke kissed her brow and, taking her arm, led her onward.

THE STENCH of the chamber was overpowering as Lady Catherine had abandoned bodily hygiene and would only intermittently allow someone to attend her. Upon hearing the heavy key turn in the door lock, she spouted off the best use of calendula extract to relieve intestinal distress.

Elizabeth took a deep breath, ignoring both the gagging of her husband to her left, and the wild mutterings of the ruined woman before her. Her dress was filthy with more than the grime of daily wear. The stale air was suffocating, charged with the force of insanity. She fought the instinct to cover her nose and mouth in order to face Lady Catherine in a position of strength.

When her visitors entered the room, the former dictator of Rosings Park stared long and hard, coming as close to the iron grill as the chains fastened to her legs allowed.

"Keeps her from kicking us," Dr Stone admitted to their unspoken question.

Elizabeth approached the bars as if entranced by the withered woman alternately cowering and screeching.

"Stay away, you!" she bellowed, shaking her first. "Have you not something better to do than stare at your betters?"

Elizabeth looked at her husband, who seemed as if he might swoon. She could not imagine the range of emotions assailing him on seeing the dominant woman in such a state. She saw Julian clap his back reassuringly, and she turned, gripping the bars separating them from the patient.

Lady Catherine tracked their movements, startling when the young woman stood before her, just out of reach.

"You!" Her screech was hollow. "How can it be? You!" She turned, eyes darting, searching. "Am I dead?" she asked to the air about her.

"No, Lady Catherine," Dr Stone replied.

"How can it be?" She stepped forward, the heavy clank of her chains hitting the floor punctuated the silence. Her eyes scanned the room. Hesitating, she returned to Elizabeth and said, "Step closer, girl. Let me see you."

Elizabeth turned to her father who stepped forward. Darcy and Julian stepped behind, ready to intervene should the need arise.

"What? You are afraid of me?" Lady Catherine cackled in delight. Elizabeth straightened and faced the demon of her youth. Her bold gaze disconcerted the patient, who unexpectedly cowered ever so slightly.

"It is I, Lady Catherine," Elizabeth said, plainly but with strength. The older woman covered her ears, her body beginning to sway as if keening for the dead. "Lady Elizabeth Aubrey Rose Elliston Darcy, daughter—"

Lady Catherine began to moan, "No!" repeatedly.

"Daughter"—Elizabeth's voice grew stronger—"of Their Graces, Philip Michael Elliston and Alexandra Darcy Elliston, Duke and Duchess of Northampton, sister to Julian Robert Elliston, Marquess of Glascomb, and…"

"…beloved wife of Fitzwilliam Darcy." Darcy stepped to Elizabeth's side. She turned and smiled.

Lady Catherine snapped her attention to her nephew, and her anger flared. "You!" she bellowed. "You traitor! You betrayed me. Betrayed your mother and uncle. You are a disgrace to the family name, and I claim you as my nephew no more."

She bared her teeth, raising both fists. Darcy shuddered until Elizabeth took his arm. Looking deeply into Darcy's eyes, Elizabeth pulled him away from the shock of his aunt's words. The duke and Julian were the ones to now exchange nervous glances.

"Lady Catherine"—Elizabeth turned to face her abductor—"what you have done and the crimes you have committed are known, and for them you are condemned." Lady Catherine shrank away, baring her teeth at Elizabeth. "But neither you nor your hatred has killed me, and the pain you inflicted has faded. Your reign of terror is over." She stepped closer, taking hold of the bars. "I have won, Lady Catherine, and I release you from my heart and from my life." Each word struck her as a blunt object, and she jerked back. "I forgive you, Lady

Catherine de Bourgh, and I pray for the redemption of your immortal soul."

"Away," the sad woman screeched, turning her back to them. "Away!" She crumpled to the floor, wrapping her arms about her and rocking.

Seeing her tormentor crumpled and in ruin, Elizabeth wiped a tear from her eye, whispered a prayer for mercy, and turned away. Mr Ralston followed the silent party from the room. Dr Stone remained to administer an extra dose of laudanum to his patient.

No one said a word until they exited the patient wing and again breathed the clean, fresh air of the open road.

ABOUT THE AUTHOR

A lifelong writer, Mary Anne Mushatt relocated to New Orleans last century, where she earned an MFA and created a documentary of oral histories in the African-American and Native American communities along Louisiana's River Road. When the levees failed, exiling her family from their home, she discovered the community of Jane Austen acolytes and began writing novels placing the beloved characters of *Pride & Prejudice* in innovative situations. *Taken* is her second published novel. As a result of one of her earlier novels, she works with a multi-disciplinary team aiding victims of human trafficking become survivors.

Mary Anne lives in New Orleans with her husband, two sons, and two dogs.

To learn more about books by Mary Anne and other great forth-coming works, please visit us at www.QuillsandQuartos.com

ALSO BY MARY ANNE MUSHATT

Darcy and The Duchess

In this 'what-if' retelling of Austen's Pride and Prejudice Elizabeth Bennet enjoys her first love with the ailing Rafael Gainsbridge, the Duke of Deronshire bringing her into the glittering world of London's high society. When tragedy strikes Elizabeth must overcome her prejudice against her late husband's dearest friend, Fitzwilliam Darcy to protect her family. Together they must move beyond their pride to earn a second chance at love.

Made in the USA
San Bernardino, CA
13 May 2020